ANARCHY

Visit Paul Henke on his website
for current titles and future novels at:
www.henke.co.uk
or email Paul at
henke@sol.co.uk

By Paul Henke

The Tears Series:
A MILLION TEARS
THE TEARS OF WAR AND PEACE
SILENT TEARS
TEARS UNTIL DAWN
SHADOW OF A TEAR

The Nick Hunter Adventures:
DÉBÂCLE
MAYHEM
CHAOS
HAVOC
TURMOIL
CORRUPTION

Also by Paul Henke
PHOENIX RISING
THE SEVENTH CIRCLE
NEVER A WINNER

ANARCHY

Paul Henke

Good Read Publishing

All the very best!

Paul Henke

First published in 2015

10 9 8 7 6 5 4 3 2

ISBN 978-1-902483-15-3

Typeset by Readers Direct, Balfron, Stirlingshire

Printed in Poland

www.lfbookservices.co.uk

Good Read Publishing Ltd

Balfron

G63 0RL

Prologue

HE WAS A large black man with a spider's tattoo on his neck. Muscular and fit looking, he had the beginnings of a paunch. Dressed in jeans and tee-shirt, he carried his spending money, along with his passport and driving licence, in a belt around his waist. The cash for the transaction was in a briefcase dangling from his right hand. His passport was British, his address the East End of London.

She was small, dainty almost, with long, lank blonde hair. Wearing torn blue jeans and a yellow tee-shirt that was in need of washing, she carried a small knapsack slung over her left shoulder containing her passport, cash, cigarettes and the heroin she needed on a twice daily basis. As always, she had a cigarette burning between the nicotine stained fingers of her right hand.

They were strolling through the Platzspitz Park in Zurich, situated behind the central railway station. Over twenty years earlier, hundreds of drug addicts had bought and used heroin and cocaine in the park every day. It had been done openly, with no interference from the police. The place had been a magnet for drug dealers and users from all over Europe and other parts of the world. They had gone there to conduct business or get their fix of choice. Crime became rampant. As many as 20,000 addicts had used the park.

Truly international, signs had been displayed in many different languages, not only European but also African. Languages such as Amharic, the language of Ethiopia, Arabic, the language of 26 different nations from Algeria to Yemen, and even Tswana of Botswana and South Africa. It had been a multi-cultural hell hole. Finally, the tolerant Swiss people had decided enough was enough. It had been agreed that the experiment hadn't worked, the once beautiful and historic park had been destroyed - degraded to mud and used needles, and it was time to take it back. The police had moved in, the addicts displaced and the park returned to its former glory. He liked the idea of using the place for his purpose.

His thoughts switched to the self-deception to be found amongst addicts. They never used the word heroin. The drug had over 200 words associated with it, such as Chasing the Dragon, Judas and even Murder One to describe a mixture of heroin and cocaine. Now, he'd heard, there was talk amongst his business acquaintances that Switzerland was going to decriminalise the use and possession of small quantities of any narcotic. If they did and it proved to be successful, would the rest of Europe follow? If so, what effect would that have on business?

The park was busy. The crowds worked in his favour. He saw the man he was looking for and also identified the two bodyguards standing immediately behind him. He knew they didn't carry guns, but they were giants, tough looking with hard eyes. The man in front was of average height, average weight, bald and looked as though he would make a genial host at a party.

The three men wore business suits in spite of the heat of the day. They were sweating. They also stuck out like sore thumbs.

The two parties had done business before. This was their fourth transaction. The Brit stopped in front of the smaller of the three Russians, and held out his right hand as though they were shaking hands and the briefcase was adroitly taken from him and passed back to one of the bodyguards.

The recipient of the briefcase smiled, nodded and said, 'The van is on the open roof of the Parkhaus Sihlquai. Everything is as usual.'

Which meant the keys were on the back wheel on the driver's side along with the parking ticket.

There was barely a pause as the black man nodded and moved on. There were no smiles, no have a nice days. Neither side believed in the hypocrisy displayed by the Americans with their false greetings and farewells.

The girl shuddered. 'They give me the creeps.'

'Forget them. Ten minutes and we'll be at the multi-storey. A nice leisurely drive across France and home tomorrow night.'

'Can't I try some of the gear first?' she asked eagerly.

'I must be getting soft. Alright. But make it quick,' he ordered.

1

HUNTER SAT WITH a mug of coffee in his hand and his feet balanced precariously on an empty, upside-down wastepaper basket. His slouching attitude hid the fact that his 6ft 2ins frame was exceptionally fit and that he kept himself in peak condition. As a Minewarfare and Clearance Diving Officer in the Royal Navy a certain degree of fitness was required. As a top operative in The International Force Against Terrorism - TIFAT - being extra fit could mean the difference between life and death and frequently had done. Apart from an ability to handle explosives and deal with bombs and mines underwater he had advanced skills only to be found in the organisation. TIFAT was renowned in the right circles for its black operations, ruthless efficiency and disregard for the rules of war. Even a healthy disregard for the law itself was welcomed by those who knew how effective they had been over the last couple of years. Many lives had been saved and major disasters had been avoided thanks to TIFAT's mandate.

The office was military standard. His desk was near the window, a chair between them. The desk was light brown wood with a phone, in-tray, out-tray and a laptop computer, currently switched off. The chair was black leather, swivelled, and was comfortable. Opposite was the door to the corridor, along the right hand side wall was a three drawer filing cabinet. The top drawer held a collection of various types and strengths of coffee. The second drawer had half-a-dozen bottles of malt whiskies, only one of which had the customs seal broken and an inch or two of the amber liquid missing. The third drawer contained various glasses. Next to the filing cabinet was a sink and small shelf containing two mugs. On it was a kettle and the latest coffee making machine. In the middle of the room was an occasional table and four reasonably comfortable armchairs. In front of his desk were two straight backed, padded chairs with arms. The walls were painted a uniform cream and the floor was polished wood. There were prints of Royal Naval battle scenes on the wall, all stemming from the days of sail and three masted frigates.

He was looking across the room at his uniform jacket hanging behind the door. He was still coming to terms with having a third stripe instead of the two-and-a-half stripes he had been wearing. Promotion from lieutenant-commander to commander had been unexpected, earlier than he could have hoped.

Above the breast pocket on the left side was the dark blue ribbon with silver cross of the George Cross, awarded for an earlier operation. He was sitting in deep contemplation, mentally switching back and forth. Stay with TIFAT or return to general service? Possible command of a frigate? Promotion at least to Captain and then, eventually, as middle age settled over his shoulders, even Admiral? It was a dilemma he had been facing for months and, unlike him, he was vacillating. He was honest with himself. His problem was his restless nature. He was never happier than when he was on an operation. He relished the challenge and the danger.

His skills were honed to a fine level, his ruthless determination a major factor in how he went about his job. Like many others in the clandestine world of special operations and the security services, he was fully aware that it was not possible to bring some people to trial. To supply the necessary evidence, obtained by some spurious notion of legality, which, if not followed to the letter of the law, frequently resulted in an acquittal. That didn't include the coercion of witnesses, death threats to them and their families and outright killings of those brave enough to step forward and be counted. Hunter thought about the incredible corruption to be found within the law itself. In some countries it was rotten to the core, in others, such as Britain and other Western countries, it was only rotten in places. Corrupted barristers, lawyers and, on occasion, even judges, meant terrorists and criminals going free. That was when TIFAT stepped in. No trial and a quick end to the problem. The trouble was, as soon as one evil individual was dealt with, another took their place. It was never ending. A conveyor belt of those who leached off others, often the weak and despairing. It was too easy to succumb to the offer of money, a good life, the promise of Nirvana that was dangled before their eyes. The reality was, it was never like that. Men and women exchanged one hard life for an even harder one.

He was all too well aware of the issues that faced the world. He often discussed these with his TIFAT colleagues. Where was the morality in what they did? Could they afford to take a moralistic stand? If they did, what would happen? How much more at risk would they be if they yelled "Halt or I fire" as the enemy shot at them.

He recognised in himself that he had a streak of ruthlessness that enabled him to kill the enemy without a second thought. Them or him. Them or the lives of the innocent. Them or civilisation. Them or a peaceful existence for the majority of the inhabitants on earth. Was that overstating it? Was that a way to justify what he did? Probably.

When it came to his career, there was a major consideration to be taken into account. Ships were required if promotion was to be earned and ships were now in short supply in today's Royal Navy.

He swung his feet to the floor, picked up the DBL - Daily Briefing Log - out of his in-tray and started going through it. There was hardly a man left on the base. They were all either on operations somewhere in the world or taking much needed and much deserved leave.

Finishing with it, he threw the log into his out-tray, stood up and stepped across to the window. He gazed down over the parade ground and across the river. On his left was the Forth Road Bridge and a little further on he could see the arches of the Forth Railway Bridge. TIFAT occupied the old naval base, HMS Cochrane, another important RN establishment axed by a government claiming a better military on a smaller budget.

It was a fine forenoon, the sun was shining and a few clouds scudded across the sky, lonely and isolated. Wordsworth had it just about right.

Hunter was contemplating going for a run and a workout when his intercom buzzer sounded and he pressed the receive button.

'Hunter.'

'Commander, can you spare me a few minutes?'

Hunter grinned, his dark blue eyes crinkling. There was no question of sparing General Macnair a few minutes - the summons was on a par with that of a royal command.

Malcolm Macnair was the Commanding Officer of TIFAT. He had been given the job because a few years earlier he had written a staff college paper on the need for an international, well manned and well armed organisation that took the fight to the terrorists. The axiom that government forces had to be lucky all the time and the terrorists only once rang loud and true throughout the corridors of power across the Western world.

The paper had been considered a wake-up call as facts and figures coupled with logical argument were presented. The paper wound slowly along those same corridors of power until it was read by the right people.

Thanks mainly to an American President, action was eventually taken. Backed by most Western governments, The International Force Against Terrorism was established. Its mandate was carefully drawn up by lawyers, politicians and senior military personnel. As was so often the case, it was a document of waffle and open to misinterpretation by anyone who read it. It allowed certain people, mainly politicians, to cover their backsides in the event of a wrong decision being made. The biggest problem they faced was with the human rights lobby. These were people who sat safely behind desks and in offices where they could pontificate on the rights of terrorists and criminals at the expense of the men and women in the field. It was an expense the lobbyists would never have to pay - with their lives or crippling injuries.

'I'll be right there, sir.'

Two doors along he knocked and went in. The room was the same colour as his own, except it was a corner office and about twice as big. The fittings and furniture were similar apart from the fact that the occasional table was bigger and on each side were two leather armchairs. The walls had also been decorated with prints of land battles set in the 17th and 18th centuries.

'Commander, welcome back. Though I must say, I wasn't expecting you for at least another four or five days. Take a seat. '

'A safari in Kenya seemed like a good idea at the time, sir, but there was only so much wildlife to track, see and shoot with a camera. After a week I was bored, so I went to the coast at Malindi and did a bit of diving.'

'Got bored again?'

Hunter grinned. 'When I saw what looked like the same brightly coloured fish for the umpteenth time waving at me, I decided enough was enough. So I hopped a plane and came home.'

'Well, I'm glad you're back.'

'Thank you, sir.' Hunter's antennae were humming. Something was up, he was sure of it.

Macnair, of medium height and build, was fit for 50 years old. He had brown hair turning grey at the sideburns, brown eyes and a slightly hooked nose - that was as a result of a game of rugby back in his days at Sandhurst.

'Coffee?'

'No, thanks sir, I've just had one.'

'There's something I'd like you to take a look at.'

Hunter waited patiently while Macnair helped himself to a strong, black coffee that sat stewing next to the window. With his mug replenished, Macnair sat back behind his desk.

'You know what we have to do.' Although British by birth, Mirza Nawaz had spent most of his life in Pakistan. His father had arrived in the UK in 1951, but after his son was born in 1961, he and his family had returned to his country of origin - away from the godless societies that were Britain in particular and the West in general. He had gone back to decency and honour, where Sharia law ruled and Islam was the very essence of their being.

His father had died in poverty a decade after they had returned. Nawaz could remember little about him except that he was a man of great piety. In less than a year his mother had remarried. As far as Nawaz was concerned, she was a whore. Her husband was twenty years older, ran a successful business and lived in a large, rambling house, on the outskirts of Rawalpindi. He already had three wives but no children. He was obsessed about leaving his business to a son. He cursed and ranted his three wives for not bearing him any children. The notion that he was to blame never entered his head. Nawaz had been officially adopted and immersed into the production of cheap clothes, using effectively slave labour, with people working in dreadful conditions for $1 a day. The clothes were sold at huge profit, the family lived in splendid luxury, the servants were treated abysmally and Nawaz had a wonderful life when compared to his first 10 years on earth. The only problem was, he hated it. His inspiration, his life focus, had been moulded by his father. His step-father berated him for his adherence to Islam, his slavish interpretation of the Quran, his deep rooted hatred of all things Western. His step-father wanted Nawaz to learn the business and to inherit it. To build it into a global empire, wielding power and influence in whatever government ruled Pakistan at the time.

Nawaz recognised the dreams of his step-father for what they were - unattainable nonsense. On his 17th birthday he walked out of the house and went to the nearest army recruiting station. In the back of his mind he had the idea that he would learn how to fight, how to kill and turn his training into a weapon against the West. Martyrdom beckoned and he relished the prospect. He had joined as a squaddie, but his intelligence, drive and known family contacts meant that he was singled out for officer training within months of joining up. His step-father had disowned him to begin with and then had changed his mind, convinced that Nawaz would come to his senses one day, leave the army and take over the reins of the business.

His step-father dropped dead of a heart attack when Nawaz was 23 and a junior lieutenant. He inherited a great deal of money. He promptly gave most of it to a little known fundamentalist organisation that had been brought to his attention by a Captain in the same regiment. The balance he used to buy a Volkswagen, his only decadent purchase. Promotion had come relatively rapidly, which he had put down to his natural ability as a leader and his above average intelligence. On his promotion to Major at the age of 32 he was made an aide to General Pervez Khan, the Chief of Army Staff of the Pakistani army and a man who was only one heartbeat away from supreme power. Nawaz was taken into his confidence. The General was known by a select few as the leader of different fundamentalist factions that he was morphing into a single, coherent force. Nawaz's generous donation to the cause had brought him to the General's attention. Nawaz's orthodox worship of Allah and Muhammad was an inspiration to his men and fellow officers. He had helped to convert many to the cause. His reward would be earthly esteem and a place in Paradise.

2

'GCHQ AND ECHELON have been trawling the ether for information and cross-referencing it with CSE, DSD and GCSB,' said the General.

Hunter nodded. That was what it was set up to do. The United States National Security Agency had created a global spy system, codenamed ECHELON. It was controlled by the NSA and operated in conjunction with Britain's Government Communications Headquarters, the Communications Security Establishment of Canada, the Australian Defence Security Directorate and the General Communications Security Bureau of New Zealand. Although these organisations had been operating together since a secret agreement reached in 1948, the deal was still kept under wraps, classified top secret. The system was fairly simple in design. Intercept stations across the world captured satellite, microwave, cellular and fibre-optic communications traffic. This traffic was then processed through the massive computer capabilities of the NSA looking for code words or phrases. This was known as the ECHELON dictionary, triggered when certain things were said or written.

There was one massive flaw that had been allowed into the system. ECHELON had been used to spy on politicians and other civilians who were not involved with terrorism or crime. It was not just foreign politicians of despotic regimes but home grown ones as well. This fact had leaked back in the fifties but had been strenuously denied at the time. Since then, enough information had come to light to prove it was true. There had also been the bugging scandal of the Press which had created such an uproar. As a result, there was a great deal of government oversight of the 5 systems. That had led to the dissemination of the facts being late, out-of-date and usually useless.

To cap it all, TIFAT now had an oversight committee also, though with a difference. The alphabetic soup that made up the world's security services were national, even if they operated on an international scale. Their governmental oversight committees had regular up-to-date reports on operations before, during and after they were carried out. As a result, the security services had to justify the planning of an operation, what was happening at each step of the way and report the final result. The politicians would also demand a cost/benefit analysis in order to justify the amount spent. The question of lives saved or ruined by injury and the potential damage avoided to property was weighed against the human rights of the enemy and the enmity of the left-wing press and its effect on political ambitions. It meant that many operations weren't authorised, were pulled after they had started or made public afterwards, usually with words of condemnation by members of an oversight committee. Any action taken was covered over with words such as "Lessons have been learnt" or "This will not and cannot be allowed to happen again."

However, TIFAT did not ask permission, report on ongoing operations, or justify results achieved. Its budget was not controlled by any one national government but came from governments across the world and Macnair was told to get on with it. What the national governments liked about TIFAT was that it was getting results, as after-operation briefings showed. These briefings were sanitised and made anodyne but the experts could read between the lines and draw their own conclusions.

Governments also liked the fact that Macnair didn't hold out the begging bowl asking for more resources based around TIFAT's results. He wasn't empire building. His concern, motive and objective were to keep the world safe from terrorists and organised crime. He knew that if TIFAT became too large, too much in the public's face, there would be a much closer scrutiny of how it carried out its work. With that would come the politically correct demanding the rule of law be enforced at all stages. The whole industry of human rights would be brought to bear down on TIFAT and it would find itself as shackled as the rest of the forces fighting to protect the free world.

What the politicians did not know was that whenever it was possible, TIFAT would raid the bank accounts of the enemy and steal all and any assets they found. This was achieved mainly thanks to the skills of the people in TIFAT's IT department, headed by Isobel Sweeney. General Macnair described the funds liberated as being recycled for the good of mankind. It meant TIFAT had state-of-the-art equipment, a sizeable operating fund and a very generous death benefit and injured benefit pension for the men and women on active service.

Now though, the British government had forced a small oversight committee on him to receive detailed after-action-reports, insisting on warts and all. Of course, he didn't supply anything like the detail they were demanding, and had told the committee that what he gave them was all they would get.

'Let me ask you something, Commander,' Macnair said, easing back in his chair, 'how many criminal gangs do you think are operating in London and the south-east?'

'The last I heard, it was at least a couple of thousand. Mind you, that was a Channel Four documentary so I took it with a pinch of salt.'

'It was pretty accurate. As you know, most are from Eastern Europe where organised crime makes the Mafia look like a bunch of delinquent children. They bring in the guns, control the drugs trade and young girls are forced into prostitution. That's just the tip of the iceberg.'

Nodding, Hunter said, 'Where's SOCA fitting into all this?' The Serious Organised Crime Agency's job was to arrest the major drug dealers, money launderers, people traffickers, murderers and those who committed serious robberies - usually where violence was involved. SOCA had a turf they protected with vast amounts of jealousy and vigour. It was often said that if they used the same passion fighting criminals, organised crime would be way down.

'We know the gangs are global and as such, SOCA is frequently powerless to do anything about them. The main problem is, the heart and brain of the beast is well protected and often not in this country. MI5 is stretched to breaking point and is also under close scrutiny by parliamentary committees. Furthermore, SOCA and the police need to apply to the courts to get warrants for just about any action they want to take. They need to disclose their information and where it came from. That makes it public knowledge within about fifteen minutes.' Macnair got to his feet and stood leaning against the windowsill, his ankles crossed, his hands either side of him clenched around the lip of the sill. 'If information is from an informer, his or her life can be put at risk and if it's from an unnamed source, merry hell is created until that source is divulged. The ordinary police forces are hamstrung. They solve less than ten percent of any serious crimes, spend most of their time filling in paperwork and are good at hassling motorists travelling 10mph above the speed limit.'

'Sir, with all due respect, we know all this.'

'I'm getting my thoughts in order.'

Hunter knew it was a trait of Macnair's to mull matters over, expressing his thoughts, looking for ideas and welcoming interjections from his audience.

'As you know, a year ago we were told that organised crime was off our watch. We were to deal solely with terrorist activities. I didn't argue at the time, due mainly to the workload we're being crushed under. However, the Home Secretary has suggested that we take a more active role in fighting organised crime.'

'Suggested?'

'She can't order us. She used the argument that due to the fact that terrorism and major crimes are often intertwined we should slip over the line and deal with gangs that were solely criminal.'

'That's what was happening when we were told to be more selective in choosing our targets. That criminal organisations were to be left strictly alone,' said Hunter.

'I pointed that out to her.'

'What did she say?'

'Her frustration as Home Secretary was making her madder by the day.'

'Madder? As in nuts?'

'As in angry. She said that she had come to understand why her predecessor had spoken so highly of us and what we can achieve if left to get on with our job.'

'But she was the one who told us to leave fighting crime to the police. The rule of law and all that.'

'Well, it seems she's changed her mind.'

'Strictly off the record, of course,' said Hunter.

'Of course. Let's get a bite of lunch and I'll fill you in on what's going on.

Just before Nawaz's 33rd birthday, General Khan pulled Nawaz into his office and explained what he wanted him to do. As Nawaz listened, he felt elated. At last, the opportunity to serve Allah in a way he had often dreamt about.

Now, he and his colleagues were in Hackney, London. They occupied two terraced houses connected by a door that had been knocked through the wall. Mirza Nawaz smirked. Without permission of the stupid local authorities. He thanked Muhammad, peace be upon him, for the fear created by what the West called political correctness. A fear of being called racist, an oppressor of the different minorities that occupied Britain from north to south. Political correctness would help him and his brethren sow more distrust, hatred and fear amongst the non-believers. He basked in the irony of it all.

'It is time, Mirza. For the zuhr.'

'Thank you. Let us pray.' The seven men got down on their knees and bowed obeisance in the direction where they believed Mecca to be. This was the midday prayer, the Dhuhr or Zuhr. One of five daily prayers collectively known as The Five Pillars of Islam in Sunni Islam and one of the ten Practices of the Religion in Shia Islam. It was said after midday. Not, as was often believed, at 12.00, but true midday, exactly halfway between sunrise and sunset. On that day, in London, midday was at 13.02. There was leeway, as to pray exactly at the right moment was impossible unless you were an Imam in a mosque. From noon until the Asr prayer commenced, a true Muslim could pray. Asr started when the shadow of an object was the same length as the object itself. There were other caveats to the ritual that constituted a Muslim's prayer regime but most of them were too complex and too demanding to be practised or even understood. That was for the Imams. The leaders of their faith. The wise men.

The six Pakistanis knelt a little distance away from the seventh man. It was a subconscious action. There weren't many blonde haired, white men in their religion. This man had converted to Islam when he had visited Pakistan for a month's holiday and stayed ten years. Like all converts, he was a fanatic.

Prayers over, Nawaz said, 'It is yet to be confirmed whether we are to strike in London or at the country home. Let us once more examine the photographs as well as the architects' drawings of both houses. Remember, we must not fail. It is of the greatest importance. *Allahu Akbar.*'

The others repeated the takbeer.

They went over the plans in minute detail, taking them well into the afternoon. Although they had been through the plans on numerous occasions already, Nawaz knew there was no such thing as being too well prepared. Especially when it came to novices like the ones in the room. In the heat of battle, mistakes were so easily made - the sort that cost lives.

When he had finished the briefing, one of the men asked, 'What about the guns? Do we have them yet?' His eagerness was evident.

Nawaz smiled. 'Yes. They were finally delivered last night. Also, if we need them, we have night vision goggles.' That brought smiles to all their faces except that of the blonde man, who merely nodded. Excitement tinged with anticipation swept through the room like a bolt of electricity. Looking at their young and eager faces, Nawaz wondered if blind faith and commitment were enough. Would it carry them through the ordeal of the attack? Would they have the stomach to carry out the killings? To step up to a man and put a bullet into his head? Looking at them, he thought he knew the answer. They would kill without a second thought. Mirza Nawaz and one of the older men exchanged glances. They were the only two professionals in the room.

'Can we see them?'

Nawaz was about to say no when he thought better of it. They were children. He would let them have their toys.

'Help me,' he ordered.

They shoved a settee to one side and Nawaz pulled the carpet away from the wall to reveal a trapdoor. He lifted it open to show a shallow recess under the floorboards. Reaching inside he took out the weapons, ammunition and goggles. He handed them around. There was awe and excitement amongst the group. One of them fumbled with a magazine and dropped it into an open box of ammunition, the bullets scattering in the hole. Sheepishly, he went down on his knees to collect them.

Nawaz managed to hold back the retort that came naturally to his lips. After all, he and his friend were the only two who would be surviving the attack along with one of the men on the other side. His instructions had been explicit.

The internet was a wonderful recruiting tool, he thought, where lies and fiction were taken as fact. He glanced at each of them. Children, he thought again. So easy to manipulate. It took effort, but he managed to keep the contempt he was feeling from showing on his face.

His mobile hummed softly and he picked it up off the table. It read *essex, underground, heathrow.* Essex meant the country house, while the Underground and Heathrow Airport were targets for the suicide bombers.

He smiled. He wouldn't be using either the London Underground or the airport for a few days. He sent one word to each of two recipients.

3

THE TWO MEN arrived at the wardroom which operated cafeteria style. They both settled on a chicken salad with boiled new potatoes. The food was pretty good, considering it was a military establishment.

'Sir, from what you've been saying, we won't be asking the courts for permission. We'll carry out illegal phone taps, mail interceptions, and break into computer data bases and so on and so on.'

'Correct.'

'What do we do with the info when we get it?'

'That'll be up to us. Major operations have been tied up in so much red tape those criminals responsible have rarely seen the inside of a court house. Sometimes, the foot soldiers end up in prison while the bosses don't even have their collars felt. If there's any danger of arrest most of them get out of the country. Usually to someplace where there's no extradition agreement. Let's face it, the world's a big place to hide in and yet it's a small one when it comes to running a criminal organisation.'

Silence reigned for a few seconds. Then Hunter said, 'Sir, we're stretched thinly as it is with the workload we have. I'm not one to complain, but there is a limit.'

Macnair's smile was more of a grimace. 'I told the Home Sec precisely that and she asked me if we wanted more people, more resources or more funding.'

'What did you say?'

'I asked her why she was asking. At least she had the good grace to look sheepish. I told her that we both know nothing else will be coming our way which is why I wouldn't ask for anything.'

'And she said?'

'That she had been expecting such a request. So I told her that we would manage with what we've got and carry out our duties to the best of our ability.'

'What did she say?'

'Pretty much what you would expect. That she was relieved. Then I had the usual rant about the whole of the country being stretched to breaking point, the legacy of the last government, the banking crisis *et al.*'

'You must have enjoyed that.'

'I let her have her say and then I told her to stop the political broadcast and keep it for the general public.'

'I take it she didn't like that.'

'She didn't. She tried reminding me who I was talking to but I pointed out that she had come to us. I also pointed out that we are not answerable to her and that I was talking to her out of courtesy. She didn't like that either. So she tried being more pleasant, though I could tell it was an effort. The irony is, I have a lot of time for our current Home Secretary. She has bigger balls than her predecessors.'

Hunter grinned. It was true. Even so, they still weren't big enough to achieve the primary objective of keeping law abiding citizens, of whatever nationality, safe from criminals and terrorists.

'Let's go back to my office,' said Macnair.

Once there, Hunter and Macnair sat at the desk, across from each other.

'This was sent to me from the Home Office. Take a look,' said Macnair. He lifted out a buff fodder from his in-tray and handed it to Hunter. Inside was a two page summary of a report about organised crime. Hunter quickly read it.

The summary stated that there were twenty-one known criminals who were currently living in the UK and who were wanted for everything from genocide to drug dealing in huge quantities. None of them were under arrest because they hadn't committed a crime in Britain.

'Pretty damning,' said Hunter, closing the folder and placing it back on the desk. 'But we knew most of it.'

'Unofficially, yes. Officially this has been kept fairly quiet, though the press occasionally make a rumpus about it when they've nothing better to do. However, that's not the end of it. Something I didn't know and that is we don't even have these people under close surveillance or any form of surveillance, come to that.'

Hunter raised his eyebrows. 'Why ever not?'

'One reason is because we don't have the resources. But it goes much deeper than that. Most of them have legitimate passports obtained from developing countries which allow them to come and go as they please. Worst of all, there's nothing we can do about it!' Macnair paused, to let the enormity of what he was saying sink in, before adding, 'They have passports in false names so most of the time we don't know if they've left the UK or if they've returned.'

'Sir, none of us can understand why we don't just round these people up and deport them. Send them back to their own countries.'

'Because many of them have been condemned to death for their crimes, hence it's against their human rights. Don't forget the massive wall of barristers, solicitors and anyone else they can find to keep them from justice. Even if anyone is arrested and brought to trial, bribery, corruption or intimidation ensures the bosses either never face a jury or the jury's been nobbled. Even here.'

'That's been the case for some time.' Hunter decided it was time to move from the general to the specific. 'I take it you want me for a job?'

Macnair nodded. 'Have you ever heard of a man by the name of Ashraf Rabbani?'

Hunter shook his head. 'No. Who is he?'

'He's a Pakistani by birth but he also has British citizenship. He has an organisation called Barzakh.'

'That's an unusual name.'

'It means a sort of life after death. The soul of the deceased is transferred across the boundaries of this life and into the spirit world. There it rests until judgement day in a kind of cold sleep. There's a whole load more mumbo-jumbo attached to it which doesn't bear intelligent scrutiny. Well, Barzakh trains youngsters to be suicide bombers. You know, the usual promises. In the name of *Allah*, eternity in Paradise, seventy-two virgins to greet them and so on.'

'What's our interest? How did we hear about him and his

organisation?'

'Information supplied by General Khan via the Home Sec.'

Hunter knew that General Pervez Khan was the Chief of Army Staff, an important and powerful man in Pakistan.

'According to the report, Rabbani funds his terrorist organisation with the proceeds of crime. It's the usual stuff from people smuggling, prostitution to drugs and arms sales. According to Khan, Rabbani is particularly ruthless.'

'I get the picture.'

'The dossier has taken a while to compile but it's all there. It seems they've had Rabbani in their sights for some time. It's now come to a head.'

'Why? What's happening?'

'In eight days time the Pakistani Government is going to issue a warrant for his arrest.'

'Does Rabbani know?'

Macnair shook his head. 'We're sure he doesn't.'

'That won't last. It can't last. You know what it's like out there.'

'I agree. Normally. Except General Khan assures me that only three people know about the arrest warrant.'

Hunter raised his brows in surprise. 'I find that had to believe.'

'Be that as it may, it's what I've been told.'

'Who are they?'

'A high court judge, the President and Khan himself.'

'What about clerks to the court? Secretaries? Aides? It's a pretty long list of people who would know.'

Macnair shrugged. 'I'm only repeating what I've been told. At the same time as the warrant is issued, HMG will receive a request for Rabbani's arrest and extradition. The problem with that is the palaver we will have to go through to hand him over. You can hear the legal arguments. If he's returned to Pakistan he'll be tried and if found guilty his punishment will be death by hanging. Ergo, the whole issue of human rights will be brought to bear before he can be deported. Our courts will be tied up for years all the way to the European Court of Human Rights.'

'Article two pushed down our throats.'

'The right to life. Applicable to everyone, even mass murderers.'

Hunter nodded. 'Okay. Why not have a quiet word with the Pakistani President? He could commute the sentence to life imprisonment.'

Macnair shook his head. 'The Home Secretary says that Pakistan has made it abundantly clear that they will not have their legal system tampered with under any circumstances. However just suppose we did get the Pakistani President to agree to the sentence being commuted, there's the added complication of Rabbani's dual nationality.'

'That's not just a complication, sir; it's an impossible barrier preventing deportation.'

'Agreed. Thanks to the information we were given by the Pakistanis, Isobel has been into the systems of just about every law enforcement organisation in Europe.'

'What did she find?'

'You know what she's like. She's had the department working on the problem for the last three days. She's cross referenced snippets of information that wouldn't stand up in a court of law but make it clear that Rabbani's up to his neck in drug smuggling as well as prostitution right across the Continent. Possibly even gun-running though we aren't so sure at this stage. Isobel is still digging. It seems he's using young girls from Eastern Europe as well as the sub-continent to act as couriers to smuggle both heroin and cocaine into the country. Many of the girls are also forced or coerced into prostitution.'

'Okay, he's a vile piece of work and I can see why something needs to be done about him, but what about, what did you call it? Barzakh? I don't get it. I've never heard of a crime boss being involved in terrorism. A contributor to the cause maybe, but active involvement? No. They enjoy life too much. Why put it all at risk? After all, if Rabbani is a fundamentalist at heart, there are plenty of organisations he can support from the Taliban to al-Qaeda. Why bother with an organisation like Barzakh?'

'I asked the Pakistanis the same questions. This came in yesterday afternoon. It appears his family lived in a village at the western end of Pakistan. They were wiped out when the Pakistani army, along with American and British forces, attacked.'

'All of them? Women and children as well?'

'Yes. It was a stronghold of the Taliban. The Taliban were actively supported by the villagers and were well integrated into the local population. The attack was house-to-house and hand-to-hand fighting. Even young kids shot at our troops. There were a handful of survivors although none of them were Rabbani's family.'

'So as a result, he hates the West?'

'Correct.'

'Okay, I can see where his hatred stems from. But his direct involvement with Barzakh makes him more vulnerable than if he was just a criminal. Presumably, Barzakh is hitting Pakistani targets and that's why they want him.'

'Correct.'

'We know,' Hunter stretched out his legs and intertwined his fingers across his stomach, 'that where the bosses are concerned, they are indispensable, while the foot soldiers are cannon fodder or in this case as in so many like it, suicide bombers.'

'Your point?'

'He's far more valuable sticking to his core activity. That is, using the organisation he's built up to supply the money and resources needed to wage war on Pakistan and the West. That way, he lives the good life while extracting his revenge. If Barzakh can be traced back to him then the Pakistanis will leave no stone unturned to get hold of him.'

'Which is what's happened. According to the Pakistanis, the village was an important staging post for Rabbani shipping heroin from Afghanistan into Europe through Pakistan. With his family there, he could trust them to keep things honest.'

'Where's the Taliban in all this? If the village is on the border with Afghanistan then the Taliban would demand its share of the profits.'

'Again, I asked Khan. He said that Rabbani also paid off the Taliban with guns and other weapons.'

'So why Barzakh? Why not support the Taliban and leave it at that?'

'According to Khan, Rabbani has the kind of personality that demands his direct involvement. It isn't enough just to give support to the Taliban. Also, Barzakh means he can control what targets get hit. He can focus his hatred and desire for revenge where he wants to.'

'I guess that makes a certain amount of sense.'

'If you're as warped as he is,' said Macnair, stepping away

from the window and sitting back in his chair. 'The village has been razed to the ground. Rabbani now has to ship his heroin the long way round, through Uzbekistan and Kazakhstan. This adds to his costs and eats heavily into his profits.'

'My heart bleeds. Was he already a fundamentalist or did he become one after what happened?'

'We don't know. He's not particularly religious, just attends a mosque when it suits him.' Macnair abruptly changed the subject. 'What's the most effective way to stop Barzakh?'

'Cut off their funding.'

'Precisely. With Rabbani dead, the organisation will probably wither on the vine.'

'I suppose there's also an argument that if we hand him over, the UK could become a target for Barzakh which we aren't at the moment,' Hunter said thoughtfully.

'Precisely. When it comes to acts of terrorism, Rabbani wants to keep his home territory safe. He now considers the UK his home. There's an added complication.'

4

'THERE USUALLY IS. What this time?'

'The Pakistanis have intelligence that the Taliban are planning a very large attack somewhere along the Afghan border.'

'There's always trouble along the border.'

'True, but not on a scale like this threatens to be.'

'Sir, its all ifs and buts. However, assuming it is true, where does Rabbani come in?'

'According to the ISI he knows where the attack is going to take place because Barzakh will be a part of the operation.' Macnair walked across the room and replenished his mug of coffee, which Hunter declined. The General, Hunter knew, took the stuff practically intravenously while he, on the other hand, had his Plimsoll line when it came to caffeine.

'When is the attack due? Do we know?'

Shrugging, Macnair replied, 'We aren't certain, except it's to be in the next month or so. Possibly less. Isobel has also discovered that Rabbani also has an extensive legitimate business as well. He even pays his taxes on time.'

'That's usually the case. After all, he needs to be able to launder his money even if most of it vanishes into the black hole of international banks. How big is his criminal organisation? Do we know?'

'It can only be guesswork but the figures are staggering. Nationally, organised crime in the UK alone has a turnover between twenty eight billion and thirty two billion pounds. That figure is put into perspective when you know that our total military budget is around forty-eight billion. The figures we have about Rabbani were supplied by the Pakistanis. Isobel has been trying to verify them, but for the moment it's proving too difficult. According to the Pakistanis, Rabbani accounts for something like ten to twenty million. About thirty percent is in southern Germany, the same again in France and there's about ten percent in Spain. Most of the remainder is scattered across Europe.'

'Anything in Britain?'

Macnair shook his head. 'Our information is that Rabbani is squeaky clean when it comes to this country. Somehow though, I doubt Rabbani can resist doing some business here.'

'If the Pakistanis are expecting an attack why not use other methods of discovering where and when? Drones? Other informers? Anything. Then all they need do is put a bullet in Rabbani's head and forget about him.'

'A number of reasons. First of all, there aren't enough drone aircraft to cover the whole border. Also, getting an informer to tell Pakistani security anything about the Taliban is virtually impossible. On the other hand, if Rabbani supplies the information we could deliver the Taliban a crippling blow.'

'So you want me to lift him. Am I right?'

'Yes.'

'If the Pakistanis want him then why not let them get on with it? I don't see a problem. There's no need to involve us. They're good at that sort of thing.' Hunter tugged at his right ear lobe, frowning.

'The first problem will be that as soon as a mission to lift Rabbani is planned, he'll probably know about it. With his wealth, his tentacles must stretch all across Pakistan. Secondly, Rabbani and his legal team would have a field day telling the world what the Pakistanis were up to.'

'I guess so.'

'Thirdly, Rabbani's lot would make one hell of a stink about the fact that he's on British soil and insist our government do something about it. About his safety and so on. We'll hear the home counties, left wing, politically correct screeching about his human rights from here.'

'From what you told me about the extradition request I have five or six days.'

'Not any longer.'

'That's short notice to plan an operation like this.' Hunter looked thoughtful, the permutations of the operation rattling through his brain. 'Who's available, sir? Are any of the lads here? I thought from the DBL everyone is either on leave or on other ops.'

'You're right. Except I've kept Jan back. You can have him for a few days then he must leave for Cyprus.'

Jan Badonovitch was a Spetsnaz with the equivalent rank of Warrant Officer. He had been with TIFAT from the very beginning. He was one of the toughest men Hunter knew. He was an expert with most forms of weapons and spoke Russian, English, Polish and had a good command of German. He was also ice cool in a dangerous and demanding situation, something he had proven time and again. His stint at TIFAT had been for two years and his time was up. However, the General had persuaded the Russian Military hierarchy that Badonovitch was an asset that was too important to lose. What nobody, apart from Hunter and the General knew, was that a bribe had been paid to the Commanding Officer of the Spetsnaz to ensure Badonovitch was seconded to them for a minimum of a further five years. As Macnair had said, $100,000 was a bagatelle when you broke it down to an annual cost. Besides which, in reality, Russia had no further use for Badonovitch or for many more like him. The decimation of the Russian military was on a scale that was equalled only by the West.

Hunter smiled. 'I hadn't realised he was still here. Good. No chance of keeping him for the duration, is there, sir?'

Macnair shook his head regretfully. 'Sorry, Commander, it's just not possible. It's imperative that the British government is not seen to be involved in any way. We don't want some sort of backlash by Barzakh in the UK. That will be a disaster. As it is, we have enough problems trying to prevent any attacks on Britain. Add a vengeful Barzakh into the mix and God alone knows what could happen.'

'Surely, once Rabbani is in Pakistani hands, there'll be no way of keeping it quiet. He will be screaming blue murder that we are responsible. The finger of blame will be pointed firmly at Britain.'

'In theory, yes. In practice, we'll deny it while at the same time the Pakistan government will say loud and clear that it was nothing to do with the UK government. That it was due to an opposing crime syndicate who was paid five million euros for delivering him to them. Nobody will believe it but we'll stick to the story.'

'How will that work, sir?' Hunter was certain his boss would have already devised the first moves in the operation. After that, it depended on the whims of the gods, coupled to Hunter's ability to improvise as things progressed. Or, more often than not, as things went pear-shaped. This operation was somewhat different from normal - he usually had a team backing him up.

'First, I want you to get near to Rabbani. Try and discover if there is anything in this Barzakh business. If so, what are they planning? Attacks in Europe? Here in the UK? Or just Pakistan?'

'I thought Barzakh had been around for a while. That they had already carried out attacks in Pakistan?'

'That's what General Khan told me. However, Isobel can't find any reference to them having made any attacks anywhere. And you know what these people are like. They claim responsibility even if they've had nothing to do with an attack. They just want the credit and the resulting worldwide accolades that come with it.'

'That's pretty unusual. Maybe they haven't actually been in existence long enough.'

'That's not according to the General. He was explicit in saying that the organisation has carried out attacks and that they've been operating for the past five years or more.'

'How do I get close to Rabbani?'

'You'll tell him you're in the business. That you've been offered a large amount of heroin too big for you to handle on your own and so you're looking for a partner.'

'Where do I tell him the stuff is coming from?'

'Bulgaria. It's being supplied by a well established crime syndicate who are making bigger moves into the West.'

'I take it this syndicate exists?'

'Naturally. Like all the best cover stories the more truth there is the better.'

'In spite of the amount, why would I want to take on a partner? Why don't I go it alone? Expand the business?'

'Apart from being a one man operation, you specialise in cocaine, supplying mainly the middle and upper classes.'

'Why am I approaching Rabbani?'

'You'd heard that Rabbani has a European wide network

dealing in heroin and that's why you want to talk to him.'

'Why would he be interested? Especially working with someone he doesn't know.'

'Greed. He's the sort of man who can never have enough, no matter how rich he is. He must have a fortune stashed away, so why not stop and enjoy what he has? However, people like him can never stop. They're addicted to having more, even if they can't spend it in ten lifetimes.'

'I suppose there's Barzakh to fund. That can't be cheap.'

'With what we think he's accumulated, funding Barzakh will be petty change. Ideological fools, some brainwashing and a few sticks of dynamite are all it takes. Some radical Imams are especially good at identifying the fools and highly adept at the brainwashing. Dynamite is cheap enough to get hold of.'

'How much heroin am I offering?' Whatever he had been expecting, the answer shocked him.

'It has to be something really enticing so I thought a street value of about three million pounds should do it.'

5

'WE ARE AGREED. We will get on the train at King's Cross,' Basel said.

'Yes,' said the teenager sitting opposite him. They were in a McDonald's near the station, eating french fries and burgers. Milkshakes were close at hand.

Basel was overweight, bordering on obesity - a testament to his eating habits and lack of exercise. Of average height and puffy looks, he had one regret. He would die a virgin. But, as he kept telling himself, that would be put right once he arrived in Paradise. Seventy-two virgins would be waiting to welcome him. He reminded himself of the traditional sayings attributed to Muhammad, peace be upon him, found in the *hadith*. Number 2,563 in the collection, known as the *Sunan al-Tirmidhi,* stated, "The least reward for the people of Heaven is 80,000 servants and 72 wives, over which stands a dome of pearls, aquamarine and ruby". So where did the idea of virgins come in? Like many educated Muslims he couldn't get his head around the idea of where they all came from. After all, weren't the servants and wives entitled to enjoy paradise as well?

He reminded himself of the meaning of his name. It meant brave. Brave like a warrior. When the time came, he would show the world just how brave he was.

Brave, just like Faakhir, licking his fingers as he reached for the strawberry shake. Faakhir, meaning proud or excellent, was in sharp contrast to his friend. He was thin to the point of emaciation. He had been blessed with classic good looks, black hair, brown eyes and a slightly hooked nose that gave him an air of masculinity and menace. The girls on the campus were forever chasing him. Forever wishing to bed him. Not the Muslim girls, of course. Just the Western sluts.

'What about Muhsin?' He was the third member of their attack squad. Meaning beneficent or charitable, he was practising playing the violin with the university's orchestra. He had a brilliant brain and a remarkable talent. Both gifts would soon be lost to the world.

Basel understood the question. 'Don't worry about him. He's prepared as well as willing. In truth, he's more than willing. He's eager.'

'Good.' Faakhir nodded with satisfaction.

'When will it be?' Basel couldn't keep the nervousness out of his voice.

'We will be told on which day. But prepare yourself, Basel, my good friend, for it will be soon.' He looked about him and though there was nobody nearby he lowered his voice, 'Many infidels will die.'

'I understand. It will be a wonderful day. *Allahu Akbar.*' He said the last two words quietly, also looking around, fearful they could be overheard.

The two of them, plus their absent friend, were shahids, an Arabic word that in Islam meant martyrs. It was used as a title for Muslims who had died while waging war in the name of Islam. It meant that if you died a shahid then according to the Qur'an you were guaranteed a place in Paradise. Basel recited the verse to himself - "Think not of those who are slain in Allah's way as dead. Nay, they live, finding their sustenance in the presence of their Lord; they in the bounty provided by Allah. And with regard to those left behind, who have not yet joined them in their bliss, the martyrs glory in the fact that on them is no fear, nor have they cause to grieve."

Allahu Akbar. Truly, God was great. He lifted his cardboard mug of strawberry milkshake and sucked hard until the liquid gurgled. He did his best to ignore the slight shake in his hand.

'Three million pounds is a lot of enticement.'

'Do you have any idea how much the stuff sells for in Britain?'

Hunter shook his head. 'No idea at all. Expensive, I suppose.'

'Comparatively, but it's cheaper than it's ever been. The most common price is between £40 and £60 per gram. In 1998 the average price was £74. Hence, in real terms, the price has dropped significantly. The UK market is supplied mainly from Afghanistan. According to the United Nations Office on Drugs and Crime the Afghanis have over 154,000 hectares of land under heroin cultivation. That produces well over 6,000 tons of opium. That refines down to about 600,000 kilos of heroin. The UNODC claim that fifty percent of the opium isn't refined into heroin. That's disputed by every law enforcement agency in the world who all agree that the UNODC is manipulating the figures for propaganda reasons.'

'Why?'

'Pretending the problem is nowhere near as great as we know it is. Pretending that the war in Afghanistan has been successful in the fight against drugs which couldn't be further from the truth. According to a BBC report, a quarter of the drugs trade in Britain is controlled by Asian gangs who are working hard at capturing the whole UK market. According to the National Criminal Intelligence Service, by Asian they mean mainly Pakistani organised crime gangs. Most, if not all, of the criminals arrested suddenly don't speak English, witnesses are intimidated and police threatened. Because of the sheer amount of money involved it's easy to see why so few court cases result in a conviction. The gangs are vicious with a total disregard for life, whether that's men, women or children. The annual turnover in illegal drugs in the UK is well over eight billion pounds. Worldwide it is a staggering two hundred billion.'

'I knew it was bad, but that's unbelievable.'

'The profit margin is huge. Heroin costs about seventeen hundred pounds a kilo to grow in Pakistan and even less in Afghanistan. Here in the West it sells for about ninety thousand pounds a kilo. It gets worse. The interception rate is now only six percent in the UK. Worldwide it's less than ten percent.'

'That's incredible.' Hunter shook his head in disbelief.

'It's all thanks to the European Union. The largest single market for drugs is still the USA. However, Europe is fast overtaking it. Once the drugs are delivered anywhere in Europe, the lack of border controls means that moving them is pretty much risk free.'

'Where do the Bulgarians get their stuff from? I need to know in case I'm asked.'

'From Afghanistan then through Turkey.'

'What about some sort of introduction?'

'All arranged. We have a legend to cover you which should work.'

'Oh?'

'Yes. You're ex-military. Special Boat Service. Thrown out after 12 years for conduct unbecoming.'

'What did I do? Have an affair with the CO's wife?'

'Yes.'

Hunter gave a cynical half smile. 'If I'm undercover will I have a new identity?'

Macnair nodded. 'Although I don't envisage any problems, I thought it safer. It will include a well worn passport.'

'You said I'll have some sort of introduction to Rabbani?'

'Yes. Ever heard of a man by the name of Dimitar Petrov?'

Hunter searched his memory. He'd heard the name somewhere. 'I remember. I read a report about him a few months back. He was ambushed last year and shot dead. His body was found in a wrecked car. Wasn't there a problem with ID? The body charred beyond recognition?'

'It turns out he isn't dead. It had been a ploy to bring rival gangs into the open. He then eliminated most of the competition. It was a slick operation. He's now the biggest supplier of drugs, weapons and young girls out of Bulgaria.'

'Where does he fit in to all this?'

'Your story is that you were the one who warned Petrov about the attack in time to save his life.'

'Why would I have done that?'

'Because Petrov is your main supplier. You've resisted taking the heroin until now, happy to deal only in coke. However, Petrov has sweetened the deal so much, as a thank you for what you did, that you feel you can't pass it up.'

'How good is my cover?'

'Not bad. It should stand up to scrutiny. The reason we chose Petrov is because he and his gang spend most of their time hiding in the mountains.'

'I thought he was successful?'

'He is, but that's only as far as it goes. The Bulgarian authorities are after him for the murder of a judge's son, although they aren't trying as hard as they could to find him. Apparently, whenever they get close, he manages to slip away due to a network of informers and supporters across the country.'

'I guess the story will hold water long enough.'

'Precisely. After all, your cover only needs to be believed for a few days. At most a week.'

'Will I have any actual drugs to give Rabbani?'

'You'll be supplying him with enough heroin to convince him it's kosher. You'll give it to him free, as a sign of good faith.'

'How much will that be and, more importantly, where will I get the heroin?'

'About half a kilo.'

'What, forty-five grand free and gratis?'

'It has to be realistic. Taking a couple of grams to prove the heroin exists is a non-starter. Also, the stuff you'll be offering is very high grade.'

Hunter leant forward frowning. 'You said it'll be about half a kilo. I take it we don't actually have the heroin?'

Macnair pursed his lips and nodded. 'Correct. Before we get on to that, let's assume for a minute we have the heroin and your meeting with Rabbani goes ahead without any hiccups. Not surprisingly, Rabbani trusts nobody. He'll want to check you out. There's another reason we chose Petrov. He has someone on his payroll whose job is to warn him if the Bulgarian authorities are getting too close while at the same time arranging drug deals.'

'How do we know all this?' Hunter looked puzzled.

'When I decided we were going ahead with the op I contacted MI6 and told them what I needed. They came back with the information. As you know, they have info on dozens of individuals and criminal gangs in their data base. I chose Petrov as he is so inaccessible.'

'If the Bulgarians know about this other man, why hasn't he been arrested?'

'His brother is the Governor of the Province where he lives and works. On paper he is a highly respectable lawyer, in reality he's about as corrupt as they come. If Rabbani tries to contact Petrov he will have to go through this man. He'll confirm that you're working with Petrov.'

'Why would he do that?'

'Simple. There's no danger to Petrov so he isn't betraying Petrov's trust. MI6 have arranged for a fee of ten thousand dollars to be paid to him.'

'Where's Rabbani now, sir?'

'He's at his house on West Halkin St. He's been there for the last ten days or so.'

'Have you fixed a meeting?'

'Yes. Tomorrow at ten hundred at his place.'

'What about my legend?'

'We've kept it simple. Your name is Nicholas Hughes. Nick for short.'

Hunter knew it made sense to keep both names and information as near the truth as possible. It meant that the likelihood of making a slip-up was significantly reduced.

'After you left the SBS you drifted for a while getting into various minor scrapes and then, more by accident than design, you started dealing in cannabis and then coke. Eventually, you teamed up with Petrov.'

'Teamed up with him or working for him?'

'You're working with him, not for him. Makes you more independent. Like I've already said, you've stuck with coke, refusing to sell heroin or to get into the big time. You've been making a more than adequate living while staying below the radar of the authorities. However, this deal is too tempting.' Reaching into a desk drawer the General withdrew an envelope. 'In here is a gold credit card in the name of Hughes as well as two thousand pounds.'

'Thanks, sir.' Hunter took the envelope. 'Supposing it all goes wrong? What do you want me to do?'

'First and foremost, get out, but if you get the opportunity then kill Rabbani.'

'And if things go according to plan?'

'I want you to take Rabbani to a quiet stretch of coast somewhere along the south. It doesn't matter where precisely. The Pakistanis will have merchant ships ploughing the area, going in and out of various ports. I'll let the Pakistanis know where you are and it'll then be up to them.'

'What about the heroin I'm using as a sample? Where's that coming from?'

'You're going to have to steal it.'

6

'IT IS HEATHROW.' She spoke excitedly. 'Heathrow,' she repeated. Abrar looked at her friends. She was a beautiful girl, with large, almond shaped, brown eyes. Her enticing figure she kept hidden under a billowing black burqa whether at home or outdoors. She wore the yashmak whenever she ventured beyond her front door, the head and face veil leaving only slits for her eyes to look through. Abrar meant devoted to God in Arabic. Dedicated to her religion and devoted to Muhammad, she believed this with all her heart. Throughout her childhood she had been known as Abi. She had grown to hate the name and from the age of 13 had insisted on being called by her full name, Abrar. Slowly, but surely, she had lost her non-Muslim friends.

The three young women sat around a low table in a detached house on the edge of Wimbledon Common. The owners of the house, Mr. and Dr. Shaban, Abrar's parents, were visiting family in Pakistan while at the same time helping to run a clinic in a poor area of Islamabad. Both were doctors. Her father was a consultant surgeon and her mother a gynaecologist. The fact that Abrar had not shown any inclination to follow them into medicine was a source of sorrow to them both. Instead, she was at university in Reading, studying Islamic history, and doing well. She would be entering her third year if she returned in the autumn. However, there was another source of great sadness to her parents and one that brought real strife into the home and that was her embrace of fundamentalism. It had started when she was 14 years old. By the time she was 16 she was devout to the point of obsession. Her parents were moderate Muslims and tolerant of other religions. They were respected by their colleagues and were unhappy that Islam was tarnished with fundamentalist ideology. They had tried frequently to dissuade Abrar of her views but were resigned to the fact that it was a losing battle. They were reduced to praying that she would grow out of it.

Her two friends, also at Reading University and doing the same course, were equally as devout though perhaps not quite with Abrar's zeal.

Maida, meaning beautiful, couldn't have been more different than her name suggested. Plain and overweight, she made up for how she looked with a fun-loving and bubbly personality. Her parents owned a corner shop in Stockport where they put in a sixteen hour day to give their son and daughter a good education and a good start in life in the country which had been so welcoming when they had arrived in the 50s. Their son had left Birmingham University and was going to be a solicitor, which made them extremely proud. What Maida was going to do her parents didn't know. However, one thing her parents had vowed. Their children would not leave university with any debt hanging over them. They would make sure of that, even if it meant many sacrifices. At the news about Heathrow, Maida's smile was not as radiant as Abrar's.

Sofia, meaning wisdom, came from a family of fundamentalists. Her father was an Imam in a mosque in Reading. He had spent his life indoctrinating hatred of all things Western into his three sons and two daughters. One son had been killed in a knife fight between a gang of Pakistanis and a gang of Africans. Another son was in Pakistan studying to become an Imam. The third son, the eldest, had left home and gone to the USA to live. He had last been in contact with his family more than two years earlier. Having built a new life he had turned his back on his father's interpretation of Islam.

Sofia's sister had been taken to Pakistan on her 19th birthday, ostensibly to celebrate the event. Instead, she had been married to a cousin, 12 years older, who she had never met. She and her husband were living in Reading, where they already had three children. She was 22 years old.

It had been a hard battle, but finally Sofia had her way. She would be allowed to go to university provided she did a degree in a subject approved by her father. There were other conditions such as the wearing of the burqa and the yashmak at all times when in public. She had agreed. It was also understood that she would also be going to Pakistan when she had qualified to be married to a man of her father's choosing. That wouldn't be happening. She had chosen a different path for herself.

'You must now destroy the sim card and phone, Abrar,' said Sofia, always the most practical of the three, 'just like we were instructed.'

'I cannot,' Abrar replied. 'I cannot find my normal phone. I think it was stolen yesterday and I still need to buy a new one. What I will do, is only switch it on when I need to. I thought,' she hesitated, rallied herself and said, 'I thought there was no point in getting a new phone with such little time to use it.'

'God is the Greatest,' whispered Maida.

They all nodded. None of them would be returning to continue their studies. None of them would be receiving a degree.

'Are you serious?'

'Of course I am,' Macnair replied with some asperity.

'Yes, of course. Sorry, sir. Where am I stealing the stuff from and more to the point, why?'

'There's no way I can get my hands on half a kilo of heroin under any circumstances. If I tried, so many explanations would be required and so much paperwork needed I doubt the operation would be a secret for more than twenty-four hours.'

'Point taken.'

'So I want you to get the stuff on the q.t. and straight away.'

'Where from?'

'A gang operating in the East End of London.'

'British, Eastern Block or Asian?'

'Home grown. Very territorial. There have been more than a few killings over the last year or two as the Eastern Europeans have tried to muscle in.'

'Fun and games all round. If we know all this, why haven't the police done anything about them?'

'The usual. Under resourced and, more significantly, genuinely incapable of dealing with situations like the one they're facing. Gun crime is rife and as you'd expect the criminals are well armed. Arresting people and finding the right evidence that will stick is near impossible.'

'How do we know about the heroin?'

Macnair took a mouthful of lukewarm coffee before replying. 'We had a bit of luck. I spoke to Bob Snow and asked him where we could get our hands on some heroin.'

Bob Snow was the Commissioner of Police in London, a personal friend of Macnair's and a strong supporter for what TIFAT was doing and how it went about its business.

'He told me to leave it with him. In less than an hour he came back to me with news of a shipment of heroin due in sometime in the next forty-eight hours.'

'How do they know?'

'He was given the heads up by the Dutch. The Dutch police wanted to know whether we wanted to make the arrests. That way, it was possible we could arrest others in the gang.'

'Makes sense.'

'The fact is, they get literally dozens of intel reports about drugs and arms coming into the country. Far too many to follow up on.'

'So how can they be sure this one is for real?'

'They can't be a hundred percent certain, they never can be, but according to Bob Snow, it's about as good as it gets. He had intended to follow up on it but they are stretched to breaking and so he's more than happy to leave it to us and he'll keep the police out of it.'

'Okay. So when do we lift the heroin?'

'Tomorrow, maybe the next day. Jan has a file on the gang with photos and background and can give you all the info.'

'Where will we be going?'

'Harwich.'

'Isn't it known as the heroin gateway to Britain?'

'So I understand.' Macnair looked at the wall clock and said, 'Time is nine thirty-five. I'll get hold of Badonovitch. Here, take this. It's the file we've put together on Rabbani.'

Hunter took the buff folder and sat looking quizzically at the General for a few moments.

Macnair nodded. 'I know. It doesn't make any sense. Which is why I want you to get close to Rabbani and try and find out what's going on. The most important factor in all this is the Barzakh connection. Ideally, the Pakistanis get their hands on Rabbani and get the information they need to not only stop any attack but also do the organisation some serious damage. If you do have to kill him it will probably damage Barzakh enough to stop the attack taking place and, most importantly, to seriously damage the source of their funding.'

Back in his own office, Hunter sat at his desk and began leafing through Rabbani's file. There was a selection of twenty photographs - some showed him in a dinner jacket, others a light fawn suit, as well as in jeans and T-shirt. According to the file he was 43 years old. He had a swarthy complexion and a droopy moustache. As his forehead stretched halfway across his head, Hunter assumed he'd grown the moustache as compensation. Apart from the photos there was nothing new in the file, just confirmation of what Macnair had told him. What was unequivocal was that Rabbani was one of the vilest men Hunter had come across. It seemed that no crime was beyond his reach. Hunter had just finished reading when there was a brief knock and the door opened.

'Hi, Nick.'

'Jan. Come in and grab a seat. Coffee?'

Badonovitch shook his head. 'I'm fine, thanks.' He had a deep voice, with just a trace of an accent. The Spetsnaz placed a blue file on the desk.

In TIFAT, there was no ceremony. Officers and NCOs were on first name terms at all levels, up to but excluding the General. There were some lines even the men and women at TIFAT didn't cross.

Badonovitch was 5ft 6ins tall and broad shouldered. He had hands like steel callipers and was immensely strong. It was a natural strength, kept honed by regular exercise. He had brown hair, a round face, straight nose and was always ready with a smile.

'You know what's going down?' Hunter asked.

'Yes. I've read the file on Rabbani we received from the Pakistanis.'

'And?'

'He appears to be a particularly nasty piece of work.'

'What's your gut reaction?'

Badonovitch knew what Hunter meant and he shrugged. 'I get the impression that, what's the saying? The pudding has been over egged.

7

BADONOVITCH PICKED UP the file and waved it. 'You want to read this or shall I brief you?'

'It'll save time if you just tell me.'

'You know about this gang in London?'

'The East End. Yes. The General told me, though he didn't give any details.'

'This came in a few days ago. It's not much, but enough. From what I've read we are dealing with a vicious, nasty bunch. It looks like they've been involved with or directly responsible for at least half a dozen deaths and the police think it's far more than that.'

'They don't know for sure?'

'No. The Met have had no complaints because most of the deaths have been Eastern European criminals trying to muscle in on the gang's territory. Though it does look like some locals have gone missing.'

'Murdered?'

Badonovitch shrugged. 'No bodies have turned up. The police report that they've interviewed people who refuse to go on the record. The police are sure the witnesses they did identify have been warned off.'

'Could those missing have just upped sticks and gone?'

'Maybe, but the police don't think so. Too much has been left behind, like families and jobs.'

'No bodies but everyone knows what's happened. Do we know who the ringleader is? How many there are altogether?'

From the file, Badonovitch flicked a photograph onto the desk. Hunter picked it up and looked at it closely. It was of a man in his late thirties or early forties, swarthy looking with a shaved head and an earring.

'His name is Winston Doolittle.'

'Doolittle as in the doctor?' Hunter was referring to the famous fictional doctor who could talk to animals.

'That's the one and Winston as in Churchill. His father was from Jamaica, his mother white and English from London. Anyway, these two are his brothers,' he flicked two more photos onto the desk, 'and this is his cousin.'

'Names?'

'The first brother is known as Goldie, because, as you can just make out,' he pointed at the man's mouth, 'he has a gold tooth. The other brother is Cuthbert, though nobody calls him that to his face.' Seeing the quizzical look on Hunter's face, he added, 'He thinks it's too poncey.'

'So what is he called to his face?'

'Bertie.'

'Goldie has the same colouring as his brother, but not Bertie.'

'Actually, all three have different fathers. As near as we can tell, Winston's father did his best to look after his family, even marrying the mother. He was killed in some sort of accident while unloading a cargo vessel at Tilbury when the boy was three years old.'

'And Goldie?' Hunter asked.

'The mother was pregnant less than three months after her first husband died. She doesn't seem to know who the man was. All we know is that he was black. Then, only two years later along comes Bertie. This time, we do know the name of the father. A hard case by the name of Isaac McShane.'

'Sounds a good Scottish name.'

'It is. He's been in prison for the last ten years for murder and is expected to serve at least another ten. Maybe more.'

'What can you tell me about the cousin?'

'Not a lot. His name is Les Adeyemi. He only moved into the area in the last couple of years. Came here from Nigeria. He's an asylum seeker demanding to be protected, housed and fed. Up to his neck in petty crimes. He says he's family. Whether he's real family or not is doubtful but you know how it is. Nobody is going to challenge the fact.'

'Political correctness at its best and purest. This stuff reads like a bad crime novel.'

'That's for sure. Anyway, they opened their own business in a small way and have been going from strength to strength ever since. These are more of the gang.' He placed photographs on the desk.

There were four women, two with long, dyed blonde hair, two with shaven heads and all four with tattoos.

'Apparently these four are as bad as the men. They've a reputation for being extremely nasty when it comes to dealing with other women. Nobody, but nobody, messes with them. Little is known about them apart from the fact they've known each other since they were teenagers and met in some child care home in Birmingham. I suppose theirs are the usual stories of broken homes, abusive fathers. Though that's guessing on my part.'

'What do we know about the shipment?'

'The heroin is expected tomorrow.' Badonovitch pointed at a photograph of one of the women. 'She's with Doolittle. We had an update. The gear is coming into Harwich on the cross channel ferry from Holland, arriving around twenty hundred.'

'Are we sure?'

'As sure as we can be. We received some info from the Dutch. Also, I was in the ops centre with Isobel and she took me through a few things. She was showing me her latest bit of kit. We've tapped into the mobile phones of Doolittle and his gang, going through their supplier. We know that when the heroin gets to Britain its being taken to a warehouse on an industrial estate near Barking, where their distribution point is located. That's about two hours drive from Harwich. Maybe a bit less. Mules arrive at all times of the day and night and distribute the drugs throughout the East End.'

'Is it only drugs or do they do anything else? People smuggling? Guns?'

'They run most of the prostitution on what they consider to be their turf and have an interest in a couple of brothels. They don't appear to do any people smuggling. They also have five pubs, two freehold and three leasehold. Some of the women work out of the pubs. You know the sort of thing - a knee trembler round the back for twenty quid. They also smuggle in cigarettes and booze but as far as we can tell, only for sale in their pubs.'

'What about weapons?'

The Spetsnaz shrugged. 'The police don't know whether they're armed or not. I doubt tomorrow they'll be bringing guns through customs.'

'I think you're right. Getting caught with a gun adds at least five years to any sentence and they'll go down for long enough if the heroin is found. What about any welcoming committee?'

Badonovitch shrugged. 'We don't know for sure. However, according to Isobel, definitely two of the brothers will be there. Maybe even all three.'

'Any ideas?'

'There's no point in going to Harwich. I think, we should take over as the welcome party in Barking.'

Hunter nodded. 'That's what I was thinking. Okay, let's go into the detail.'

'You're travelling Crab Fat Air,' said the General, using the widely used military term for the Royal Airforce. The word wasn't used in a disparaging fashion. Quite the reverse. The RAF had pulled TIFAT's chestnuts out of the fire on at least half-a-dozen occasions. 'You fly out in the morning for Brize Norton. It's a lucky coincidence, but there will be a Tristar arriving at Leuchars later today, from an exercise in the States. The crew are staying overnight with an early morning departure. I'll sort out the details and get them to you.' Macnair paused, 'Any questions?'

Hunter and Badonovitch exchanged glances and shakes of the head. It was Hunter who answered for both of them. 'No, sir. We'll collect our gear from the armoury.'

They left the office, went down the stairs and out onto the parade ground. There was very little wind with the temperature in the high twenties.

Hunter stopped in front of the door to a low, windowless building. He used his swipe card and dragged open a heavily constructed door. There were four cages in front of them. 'Have you seen this? It came in last week.' He reached in and lifted down a short, thick stick about 8ins long with a foam grip. He flicked his wrist and a length of black chrome sprung out of the bottom lengthening it to 21ins. It was a nasty little weapon when your opponent was bigger and with a longer reach. 'This is an ASP 21F. It could be useful in certain situations.'

'I'll take one.'

'These arrived last week.' Hunter lifted down a dark green, Kevlar vest and offered it over.

Hefting it in his hand, Badonovitch said, 'This is light. What's its stopping power? Any idea?'

'As good as the old one.'

'Pretty impressive. This must be at least half the weight and thickness.'

According to the report Hunter had read, the vest could stop a 9mm Parabellum round at 10m although the recipient would be thrown off his feet and suffer a nasty and painful bruise or possibly cracked ribs. However, a shot in the back was something else entirely. A bullet to the spine could break it. A normal bullet would enter a body and exit it with very little reduction in velocity. The tissue damage was relatively small and if the bullet missed any vital organs and medical help was near at hand, there was a very good chance of the shot person surviving. The Kevlar vest often didn't stop the bullet, but significantly reduced its velocity. However, if the bullet was a hollow-point, then the vest was far more effective. A hollow-point was designed to flatten out when it hit the target, decreasing penetration but at the same time destroying far more tissue. The traumatic wound and level of bleeding meant that the target was less likely to survive. The hollow-point was also used where collateral damage was to be contained, the bullet entering the target but often not exiting it. On impacting the vest, the lead spread and didn't enter the body. On more than one occasion, both men had seen how effective a vest could be. Even so, luck played a major part in surviving the shot. The vest was no good against a head, arm or leg wound.

'It is and it's a lot more comfortable. Thanks to their thinness, they're also more difficult to spot than the old ones.'

Badonovitch tried on a couple of vests and chose one. Moving his arms and torso he announced, 'I see what you mean.'

They moved on to the next cage. 'New tasers. Four million volts, rechargeable and no batteries to bother with.'

'Jim has been busy.' Badonovitch was referring to Major Jim Carter, ex-Catering Corps, ex-paratrooper. He was responsible for the supply of gear needed by TIFAT. Thanks to the assets they had lifted over the previous couple of years, finance wasn't an issue. He could afford to and hence did, buy the best.

8

Hunter opened another cage that contained shelves holding rows of handguns. They were of various makes and sizes from countries all over the world. He reached out and lifted one down. 'Jan, try this,' he said, handing it over. 'It's an American Government Colt Pocketlite. Another new addition to the armoury.'

The teams spent a lot of time on the firing range. All of them could shoot extremely well with one hand, be it their right or left, and reasonably well with the other.

Badonovitch hefted the gun in his right hand. Weighing only 418g, it was practically half the weight of any other handgun on the market.

Flicking down the safety on the top left of the frame at the rear, Badonovitch drew the slide back. Holding 7 bullets of 9mm, it was a formidable weapon for its size.

'Stopping power?'

'See for yourself,' said Hunter. 'I'll be taking one.'

'I'll give it a go,' said Badonovitch. He lifted a silencer off the shelf.

Hunter checked over his own Pocketlite. Then they crossed to a door that was situated at the other end of the armoury. Hunter flicked some switches, opened the door and they stepped into a soundproof room. It was long and low, stretching about 60m. If greater distances were required, then adjustments were made to the size of the target to simulate the range to the target. The room was 8m wide and had firing positions for 5 shooters.

Gone were the old crouching soldier targets. Instead, there were different shaped civilian cut-outs of all shapes and sizes, men, women and children. They had different clothes, western dress as well as ethnic religious outfits.

Badonovitch pressed a button and a target slid across to hang in the middle of the far wall. Behind the target the wall was lined with a thick layer of a polyurethane based plastic, replacing sandbags. The plastic was not only equally effective but saved the necessity to sweep up the sand and replace the sandbags.

The cut-out was that of a male Caucasian, standing face on with a briefcase in his hand.

Badonovitch had filled the magazine and fitted the silencer as they had walked through. Hefting the gun in his right hand, he placed his left hand under the grip to reinforce the steadiness of his aim. 'Mouth,' was all he said. He pulled the trigger. The gun made a cough and bucked in his hand.

Hunter was looking through a fixed telescope at the target and said, 'Spot on.'

'Forehead,' Badonovitch said and fired. His hand dropped to his side, the revolver pointing at the floor.

'Dead centre.' But then Hunter hadn't expected anything else.

'Good gun. I like it. I'll take it with me.'

Badonovitch fired three more rounds in quick succession, holding the weapon with his right hand, not steadying it with his left. He then flipped the gun into his left hand and fired the last two shots.

Anyone in the security services, including armed police, when tackling suicide bombers operated under a directive and code known as Operation Kratos - named after the Greek demi-god Kratos meaning strength or power. This meant head shots without warning. Explosives used by suicide bombers were highly sensitive and a shot to the chest could easily detonate them. The term Operation Kratos was no longer used by the police for political reasons but was still used by TIFAT.

The two men spent the next hour shooting at targets of different shapes and sizes. There were innocent people alone, terrorists hiding behind men, women and children all in different places and positions. It was good training but they knew it was no substitute for the real thing. Hesitation could get you killed. Precipitous action could get the innocent killed. It was a very difficult and fine balancing act - one they practised regularly. Sometimes they made mistakes, most of the time they didn't. When they did, they analysed their reactions, thoughts and decisions, trying to work out what they could and should have done differently.

They finished shooting and returned to the armoury where they cleaned the guns and reloaded them. Compared to the regular army, like other special services regiments all across the world, they fired more rounds in a month than the regulars did in a year, even two. They fitted bumbags around their waists.

They knew that carrying a weapon in a holster strapped to the waist was a non-starter. Any keen-eyed member of the public spotting the gun would either have a fit or call the police. Or more likely, both. The next thing would be an armed response unit from CO19 pointing their guns at the carrier. Then would come the explanations, proof of identity and the display of the permit to carry a weapon. All of which was time consuming and, more importantly, could easily lead to the blowing of an operation. Therefore, the best option was to carry the gun in such a way that it couldn't be seen. Hence the bumbag.

The bag was slightly deeper and thinner than the ordinary type. It fitted comfortably around the waist and with the bag at your back and under your jacket, couldn't be seen. It was not designed for a quick draw.

They both added a spare magazine to their bags.

'I'm going for a run,' said Hunter. 'What about you, Jan?'

'Swimming.'

9

KATHLEEN SUMMERS WAS worried. She re-read her notes. Like all freelance journalists who specialised in international politics and terrorism, she had useful contacts. Omar was high on her list. He was an analyst in a bank. He monitored the value of shares of the world's largest companies. He looked for reasons to invest in them or divest the bank of the shares in an effort to increase the return by even a fraction of a percent. Like he had told Kathleen, every fraction counted. He hated terrorism with every fibre of his being. He denounced the act as well as the perpetrators at every opportunity, provided, not unreasonably, that it was safe to do so.

He had visited her the evening before and passed on information which, if true, needed to be in the hands of the authorities as soon as possible. Her dilemma was that the info was sensitive enough that she could be stopped from having her article published. Which would mean weeks, or more accurately, months of work down the drain. When all was said and done, she had her rent and other bills to pay.

Getting up from her desk, she went into the small kitchen attached to the living/dining area. A cup of herbal tea was needed. She put the kettle on and browsed through the various teas she'd accumulated. Peppermint. That would be refreshing enough. While the kettle boiled she went through to the bathroom.

The flat was on Oakhill Street, in Wandsworth, on the fourth floor of a pleasant five storey building. There were two bedrooms, both en-suite. She'd chosen the place as it was not far from the Underground station of East Putney. She loved London and was living as close to the heart of the capital as she could afford.

Kathleen was 5ft 9ins tall, had a good figure, neither fat nor thin, black hair, hazel eyes and dimples when she smiled. With a Pakistani father and a white Birmingham mother, she had the kind of soft skin and colouring that many women around the world not only yearned for but spent a small fortune trying to achieve. As she washed her hands, she looked at herself in the mirror. She saw that she was developing crow's feet at the corners of her eyes. She reached for the latest wonder cream that would smooth her skin once more. Her smile was cynical in the extreme but she felt better for using it.

Back at her desk, she cupped her tea in her hands while she looked at her notes. What she had learnt was too important to waste time on self pity. She needed to do something. But what? It was a question that had been haunting her since Omar had sent his e-mail.

According to him, three Muslim girls were intending to commit suicide wearing explosive vests. In London? It was unthinkable. But then she thought back to 7/7. Unthinkable? It was the wrong adjective.

If bombs did go off and people were killed and injured then prejudice, hidden beneath a veneer of civilised behaviour in the West, would bubble to the surface. Prejudice would turn to hatred - on both sides. A tiny minority was ruining the lives of hundreds of thousands of decent, ordinary Muslims, usually Pakistani.

The terrorists were a cancer in society, a nasty boil that needed lancing and the puss removed.

In her early days as a journalist she had tried to give a balanced view. She had written time and again about the rights of the perpetrators of the atrocities and not the rights of the victims. The clarion call had been the right to free speech. The right to be heard, no matter what they said about the deaths of British troops and the insistence that suicide bombers must have had a reason for doing what they did. Those arrested for terrorist crimes had the right to a fair trial and if found guilty to a just and reasonable punishment.

Then her close friend, Andrea, visiting her from Wales, had been killed in a bomb blast as she walked away from Green Park Underground Station. She hadn't even been near the blast. Others, closer, had survived. A small chunk of brick had flown through the air like a bullet and struck her on the back of the head. She had died an hour later, in hospital, with brain damage so bad that if she had lived she would have been a vegetable for the remainder of her life. Holy Jihad had claimed responsibility.

Afterwards, the tone of Kathleen's articles had undergone a radical shift. Her understanding of the plight of the victims had finally bubbled to the surface through the dark and malignant swamp that had clouded her judgement. Her articles were well researched and well written. She was often castigated by a tiny, but vocal, minority of Muslims while others, the majority, pointed out the honesty of what she had written. It was a fine balancing act, to use harsh yet honest words where they were called for whilst not insulting Muslims in general and those of Pakistani family origins in particular.

She groaned again. She wasn't particularly religious and, truth to tell, knew very little about any religion, not even her own. However, she was sure of one thing. No God and no prophet from any dissuasion, would want things to be the way they were.

She had thought about going to the police. But who would listen to her? Who would believe her? Not only a freelance journalist but to cap it all, one who hadn't always been complimentary about the heavy handed tactics of the police. They'd think she was stirring up trouble just for the story. Even if they did believe her, what actual proof did she have of anything apart from the hearsay supplied by Omar? With that thought she sat up straight. There was one thing she could do. A name flashed across her mind - that of an officer in the Royal Navy. She'd rather liked him, even if he was shallow and incapable of a meaningful relationship. Especially as he would never talk about his work. He claimed to be a desk-jockey at that place in Scotland. She never discovered what he actually did but she was positive that driving a desk was not it. There was something about him. He had an awareness that was uncanny.

Her ultimatum had been childish. A relationship with her or his stupid job. He'd shrugged, kissed her cheek and said goodbye. Just like that. There one minute, gone the next. She hadn't wept. Just been miserable for a week or so until she put the whole thing in perspective and shoved the memory of him to the back of her mind.

The place in Scotland had something to do with fighting terrorism. He'd know who to contact, what to do. She hoped. She hesitated. What if she was making a fool of herself? She couldn't bear the idea. Not in front of him. She had another thought that struck horror through her breast. What if he assumed she was using it as an excuse to contact him? Commonsense raised its head and told her not to be so stupid. Their short, sharp affair had been too long ago.

Still, she told herself, she'd have to give it more thought before she went off half-cocked.

The following morning, a staff car took Hunter and Badonovitch to Edinburgh Airport. It was an early start from Rosyth though the plane wasn't due to leave until 09.00.

The RAF station, situated at one end of the airport, had its own gate and security. Their ID cards got them through the gates. They drove around the periphery of the field and drew up at the door to the control centre. The addition of the RAF was a result of the closure of Leuchars in Fife, a move by the politicians that the military had objected to strongly.

Grabbing their kit out of the boot of the car they walked into the building and were directed to the briefing room. There was a lieutenant running through the flight plan for the benefit of the crew. The plane was an air-to-air refuelling Tristar from 216 squadron. They learnt later that the plane and crew had been on exercise in the USA for a month, at a base near San Diego.

Introductions to the crew were brief. There was a full contingent of 9, 6 men, and 3 women.

A woman bearing the rank of Squadron Leader stepped forward. 'How do you do, sir,' she offered her hand. 'I'm Brenda Baxter. I'm in command.'

As he took it, Hunter shook his head. As a Royal Naval Commander he was a rank above Squadron Leader but never one to stand on ceremony and being in civvies, said, 'Pleased to meet you, Brenda. Call me Nick. This is Jan.'

'Ma'am,' Badonovitch also shook her hand.

Squadron Leader Baxter was about 5ft 8ins, with a round face and a ready smile. She was attractive but behind the smile Hunter could see the toughness that would probably take her to far higher rank. The overalls she wore did nothing to hide her curves and glancing down Hunter caught the glint of a wedding ring.

Smiling, she said, 'Yes, I'm married. To an RAF doctor.'

Hunter had the good grace to smile and said, 'Pity.'

The lieutenant who had given the briefing asked, 'Is that okay, Ma'am?'

'Yes, thanks, John. We'll get some coffee, check the weather and get going.' She looked at Hunter and said, 'We're doing three circuits before we head south. Flight Lieutenant Oldsmith will be skippering.'

'That's fine. We're in no particular hurry.'

With a coffee in his hand, Hunter watched as the weather map was pulled up on a computer and displayed on a screen on the wall. He could see that high pressure sat over the country promising fine weather but with a possibility of the odd thunderstorm in the late evening.

'Ideal,' said the Squadron Leader. 'Let's go!'

Grabbing their kit they left the building and crossed to the plane. A member of the ground crew reported that the plane was ready and they climbed aboard.

Take-off was smooth and in short order. The three landings, by contrast, were met with a heavy thump onto the concrete runway, and then they were heading south. An hour later it was announced that they were lining up to land and that everyone was to take their seats and fasten their seatbelts.

Descending from the plane, Hunter said to Squadron Leader Baxter, 'That landing was the best of the four. Feather light.'

'Thanks. It was my last one.'

'You were piloting the plane? Why is it your last one?'

'I'm pregnant. Three months. I'm going to be a camp follower for a few years.'

Hunter smiled. 'There was me thinking you were destined for greater things.'

Brenda smiled in return. 'So my CO said. It came as a big surprise to him but it's what I want. I like the idea of staying at home for a few years and raising a child or two. Besides, what's there to stay in for? The RAF is being decimated. It'll be as inconsequential as the Royal Navy in a year or two.'

'Inconsequential?'

She looked up at him. 'Isn't it the case? Why are you in TIFAT and not bucking for command and promotion?'

Hunter nodded. 'Fair point and of course, you're right. It's why

I want to stay where I am. I can do a lot more good in TIFAT than if I return to general service.'

'Precisely.' They were approaching the main building and Brenda stopped and held out her hand. 'Good luck, Nick, whatever you're doing. If you go round the side you'll find a staff car waiting.'

'I hope all goes well,' said Hunter. 'I think your husband is a lucky man.'

She smiled. 'So my father keeps telling him and one day he might believe it.'

Hunter and Badonovitch walked away.

The car took them into Oxford and dropped them at the railway station. There they rented a BMW. By 12.45 they were heading out of the city for the M40.

The motorway was bumper to bumper, the traffic crawling along barely above 20mph. The reason became obvious when the road tapered to a single lane due to a three car pile-up at junction 4, the High Wycombe turn-off.

Once the accident was behind them the traffic returned to normal and Hunter wound the car up to 80mph.

Hunter glanced at the dashboard clock and said, 'Just coming up to fifteen thirty. Plenty of time.'

Badonovitch reached into his coat pocket, extracted a piece of paper and said, 'This is the full address.' Reaching for the satnav he keyed in the postcode. After a few seconds the dulcet tone of the woman who spoke so enticingly began giving directions. The first thing she did was nag them that the speed limit was 70mph. Hunter eased up on the accelerator. At 75mph she shut up.

'Nick, have you thought anymore about moving off the base?'

'Yeah. I did toy with the idea of finding my own place in Balfron, you know, where my parents live, but I decided it was too close to them. Visiting the village is one thing, living there is quite another.'

'So what will you do?'

'Edinburgh is one option, Dunfermline another. But right now I'm thinking about buying a boat and living on it in one of the marinas. My cousin, Richard, refurbished an old boat and made a fantastic job of it. Though he's sold it and now lives in Leith. A boat appeals to me. I need to make up my mind. What about you? I thought you and a couple of the others were looking to find a place.'

'We were. But then, life on the base has its plus side. All the comforts and no commuting.'

'And no female company.'

Badonovitch grinned. 'True, but the women have their own places. That'll do for now.

'Damn it to hell, here we go again.'

The traffic ground to a halt just before the M25. They crawled along until they finally reached the junction. Hunter turned onto the other motorway and headed north. The satnav went berserk. After a few minutes Badonovitch switched it off.

'Good,' said Hunter. 'We can put it back on when we get to the M11.'

The question of somewhere to live led his thoughts down a track he'd contemplated a few times already. Why not get a boat of some description? Not, he told himself, a sailing boat or any kind of yacht, but something with a couple of engines. There were plenty to be had and at a reasonable price as well. He'd have a browse through a few magazines and see if there was anything that took his fancy. Which was, he acknowledged to himself, a means of procrastinating over the decision. A feature that was highly unusual for Hunter, who was normally so decisive.

They stopped at South Mimms services for a break and a leg stretch. They waited until nearly 19.00 when the afternoon rush hour traffic had died down to something more reasonable before climbing back into the car and heading east. Badonovitch drove while Hunter reset the satnav. This time, they followed instructions and hit the M11 half-an-hour later. They turned south.

'End of the M11 only two miles. We should be there pretty soon,' said Hunter. 'Sunset in an hour. Let's go and take a look if anyone's there yet.'

It wasn't long before they were on the North Circular. They came to a roundabout and were instructed to turn left then right onto the A123. They passed Barking Abbey, then the town centre and were directed onto King Edward's Road.'

'Pity the area doesn't live up to its posh street names,' said Badonovitch. 'Look at the rubbish around the place. Ah, see that pub on the corner? That one belongs to the Doolittles.'

They passed the Merry Duck. It looked shabby with a pavement full of people outside the door having a cigarette. The ground was littered with butts.

'What a dump,' was Hunter's opinion.

The satnav said, 'Turn left at the next junction.' They continued going where they were told. Finally, they turned into a run-down industrial estate that stretched back half-a-mile and had roads off to the left and right. The place they wanted was at the end.

Before getting there, Badonovitch pulled into a side road and turned the car. 'Dark in fifteen.'

'Yeah. I'll take a quick look and be back in ten.'

Out of his holdall Hunter took a leather shoulder holster and put it on. He took the Pocketlite out of his bumbag and slipped it into the holster, fitting it snugly to his left side, the grip forward. He buttoned up his jacket. He was wearing a black, single breasted, light weight safari style jacket that easily covered the weapon.

He walked away, turned the corner and ambled along the pavement. He passed jerry-built, 1960's style concrete slab buildings with flat roofs. Some were in blocks of three; others were larger, single units. All were single storey, with dirty windows that were well protected with metal grills. He couldn't tell if any of them were in use. There were scores of black, plastic, rubbish bags as well as individual items of litter scattered all over the place. It looked as though the local population used the estate as a rubbish dump. He counted three mattresses, two fridges and a three piece suite.

The light was fading fast. He paused at the next corner. A stone's throw away was one of the biggest buildings he'd seen on the estate. It stood in isolation, with a concreted parking area surrounding it. In front was a double door, while to the left was a roller shutter for vehicles to pass through. It appeared big enough to take a 15 tonne lorry.

There were two windows on the other side of the door, each with a metal grill. The place was in darkness and appeared deserted. Hunter went back the way he'd come. He stopped near the car. It was empty.

'Jan?'

'Here,' the voice was virtually in his ear. Badonovitch stepped from behind a discarded cupboard where he had been kneeling. 'Anything happening?'

'Couldn't see anybody. There's a side door as well as a roller shutter door for vehicles. Two windows are protected with grills. There are probably more windows around the back.'

'Shall we take a look?'

'Yes.' Hunter reached into the boot of the car and opened his holdall. He extracted a small, folded up nylon shoulder bag. He slipped the carrier strap over his neck and under his arm and slid the bag behind his back.

As it grew darker rats began to appear, only the odd one at first but soon they were too numerous to count. They were bold, unfazed by the two men walking down the middle of the road.

'Have you ever eaten one?' asked Badonovitch, nodding towards the rats.

'No. Have you?'

'Yes. Part of the training. In a stew. Not bad actually. Virtually fat free.'

'Somehow, it doesn't appeal.'

'Agreed, but if you're hungry enough, you'll eat anything.'

They came to the end of the road, cut off by a collapsed wire fence on the other side of which was an overgrown patch of ground. Slowly, they made their way over the weeds and dirt and picked their way around yet more rubbish. In the background they could hear the hum of traffic and, intermittently, the throaty roar of a speeding bike.

A few minutes later they stopped behind the Doolittle property.

'A door and two windows,' Badonovitch said softly. 'Looks empty.'

'Okay, slow and easy. Let's go.'

Both men took out their pistols and screwed on silencers before they closed in on the building. They approached the backdoor. Hunter tried the door handle. He wasn't surprised to find it locked. Badonovitch was trying to look through a window.

'Can't see a thing,' he whispered. 'They're too dirty.'

'You go left, I'll go right.'

There was little light to see anything by. The street lights had been smashed at some point, leaving a distant glow around the estate from the lights on the main roads.

The building was about 40m by 40m. It was of the same concrete slab construction as the rest of the estate with here and there, fresh concrete repairs.

Minutes later they met at the front door.

'Nobody,' said Hunter. 'Notice the lock?'

'Yeah. A Lever Deadbolt 2. Which is roundbolt operated. That's a serious bit of kit. Same with the roller doors.'

'We'd better go round to the back. I noticed it's a mortice lock. That won't be a problem.'

At the back door, they pulled on cotton gloves, flexing their fingers, trying to get them comfortable. From his nylon bag, Hunter extracted a small tool that looked like a replica of a gun. He selected one of its blades, pushed the end into the lock, jiggled it, felt it engaging and pressed the trigger. There was a slight vibration and then the tongue of the lock slid back. Pulling the door open a crack, he used a pencil torch to look around the edges.

'Anything?'

'Looks clear.' He inched the door open further but still there was no sign of an alarm. 'Okay. Let's go.'

They moved slowly and cautiously. They were in a short passageway with a door left and right. A glance in each showed them to contain toilets, surprisingly clean.

Through the door at the end they entered a large open space. There were no windows and so it was pitch dark. Badonovitch scanned the place with his pencil torch.

'They're using it, no question,' said Badonovitch. 'Look at the scales. See that reddish brown powder that's been spilt over there?' He pointed at a light covering of dust in an otherwise spotlessly clean environment.

Each side of the room contained a Formica topped work table surrounded with bar stools. There were sixteen stools in all, in front of which stood the kind of electronic scales used to weigh small amounts.

'Take a look at these,' said Hunter, 'boxes of sachets. There must be tens of thousands in this lot.' He lifted out a handful of plastic, self seal sachets. 'Just right for a few grams of heroin.' The boxes were stacked 2m high and three wide in the corner opposite the door. 'Let's see what else is here.'

They went through the remaining door that led to the front of the building. Here there were two doors, one either side of the double doors. The one on the right held a desk, a chair and a filing cabinet but nothing else. From the dust on the surfaces it was obviously not used. The other door led into a small kitchen with a fridge, a cooker and an electric kettle. A glance in the fridge showed there was a half empty plastic bottle of milk. Hunter took it out and checked the date stamp.

'Use by date is three days from now.' Replacing the bottle, both men returned to the corridor.

'Look at this.' Badonovitch was pointing at the front door. 'Typical. State of the art alarm plus one of the best locks on the market in the front and the back virtually an invitation to enter.'

It was at that moment they heard a key turning in the lock.

10

THERE WAS NO need to say anything. They pulled ski masks over their faces. Hunter pointed at the door to the main room while he went into the office on the left. The front door opened and he heard somebody come in. Lights came on followed by the bleeping of buttons as the alarm was switched off.

A gruff voice with the unmistakable cadence of someone from Africa asked, 'How much longer?'

'Flo said twenty minutes.' The reply was East End of London.

'That stupid cow. She wouldn't know if it was twenty minutes or two hours. Especially if she's rat faced.'

'I'll give him a call and double check.' There was a brief silence. 'Win? How long? Right.' Breaking the connection, he said, 'They'll be a couple of minutes. Go and open the doors.'

Hunter heard the door to the main room open and close. He opened the office door and looked out. He couldn't see anybody. He followed after the two men. He cracked open the door and looked in. The lights were on and the roller doors were rattling open.

Badonovitch was behind the boxes with the sachets. He looked out and saw Hunter. One of the men at the roller doors was Goldie, the other Hunter recognised as the cousin, Les Adeyemi. Goldie had his hand pressed on a green button to raise the rollers. The other man was standing beside him, dangling an automatic rifle in his right hand. It was, thought Hunter, an Italian Beretta. About as modern as they came.

The noise of the doors echoing around the walls masked any other sound. Hunter pointed, drew his gun and stepped into the room. Badonovitch came out from behind the boxes and stepped silently across the floor. Hunter veered to the right, the targets on his left, while Badonovitch moved straight towards them. The doors stopped, silence descended. The rubber soled shoes of the two men from TIFAT made no sound but then Badonovitch' shadow hit the wall and the man with the rifle began to turn around. He saw the frightening figure of Badonovitch wearing a black ski mask only paces away. His look registered shock. He had no idea Hunter was behind him.

The man's gun was still pointing towards the floor when Hunter smashed him across the back of his head with the butt of his pistol. Hard. The man collapsed onto the concrete, smashing his chin into the bargain.

Goldie displayed courage or stupidity when he leapt at Badonovitch. It wasn't a fight as such, more a choreographed farce. Badonovitch waited, stepped to one side as Goldie almost reached him, kicked him very hard in the stomach and used the butt of his gun on the back of Goldie's head. He went down as though he'd been poleaxed.

'Help me get them into the corridor,' said Hunter. He unceremoniously grabbed his victim by the back of his collar and dragged him across the room, with Badonovitch following close behind. As he stepped through the door to the front, Hunter flicked off the lights, plunging the main room into darkness. From his nylon bag, Hunter took a handful of tie wraps and they used them to secure the arms and legs of the unconscious men.

'There's a car coming. I just saw its lights,' said Badonovitch, as he finished with the wraps.

'Okay. They'll wonder why the lights aren't on but I doubt they'll be suspicious seeing as they've only just spoken to Goldie. We'll wait until they get out and then take them.'

It wasn't a car but a white van. In the reflection of the headlights they could see two people. The driver's door opened and Winston Doolittle stepped down. He was still dressed in the tight fitting T-shirt and figure hugging jeans he'd had on in Zurich. Stepping across to the door, he flicked the light switch and pressed the button to close the roller shutters. 'Goldie? Where the sodding hell are you? Les?' There was anger in his tone.

Another person stepped around the side of the car. From his hiding place, Hunter could see it was a woman, with long lank, died blonde hair, a nose ring and half-a-dozen rings in both ears. She was sucking deeply on a cigarette.

'Flo, go and see where the hell they are.'

She walked towards the door where the TIFAT men stood.

Badonovitch pointed at himself and shifted to one side of the doorway while Hunter moved behind the door.

The door swung wide open and the girl stepped into the dark. She barely had time to register the two bodies on the floor when Badonovitch wrapped his left arm around her, pinning both her arms to her side. She took a deep breath to scream but before she could he clamped his right hand hard across her mouth, squashing the cigarette against her cheek and pinched her nostrils at the same time. Lifting her off the floor he held her tightly as she squirmed, first to free herself and then for a few seconds with total panic as she began to lose consciousness. Hunter pushed the door shut, cutting off the light.

They heard Winston Doolittle yell out in real anger and then his voice grew louder as he stormed across the room. Badonovitch had put the girl's body on top of the other two just as the door was thrown open.

The man stopped in utter shock. His mouth dropped open but before he could speak Hunter hit him across his throat with the edge of his hand. It was a carefully controlled blow. Too hard and his larynx could be crushed, too soft and he could try retaliating. He needn't have worried. Doolittle gasped, clutched his throat and collapsed to his knees.

Hunter grabbed Doolittle's left leg while Badonovitch took his right. They yanked him hard so that he fell face down and dragged him back into the big room. Doolittle's chin scraped along the concrete for a few metres until he managed to lift his head up. He was gasping and swearing at the same time.

'Jan, we don't want to be disturbed, use the tie wraps on the girl.'

While that was happening, Hunter stood and watched as Doolittle struggled to sit up, massaging his throat, gasping for breath. He glared his hatred at Hunter, looking around the place, his face a picture of bewilderment.

'What do you want?' he croaked.

'The heroin you brought over on the ferry from Holland.'

'What heroin?'

'Tut, tut, tut,' Hunter spoke in mock sorrow, shaking his head. 'That won't do at all, Winnie old boy.'

'You know who I am so you'd better believe it when I tell you get out. Or you're dead.'

'Hear that? Either we leave or we're dead.'

Badonovitch laughed as he walked back across the garage towards them. Doolittle continued massaging his throat with his left hand and placed the palm of his right on the floor.

Both Badonovitch and Hunter had put their guns away so Doolittle had no idea they were carrying. All he saw were two individuals, both smaller than him although the one standing in front wasn't that much shorter. He bent his right leg so that the sole of his foot was flat on the floor while his left leg was angled to the left. They'd regret what they'd just done.

It was obvious that Doolittle was about to push himself up and attack. Just as he tensed his body, Badonovitch stamped heavily on the back of Doolittle's hand, breaking a bone or two, the crunch loud in the quiet room.

Doolittle screamed. He began cursing, nursing his right hand to his chest, tears welling up in his eyes.

'Where's the heroin?' Hunter asked in a good natured manner.

The response was a mouthful of invective. After a minute or so Doolittle gasped out, 'What H? I'm telling you, I don't know what you're talking about.'

'Jan,' Hunter gestured with his head.

Badonovitch crossed to the white van and opened the back doors. It was full of boxes. He pulled out the first and ripped the top open. It was packed with Belgian chocolates, which he scattered across the floor. He did the same with the second box. He continued working his way through the boxes. There were cartons of cigarettes, cigars, rolling tobacco and cases of booze.

The cases of liqueur were opened and bottle by bottle flung against the nearest wall where they shattered into small pieces. The pungent smell of alcohol came wafting through the air.

'I told you, I ain't got no H,' Doolittle gasped, rocking gently back and forth. As the pain subsided, his courage returned. He asked again. 'Do you know who I am? Get out while you can. Go on. I'll forget all about this. Or...' he tailed off.

'Or what?' Hunter said. 'You'll set your animals onto us? Please do. I'd love to meet them.'

'You'd end up in a box. Alive,' said Doolittle through clenched teeth.

Hunter shook his head. 'Listen, Winnie, the lot we work for make your crowd look like girl guides. So watch what you say or I'll break your arms.'

'You wouldn't dare,' Doolittle sneered.

The last box was thrown out. Badonovitch jumped down from the back and shrugged his frustration at Hunter.

'Last chance to tell us, Winnie. Or you'll really regret it.'

'Not nearly as much as you will,' said Doolittle glancing a second time at his watch.

Hunter realised he was expecting others to arrive and so he took out his Pocketlite and placed the end of the silencer on the top of Doolittle's right foot. The anger and hatred was replaced on Doolittle's face by fear. Hunter didn't say a word, merely pulled the trigger.

The plop of the gun was drowned out by the other man's scream. Hunter stuffed the gun into Doolittle's mouth, breaking one of his front teeth.

'Shut up. Last chance. Understand?'

The man nodded, gasping as the gun was removed. 'In...in a compartment under the driver's seat.'

'On the floor or part of the seat?' Hunter asked.

'Part of the seat.' Doolittle shuddered. 'Christ, help me. Give me something for the pain.'

'What do you want? How about a bullet in the head? It's guaranteed to take away any pain.'

It had been arranged that as soon as Hunter and Badonovitch were finished, Macnair would tell Bob Snow who would send in SCO19 - Special Crime and Operations Division of the Metropolitan police. They would be supplying armed support for the Flying Squad whose main task was the investigation of armed robberies and the prevention of other armed crimes. They would be arriving mob handed. TIFAT's involvement would be known only to the Commissioner. It had been decided to leave as many of the gang alive as possible. Information would be gathered and collated and prosecutions would take their course. Bob Snow had made the point to Macnair that when one gang of rats were exterminated, another took their place. It was a never ending war. A situation that Macnair all too readily recognised.

Badonovitch said, 'Found it!' He stepped triumphantly around the back of the van.

It was just then that they heard a commotion from the front of the building. Hunter looked around. In spite of his pain, Doolittle still managed to smirk.

Badonovitch flicked off the light as he drew his gun and glided across the floor to stand with his back to the wall, directly facing the door. One of the trestle tables stood between him and the door.

'Now what are you...' Doolittle started to say when Hunter kicked him in the side of the head. Doolittle flipped over on his side and went out like a light.

The door smashed open and three people appeared, silhouetted against the light in the corridor. Each move they made showed they had no idea how to handle themselves. The first two men were carrying handguns. Neither Hunter nor Badonovitch could see the hands of the third man.

Badonovitch fired. He shot the right knee of the first man who yelled out as he went over onto his side, smashing into the concrete. The man pulled the trigger of his gun and Badonovitch went staggering sideways. The man dropped his gun, clutched his leg, and started screaming.

Hunter's shot was into the thigh of the second man, smashing his femur. He went down with a yell of pain while at the same time pulling the trigger of his semi-automatic. He wasn't aiming, just pulling the trigger in reaction. In seconds, the gun clicked empty.

The third man stood still, clearly unsure what to do.

'Lift your hands into the air,' said Hunter, 'and don't move.'

The man did as he was told. His arms were shaking, fear etched deeply on his face. He moaned and a damp patch spread across the front of his trousers and urine trickled down his leg.

'Are you alright?' Hunter asked.

'Yeah. The bullet scraped my side and along the vest.' Badonovitch put his hand under his right arm and rubbed. 'No damage. Hardly a bruise.'

The man that Badonovitch had shot was scrabbling one handed for his gun which was about a metre away. His other hand was clasped tightly around his knee, the blood pumping out between his fingers. There was no doubting the injured man's courage.

Hunter stepped across the floor and kicked the gun away. Looking down, he saw it was Cuthbert, the third brother. 'Don't move, Bertie. I don't want to waste another bullet.'

In response he received a mouthful of abuse interspersed with loud groans. Badonovitch checked the other wounded man. He was sitting up, both hands wrapped around his thigh, groaning loudly. Hunter realised that if he didn't get help soon he would bleed to death. Neither Hunter nor Badonovitch recognised him.

'What...what do you want?' asked the man with his hands in the air.

'Nothing,' said Hunter. He picked up the bag of heroin that Badonovitch had put on the side of the trestle table, hefting it in his hand. There was at least half a kilo, possibly more. He carefully made a small hole in the top. Taking a piece of absorbent paper out of his pocket, he sprayed it with a substance from a thumb-sized aerosol can. He sprinkled some of the dust onto the paper and watched it turn deep blue. Satisfied, he took the nylon bag off his shoulder, put the heroin into it and replaced the bag.

'Okay?' Badonovitch asked.

'Definitely heroin but I'm not sure how pure it is. It needs further tests. Come here.' Hunter gestured at the unhurt man and walked towards the van. The man followed slowly, dragging his feet.

Hunter became impatient, stepped back, grabbed the man by the front of his T-shirt and pulled him forward. 'That's where we found the heroin,' he pointed at the driver's seat. 'Are there other hiding places?'

'Don't tell him, Vince,' yelled out Cuthbert.

'Wrong thing to say,' said Badonovitch. 'If you'd said no there aren't then there's a possibility we'd have believed you. But don't tell him?' Badonovitch shook his head sadly, as though at a recalcitrant child, 'It means there are.'

'Are there?' Hunter asked.

'I...I'm not saying,' Vince gasped. 'Please don't make me. If I do, they'll kill me.'

It seemed to Hunter that the man was more frightened of the Doolittles than him. Which said a lot for the power and fear the brothers engendered in the area. With the possibility of others arriving, there was no time to waste. He opened the bonnet to the van and ripped out a handful of wires, disabling it. While he did so, Badonovitch tie-wrapped the man known as Vince. He then searched each of them and took their mobile phones, smashing them underfoot.

'Okay?' Hunter called out.

'Ready.'

Cuthbert asked between clenched teeth, 'Who are you?'

Neither man bothered to reply.

'Right Jan, let's go.'

Once outside, they removed their ski masks and gloves as they walked briskly towards their car.

Minutes later they were on the A13.

'Where to?' Badonovitch asked.

'The roads are quiet enough, so can you drop me in the city? King's Cross?'

'Sure, no problem.'

'I'll call the General and bring him up to date.' Hunter speed dialled Macnair. The phone was answered before the second ring. He briefed him on what had happened.

'The shootings can't be helped. I'll let Bob Snow know. What about the heroin?'

'It seems to be fairly pure though I can't be sure. It's at least half a kilo from the feel of it. If there's any more in the van then the police can find it.'

'Well done, both of you.'

'If help doesn't arrive soon, then one, possibly two of them could die. The one I shot was bleeding like a gutted pig.'

'It can't be helped. I won't lose any sleep over it. Tell Jan to go back to Brize Norton. I've arranged for transport back here for first thing in the morning. He's flying out to Cyprus tomorrow evening from Edinburgh. I've arranged with Hertz for them to pick the car up at the base. Tell him to leave the keys with the guards at the front gate.'

'Right, sir. Is there anything else? No? Then goodnight.'

11

AN HOUR LATER the car stopped. Hunter and Badonovitch shook hands. 'Good luck in Cyprus,' said Hunter. 'How's your side?'

'Fine. It's nothing.'

Hunter knew that even if it was hurting like hell, Badonovitch would never say so. Hunter climbed out, opened the rear passengers' door and hefted out his grip. 'See you, Jan.' He slammed the door shut.

It was half past midnight. The Cunningham Hotel, where he was staying, was a 30's style gray stone building. As he approached, a taxi drew up and disgorged two passengers. Hunter followed them through the door and across the gloomy foyer. He went up to the desk which was still manned even at that late hour. He gave the girl his credit card for swiping and signed the register.

The room was en-suite and bog standard. Enough space for a double bed, dressing table with a mirror behind and a chair in front. On it was a kettle with 4 sachets of coffee and 4 bags of tea, along with longlife milk in small cartons. A built-in wardrobe was big enough to hold half-a-dozen hangers.

He took a shower, brushed his teeth, climbed under the duvet and was asleep in minutes.

The next morning, he went down for breakfast. Dressed casually in an open-necked white shirt with a single-breasted blue blazer and gray trousers, he looked like a tourist. He had cereal and toast. A full English was the last thing he wanted. The coffee was insipid, the orange juice from a carton.

Although his appointment with Rabbani wasn't until 10.00, he set off for West Halkin St. just after 08.30. Unlike most of London it was relatively quiet, but as the street led off the western corner of Belgrave Square that was only to be expected. He sauntered past the embassies of Bahrain and then Serbia and Montenegro. The Spanish Embassy was on his left, as was the

Austrian Embassy and then he turned into West Halkin St. The house he was looking for was an imposing 3 storey building that he easily identified.

He continued past until he reached the Halkin Arcade. He entered a coffee shop. Sitting at the window, savouring a large Americano and appreciating the caffeine, he had an unobstructed view of the house.

The street remained quiet, the odd taxi dropping off or picking-up a fare. There was the occasional passer-by, more often than not with a small dog on a lead.

It was around 09.15 before he saw anyone enter the house. A Caucasian male with short, white hair, broad shoulders and fit looking. He had a bulbous nose, thick lips and a poor complexion as though he spent very little time in the sun.

A few minutes later Rabbani came out. He was instantly recognisable. He was wearing a lightweight, gray suit and black, open necked shirt. Incongruously, he was wearing brown moccasin shoes and as an affectation, he carried a walking stick which he swung with a flourish. Behind him came a second man. It was the man who had just entered the house. He stayed a few paces behind Rabbani, his head never still as he looked in all directions, including behind them. It was obvious he was a bodyguard.

Hunter studied Rabbani as he walked past the window. He was about the same height as Hunter and a bit older looking than his photograph. His hair had receded further while his neat moustache still reached down to his chin. His clothes were immaculately tailored but didn't hide the fact that he was developing a paunch.

He watched as Rabbani walked around the Square and started on a second lap. The bodyguard stayed the same distance behind. When Rabbani completed a third lap, he returned to the house. Hunter concluded Rabbani had simply been out for a morning constitutional stroll.

It was 09.55. Hunter intended being late to see what sort of reaction he invoked - if any.

At 10.15 he rang the doorbell.

The door opened almost immediately. It was Rabbani's bodyguard. He looked tough and close up he appeared to be in his mid thirties. He was wearing a black suit and an open-necked white shirt. The jacket was buttoned and tight fitting. Hunter could see the man wasn't armed.

'My name is Hughes and I have an appointment with Mr. Rabbani.'

Without saying a word, the man moved to one side and indicated for Hunter to enter. Stepping inside, Hunter found the house to be refreshingly cool.

The hall was large and imposing. A stairway was a good 8m away, lining the right wall. A door led off to the left and another to the right while directly ahead he could see the corner of a third door. The hall was painted a pleasant blue the colour masked beneath the paintings covering the walls. Their frames were highly ornate and gold coloured.

'Please to stand still.' The man took out an electronic wand and waved it around Hunter. At his right pocket there was a bleep. Hunter reached into it and lifted out his mobile phone. There was a nod of acceptance and he replaced it inside his jacket. There were no other bleeps.

Looking about, he noticed a second man sitting in an archway in the left hand corner of the hall. Hunter assumed he was armed.

'Follow me.'

The man spoke with an accent Hunter couldn't quite place but knew to be Eastern European - possibly Russian or Polish. He moved with an easy grace and had that way about him that suggested ex-special forces.

As they crossed the hall and went up the stairs, Hunter studied his surroundings. Up close he could see the brush strokes on the paintings and so there was little doubt in his mind that they were originals. The scenes were of the Middle East or Pakistan. The former showed mainly camels, oases and sand dunes with the occasional man in Arab garb or a woman completely enveloped in the burka. The scenes of Pakistan were more vibrant, each painting giving the impression of activity.

Pausing a second or two to look at a painting, he glanced down and saw that the front door and the windows were wired with burglar alarms. At the top of the stairs the man stopped and looked back, glowering at Hunter.

'Nice paintings,' Hunter gestured, continuing up the stairs.

The man stepped across to the door facing them and knocked. He didn't wait for a reply but turned the ornate handle, opened the door and waved Hunter through.

The room was imposing with a high ceiling. Opposite the door, in front of a window, Rabbani was sitting at a desk with his back to the window with another man sitting opposite. This man twisted his head to look at Hunter. An empty chair was next to him.

Three settees were placed around a low table on the right. To the left was a sideboard with a coffee machine. The air smelled of freshly made coffee and stale cigarette smoke. More paintings crowded the walls.

'Mr. Rabbani,' said Hunter walking across the room, his hand outstretched. 'Apologies for being a few minutes late. I was unavoidably delayed.' Shaking hands, Hunter couldn't help noticing that Rabbani's was flabby and soft.

'Think nothing of it, my friend. It is good of you to join us. Let me introduce my colleague, Mr. Yassin.' Rabbani's smile exposed his nicotine stained teeth but didn't reach as far as his eyes.

Yassin shook hands but made no attempt to remove the scowl from his face. He was short, round faced and heavy gutted. He also had a moustache drooping either side of his mouth, but in his case his hair was thick and untidy, his sideburns long and gray. He didn't say anything.

'Please, take a seat,' Rabbani indicated the empty chair. 'Coffee?'

'Thank you. It's been a while since breakfast.'

Rabbani stood, walked around the desk and went over to the coffee machine. He placed a cup under the nozzle and pressed a button. There was a whirling and grinding noise followed by the gurgle of the coffee as the cup filled.

'Milk? Sugar?'

'Just milk, thanks.'

Rabbani came back with the coffee and handed it to Hunter. Sitting down, he flipped the lid on a gold box and offered Hunter a cigarette.

'I don't, thanks.' He took a sip of coffee and added, 'Excellent.'

'It's Arabian. A blend I have made up at one of the specialist shops nearby. I am addicted to caffeine as well as nicotine,' he smiled, lighting a fresh cigarette with a gold lighter. He inhaled deeply and said, 'The cigarettes are specially rolled for me as well. I like to think of myself as a connoisseur of coffee and tobacco.'

Yassin took out a packet of cigarettes from his jacket pocket, used his own lighter and inhaled just as deeply.

'I was admiring your paintings as I came up the stairs.'

Rabbani waved the cigarette in front of him in a dismissive gesture. 'All original, all very expensive and all a good investment, though I have no intention of selling any of them. Collecting them is a passion of mine. Now, why did you want this meeting?'

'I want to discuss the prospect of us doing some serious business together.'

'I have many interests that range across the world. Why should I wish to do business with you?'

'The size of the profits?' Hunter suggested.

'That is a major consideration, of course. In what line are we talking about? Computers? Mobile phones? A new type of car? Electric perhaps?'

Hunter took a sip of coffee and stayed silent for a few seconds after the other man had finished speaking.

'First, I had no idea you dealt in any of those things, but we both know they aren't why I'm here.'

'Why are you here, Mr. Hughes?'

'I'm talking narcotics.'

'I don't deal in narcotics.'

It was more or less what Hunter had expected him to say.

'Then I am sorry to have wasted your time.' Hunter placed the cup and saucer on the desk and stood up. 'I was obviously misinformed. I shall let my supplier know.'

'Who is your supplier?'

Hunter looked quizzically at the other man and then shook his head. 'Never mind who he is. You're not interested in doing business so I bid you good day.'

'Wait. Please. Sit down. You have made me curious. Let us discuss matters.'

'What's there to discuss?' Hunter asked, though he sat back

down and lifted the cup and saucer off the desk. Raising the cup to his mouth, he took a sip.

'Let us not be too hasty, my friend. We can discuss matters like businessmen.'

Hunter sat back and crossed his right knee over his left. 'Mr. Rabbani,' he kept his tone neutral, masking the disdain he felt for the man opposite, 'I have other contacts I can speak to. I was told that for a shipment the size of the one I am offering, you would be the man to deal with. That you would be able to take advantage of future deliveries as well. If that isn't so,' Hunter shrugged, 'then I am evidently wasting my time and yours. For which, incidentally, I apologise.'

Rabbani was looking at Hunter through slitted eyes. 'No apology is necessary. However, Mr. Hughes, let me first assure you that no business is too big. Nor would it be too frequent.'

By baiting Rabbani, Hunter had the desired reaction. The man had an ego to match his moustache.

Rabbani added, 'What are we talking about? I hope it's not anything such as skunk. There's little profit in weed nowadays.'

'It's not.'

'Coke?'

'Heroin.' Hunter reached into an inside pocket and threw a small sachet of reddish brown powder on the desk.

Rabbani looked at it. 'Afghani. This is some sort of joke, right?' His sneer was evident.

'No,' Hunter shook his head. 'It's no joke. That's a sample of a sample. I will supply half a kilo of grade A heroin for you to have analysed. Hell, as far as I'm concerned, you can even use it yourself.'

'I do not use drugs, Mr. Hughes. Mr. Yassin, perhaps you will be good enough to take this sample and check it's purity.'

'Yes, sir.' Yassin stood and took the packet. 'I will be twenty minutes.'

'Thank you, Mr. Yassin,' Rabbani called to the retreating figure. He looked back at Hunter, 'Would you like some fresh coffee?'

'No, thank you. Why will he take so long? We both know it's easy to check if it is heroin.'

Rabbani nodded. 'It is quick and simple to check if a substance has only traces of heroin but it's purity takes longer.'

Hunter nodded, put the cup in the saucer and placed both on the table in front of him before getting to his feet. 'I'll be going. However, I will come back in one hour. If you like what I have, I will make the necessary arrangements to give you the remainder of the sample. A half kilo as a sign of my good faith. Consider it a gift from me.'

Rabbani's voice was harsh and cold. 'I would prefer it if you remained here, Mr. Hughes. If you don't mind.' The smile still contained no warmth.

Hunter knew that if he meekly gave in, the other man would continue to give instructions, instead of making requests. He would see himself as the superior of the two of them.

Smiling, he leaned forward and put both his fists on the desk. He spoke softly. 'I don't think so, Mr. Rabbani. I will be back in about one hour. I am here to do a deal with you,' he spelt it out, 'as equals.'

It was obvious that Rabbani didn't like that idea but said nothing, merely nodded.

Standing up straight, Hunter spun on his heels and stalked from the room. He glanced back at the other man in time to see the anger on Rabbani's face.

He took the stairs two at a time. Smiling at the man by the door, he said, 'I'll be back in an hour.' He let himself out and walked briskly along the pavement. He'd had enough coffee and so decided to go for a stroll, enjoying the sunshine and fresh air.

12

HAVING ESTABLISHED HIS independence by arriving late and leaving of his own accord, Hunter was back exactly 60 minutes later. His welcome was the same. The tableau in the room was identical to when he had first arrived.

'Ah, Mr. Hughes, do sit down,' Rabbani greeted him. 'The product is of excellent quality. Eighty percent pure. Do you have the rest?'

Hunter nodded. 'Naturally. Though not with me.'

'Why is that?' Rabbani narrowed his eyes, his anger showing through the veneer of civilisation he cloaked himself in. Hunter wondered briefly if the man had a problem with anger management.

'I will deliver the remainder of the heroin in two days when you can have its purity checked again. By then, we should have worked out a plan of action.'

'A plan of action? That seems an odd way of putting it. I don't understand.'

'Mr. Rabbani, I may be representing someone but I am not employed by him. He has made me a very lucrative offer which enables me to do business on highly favourable terms. Like I said, I knew of you, hence this meeting. However, as you know only too well, you aren't the only player in town.'

'So why me in particular?' Rabbani leaned back and sucked heavily on a cigarette.

'There's no reason. If you don't want to do business then I couldn't, quite frankly, care less. If you do, then we can proceed.' Hunter shrugged, a man without a care in the world.

Rabbani could call his bluff and he would have to back-pedal. If he did, then Rabbani would assume the upper hand and make Hunter's plans more difficult to implement. 'Do keep in mind that we are talking about a very considerable profit.'

Rabbani nodded. 'How big a shipment are we talking about?'

'Street value?'

'Yes. Let us say street value.'

Hunter nodded. 'At least three million.'

'Euros or pounds?'

'Does it matter?'

Rabbani chuckled, still without mirth. 'How do I know this isn't a set up?'

'By whom?'

'The authorities.'

'The police?' Hunter looked surprised.

'Police, MI5 even MI6. How can I be sure?'

'Three million pounds worth of heroin is how. No police force in the world can afford to use such a large amount of bait.'

Rabbani nodded. 'What you say is true.'

'I appreciate what you're saying. So far, you've broken no law that I'm aware of. Let us move step by step. Feel each other out as it were. I am sure that whatever you do will not be directly connected to you.'

Rabbani seemed to consider the suggestion before he nodded, much to Hunter's relief. Hunter was sure that greed had taken the upper hand.

'If it is the street value, what sort of percentage profits are we talking about?'

'You and I know that a number of people have to be paid to make a deal like this work. I don't wish to risk imprisonment for the sake of a few additional percentage points of profit. You and I can discuss the matter at your convenience.'

'Why not now?'

Hunter shook his head. 'I'm sorry, but it's not convenient. However, this evening would be, if it suits you.'

Rabbani lit a fresh cigarette. 'Do you know the Blue Parrot Club, near Victoria Bus Station?'

'No, but I can find it.'

'Shall we meet there at, say, eleven o'clock?'

Hunter nodded and stood up. 'Once we agree a deal I will supply the half kilo. You test it first and then we will discuss the main delivery. The how and the where. Like I have already said, I want to proceed one step at a time. I'm in this for the long haul and we need procedures in place. There is too much profit to take risks. We need to meet and make the necessary arrangements. I hope you're of the same mind.'

Rabbani nodded. 'Most assuredly. If the terms are attractive enough then it should be highly lucrative. For future transactions we must have mutual trust.'

'Precisely.' Hunter stood up and offered his hand. Rabbani stood up and shook it. Merely nodding to Yassin, Hunter left the room.

Moments later, he was in the street and strolling towards the Square. He was pretty sure that he was being followed. Should he lose the man, lead him a merry dance or confront him and tell him to get lost? While he thought about it, he wandered up to Knightsbridge, past the French Embassy and crossed the road to Hyde Park.

By then he knew he was definitely being followed by the man who had been sitting at the back of the foyer. He was pasty faced like his colleague, though tall and thin, with black hair reaching over his ears. It seemed to Hunter that the man wasn't much good at his job.

Going through the Prince of Wales Gate, he passed the putting green and headed over to the Diana, Princess of Wales Memorial. Walking past, he stood by the Lido and the Serpentine, looking down at the water. He was contemplating what to do. The man was sitting on a park bench about 200m away.

Hunter made up his mind. He would continue to negotiate from a position of strength. He looked at his watch, turned on his heel and marched towards the man, not looking at him but passing within a few metres of where he was sitting. The man, taken by surprise, didn't move but looked away.

Likewise, Hunter continued not to look at the man. He was behind the man's left shoulder and out of his direct line of vision. Nobody else was taking any notice of either of them and Hunter suddenly veered to his left and came up directly behind the seated man.

Clamping his hand around the man's throat, Hunter squeezed and as the man jerked and grabbed Hunter's hand with both his own, Hunter bent down and hissed, 'Don't move or I'll squeeze very tightly.'

The man grasped at the fingers around his neck and tried to

pull the hand clear. It took a great deal of effort by Hunter, but his fingers didn't move.

'Tell Rabbani I'll be there this evening. If he sends another one of you goons to follow me the deal is off. Do I make myself understood?' There was no response. 'Do I? Nod if you understand.'

The man's head jerked forward slightly and back.

'Good. Go away.' He let the man go.

The man stood up with alacrity, massaging his neck, glaring at Hunter. He said a few words that Hunter recognised as Russian but didn't understand. However, it was obviously pure invective. He was an inch or so taller than Hunter and looked as though he knew how to handle himself. Hunter realised it was the unexpectedness of his move that had made it relatively easy.

'Oh,' added Hunter, 'and no hard feelings.'

The other man said nothing, made no gesture of understanding, but hurried off. Hunter wondered what he would actually report to Rabbani. After all, he hadn't exactly handled things in a way that his boss would approve.

Hunter strolled around the Serpentine and along to the pier. It was beginning to warm up and he took off his jacket and slung it over his shoulder. He was carefully checking his surroundings, ensuring nobody was taking any undue interest in him. There didn't appear to be, but he decided to make sure. He wandered into Harvey Nichols immediately grateful for the refreshing, air-conditioned atmosphere.

After browsing for 10 minutes or so, he was finally satisfied. Returning to the Cunningham, he phoned Macnair. The call was answered immediately. 'Sir?'

'How did the meeting go?'

'Okay, I'd say.' He gave a detailed report.

When he was finished, Macnair chuckled. 'Good. You played it just right. You saw only the three men? Two bodyguards and this Yassin?'

'There could be more. It was Yassin who took the heroin away for analysis but whether or not he did the testing I have no idea. By the way, what happened in Barking?'

'Bob Snow rang. They arrived in time. The man you shot in the thigh is one of the cousins.'

'How is he? Have you heard?'

'Yes. Bob's just off the phone. He said the man will live, but his leg has to be amputated just below his hip.'

'I'm sorry to hear that.' There was little conviction in Hunter's voice.

Macnair chuckled. 'If you saw his record sheet you wouldn't be. He really is a piece of work.'

'And Cuthbert?'

'The knee joint is shattered. It means another amputation, this time just above where the bullet hit.'

'Tough. What about the others?'

'Goldie has a broken jaw. The girl is fine, and so is a man named Vince.'

'Winston?'

'He'll walk with a limp for the rest of his life.'

'Good. What's going to happen to them?'

'The police got nothing from any of them. They claimed they're innocent and were attacked by two masked men without any reason.'

'Was any more heroin found?'

'Yes. In special compartments under the floor of the van they found another kilogram.

Hunter chuckled. 'And they claim to be innocent?'

'Farcical, I know. However you stack it up, the lot of them will be enjoying quite a few years at the pleasure of her Majesty.'

'That sounds good to me.'

'So all's well that ends well as far as the Doolittles are concerned.' They said their goodbyes.

Hunter lay down on the bed, hands behind his head, thinking things through. He was still working it out when he fell asleep. Years of training had ingrained into him to sleep whenever possible. You never knew when you'd need it.

He slept soundly for the best part of 2 hours. When he awoke he decided to go downstairs to the restaurant for a cup of coffee rather than make his own. He just hoped it was better than the one he'd been served at breakfast. As it was just after 18.00 the bar was already beginning to get busy. The clientele were mainly foreign tourists, judging by the mix of languages. Ordering a coffee, Hunter sat in a corner, facing the door, his back to the wall.

He was now dressed in an open necked, gray casual shirt, black trousers and a gray coloured jacket. The shirt hung outside his trousers and covered his bumbag nestling against his gut. The Pocketlite sat snugly and comfortably inside.

He lingered over his coffee. The bar began to get packed and when three people sat at his table without so much as a by your leave, he left. He strolled along the pavement to the Underground, working his way through the crowd that was slowly but surely thinning out as the evening progressed. He bought a ticket for Victoria and went down to the platform. The train came in and he fought his way on with the commuters who were desperate to get home and out of the stifling heat.

At Victoria, he went to the information office for directions to The Blue Parrot. It was less than a 10 minute stroll.

Outside the entrance to the club he read that it was guaranteed to be as good as a visit to Rick's in Casablanca. The film was one of Hunter's favourites.

Opening hours were from 21.00 until 04.00. Entry was £20 with a free cocktail. The door was protected by a steel shutter and there were no windows. He walked along to the edge of the building and up an alleyway which, much to his surprise was relatively free of rubbish and clutter. There were windows along the wall, each with iron bars as well as a fine steel mesh. Even so, Hunter suspected that local glaziers were kept pretty busy. He passed an emergency exit and went around the back where he found another two doors as well as a window also protected from damage. The fourth side of the building had no windows but another emergency exit. The owners obviously took their obligations for the safety of their patrons seriously.

Killing time, he walked slowly along the street. Thunderclouds were gathering and he figured he had only minutes to find shelter. As he stepped through the doorway of a busy pub the heavens opened and the rain came down like a waterfall.

The pub was modern Olde Worlde with a range of cask ales on offer. Though he was sorely tempted, he sipped an iced water which cost about the same as a decent pint of beer. Leaning on the counter, he wondered what the evening would bring.

The rain was lasting longer than he'd expected and so he

ordered a mediocre fish pie dinner washed down with yet more water. When the rain finally stopped, the club had been open for 50 minutes and so he headed back.

There were two doormen. Big men who had obviously enhanced their stature using steroids while working out at a gym. They nodded at Hunter, but said nothing, as he walked through the glass, double doors.

Inside, a full-size cut-out of a very large man - Signor Ferrari, alias Sydney Greenstreet, welcomed all visitors to The Blue Parrot.

13

THERE WAS A reception area, a place to hand over any unwanted coats and an attractive cashier who relieved visitors of their £20. He thanked her for his entrance ticket when she informed him that he could exchange it at the bar for a special Blue Parrot cocktail. Nodding his appreciation, he walked through a set of double doors.

It was like stepping into another world or a film set of a 1930s film.

The walls were covered with photographs of Rick Blaine, alias Humphrey Bogart. Then there was Ingrid Bergman, Paul Henreid and Conrad Veidt in his Nazi uniform. There were many photographs of Sydney Greenstreet wearing a fez and sporting a fly whisk.

Music was playing in the background. It was the tinkling of the piano and Dooley Wilson, who played Sam, singing As Time Goes By. Hunter knew that Hal Wallis, who produced the film, had considered having Wilson's voice dubbed but in the end didn't bother. However, as Wilson was a drummer and not a piano player, the piano was played by somebody else.

It was a large room. One wall was lined with a bar with a foot rail running its full length. The bar was well stocked with just about every drink known to man. There were a couple of bar tenders, young girls, each wearing artificial smiles and tired looks.

'Your cocktail, sir?'

Hunter looked at the dark blue, iced drink and managed not to shudder at the sight of it. 'No, thanks. I just want an iced water.'

'Yes, sir.' She opened a bottle, poured its contents into a glass, added ice, handed it across to Hunter and said, 'That'll be £8.50, sir.'

Hunter nodded nonchalantly as he handed over the cash. There was no doubt the place was licensed to print money. A few customers had arrived already, though not many. He guessed the majority would appear as the pubs began to close.

He crossed the room and sat at a table in a corner. There was seating for at least 200 people, a stage to his left had musical instruments but no musicians and an archway opposite led to a casino. In the ceiling were slowly rotating wooden fans which were obviously for show, the temperature being regulated by air-conditioning.

To his right was a booth with seating for 8, possibly 10 customers. It was roped off. The place reeked of money. It was an opulent set-up with, he had to admit, something of a welcoming feel to it. He wondered who owned it.

Water in hand, he stood up and wandered around. He identified two of the emergency exits and found a third at the end of a short corridor that led to the Gents' toilets. As the Ladies' was across the other side he assumed there was another exit to be found there.

Walking under the archway to the casino he stopped to look at what was available. There were two roulette tables, two blackjack tables and one table for poker.

Through an archway opposite, he saw a dance floor that was in darkness. He was aware the ceiling was lined with cameras. They were unobtrusive and not very noticeable.

He returned to his seat and watched as the place filled up. Champagne corks were beginning to pop and things were getting rowdier by the minute. A wine list had appeared on the tables and out of idle curiosity he glanced through the one placed in front of him. The cheapest plonk was £35 a bottle, Champagne ranged from £65 to £235 and a double whisky set you back the same price you'd pay for a bottle of malt in a wine merchants. The prices suggested that money was no object to the clientele. Perhaps the majority of those using the place were city bankers, Hunter thought, cynically. By now, the barmaids had increased to eight, all with the same false smiles and worn out looks.

A four piece band appeared, spent a couple of minutes tuning their instruments and began playing a speeded up version of As Time Goes By.

His watch showed 23.30 making Rabbani half an hour late. There was a commotion at the door and Hunter looked across

the room to see what was happening. The doors were practically
thrown open and held back by two of the female staff. Rabbani
stalked in followed by Yassin, the same two men Hunter had seen
at the house and three well-dressed young girls. He wondered
if the bodyguards had anyone to relieve them or if they were
permanently at Rabbani's beck and call. Such a grand entrance
surprised Hunter.

The maitre d' rushed across the room, virtually bowed to
Rabbani and led him across the room to the roped off booth.
With a flourish he unclipped the rope and ushered the party into
their seats.

No orders were given. Waitresses appeared with trays bearing
Champagne, opened the bottles and poured. Rabbani and the men
sat watching silently, the girls with a good deal of giggling and
gesticulating. They, at least, appeared to be enjoying themselves.

Hunter sat where he was for a few more minutes. One of the
waitresses walked close by and he gestured her over. 'Can I have
a whisky and soda, please? The Glenfiddich. Single shot, same
amount of soda, one ice cube.'

'Yes, sir. Certainly, sir.'

She scurried away while he kept looking at the pantomime that
was being played out in the booth. The waitress returned and
Hunter handed over £15 and told her to keep the change.

As she thanked him, he added, 'By the way, who's that man
over there? The one you're all fawning over?' He nodded towards
them but even as he asked, the penny dropped and he knew what
she was going to say.

'Sir, that's Mr. Rabbani. The owner.'

Hunter smiled and nodded his thanks. He was looking across
the room when the man he'd encountered in the park looked
towards him, saw him and spoke to Rabbani. He looked over
and waved at Hunter to join them. Hunter stood up, picked up his
drink and wandered across.

'Do sit down, my friend,' Rabbani greeted him.

Smiling his thanks, Hunter slid into the booth opposite Rabbani,
alongside one of the girls. A glance told him that the three girls
were high on some drug which he guessed was cocaine. He
doubted any one of them had reached their 21st birthday.

Hunter lifted his whisky and soda in salute and said,

'Congratulations. I like your club. You have created just the right ambience.'

'Thank you. It is highly profitable. I have similar clubs in Manchester and Glasgow.'

'I thought we were going to discuss a little business.'

'We are.'

'Not in front of these girls,' Hunter shook his head.

'They don't speak English. I can guarantee it.' As he spoke, Rabbani reached inside his coat pocket and took out a gold cigarette case. Placing a cigarette in his mouth, one of the guards reached across with a gold lighter and clicked the flame into life. Rabbani inhaled deeply.

'What happened to the no smoking ban?'

'That, my friend, is for the customers and is strictly enforced.'

Hunter nodded his acceptance of the statement. 'This is an excellent way to distribute drugs. Both coke and heroin.'

Rabbani shook his head in mock exasperation. 'Certainly not, though others have tried. This is not only legitimate but clean. Anyone found selling or distributing drugs here will never do it a second time.'

'What, the force of the law too much?' Hunter raised a quizzical eyebrow.

'My friend, you know and I know the law is virtually powerless in situations of a little drug selling or using. A small fine, a tap on the wrist. No, I ensure the people involved don't do it a second time. My regular customers are aware of the displeasure of the management and, on the whole, are discouraged from using or selling drugs when here. The occasional aberration is quickly dealt with.'

'Looking at this lot, it must reduce your clientele on a regular basis.'

Rabbani shook his head. 'You'd be surprised. Of course, many are high before they get here, which suits me admirably.'

'Less inhibited, more expensive drinks bought and more gambling?'

'Precisely.'

Hunter was impressed in spite of himself. He lifted his glass in silent salute, took a sip and replaced the glass on the table.

'Is that whisky?'

'Yes. With soda.'

'Let me get you one.'

'I still have this,' he indicated the table in front of him.

Rabbani smiled. 'If that is the house whisky then it is the supermarket's own brand. Let me get you a decent malt.' He gestured and the maitre d' appeared within moments. 'What would you like?'

'Do you have a Strathperth?' It was a superb malt with the added advantage of the distillery being owned by his family.

'Yes, sir. I shall bring it right away.'

'Also, bring me a small bottle of soda water with ice on the side.' Then, he added as an afterthought, 'Please.' Hunter liked to mix his own drinks. The one he had been served was too diluted for his taste.

'Yes, sir. Certainly, sir.' The man's tone and the way he bowed his head was a lesson in obsequiousness.

While they waited for the drink, Hunter said, 'The combo is very talented,' he nodded at the stage.

'I employ only the best and I pay them a decent wage. That way I buy loyalty as well as talent.'

'That is a good maxim by which to run a business. Any business. Legal or illegal,' he added for good measure.

'Thank you. I have to thank Mr. Yassin for his sound advice when it comes to such matters. He ensures I stay on the straight and narrow when it comes to making a profit.'

Hunter looked at Yassin, raised his glass in salute and took a sip, barely wetting is lips. The new drink, at least a double, appeared in short order. Hunter added a small amount of the soda, dropped in one ice cube, raised the glass to Rabbani and took an appreciative sip. 'Excellent.'

While this ritual was being played out, the three girls were continuing to giggle, two with a hand in Rabbani's lap while the third had her hand in the lap of the tall thin bodyguard. The second bodyguard, along with Yassin, were ignored.

The background noise was a constant hum, the music was pleasant but not intrusive and people were obviously enjoying themselves.

'When does the dancing start?'

'Not until midnight, after the patrons have relaxed and their inhibitions are reduced.'

'I say it again. I'm very impressed. No wonder it's so popular. Though the prices are a bit steep.'

Rabbani smiled, but as usual, only with his mouth. 'It helps to keep the riffraff out.'

Hunter nodded, as though agreeing with the wisdom of such a policy. Then he waited, wanting to hear what Rabbani had to say. Rabbani appeared to be of the same mind as he also said nothing. Hunter took another sip of his Strathperth.

A few minutes more passed until finally, Rabbani said, 'Shall we get down to business?'

Hunter noticed that Rabbani had not taken a drink of the wine in the flute glass in front of him and neither had Yassin. The two bodyguards didn't even have a glass in front of them. The girls had flutes of sparkling wine that Hunter assumed was Champagne. Or perhaps they were drinking a cheap sparkling wine, poured from a Champagne bottle.

'By all means. What did you have in mind?'

'I am waiting to hear what your offer is.'

Hunter shrugged. 'I have agreed a price with Bulgaria. It's based on today's prices. We are talking about a regular shipment and the market can go down as well as up. The former being more likely if we bring in a lot of good stuff. So we need to be talking percentages as opposed to fixed amounts.'

'But that is not usual, my friend. It is more common to agree a price and work to that.'

Hunter nodded. 'Yes, that's so. But I for one do not wish to meet and discuss prices whenever we have arranged a further shipment. I don't want you to yell blue murder if there's no profit because we agree a price and the bottom's dropped out of the market. Likewise, I don't want to be caught in the middle either.'

Rabbani sat in silence. Then he looked at Yassin and engaged him in conversation. Hunter recognised a few words and knew they were speaking Urdu. After a few minutes of dialogue, he turned back to Hunter. 'Mr. Yassin says that what you say makes a great deal of sense. A disagreement between partners is the most common reason for a lucrative business to go belly up.'

'Precisely.'

'I like what you tell me, Mr. Hughes. Or may I call you Nick?'

'By all means, call me Nick, Ashraf.'

'Let us drink to our friendship and our business. May it make us a great deal of money.'

They clinked glasses, both smiling, both with cold eyes.

'So where do we start?' Rabbani asked.

'I'll deal personally with the price paid to my, or I should say our, supplier. It will be on a per kilo basis for each shipment. We'll work from that.'

Rabbani nodded. 'Yes. I think that is more than acceptable.'

'In the meantime, I will supply you with the remainder of the sample for analysis.' Hunter picked up his glass and took another tiny sip. 'Ashraf, this is a long term arrangement when the real money will be made. We'll move slowly and steadily to give us time to trust one another.'

'That is the way I like to do business, though not too slowly.'

'I agree. Not too slowly.'

Hunter reached down to his thigh and picked up the hand of the young lady sitting next to him, smiled briefly at her, shook his head and placed her hand in her lap.

She pouted in a childish manner and turned her attention back to the tall, scrawny guard with the silver hair who was sitting on her other side.

'You are not interested?' Rabbani nodded at the girl.

Hunter smiled. 'I never mix business with pleasure and this is a business meeting.'

Rabbani nodded. 'Just so.'

At that moment, the band stopped playing and, thanked by a smattering of applause, left the stage. Rock n' roll music struck up and the dulcet tones of Elvis Presley wafted through the air. Hunter glanced at his watch. It was midnight. Rabbani ran an efficient and tight ship.

'How do you propose that we get the remainder of the sample?'

'I can deliver it tomorrow,' Hunter replied.

Rabbani appeared to be thinking about it, and then he smiled and nodded, 'That is suitable. Would ten o'clock in the morning be convenient?'

Hunter shook his head. 'Sorry, but no. I have something to do in the morning. How about two o'clock?'

'Fine. If you will excuse me.' Rabbani stood up and immediately the short haired, squat bodyguard did the same thing. Both men walked towards the Gents.

Rabbani was evidently a very cautious man. Here he was, in public, in a busy club, and yet he still felt the need for protection. Was there any significance or was Rabbani just being careful? It was hard to say, but Hunter decided it was probably the latter.

When the men returned and Rabbani had resumed his seat, he said, 'You do not wish to try your luck gambling? Or dancing? There are many attractive young ladies here.'

Hunter smiled. 'I don't gamble. Ever. Also, I don't care for these type of young ladies. They are probably expensive.'

Shrugging, Rabbani said, 'Not as expensive as wining and dining for days, possibly weeks, before you get your way.'

Hunter nodded. 'True. But I enjoy the chase. It appeals to my primeval instincts and when I succeed, those instincts are satisfied. The chase is often more thrilling than the capture.'

Rabbani laughed. 'You may be right. Me, I cannot be bothered with the chase. I like to achieve the result and the quicker the goal is reached, the better.'

'I can understand that. We should make a good partnership. Me slow and careful, you pushing for results.'

Again, the other man laughed and nodded. 'Would you like another drink?' He indicated Hunter's barely touched glass.

'No, thank you. I must be going.'

'Surely not! Stay and enjoy what is left of the evening.'

'Sorry. I have phone calls to make and e-mails to send. My business is on a global scale though, I admit, not nearly as grand as yours.'

Rabbani nodded, appearing to accept the compliment as his due.

Hunter had achieved two things with that one sentence. First, he had hinted at the fact that he wasn't a two bit hustler trying to break into the big time. Second, he had acknowledged the size of Rabbani's enterprise by comparison and hence flattered the man's ego.

'Now, I really must go. I'll be in touch.' Hunter stood up and smiled at Rabbani, ignoring the remainder at the table.

Rabbani acknowledged Hunter with a slight nod and then turned away from him.

Hunter walked towards the exit. Having been associated with Rabbani, the manager fawned over him as he reached the door, personally holding it open and bowing from the waist. Hunter nodded and slipped £10 into the man's hand. The manager's obvious disdain at such a paltry sum made Hunter chuckle as he left the building.

14

OUTSIDE, IT WAS warm but clear. The earlier mugginess had been washed away by the thunderstorm and it was a pleasure to be outdoors. He stood for a few moments, savouring the night. It would, he thought, be a perfect night to be sailing across the Channel, to a French fishing port or even going as far south as Portugal.

He slipped across the road and into a dark alleyway he'd scouted earlier. Standing in the deep shadow he watched the door. Although patrons were going in, none were coming out. Neither did either of the bodyguards.

Satisfied he wasn't being followed, he stepped out from the alleyway and hailed a taxi. On the journey back to the hotel, Hunter contemplated what he should do next. Timescale was the main issue at that point. He'd give it two more days and then, come hell or high water, he'd make his move.

Back in the Cunningham there was a night porter who served him a large whisky with a dash of soda and ice. He took it with him to his room. This time, he enjoyed more than a mere sip.

He lifted his grip out from the wardrobe. The bottom of the bag was false and had a compartment about 1.5cms deep. He emptied its contents onto the sideboard and checked over each item. The listening bugs were state-of-the-art. Made of plastic, they were undetectable to anyone waving a wand over him. They were the size of a penny piece and just as thick. If pressed against a hard surface, a small bubble in the middle of the back popped and a highly effective glue seeped out. The bug stuck instantly into position. The receiver/transmitter was about the size of a cigarette packet and could be fixed in the same way. The bugs could transmit up to about 100m, but if there was a wall intervening that was cut by at least half. The transmitter, on the other hand, operated through the mobile phone system. As a result, it could broadcast anything picked up by the bugs to anywhere in the world. Furthermore, each bug was used on a slightly different frequency. This meant there was no overlapping of recordings and so whatever was said didn't become scrambled. The receiver was at TIFAT HQ.

Once he was satisfied that the kit was in working order, Hunter finished his drink before getting ready for bed.

Breakfast was a leisurely affair of scrambled eggs and bacon. The remainder of the morning he spent wandering the streets and visiting a couple of coffee shops. Hunter arrived at West Halkin Street with time to spare. He sauntered down the other side of the street to Rabbani's house. Opposite the front door, he paused. It took him only seconds to press the transmitter under a window ledge. Unless someone went looking for it, the device was virtually impossible to spot.

It was 14.00. Hunter crossed the road and pressed the doorbell. The door was opened by the silver haired bodyguard whilst the other guard sat on the chair.

The wand was waved over him, there was no bleeping and he was allowed to enter.

The man didn't say a word. He merely turned and headed for the stairs.

Hunter stayed a few paces behind. As he trod on the lowest step of the stairs, he placed his hand on the banister and squeezed his thumb on the underside. The bug he'd been holding was instantly stuck into position. Anything said in the foyer would be picked up and transmitted.

When he reached the next floor, he did the same again. The guard knocked on the door and opened it. He gestured for Hunter to enter. Rabbani and Yassin were sitting in the same seats as previously.

'My dear Nick, welcome.'

'Ashraf, good afternoon.' Reaching into each of his jacket pockets, he removed two plastic bags containing a reddish brown powder and handed them to Yassin. 'Mr. Yassin, if you would care to analyse these.'

Yassin stood up, nodded at Hunter and left the room.

'He is a man of very few words,' said Rabbani. 'But then, I don't pay him for his entertaining company.'

'What do you pay him for?' The question was asked nonchalantly as Hunter placed the palm of his hand under the desk with his thumb on top. He squeezed the bug into position.

'Mainly his legal advice.'

'Not for his ability to carry out a chemical analysis of drugs?'

Shaking his head, Rabbani said, 'Certainly not. He would be most offended at such a suggestion.'

Hunter looked quizzical. 'Then who does the analysis?'

Seeing Rabbani hesitate Hunter raised a hand, palm outwards and answered his own question. 'No! Don't say a word! I don't want to know and nor is it my business. Please excuse me asking.'

Rabbani chuckled. As he lit another cigarette from the stub of the one he was already smoking, he said, 'Not at all. I don't mind. It's the chef.'

'The chef?' Hunter couldn't keep the surprise out of his voice.

'Yes, the chef. He's a good cook as well as an expert at analysing drugs. May I offer you something? A drink? Or a coffee?'

'No, thanks. I'm here to discuss our deal. Once we're agreed we can socialise.' He smiled to show there was no insult intended.

Rabbani sat back in his chair, dragged deeply on the cigarette, leant forward and flicked the ash into an ashtray at his right elbow. It was a classic delaying tactic while he thought about his response, though he'd obviously decided on an offer.

'You will be the middle man. Will you be handling the merchandise yourself?'

'I don't think that's relevant.'

'I am sorry,' there was no apology in his voice, 'but I think it is. It enables me to gauge your likely expenses. As I see it, you will arrange a delivery place while the supplier will make the drop. My men will take it away. I cannot see any risk on your part nor any work, come to that.'

Hunter shook his head. 'That is of no importance. I have to see that the supplies arrive safely and where we want them, make the pay-off and then ensure your men collect the stuff. Once they have their hands on it, your well-oiled, European wide, distribution network does the rest. As always, you're clean.'

Rabbani said nothing for a few seconds and then asked, 'What percentage do you want?'

'Ten percent of the street price.'

'Don't be ludicrous. That's far too much.'

'I don't think so. I will have expenses as well as risk.'

'But nothing like what I'll be facing,' Rabbani protested.

'Ashraf, I know only too well how you've covered yourself. It's one of the reasons I came to you in the first place. Your underlings make all the necessary arrangements and payments, while ensuring the cut-offs and deadends are foolproof.'

'Nothing is foolproof,' Rabbani said coldly.

'Maybe not, but your organisation is close to it. You feed it at one end and take your profits at the other end.'

'That may be so, but the whole point about dealing with the product we are talking about is the size of the profits we are able to make. You wish for too much. What about the supplier? What does he wish for?'

'Twenty percent of street price.'

Rabbani thought for a few seconds and then nodded. 'That I agree to pay the producer. However, you demand too much.'

It was all sham but because of what was at stake, Hunter couldn't be seen to be giving in too quickly. The discussion went back and forth until Hunter agreed to 8%. There followed a further debate on how street value would be established until, as a concession, Hunter agreed to let Rabbani report the price. After all, as each of them conceded, this was a long term venture.

Finally, they shook hands. Rabbani's smile was wide and genuine. He was very happy with the potential profits he would make.

Just then, Yassin returned. He nodded to Rabbani and said, 'It is the same.'

'Thank you, Mr. Yassin.

Hunter smiled. 'As I said, please keep the half kilo as a sign of my good faith and as a seal on our bargain.'

'Thank you, Nick.' Rabbani showed his nicotine stained teeth and, not having had a cigarette in at least five minutes, took one out of the box on his desk, lit it and inhaled deeply.

'They'll kill you one day,' said Hunter.

The response was a smile. 'We all have to go sometime. There is nothing more certain than death and taxes. The first I cannot prevent, but I can hope it will be later rather than sooner, the second I can avoid. It is the way of the world.' On that philosophical note he shrugged his shoulders. 'Now there is one more thing I wish to know. What is the name of your supplier?'

Hunter narrowed his eyes and stared at Rabbani, saying nothing.

'Come, come, my dear Nick. If we are to enter into such a large deal there must be trust on both sides.'

Hunter had hoped Rabbani would ask and check it out.

Rabbani said, impatiently, 'Well? Do you not trust me?'

Hunter shrugged. 'We have come this far, Ashraf, so I think there can't be any harm in telling you. He is a Bulgarian by the name of Dimitar Petrov. I must warn you not to make any enquiries with the police in Bulgaria. He's a highly wanted man.'

'Then how can he operate? How can he supply us?'

'He's well connected and has his ways. You know how it works.'

The enigmatic reply appeared to satisfy Rabbani who merely nodded. 'Will he be happy with our agreement? Or is he going to want to negotiate some more?'

Hunter shook his head. 'Let's say we are within the parameters that I agreed with him and leave it at that.'

There was a flash of anger and then Rabbani forced a smile and nodded.

Hunter said, 'I'll contact Petrov and tell him the arrangement and be back to you within the hour. Will that do?'

'It will have to, won't it? Are you sure you can trust this man?'

'Of course. Otherwise I wouldn't be here wasting my time or yours. I've been doing business with Petrov for a few years and I've never let him down and he's never let me down. By the same token, I don't expect to be let down or cheated by anyone either.' His voice hardened. 'I'd take very unkindly to that happening.'

Rabbani flicked ash into the overflowing ashtray by his elbow and asked mildly, 'Is that a threat?'

Hunter looked into his eyes. 'No, of course not. Using threats is a bad way to start a business relationship. It's been said of Nick Hughes that's he's a good friend and a really rotten enemy.'

Rabbani laughed. 'It's also been said of Ashraf Rabbani. Come, that's enough of the theatricals. What are you doing tomorrow evening?'

'Why?'

'I thought we might have a party to celebrate our partnership.'

'At your club? It's not my scene.'

'I was thinking of us going to my house near Southminster.'

'Where's that?'

'Near Burnham-on-Crouch.'

'I know Burnham.'

'Afterwards we can spend the day at sea. Get to know each other better. Perhaps go across the Channel in my boat. Have a day or two in France.'

'Your boat? What do you have? Sail or power?'

'Power. A Sunseeker Manhattan. I do not have the patience to sail. Me, when I want to go from one place to another, I like to go as fast as possible.'

Hunter nodded. 'I can appreciate that.'

'This is the boat.' He turned a framed photograph sitting on his desk to face Hunter. There was Rabbani in full yachting regalia standing on the open bridge. 'Talisman.'

'She's beautiful.' The boat was in the £1,500,000 bracket.

Rabbani smiled. 'The boat is seventy two feet and two inches or twenty one point three eight metres from bow to stern. It is five and a half metres at the beam and with a depth of just over one and a half metres below the water line. It will do a maximum of thirty one knots and cruise three hundred miles. It sleeps eight in en-suite accommodation and has room for two crew members.'

Hunter smiled in return. 'You sound like a sales brochure.' He spoke lightly, not wanting to insult the man in any way. 'Do you have any crew?'

'Certainly. Two of my countrymen. I have them deliver the boat where and when I want it but they are also very useful for other things.'

'Where do you keep her?'

'In the harbour at Burnham-on-Crouch.'

'Do you mean the marina?'

'Ah, yes. The marina.'

'That's a nice place to have a boat.' He looked at his watch. 'I need to go. Tomorrow sounds like it could be fun. Who'll be there?' he asked the question as nonchalantly as he could.

Rabbani narrowed his eyes. It was obvious that he did not like being asked such a direct question. Hunter realised it and said hastily, 'All I meant was how many will be there and are there going to be any women? Or is it just drinks with a few friends?'

Rabbani visibly relaxed. 'It will just be myself, Mr. Yassin, Boris and Oscar. I would tell you their surnames but they are virtually unpronounceable, especially by me.' He chuckled, self-deprecatingly. Hunter knew it was a complete act. 'There will also be the two crew from my boat, but that will be all. Of course, there will also be the ladies. One cannot have a party without ladies.'

'A select few indeed. Don't bother with a lady for me. I like to choose my own. Incidentally, which is Boris and which is Oscar?'

'Boris is the shorter of the two and Oscar has white hair.'

'Thanks. What's the address and what time?'

Rabbani picked up a pen and scribbled on a piece of paper. 'This is the address. The house is a mile south of Southminster on the B1021. You can't miss it. The gates to the property are on the left. The name on the post is Little Oaks. Come any time after eight o'clock.'

On that note, Hunter left. Although he took the precaution of ensuring he wasn't followed, he needn't have bothered. Nobody was so much as watching him.

The two men spoke Urdu. Rabbani raised his eyebrows to Yassin. 'Well?'

Yassin shrugged. 'He appears to be genuine. The amount of heroin he has given us is significant. I see no reason for a man like that to take such action if it wasn't true. But even so, I don't trust him completely.'

'You don't trust anybody completely which is why you're very useful to me.' Rabbani made no effort to take the sting out of his words. 'I don't have your doubts, but then you have enough for both of us. I cannot see any reason for doubt. He has no way of tricking us. We don't pay until we have distributed the product.'

'There is a British saying, never look a gift horse in the mouth.'

Rabbani smiled. 'Like most British sayings it makes no sense. Is it possible he has something to do with the law?'

Yassin shook his head. 'Ashraf, when did a law enforcement agency anywhere in the world hand over half a kilo of heroin?'

'That's what I've been telling myself. If we have him with us in Essex and on the boat we should have enough time to decide about the man. Like you, I can see nothing wrong.'

'What about this man, Petrov?' Yassin asked.

'We need to find out more about him. Can you arrange that?'

'Yes. It shouldn't be too difficult.'

'In time for us being on the Talisman?'

'That shouldn't be a problem.'

'Good. Either we have an enjoyable time or Mr. Hughes will be swimming with a heavy weight attached to his feet.'

'Did you send the message to Abida?' Rabbani enquired.

'Yes. She says she is looking forward to you arriving and so are the children. She plans a big celebration with all your relatives and friends there.'

'She always does,' said Rabbani dryly. 'No doubt all three of my wives will be bickering about who will do what.' He shook his head. 'Allah be praised I am not at home that often or for that long.'

Over 400 miles away, Macnair switched off the translation machine. The recordings made in London were in Urdu. The machine was near perfect in translating the Urdu into English. It was a clever bit of software Isobel's team had been working on for some time. Translators couldn't be hired as the messages were far too sensitive for anyone outside TIFAT to hear them. They were now able to translate a dozen languages into English, with more coming on stream. Macnair was toying with the idea of patenting the software through an off-shore company. The income would come in very useful to TIFAT.

His smile turned to a scowl. What he'd just heard didn't make sense when taken in the context of the rest of the information he had. He stood up and paced his office thinking through the implications. After awhile he stopped next to the coffee machine, poured a coffee, added milk, took a mouthful, grimaced and poured it down the sink. Making himself a fresh pot., he came to a conclusion. Somebody was lying. But who?

15

WHEN HUNTER ARRIVED back at his hotel he telephoned Macnair, 'Hello, sir. Are the bugs working okay?'

'Yes. Loud and clear except for the first one. It's more muted with an echo but we've filtered it and it's understandable.'

'That's the one in the foyer. Could you hear me and Rabbani?'

'Yes, no problem.'

'What about Boris and Oscar? Anything useful?'

'So far all they've talked about are some women they're to collect tomorrow afternoon from Chelmsford.'

'What did Rabbani and Yassin have to say?'

'That was rather illuminating. Rabbani spoke about having three wives.'

'That doesn't make any sense. I thought the Pakistanis said that his family had been wiped out?'

'So did I. That's evidently untrue. I'll try and check out the timeline. It's possible his first family was killed some time ago. But even so, if he's got three wives he's a fast worker.'

'Incidentally, if you don't come up to scratch they intend sending you swimming in the Channel with weights around your feet.'

Hunter ignored it. 'Do you have any information on Yassin?'

'Some. He left Pakistan at the age of five and came here with his parents. The father opened a corner shop. The local Paki's, opening at six o'clock in the morning and closing at midnight. Gave a great service to the community. He worked extremely hard wanting only a good life for his child.'

'No brothers or sisters?'

'None that we can find. His father lived long enough to see his son go to university but the poor sod dropped dead of a heart-attack. Yassin spent two years at Lancaster University taking law, hoping to become a solicitor.'

'I thought he was a solicitor.'

'No. He's a lawyer in international law.'

'How did that happen?'

'To be fair, Yassin hasn't had it easy. Or at least, he didn't as a young man. Just after his father died, his mother returned to Pakistan. We believe that she was to become the third or fourth wife of one of her late husband's brothers. As you know, not uncommon in Islamic countries. She died not long after arriving there. Because she was a British citizen, a death certificate was required and eventually one was forwarded. It was suspected that she committed suicide rather than marry the brother.'

'All that must have had one hell of an effect on Yassin.'

'It did. We've had access to the University's records and it appears as though he went off the rails about then. It was the usual sort of thing. Drinking too much, unpleasant arguments with other students, boycotting lectures, not doing his assignments. The reality was, he quit about a week before he was going to be chucked out.'

'So how did he become a lawyer?'

'He went back to Pakistan to the university of Karachi. He continued doing law. It appears he only just managed to get his degree.'

'Do we know how Rabbani and Yassin know each other?'

'They appear to be distant cousins.'

'Has Isobel managed to get into Rabbani's mobile phone?'

'She's still trying. She thought she'd managed it once yesterday but there's nothing there now. He's obviously cagey and changing his SIM card on a regular basis. Have you decided what you're doing yet?'

'Not as such. However, things have been made a lot easier with Rabbani out of London and in a quiet part of the world. The problem of getting rid of his bodyguards and any other hangers-on hasn't changed. However, being in the house means I probably won't get a better opportunity.'

'I concur.'

'Any chance of getting my hands on some Kolokol-1?' Hunter was referring to an opiate derived gas, made up of fentanyl and the highly potent carfentanil. It was effective within one or two seconds and took very little of the gas to render the person who sniffed it unconscious. It was effective for about 10 minutes.

The only after effects were a mild headache and a feeling of nausea. It had been developed at a secret military establishment near Leningrad in Russia back in the 1970s and was still in use, particularly in the event of a hostage situation.

'Yes. I'll also send some of the Benedrone our cousins across the Pond have developed.'

A single 1cc ampoule of Benedrone could put an average sized person to sleep for at least 6 hours, sometimes longer. The side effects were a worse headache and more nausea than that caused by the gas, sometimes resulting in actual vomiting.

'That should do.'

'What are you thinking?'

'My best bet is to deal with the bodyguards and the rest of them at the house, take Rabbani down to the marina and take the boat. Alternatively, if I don't get the chance, I can take Rabbani up on his offer of a day at sea and try there. The drawback to that is having to keep an eye on the bodyguards and crew once I make my move. If that happens then the sooner I hand them over to the Pakistanis the better. If I take the boat, then I can easily get to any ship in the Channel. Job done. It couldn't be easier.' Apart from the fact, he thought, that anything and everything that could go wrong probably would - it was Sod's law.

'Okay, let's work around that. Incidentally, we've had word that the attack on Pakistan will be in about six weeks. It's still very sketchy but you know how it is. Information is dripping through all the time. Whatever's going to happen, we supply Rabbani and that's our commitment over and done with. The rest is up to the Pakistanis with help from the Americans and some from us. It's coming up to five o'clock. I'll send a car and a couple of drivers and get the stuff to you first thing in the morning. It'll be at reception waiting for you.'

'Okay, thanks, sir.'

With that, the connection was broken. For Hunter, the evening dragged. He went out for a walk. It was still warm and getting muggy again after the storm of two nights earlier. He ended up in a pub with a pint of real ale and, much to his pleasant surprise, a very good steak and salad.

In the morning, he shaved and showered. He dressed in black trousers and a white shirt, before going down to reception where he collected the parcel that had been left for him. Back in his room, he opened it. The first thing he saw was the gasmask. It was the new type TIFAT had only just had delivered. The lightweight filter fitted over the nose and mouth and was much smaller than the older model. As a result, it was easier to carry and to conceal and was also more comfortable to wear.

The aerosol of gas had a long, thin tube which could be attached whenever it was needed. The tube could be shoved under a door, through a lock or into an air-conditioning system. The button was pressed for about five seconds. It worked like a body deodorant and even looked like a deodorant down to the label on the canister which promised a new and refreshing smell.

'You'll be interested to learn that Rabbani has been busy,' Macnair greeted Hunter on the phone.

'In what way, sir?'

'Yassin phoned a number of news agencies such as the Bulgarian Gazette and News Network and checked out Petrov. He found a reporter working for the network who assured Yassin that he could supply a contact for Petrov. In exchange he wanted five thousand euros.'

'Did he get it?'

'No. They haggled and the reporter settled on two thousand. Yassin arranged an immediate transfer of funds and less than an hour later had the lawyer's contact details.'

'Then what?'

'Just like we planned. The lawyer made it clear to Yassin that he was fully aware of the deal and that Petrov and you had been in cahoots for some time. Yassin was told in no uncertain terms that the whole thing would happen only through you, or there'd be no deal.'

'I take it Yassin wasn't too happy.'

'Yassin tried bluster. He was told to shove it where the sun doesn't shine and our man hung up on him. Needless to say, Rabbani has decided to go along with things the way they are. Although it's only for now.'

'Moving on, have we picked up anything about Barzakh?'

'Not a thing.'

'You know, sir, when it comes to the whole terrorist bit, I'm not so sure about Rabbani. Having met him, I just don't see him as a leader and paymaster for an international terrorist organisation.'

'It's got me puzzled as well. Yassin and Rabbani talk about their crime organisation but nothing about Barzakh. Yet according to the Pakistanis, Rabbani is highly active funding and even directing Barzakh. By the way, did you get the gear?'

'Yes, sir. I've just been looking through it.'

'Good. You have ten needles loaded and ready to go. Each one is a double dose. According to our people that should knock the recipient out for as long as twenty hours.'

'I thought a single dose was good for six?'

'It is. But double the dose has at least a tripling effect. Nick, good luck. I'm sorry there's no back-up.'

Hunter replied cheerfully, 'That's okay, sir. I don't think I'm going to need any.'

They said their goodbyes. Hunter put on his jacket and went down to the restaurant for breakfast. Whilst waiting to be served, he used his iPhone to find out the times of trains to Burnham-on-Crouch. From Liverpool Street Station there was a train at 13.35, arriving at 14.47. That would do.

He packed his grip, barely managing to stuff everything into it. He had left the nylon bag with Badonovitch. He hadn't thought he'd be needing it. He checked out. It was only a few minutes before 10.00 and Hunter decided to walk to the station. He set off for the Embankment, strolling along the pavement. It was crowded with tourists, speaking dozens of different languages.

Passing one shop that sold various types of bags, he went inside and purchased a small rucksack.

Outside again, in the distance, he could see HMS Wellington and a little further along, HMS President. When he reached the second vessel he went onboard, bought a coffee and sat at a window seat. He contemplated what he was going to do. He knew that no plan was set in stone. There were too many variables and so he would be playing it by ear. Which was nothing new.

When he finished his coffee, he went into the Gents toilet. He transferred the kit from his grip and put it into the rucksack. Slinging the bag over his shoulder, he picked up his grip and continued on his way. At London Bridge he turned north for Liverpool Street.

In the bustling station he bought a return ticket for Southminster. If Rabbani had Hunter's gear searched and a single ticket was found it could lead to questions as to why it wasn't a return. Not that a ready answer wasn't easy to come by, it was just easier not to have to lie.

The train was busy, though not packed, and it arrived at precisely 14.47. Although there was a line of taxis outside the station, Hunter decided to walk. He had plenty of time to kill.

The road was narrow, hardly more than a typical country lane but wide enough for cars to pass each other. It was deserted of traffic but Hunter could hear a tractor or two chugging in the fields. On his right he saw a large house, sitting on a hillock, with well kept lawns spreading out before it. He passed open, imposing gates, on the other side of which was a well laid track leading up to the house.

Hunter caught a glimpse of the name. Little Beeches. As he couldn't see a beech tree anywhere he thought the name ironic.

It was.

16

HUNTER TOOK A closer look at his surroundings. A high stone wall marked the boundary for the property, but that was all. It wasn't designed to keep anyone out. The gates were standing open and he walked slowly towards them. There didn't appear to be any cameras. There may have been heat or movement sensors, but if there were, he couldn't spot them.

It was a few minutes after 18.00 and so he walked along the lane, keeping the house and grounds on his left. There was a drainage ditch about half a metre deep running the length of the wall, overgrown with nettles and brambles. He stuffed both bags into it and arranged the foliage to cover the spot. He continued along the lane. He adjusted his bumbag and unzipped it. His coat was undone. The Pocketlite wasn't as accessible as in a holster, but good enough.

The wall turned at right angles and he followed it. He stepped over the ditch and into woods that stretched up the gentle hill for a few hundred metres at least. There was little undergrowth and he walked easily alongside the wall. He was looking for a vantage point from where to view the house. After about 300m, he found a spot where a few stones were missing and were covered in undergrowth on his side of the wall. He nudged one of the stones, checked it was firmly embedded into the ground and stood on it. He raised his head above the gap.

He was side on to the house which was at least 400m away, maybe closer to 500m. It was mainly lawn. Halfway across there was a gazebo. Even at that distance he could see that it was a substantial wooden construction, circular, maybe octagonal. He thought it could be about 5m in diameter. It had 6 uprights, was open all around but had a low fence about 1m high. He couldn't see the steps so they had to be on the other side. Beyond the gazebo he could see a low hedge, a metre high and stretching half the width of the lawn. Way over to his left, half hidden by the slope, he could see the top half of a large tree.

After twenty minutes he saw no one and nothing of interest.

He stepped down off the stone and continued along the wall. After about 800m he arrived at the brow of the incline when the land curved gently down the other side. He could see that the trees ended just after the brow and he decided not to waste anymore time but to retrace his steps.

He returned to the road. It was time to make his appearance at the house.

He found the bags and lifted out the grip. Hefting the bag in his left hand he returned to the entrance to the grounds, stepped between the gateposts and began to stroll along the driveway. He had left the rucksack behind. He couldn't be sure that there were no cameras and to be seen entering the grounds with two bags and arriving at the door with only one was asking for trouble. Any bags he had with him were bound to be searched. The contents of the rucksack could never be explained away.

The tree was an ancient looking oak, standing in splendid isolation in the middle of the well tended lawn about 200m away on his right. On his left was a field of pasture with sheep pock marking it and, in the distance, he could see a tractor trundling over the brow of the hill and out of sight.

It was another warm and pleasant evening. Sunset was an hour or so away, a few clouds were scudding across a blue sky and high above, white trails of aircraft vapour could clearly be seen. The birds were singing as they went about their business, creating a happy sound. On one level, Robert Browning had got it right. *God was in His heaven and all was right with the world.* But then, on another level, Reginald Heber also got it right with one of his hymns. *Though every great prospect pleases, and only man is vile.*

Approaching the house, he could see that it was more like a mansion. In the centre was a large front door with a portico. Above the portico was a window about 4m wide and 3m high. The columns either side added to the building's imposing grandeur. There were five windows either side of the door and upstairs he counted a further ten. The walls were stone, probably granite, he guessed. The house looked as if it had been there for at least a couple of hundred years. To the left was a substantial garage. He could see three cars, all facing out and ready to go. He quickly stepped inside and looked at the ignition in the nearest car, a top of the range BMW. The keys were there. He was sure they would also be in the Range Rover and the convertible Audi A4 Cabriolet. A glance round showed the place contained the usual paraphernalia to be found in a garage. A workbench was at the back, along the full length of the wall. It had a vice on one side and the wall was lined with useful tools. In a corner was a large lawnmower, the sort you sat on, and next to it were other gardening implements. It was neat and tidy and the tools looked as though they were in regular use. On one side, was a fridge next to a waist high cupboard on which sat an electric kettle. Alongside that was a Calor gas heater, a table and four chairs. It was basic, utilitarian and adequate.

He stepped back outside. The drive swept around in a circle in front of the house with an ornate garden in the centre, like a well-tended roundabout. There were numerous rose bushes displaying magnificent colours from pink to deep red. He couldn't see what was to the right of the house but on the left was another large and well tended garden area. The gardeners had their work cut out and obviously did a good job.

He buttoned up his coat, effectively hiding the bumbag. He rested his right thumb on the top of the button at his waist, his fingers underneath the cloth. Undoing the single button to get his hand on the Pocketlite added about a second to the draw. It was a move he had practised often enough.

Having noticed the cameras above the portico he fully expected the door to be opened before he reached it. It was.

The man who opened the door was portly, ramrod straight and was doing his best to appear intimidating. He had gray tufts of hair around a bald crown, his face was cherubic, his eyes cold and there was no welcoming smile. He was, however, wearing the clothes a butler would have worn half a century earlier. The effect of a black coat, with a tail down to his knees, a black waistcoat, white shirt with a black bow tie, and gray and black striped trousers - although no white gloves - was spoilt by two things. The first was that the man was carrying a gun at his waist, though hidden beneath his coat and secondly, he was obviously of Pakistani origin.

'Mr Hughes, I presume?' His accent confirmed he was from Pakistan.

Hunter nodded and smiled. 'That's right. Who might you be? Jeeves?'

The man looked at him blankly for a second and then said, 'No, sir. My name is Matthews.'

'Matthews. Right.' The name definitely didn't fit and Hunter decided it was for butlering duties only. 'Is Mr. Rabbani at home?'

'Yes, sir. He's on the patio. He said to take you through the instant you arrived. I shall see to your bag, sir.' He held out his hand, giving Hunter no option but to hand it over.

Stepping through the door, Hunter entered a foyer which was larger than the ground floor of most four bedroomed houses. The window above the portico stretched the width of the room and allowed in a great deal of light, making the place feel spacious and open. The floor tiles were black and white, with rugs incongruously scattered across them. On the left, just inside the door was a table for hats and gloves and alongside it an umbrella stand with half a dozen brollies sticking out. The walls were oak panelled and painted a light brown. The numerous paintings on display were all of British scenes. Some were of rural landscapes while others were of old battles, on land and at sea. In the battle scenes, the British appeared to be over-whelming the French, though a few were scenes between red-jacketed troops armed with rifles fighting half-naked, spear carrying, African tribesmen.

The paintings stretched the length of the walls and reached up to the ceiling. The room would have done the National Gallery proud, provided they were all originals, which somehow, Hunter suspected, was the case.

One painting in particular caught his attention. It looked like a scene from the Battle of Trafalgar, when the British triumphed over the French but lost Lord Nelson. His eyes wandered to the alarm system. The door was wired, as were the two windows.

He had expected a wand to be waved over him as it had been back in London, and he would have handed over the Pocketlite with no argument. Any questions on why he was carrying it would have resulted in a hard look, a deprecating smile and an instruction to Matthews to work it out for himself. As it was, nothing happened and he rethought his strategy.

'The dining room is through there, sir, where breakfast will be served.' Matthews pointed to the left. 'Next to it is the lounge where drinks are normally served in the evening and teas and coffees during the day. That door,' he pointed to the right, 'leads to Mr Rabbani's study. The one opposite is my pantry and quarters. It is strictly forbidden for any guest to enter. I hope that is clear, sir.'

'Perfectly, thank you.' What a pretentious prat, thought Hunter and then changed his mind. Pretentious, yes, a delusional and dumb idiot, no.

'Your bedroom is up the main stairway,' this time he merely inclined his head, 'you turn right and go along the corridor to the second door on the left. You will see that it is called the Blue Room.'

'Okay. I'll go up now,' said Hunter. 'To freshen up.'

'I am sorry, sir, but Mr. Rabbani was most insistent that you join him as soon as you arrived.'

'In that case, I'll be delighted. But first I'd like to use the washroom.'

'This way, sir.' He followed the butler behind the stairs who pointed at another door. 'That is the washroom, sir.'

'Thank you.' Hunter went inside and locked the door. It was a fair sized room, the walls lined with tiles, artfully and pleasantly designed.

He had decided to hide the Pocketlite. He could still be searched by Rabbani's goons. There were two wooden, waist high cupboards. One had doors, the other drawers. The one with drawers contained bath towels and he placed the gun at the back of the lowest drawer amongst the towels. Next, he flushed the toilet, washed his hands, unlocked the door and stepped out.

'Lead on, Matthews,' he said with a smile. In response, he received a black eyed nod of total indifference.

'Yes, sir. Your bag is there, sir,' Matthews pointed at a neat row of cases lined up against the wall, his grip at one end. 'They belong to the other guests, sir.'

He was led into the lounge. It was a large and imposing room, beautifully decorated and tastefully furnished with occasional tables, a sideboard on which stood a silver tray with crystal glasses and two decanters. From the colour of their contents, he guessed one was port and the other whisky. There were green leather chairs and settees, the walls were papered with a faint flowery pattern and lined with paintings of English fox hunting scenes.

Rabbani obviously liked his paintings. The scenes also suggested that when he was in the country he liked to play the English squire. The butler walked across the room towards a pair of French windows. They were wide open and voices were drifting in, along with the faint aroma of smoke and cooking.

When he stepped outside, Hunter was stopped by Boris who waved a wand over him. So, Hunter thought, actual arrival in the august presence was when you were checked for weapons. The bleep at his inside left breast meant he had to open his jacket, remove his mobile and show it to the Russian. Boris then waved the wand in the area a second time and, receiving no response, Hunter was allowed past.

'Nick, my dear fellow,' Rabbani greeted him, walking across the patio, his hand outstretched, his smile as usual not quite reaching his eyes. 'Let me introduce you to some of my other guests. But first, let me offer you a drink. What would you like? Wine? A beer? Or something stronger?'

Hunter looked at the white jacketed waiter hovering nearby, 'A beer, please. Cold. In a bottle.'

The man said nothing, merely inclined his head in acknowledgement. He had two things in common with Matthews; he looked Pakistani and was armed. Though in his case, he appeared to be more in his thirties than his fifties, and was also smaller and fitter looking.

'Ah, this habit of drinking beer from a bottle when there is such a thing as a glass never ceases to amuse me. So uncivilised. Here's your drink. It is produced by the Murree Brewery of Pakistan. I hope you like it.'

Hunter took it with a nod. The patio could easily have held thirty people, instead there were twelve.

The bottle was cold and Hunter took a mouthful of beer.

'What do you think?'

'Not bad. Not bad at all.'

'Let me make the introductions. Mr. Yassin you already know,' he began by stating the obvious. 'As well as Boris and Oscar.'

The three men inclined their heads but kept straight faces and didn't offer their hands. 'This is Mr. Jamil, and this is Mr. Mady. They crew the Talisman.'

'How do you do?' Hunter held out his hand. He shook hands with the first man, 'Mr. Jamil, is it?'

'Yes. How do you do?' Tall, slim, Pakistani and carrying a gun under his coat. His hands were soft, his handshake limp. He looked somewhat ludicrous in a double breasted blazer and white trousers, with a yachting cap perched to one side of his head.

'Then you must be Mr. Mady.' Hunter shook hands with the other man who was similarly outfitted. He was a few inches shorter than Jamil, also slim, also a Pakistani. His gun was not quite as obvious as his coat hung more loosely.

'Now come and meet the ladies.'

Rabbani led him past a white clothed table, laid out for a banquet. On it were bowls of salad, baked potatoes, cheeses, cold meats and crusty bread. Matthews was a few metres away tending to a large, charcoal burning barbecue. On it were strips of succulent looking steak and the wings and legs of chicken that had been marinated in a brown sauce. There appeared to be enough to feed the five thousand, give or take a few hundred.

Five young women were standing further along the patio. Hunter guessed they were all younger than 20. Each was wearing a low cut blouse or dress, showing how well endowed they were. Two were brunettes and three were blondes. One of the blondes was natural, while the other two came with the aid of a bottle. They all wore too much makeup. Hunter realised all five of them were high on something. He presumed it was cocaine.

They were giggling, each holding a flute of Champagne. As the two men approached, all five of them looked pointedly at their crotches.

'Ladies, I'd like you to meet a very good friend of mine,' Rabbani announced. 'This is Nick. I shall leave you to make your introductions. Excuse me, ladies.' As he turned to walk away Hunter caught the smirk on his face.

The five women turned their attention to Hunter. The natural blonde took his right arm and held it tightly, preventing him from lifting his bottle of beer to his mouth, while one of the brunettes took his left arm and rubbed herself against him.

'Hello, Nick. I'm Sharon. Mr. Rabbani told us we should take especially good care of you.'

'I'm Cindy,' said the blonde. '*Especial* good care,' she emphasised the word.

The other three stood in front of him, grinning inanely. The two on his arms appeared to be the least spaced out.

'Thank you, ladies,' he tried to take their hands off his arms but they were holding him too tightly. After a few more moments he said, 'Thank you, but no thanks.'

He bent his left arm up and pushed the hand of the woman on his right so that she was forced to let him go. He transferred the beer to his left hand and did the same to the other woman. Women? Hunter thought. More like children.

17

RABBANI WANDERED BACK over. 'Are my girls not to your liking, Nick? Or perhaps you are like Mr. Yassin and have taken a vow of celibacy?'

Hunter glared at Rabbani. 'First of all, I have taken no such vow. Second of all, I like a woman to be closer to my age and third of all, I like to pick the woman I am going to sleep with. I hope that is clear enough?' He then broke into a beaming smile, as though he hadn't meant for his words to sound as harsh as they did.

'My dear fellow,' Rabbani broke into a smile of his own, 'of course I understand only too well. But it means it will be a long night without female company to keep you amused.'

'I think I can survive,' said Hunter, well aware of what the other man was doing. If Hunter had succumbed to the charms displayed, it would have shown a weakness which Rabbani would have somehow done his best to exploit.

Matthews called out something in a foreign language.

'I tell Matthews not to speak Urdu in front of guests, as it is so rude, but he forgets. Good help is so hard to find nowadays, don't you think?'

Hunter wondered if he had stepped into the set for filming a soap opera or was it simply a mad house? Whatever it was, he was sure Rabbani wasn't expecting a reply.

'He says the steaks and the chicken are ready. Come, my dear Nick. Matthews makes superb marinades, one for beef and the other for chicken. That, of course, is necessary due to the more delicate flavour of the poultry compared to the cow. Ladies, come along.'

He led the way towards the table. 'Please sit there, next to me,' he said, indicating a seat on the left hand side. 'I like to sit with my back to the wall. Any wall.'

Hunter smiled his acceptance. 'Thank you.' He placed his beer next to the place setting.

'But come, we must get our food. Here, let me help.' Taking a plate from a table next to the b-b-q he handed it to Hunter. 'As you see, the food is cooked over charcoal, none of that gas rubbish here. Isn't that right, Matthews?'

In reply, the butler inclined his head in deference whilst lifting up a succulent piece of steak and placing it on his master's plate.

'Thank you, Matthews, that will be all for me. Come, Nick, choose.'

'I'll take the steak as well, please,' he smiled at the man who was now wearing a white apron having removed his jacket. Not surprisingly, there was a sheen of sweat on his brow for the evening was warm without a cloud in the sky and the air was still.

'Rare, medium rare, medium or well done, sir?'

'Just as it comes,' he replied.

'Nick, that will never do. You must pick. Matthews is rightly proud of his culinary skills and as anyone who has used a b-b-q knows, to be able to cook meat as precisely as that over a charcoal fire takes real skill.'

'You are quite right. In that case Matthews, I'll take the medium rare.'

The man picked up a piece of beef and deposited it on the plate Hunter was holding out.

'Thank you.'

'Take some chicken as well, Nick. I can promise you that you will never have tasted anything so good in your life.'

'Ashraf, you are too kind, but no thanks. With all the other food on the table this is more than sufficient.' Hunter helped himself to salad and a baked potato.

The two men took cutlery and walked back to their seats while the remainder of the company grabbed plates and jostled each other to get served. However, instead of dishing out the meat, Matthews offered the tongs to one of the girls, untied his apron, threw it over the back of a chair and left the patio. Hunter deposited his plate on the table before sitting down. He then put his hands either side of his chair, the cutlery still in his right hand. The extra knife he had lifted he slipped under his thigh before placing his hands in front of him and switching the fork from his right hand to his left.

The girl named Cindy was giggling as she stepped around the fire, opening and squeezing the tongs. 'Now, who wants what?' As if that was a funny question, she burst into more giggles.

'What do you think of your steak, Nick?'

'Superb.' He put down his knife and lifted the bottle of beer in his left hand, taking a swig. Rabbani was looking at his plate, concentrating on cutting his steak. Hunter put his right hand by his thigh and surreptitiously slid the steak knife into his trouser pocket. The blade was 4ins long, pointed and very sharp. He had a specific use for it later.

'Thank you.' Rabbani inclined his head as though the compliment was for him and him alone. Then he added, 'I shall pass on your comments to Matthews. I am forgetting my manners as a host, forget your beer, and do try some of this excellent wine.' He picked up a bottle of red wine. 'This is a Merlot from my own vineyard in Arroyo Grande, California. Contrary to popular belief, many fine vintages come from America. Some of the older ones command very high prices on the open market. As much as, or if not more, than European wines.' He poured wine into the glass at Hunter's elbow. The others at the table were imbibing freely, though Hunter noticed that Rabbani, although he had a glass of the Merlot next to his plate, barely touched it. Even the bodyguards were drinking bottles of beer. It appeared that Rabbani and his staff let their guard down when in the countryside.

Hunter raised his glass in a toast and sipped. 'Excellent. First class.'

'Thank you. We sell it at $80 a bottle to the wholesaler. In restaurants one can pay as much as $300, if not more.'

'I'm impressed.'

'Of course, we make other wines as well. The stuff the supermarkets want. Wine for the peasants.'

Hunter nodded with a slight smile. 'Each to their own, I suppose. Though having drank some very expensive wines, I think many are overrated.' He paused before adding, 'Of course, it goes without saying, not this one.'

'Thank you, you are too kind.' Rabbani had a lighted cigarette burning in an ashtray on his left side from which he took a deep drag after each bite of food.

'What about you, Mr. Yassin? Are you enjoying your chicken?' Hunter asked the man sitting opposite him.

'Yes. As always, it is very good. The recipes of your famous television chefs are closely followed by Matthews.'

'Mr. Yassin, my dear fellow, you should not give Matthews' secrets away like that. Not even to such a highly revered guest as Mr. Hughes.'

The other man shrugged expressively, cut off a large piece of chicken and stuffed it in his mouth. While chewing, he closed his mouth about one bite in three.

The two men from the boat were imbibing freely, though only picking at their food. Hunter wondered about their relationship.

'An incident occurred a few nights ago that shows we are in a very dangerous line of work,' said Rabbani, 'and deserve our profits.'

'Oh? Why? What happened?' Hunter raised his eyebrows in query.

'An organisation we have had a few dealings with in the past was attacked and nearly two kilos of H was lost.'

'Does that present a problem?'

'No, not at all. Like I said, we only had a few minor dealings and that was some time ago.'

'Where did it happen and what happened?'

'Near Barking.' He waved his hand. 'A robbery. Guns were involved. Some shooting. The police turned up after it was all over and found the heroin. I have been told that another group is already entering the area. Apparently they are from Somalia and claiming asylum. You have to agree they are an enterprising people. Amoral and ruthless of course, but enterprising. Luckily, there is an endless supply of users and many who are willing to take the risk to supply drugs of all sorts.'

'Doesn't that mean competition? And competition is bad for business.'

'Not at all, my dear fellow, not at all. Some competition is good. I encourage it. They get people addicted and help to create a wider and deeper customer structure. Then, when the time is right, some of the suppliers go out of business and those of us who are better positioned, better protected, better financed, better connected plus a whole lot of other attributes, can step in and take-over.'

'A sort of company take-over without the hassle and expense.'

'Oh, there is some hassle. But nothing we are unable to deal with. Freelance help is readily available and so much cheaper than permanent employees. They are such an expense as well as a nuisance. After all, it is far better for people to know as little as possible about one's business, don't you think? Except for your most trusted aides, of course.'

'Of course,' Hunter inclined his head. 'I take it Mr. Yassin is in that position.'

'Naturally. I rely upon him a great deal.'

'He strikes me as being a loyal, I was going to say servant, but I meant employee.'

During this repartee Yassin had been concentrating on cutting his chicken and eating quickly, as though he hadn't tasted food for a week. He took no overt interest in what his boss and visitor were saying though it appeared to Hunter that he was taking in every word said.

'It is very important to have at least one person you can trust, otherwise you will be unable to handle all the work on your plate.'

Matthews approached the table with a tray balanced on his left hand covered with a napkin. He leant over Rabbani's left shoulder, took hold of a corner of the napkin and flicked it to one side.

Nestling in the middle of the tray was Hunter's Pocketlite and silencer.

They travelled in two cars, three miles apart. Made by a Japanese manufacturer in Derbyshire, the cars were old, small and cramped. There were three men in the lead car and four in the one following. They all wore dark clothing and each carried gloves in their pockets.

Tension was beginning to grow as they approached their destination. Mirza Nawaz, in the lead car, was sitting next to the driver. He had briefed them relentlessly. The briefings were followed by questioning. Non-stop questioning with one objective in mind. The survival of one of the targets. He hoped his threats and promises had been enough to ensure the men with him didn't overreact.

He was beginning to get nervous himself. It was one thing to execute an operation in his own country but something entirely different in a foreign land. Also, inside the trunks of the cars was enough weaponry to ensure at least 10 years in a top-security British prison, so it was not surprising he was anxious. He was fully aware of the fact that if he made a hash of things he and his family would regret it bitterly. There were never second chances with the General. Excuses were rarely tolerated; mistakes dealt with in a manner that usually resulted in a slow and painful death. If the cock-up was considered big enough then the miscreant was forced to watch as punishment was meted out to his family, though in their case they would be lucky - a bullet in the back of the head was quick and painless. The General considered it was the most effective way to establish control and ensure outstanding performance by his troops. It also made for a very high degree of loyalty.

He thought about the upcoming attack. It was a military operation even if men with him weren't trained troops. They were ready enough. They were ready to die for the cause and die they would. He was to make sure that happened. One thing he was confident about, an overwhelming and totally unexpected force inevitably won the day. Today would be no exception. Nobody in their right mind would expect an attack by an armed gang willing to kill or be killed without a moment's hesitation.

For all his rationalising, at times like these, doubts usually raised their ugly head. Had he made the right decision to throw his lot in with General Khan? At the time it seemed the right thing to do. The glory! The kudos! The fame! The words tumbled through his mind. He would be an important man in the General's new regime. His family would have a good life. They would be respected. Revered, even. They would live in a big house. Have luxury cars to drive. The future was bright. He knew it. He could feel it.

Nawaz came out of his reverie and looked at the countryside. 'How much further?' he asked.

The young man driving answered nervously. 'About twenty miles.'

Nawaz craned his neck and looked at the speedometer. It was

showing 60mph. 'Slow down to fifty. We don't want to get there too early.' He paused and then added, 'You are sure about the position of the gazebo and the distance to the house?' He knew he was asking the questions out of nervousness. He just hoped the other two didn't realise it.

'Yes,' the young man replied, licking his lips.

Nawaz knew the driver was nervous. Apart from himself, none of them had killed a man before. Never mind six or even eight people.

'It is just like we told you,' said the driver. 'You have seen the Google Earth photographs,' he began, then he stopped speaking.

Nawaz didn't rebuke him for his insolence. The idiot would be dead in a few hours so there was no point in reaming him out, even if the man's insolence made him white hot with fury.

Instead, he said in a reasonable tone, 'You are quite right. But a good planner always thinks ahead. Thinks about all the things that can go wrong and makes allowances for them. This is vital if he is to bring his troops back home to glory and to fight another day.'

The driver nodded furiously, a smile plastered across his face.

Nawaz managed a smile that was more like a grimace but went unnoticed by the driver who was gripping the wheel tightly, staring ahead. 'Good.' He tried to look relaxed while he ran through the information he had in his head. The alarm at the back door would be cut inside the house. Their contact had been adamant that there was no way he could reach the alarm system and turn it off, which would be neater. It didn't matter. Also, the door would be unlocked. He knew which rooms the men would be occupying, the women would be shared out amongst them. He counted targets. Rabbani, the two bodyguards, two men from the boat, the butler, the waiter, Yassin, the five women and the stranger. Too bad the stranger had chosen the wrong day to visit. Nawaz hoped he had enjoyed it as it would be his last.

That made fourteen people in all. Thirteen to die, one to live. If all went smoothly that would leave his own men to be taken care of. That would be easy. They were fools and the best contribution they could make for the cause was to die. British Muslims killing a Muslim businessman? Why? What was going on? Who was behind it? Who killed them all? Forensics would have a field day matching bullets, trying to fathom out the unfathomable. According to their contact the inhabitants in the house would be sleeping soundly after too much alcohol and too much activity with the prostitutes. The whole operation could not be easier.

This time, Nawaz's smile was more genuine. By the time the stupid British had managed to figure anything out it would be far too late. Their objective would have been achieved. The General was a clever man and a great leader.

As they went deeper into Essex he prayed. That was all that was left for him to do.

Hunter didn't as much as blink. However, he did wonder how the hell Matthews had found it. Were there hidden cameras around the house or did Matthews conduct a search of the toilet as a matter of routine? Either way, it didn't matter.

Rabbani reached over and picked it up, hefting it in the palm of his hand. 'A very nice toy,' he said, before looking deadpan at Hunter.

'It's no toy, believe me.'

Rabbani was holding it in such a way as to be almost, though not quite, pointing the gun at Hunter. 'Oh, I believe you, Nick.'

The noise from the other end of the table was dying down until there was complete silence. The loudest sounds were the various calls of birds singing for their supper.

Hunter used his peripheral vision to see what the others were doing. One of the men from the boat was the nearest, then two of the girls and then the other boatman. The bodyguards were sitting with their backs to the house, able to react should anything happen. Hunter was unable to see either of them. His response would have to depend on sound, not vision.

The other man who had been serving drinks was standing at the makeshift bar. It was a frozen tableau. Whatever happened in the next minute or less would determine what he was going to do. One thing was in his favour - the safety, on the left side of the gun, was on and he was less than a metre away.

'Perhaps you would like to explain?' Rabbani asked, pleasantly enough.

'Explain what?'

'Why you brought a weapon into my house?'

'I don't go many places without it. Like you don't travel without those two,' he jerked the thumb of his left hand over his shoulder.

'But I take it as an insult that you find it necessary to come here with a weapon. Even one as small as this.' There was a look of...what, on his face? Contempt? Superiority? No. Smugness with a tinge of contemplation as he stared at Hunter.

'You can take it anyway you like.' Hunter had decided how he would react. 'You will notice I didn't bring it out here. Which is what I would have done if I had intended any harm to you. Instead, I put it in a pretty inaccessible stowage.'

'Why not just deposit it in your bag?'

'I didn't want it found, because one thing I am damned sure of, Matthews will have searched it.'

'That is true. Then he would have found it and shown it to me earlier.'

'To achieve what? Disharmony in our burgeoning business arrangements? I figured it was better all round that the gun be left out of the way until it came time for me to leave.'

Rabbani sat for a few moments apparently in contemplation of what Hunter had said. The gun was pointing a bit further down and to the left, no longer in his general direction. The safety was still on.

It was then that Hunter heard a chair scraping behind him. It was enough. He didn't trust Rabbani in any way. He had been relatively sanguine about Rabbani's intentions because of the good news Macnair had imparted to him. TIFAT had recorded the two Pakistanis discussing Hunter's future. It was good in the short run, bad in the long run. Hunter would not be killed until after the first drugs run. That would enable Rabbani to establish his own credentials with Petrov. Once he'd done so, with Hunter dead, there would be far greater profits for Rabbani. Yassin had expressed delight at the plan when it was outlined by his boss.

His options raced through Hunter's brain like a lightning bolt. Stay where he was, make no movement and wait. Or act now. Over the edge of the table. Grab Rabbani and use him as a shield. Take the gun back. Take off the safety. Shoot the others. Or stay still and bluff it out? Should he talk about the deal? That it would be lost if he was killed? He knew he had no choice. If he tried to make a move, he would be dead before he even got to Rabbani. The Russians were professionals, of that he had no doubt. Also, there was the problem of killing someone in front of the girls. If he was shot, one of the girls would talk about it sooner rather than later. So the girls would have to die as well. And for what? Because a pistol was found hidden in a virtually inaccessible location?

Hunter neither smiled nor scowled. He kept a straight face. He didn't argue his case and he wasn't going to say please because on balance it made no sense for Rabbani to have him killed. Later, yes. Now, no.

Rabbani made a gesture with his hand to someone behind Hunter then beckoned to Matthews. The butler held out the tray and Rabbani placed the revolver on it. The white cloth was folded over the gun.

Rabbani turned back to Hunter. 'I shall return the gun when you leave.' His smile carried no hint of merriment. 'I hope you don't mind.' It wasn't a question, it was a statement of fact. He waved his hand again and Matthews walked away, ceremoniously holding the tray in front of him.

Hunter shrugged, aware that whether he minded or not was immaterial. Chairs scraped on the stone and he looked over his shoulder. Boris and Oscar were replacing their guns in their holsters as they sat down. Both men were staring at him. Hunter smiled but received only deadpan looks in return.

Hunter decided to show Rabbani that he wasn't intimidated by him and looked Rabbani in the eyes. 'Whether I object or not is irrelevant,' he said curtly, 'but I shall leave with it.'

'Of course, my dear fellow, of course. Now, let us have some more food and wine.'

'No, thanks, I'm fine.' He changed the subject completely, injecting a note of friendly banter into his voice. 'This is a grand house. Beautifully furnished and decorated from what I've seen of the place. I take it the rest of the house is the same?'

'Naturally. I hired the finest interior decorators I could find. As you see, not in any modern style but from a time when style meant elegance and permanence.'

'Tell me, are you the art connoisseur? Your collections in London and here are superb. Even I recognise the fact.'

This time, the smile was followed by a chuckle of genuine mirth. 'No. I know nothing about art. I hired an expert and told him what I wanted. You see the results.'

'The refurbishment and the artwork must have cost a fortune,' Hunter said, as though he was being naive. 'Millions.'

Rabbani nodded. 'Over fifteen million in fact.'

Hunter gave a soft whistle. 'That's a lot of money.'

'There is no point in having wealth unless you spend it on beautiful things.'

It was a contrite statement to make, but not one Hunter would argue with, so he nodded and smiled in return. 'It's why we're in the business we're in.'

'Precisely.'

'May I ask, do you have family?'

'Why? Why do you want to know?'

Rabbani slipped in and out of his moods for no reason at all. He was mercurial. From good humour to anger to petulance took mere seconds. Hunter wondered if he was using some sort of drug.

'No reason. I'm merely making polite conversation. If it's private information then please, don't tell me.'

There was silence for a few seconds and then Rabbani smiled again. 'I do not object to telling you. I have three wives, six sons and two daughters all living in Pakistan.'

Hunter smiled in return. 'That's a big family. Do you see them very often?'

There was a flash of something across the other man's face and Hunter raised his hand. 'Sorry, sorry,' he repeated. 'Forget I asked.'

18

THE ANSWER WAS pure fabrication if Rabbani's family had been wiped out like the Pakistani government had said. Even if it had been some years ago it had hardly given him enough time to find three wives and have six sons and two daughters. What did lying achieve?

'No, I don't mind. I will tell you. I go to Pakistan once a month. I see to some business and visit my family. I like to think of it as a combination of duty and pleasure, but,' he added with a genuine smile, about the first that evening, 'it seems to be more like duty every time I go there. You? Do you have a wife?'

Hunter shook his head and repeated the fiction. 'I was married but it seems like a long time ago now, so much water having flown under the bridge. But like so many marriages these days, it didn't work.'

'Children?'

'No. Thank goodness. No kids.'

Rabbani said, 'You see! The Islamic way is best! You marry once, have a child or two. You get bored and so you find another wife. The same happens again and so you take a third.'

'Then a fourth. Will you be doing so?' Hunter smiled good naturedly.

'Of course. It is very simple. We are allowed a fourth and final wife, praise be to Allah, and such things should be taken advantage of.'

'I'm not sure most of us in the West would agree. One at a time seems to be more than sufficient.'

'What about those men and women who take lovers? At least our relationships are open for all to see.'

Hunter nodded portentously as though giving the matter some thought. 'You're probably right. But it can be very expensive.'

Again, Rabbani's chuckle was genuine. 'That is true. However, it is well worth it. I shall find a suitable successor from amongst my children. One of my boys will take over my empire. With great wealth comes great responsibility. He will need to be educated and trained. It is very important.'

'A sort of clan Rabbani,' Hunter said with a straight face. The information he was gathering made a nonsense of Rabbani's reasons for creating Barzakh.

The other man looked at him sharply for a second or two, then answered seriously. 'Precisely. With four wives and many children it will not take many generations to establish a strong and influential family, or as you called it, a clan.'

'Sorry, I must have misunderstood. I thought you said you only had three wives,' Hunter raised his wine glass and took a sip.

Rabbani continued to ignore his wine but drew deeply on his cigarette. The ashtray in front of him would have been over flowing long ago if Matthews hadn't kept emptying it. 'I shall be marrying for a fourth time in five weeks.'

'I hope the lady is young and pretty.'

'She is eighteen and very beautiful. She should bear me many fine sons.'

Hunter didn't bother pointing out that with six sons already, why have more? For Hunter, the next hour dragged by. Rabbani and Hunter stayed sober, neither drinking any more alcohol. The others were becoming noisier and more boisterous as the evening wore on. It was pleasantly warm and three of the girls were now topless.

Finally, Hunter decided it was late enough so that he could leave. 'If you will excuse me, I shall bid you goodnight.' He stood up, pushing his chair back.

'Not staying to watch the amusement? Or to join in?' Rabbani smiled at him.

'No, thanks. I've already told you. I prefer my women more mature.'

Rabbani nodded as though in complete understanding. 'Oh, just one thing. Please do not wander through the house after midnight.'

'Oh? Why is that?'

'The house is alarmed.'

'What if I need the bathroom?'

Rabbani appeared to contemplate the request for a moment or

two. 'I understand you to be in the Blue Room. Unlike some of the other rooms, yours isn't en-suite. The bathroom is directly opposite. All windows and doors downstairs are wired. Upstairs, you may cross the corridor to the bathroom but do not wander any further.'

'Okay! No problem.' Hunter turned to go and then paused as if with another thought. 'Ashraf, it is so warm I shall wish to open my window. To let in some fresh air.'

Rabbani inclined his head graciously, as though bestowing a favour. 'Naturally, you may open the window to your bedroom. That is not alarmed.'

'Thank you.'

He didn't bother bidding the others goodnight. He entered the house, started across the foyer, picked up his bag on the way and went up the stairs. At the top was a T junction. The lights were on. There was a long corridor to the right that stretched to the outside wall, where there was a floor to ceiling window, about 3m wide, the width of the corridor.

The corridor to the left was about 10m long with no doors. He took a quick look. At the end, the corridor turned sharp left where there were doors left and right with a single door at the end. He retraced his steps and walked along the strip of beige carpet running the length of the corridor towards his room. The walls were painted white and between each door was a series of paintings, showing scenes of debauchery.

Past the stairs, Hunter paused at the first door on the left. The sign on the door said Pink Room. The lettering was ornate and gold coloured on a brown wooden tablet. He opened the door and felt for the light switch. He flicked it on. The room was big. It held a king sized bed capable of sleeping three, a chest of drawers, a wardrobe and an occasional table with an easy chair next to it. There was a sink, a mirror on the wall and a low cupboard on which sat a kettle, two mugs and three ornate biscuit tins. It reminded him of the rooms found in a bed and breakfast guest house. Apart from the walls. They were pink and covered with paintings of more lewd scenes. They could be summed up in one word - tacky. Which was in sharp contrast to the rest of the house. There didn't appear to be anyone occupying it.

The curtains were open though the night was dark; he knew

the view was to the front of the house.

The room opposite was the Green Room also with an ornate sign. He opened the door and switched on the light. It was identical to the Pink Room except the decor was in different shades of green. Through the window he could see the back of the house. The next room on the left was his. He ignored it and opened the door opposite. There was no name on the door. It was a well fitted bathroom with a bath that could easily fit three people. The shower could have held half a soccer team with comfort and was one of those that sprayed water at you from all directions. The fittings were gold, the walls were white tiles. There was a double sink; above each was a small cupboard with a mirror for a door. Hunter opened one and saw that it held shampoos, soaps and even a tube of toothpaste. If the shower could take half a soccer team, the rest of the room could hold the other half.

The next room on the left was the Amber Room. The decor was surprisingly restful. On the right was the Yellow Room. It appeared to Hunter to be slightly smaller than the other two but was furnished the same. This time the decor was garish and not a room Hunter would wish to spend any time in.

Opposite the Yellow Room was the Brown Room. It was the mirror image of the other except the colours blended in a more harmonious fashion. There were women's clothes scattered on the bed.

Hunter returned to the Blue Room. He opened the door and switched on the light. He was gratified to see there was a key in the lock. As he expected, everything was blue. The walls were light blue, the carpet royal blue and the bedspread a very deep blue. He flung back the cover to take a look. Underneath was a continental quilt with a dark blue floral pattern. He placed his grip on the table and opened it. A quick glance proved that Matthews had rifled through it. There had been no attempt to hide the fact.

He locked the door before carefully and methodically searching the place. There were no microphones or cameras in the chandelier that hung from the middle of the ceiling, nor anywhere in or around the wardrobes, the dressing table or the upright chair in front of it. The mirror behind the table wasn't fixed to the wall but was mounted on the table so it was impossible to conceal a camera there. Finally, there was only one place left to examine and that was in the radio clock. He took the knife and carefully undid the 4 screws on the base. There was nothing out of the ordinary that he could see and he replaced the cover. Even so, he wasn't going to take any chances. He unplugged it from the wall and shoved it under the duvet before switching off the lights.

Picking up the chair, he placed it next to the window. He'd already confirmed there was no alarm system and he slid the bottom half of the window open, careful not to make a noise. The sun had long set, the sky was clear and there was a pleasant scent of the countryside in the warm air. He sat with his elbows on the sill, looking across the grounds to the boundary wall which he could just make out in the distance.

He stayed there, contemplating what he would do next. The moon was now a slither on the horizon but coming up fast. Within minutes it was casting a dim shadow at the foot of the oak tree. Okay, which way? Into the garden, through the other side, stay low and head for the grand old tree? No, that wouldn't work. Anyone looking through one of the front windows would spot him. That meant going along the front of the house, staying close to the wall, then diagonally away from the corner, keeping it aimed at his back. That reduced the chances of being seen by a casual observer or anyone on guard inside the house. In front of the low hedge were well tended circles of cultivated garden, about 5m in diameter, with spectacularly coloured flowers, none of which Hunter could name. Even in the poor light he could distinguish bushes of white, pink and purple rhododendrons, a species of plant he did recognise thanks to the ones his mother cultivated at their home in Balfron. The shrubs would give reasonable cover. After that was the gazebo. That would be the way to go.

He sat and absorbed the serenity of the scene and the night. Then he heard a noise and listened more closely. There it was again. A cough followed by the sound of a throat being cleared. He leant further out of the window and sniffed. The atmosphere was heavy with the scent of flowers. Then he caught the faint smell of cigarette smoke. He looked down to his left then right. The portico was to the right and leaning against the nearest column he could just make out the feet and bottom half of a pair of legs. The waiter was between Hunter and his bag of equipment. To smoke when on guard was a stupid thing to do. Not only could the glow of the cigarette be seen from a distance but the person inhaling also had their vision degraded. Finally, the smell of smoke was always a potential give away.

The peace of the night was broken by loud music coming from the other side of the house. The party was evidently hotting up. Looking down he saw that the waiter was becoming restless as he levered himself off the column, walked away and a minute or so later came back into sight.

It was time for Hunter to make his preparations. The ground was 8m down. He unhooked the curtains from their railing and, using the steak knife, cut them into four strips which he tied together using a reef knot. The result was a makeshift climbing rope more than long enough for his needs. When he was ready, he would drag the bed across the floor to use as an anchor.

He looked at his watch. 23.50. He lay down on the bed, closed his eyes and dozed off. His mental clock woke him two hours later. He lay listening to the silence. A stanza from his favourite poem came to mind. It was *The Listeners* by Walter De La Mare - *But only a host of phantom listeners That dwelt in the lone house then Stood listening in the quiet of the moonlight To that voice from the world of men.* Moments later his thoughts were interrupted. He heard noises outside in the corridor that he identified as the guests making their way to their bedrooms. From the giggles and grunts it didn't appear as though many of them would be sleeping alone. Eventually, silence cloaked the house. Hunter glanced at his watch. It was 02.17.

Climbing off the bed, he crossed to the window. He looked down. He couldn't see the guard. Maybe he was sitting under the portico or wandering around the grounds trying to stay alert? Certain factors were in Hunter's favour. With the house quiet, the alarms set and everyone gone to bed, a guard naturally relaxed. His mood and alertness fell into the cadence of a tranquil night. Natural tiredness also took its toll. Coupled with that, was the fact that trouble wasn't expected. There hadn't been any in the past, so why tonight?

Finally, it was 03.20 and time to make a move. He took off his white shirt, adjusted the Kevlar vest and pulled on a black T-shirt.

He buckled on his bumbag and adjusted it to sit comfortably around his waist. He placed the steak knife in the bag. For the moment it was the only weapon he had. Next, he slipped on his lightweight black cotton jacket. He checked the pockets. His top left pocket held his fake driving licence and credit card. He buttoned the flap. His top right hand pocket held a wad of money. There was nothing left in the room that he needed. For the last hour he hadn't seen a sign of the guard. There had been no smell of cigarette smoke, no coughing, no shuffling of feet or rustling of clothing.

The bed was on casters and easily slid across the room. He slipped the curtain around the leg nearest the window and dropped both ends down the outside wall. He didn't wait to see if there was actually anyone below. Speed was now of the essence. He climbed out of the window and went down rapidly hand over hand. His feet touched the ground and he crouched before moving towards the gloom of the portico. He couldn't see anybody. He stopped behind the first pillar. He sniffed. Cigarette smoke. On the other side of the portico someone was sitting on a folding seat. It was the waiter.

The figure yawned, then stretched his arms above his head. He sucked deeply on his cigarette, the tip glowing brightly. Hunter stood still. The man shook his head and stood up, turning away from Hunter. Three paces and Hunter was behind him. The waiter was turning his head when Hunter reached him. Hunter slammed his right forearm across the man's throat, his left arm behind the man's neck; he gripped his arm just above the elbow and jerked the waiter's head forward. The neck snapped. The gun he was holding dropped to the ground with a clatter.

Hunter regretted what he'd done but knew there had been no alternative. Tying people up and gagging them was all very well in books and films but there was a high risk of that person getting loose or working the gag free and yelling for help.

Picking up the gun, he looked at it closely. He'd used quite a number of different guns in his time but this one was unknown to him. He realised it was a sub-machine gun of some kind. It had a fairly bulbous nose, was only about a half metre or so long and wasn't particularly heavy. For all that, it was a serious piece of kit. Fear of a prison sentence for possession obviously didn't bother Rabbani and his thugs.

Returning to the curtain, he grasped one end and tugged, threading it from around the leg of the bed to land in a heap at his feet. When it came time to get back inside he would use the ladders in the garage.

He wasn't going to leave the body where it was in case there was a relief guard. If there was, anyone looking for the waiter would assume he had gone to the toilet or for a walk to help stay awake. At least that would delay matters even if only for a few minutes, and minutes could easily mean the difference between life and death.

He slung the curtains over his shoulder and then grabbed the body by its belt and half carried, half dragged it along the front of the house. After only a couple of paces he realised that the man's shoes dragging along the ground were making too much noise. He bent down on one knee, grabbed an arm and thigh and lifted the body over his shoulders. Picking up the gun, he stood and listened. Nothing. He continued walking; the weight of the man and the bulk of the curtains hindered his movements only slightly.

At the corner he paused, looking up and along the side of the house. There were no second storey windows but there were three windows at ground level. He lowered the body and curtains to the ground and walked slowly along the side of the house. All the curtains were drawn and no lights showed.

The gazebo was about 100m away. Returning to the corner, he knelt and slung the body over his shoulders, grabbed the curtains and headed towards the garden and the hedge. Once he was behind the hedge he felt safer and moved more quickly towards the gazebo. It stood about three-quarters of a metre off the ground, on sturdy pilings. There were three steps to climb. Hunter dumped the waiter's body under the floor, behind the steps and shoved the curtains in after it.

He climbed the steps and took a look around. It was octagonal, with a table surrounded by 6 chairs in the middle. The place was immaculate with plenty of space.

19

HUNTER LOOKED BACK at the house. It was still quiet. No alarm had been sounded and the house remained dark. Satisfied, he looked closely at the gun he was holding. He remembered the words of his small arms instructor. He used to say that all you really needed to know about any weapon was where the safety catch was to be found, was there a bullet in the chamber and then he would add for good measure, and for the less intelligent, where the trigger was and which end the bullets came out. However, he then went on to say that any professional needed to know more. The wrong guns in the wrong place had been known to cause major problems, ones that meant the difference between life and death. The SA80 came to mind. It had proven a disaster during the first Gulf war, often jamming due to a few grains of sand. Hunter needed to know what he was holding.

It took a few seconds, but then he recognised the initials G.D.P.S. alongside the serial number. South African. Not surprising, thought Hunter. The country was a major arms manufacturer and supplier to most of the third world - especially to terrorists operating in the Middle East.

Something connected in his memory and he knew he was holding a BXP. It was, Hunter knew, a clever and versatile sub-machine gun. The bulbous end meant there was a silencer attached. He unclicked the magazine and saw that there were about thirty rounds of 9mm Parabellum cartridges. He looked closer. Both sides had a safety catch so that the gun could be operated using either hand. Up was a green dot for safe; down was a red dot for fire. He couldn't see a fire selector which normally meant that by pulling the trigger to the first stop, a single round was fired, while all the way back and it fired on fully automatic. The safety had been on green.

He hefted the weapon in his hand. It was finely balanced, the grip under the barrel giving it a steadiness often missing with similar guns. Bending down, he tapped the waiter's pockets and found a second magazine which he transferred to his own pocket. Now all he had to do was get down to the gates, collect his kit, return to the house, knock everyone out using the gas and then put them under using the hypodermic. As easy as ordering an Americano at Starbuck's.

A glance at his watch showed that eleven minutes had elapsed since he'd dropped out of the window.

The landscape was brightly bathed in moonlight and he set out at a run. He looked like a jack rabbit. He jinked left and right, taking irregular steps. It made for a more difficult target. Not that he expected anyone to shoot at him. He held the BXP underneath the trigger guard in his left hand, the weight evenly balanced. The safety was pointing to red, the gun primed to fire.

In under a minute, Hunter was back at the gap in the wall from where he had been observing the house. He paused, knelt by the wall and looked back. He still saw nobody and nothing untoward. He climbed over the wall, landed softly and stopped to listen.

All around him he could hear the calls of birds, disturbed by his arrival.

There were no other sounds. The moonlight was dappling through the trees, casting eerie shadows, giving him a feeling of safety. He made his way carefully through the woods to the road. Once there, he jogged towards the gates. He arrived at the spot where he'd hidden the rucksack and recovered it. Slipping the straps over his shoulders, he retraced his steps to the wall where he paused, examining the landscape before him. Even if everything was quiet he wasn't going to rush it.

He could clearly see the gazebo. Nothing seemed to have changed. Scrambling back over the wall, he stopped for a moment. He slung the BXP's carrying sling over his right shoulder and, with the stock folded, held the gun by its grip in his right hand. His finger was on the trigger but the safety was on. He sprinted across the lawn, bent double, heading for the gazebo. He stepped inside and knelt on one knee at the railing while he examined the ground ahead. The moon was bright enough for him to see clearly all the way to the house. There was nothing stirring. There were no lights showing and no activity as far as he could see. From that he surmised nobody had yet missed the waiter. Hunter ran to the low hedge. Again he knelt and studied the terrain. It was as quiet as the grave. He paused for about 15 seconds and then ran for the corner of the house. His next move was to go around the front of the house, under the portico and to the garage to get the ladders. At that second his plans changed.

Nawaz was as satisfied as he could be. Tension was high as the six men stood at the backdoor. The seventh, the convert, had been sent to the garage. If they needed to get out in a hurry they would be running down the drive towards the gates and the farm lane where they had parked their cars. The man in the garage would cover their retreat. Not that retreat was an option. If they failed in their mission, better to die there than to admit failure to the General.

On the other hand, Nawaz had no intention of dying. The man in the garage was to cover his retreat, not the rest of the team's. Because if they were forced to abandon the attack, if they were beaten back, none of the others would survive, he would make sure of that. He would get away and hide. Where and how he hadn't given much thought to, but the idea gave him some comfort.

He tried the door handle. It turned. He pushed the door. It didn't move. He pushed again. It was locked. The imbecile in the house hadn't unlocked the door. Had he disarmed the alarm? Surely he could not, would not, have done one without the other? Another thought came to him. Perhaps someone had noticed the door was unlocked and locked it again? If the man inside had done his job properly then the alarm would be set but the wire cut. That would mean anyone checking the alarm would think everything was in order. He hoped. All would go according to plan, *Insha'Allah* - God willing. The top half of the door was panes of glass about 20cms square. He cursed the man inside again and then hit the pane of glass next to the handle with his left elbow. Nothing happened. He rubbed his elbow. It was sore.

He used his revolver and tapped the glass with the butt. The glass shattered. He waited a few seconds. There was no alarm, no flashing lights and no yells. He used the butt to clear the glass from around the frame and he reached in for the key. It was in the lock and he turned it.

The faint tinkle of breaking glass was unmistakable in the still night. The noise came as a complete surprise. It came from the back of the house and sounded like a window breaking. That would mean somebody was trying to break in. Any second now the alarm would sound, all hell would break loose and his plans would be ashes. Maybe in the pandemonium he could get away with it. He could dump the BXP and let one of the others find it.

He waited all of two seconds before he realised that the alarm should have sounded. That meant the system was either for show or the intruders knew what they were doing. The former he discounted. That wouldn't be Rabbani's way. So they were professionals. Except they had made a fundamental error. If the attack went wrong and Rabbani was able to make a run for it then the likelihood was he'd come through the front door, not the back where the attackers were. A sniper in the gazebo, with the right weapon, would have been ideally placed to shoot Rabbani. So perhaps they weren't so professional after all. Or maybe there weren't enough of them. But if they had done their homework they would know there would be about a dozen people in the house, possibly more. Or maybe it was merely a burglar trying his luck. No. A burglar would have done his home work and would know the house was full of people. It was still possible it was a single attacker with one objective and that was to kill Rabbani. If he knew the layout of the place and which was Rabbani's room, it wouldn't be that difficult to put a silenced bullet through the target's head. The permutations were so complex there was only one thing to do.

He sprinted for the back of the house, went down on one knee and peered around the corner. He was in time to see somebody enter through the kitchen door. He stayed where he was for a few more moments until he was as satisfied as he could be that there was nobody else. He stepped silently onto the patio and made his way towards the kitchen. He had to step around the tables and chairs, impressed that the remains of the b-b-q had been cleared away. Looking around, no one would have believed that a party had taken place only hours earlier.

At the kitchen door he knelt down on one knee and looked inside. With the moon in front of the house, the room was in deep gloom but not pitch dark. It appeared to be empty but Hunter wasn't going to take any chances. He stayed where he was, listening. It was so quiet that he would be able to hear somebody breathing. He heard nothing. He was as sure as he could be that the room was empty.

The door opposite was open. Hunter could see shards of glass on the floor and he stepped round them. He crossed to the door. Now he was inside his eyes were becoming more accustomed to the darkness. Coupled with the fact that moonlight was streaming in through the window above the front door it was easy to make out two men. One was just stepping onto the stairs; the other was halfway across the foyer.

They were wearing night vision goggles.

Hunter was about to follow them when the door to Matthews' pantry opened and Matthews appeared with a gun in his hand. With no alarm going off, Hunter assumed that the butler must have heard something. There was no warning. Matthews aimed and fired without a second thought. The shot, using an unsilenced revolver, was loud in the confined space. The round hit the intruder in the chest and blew him off his feet. Matthews was yelling in Urdu, walking towards the stairs, when the body on the floor moved. An arm was raised, a gun was pointed and the trigger was pulled. Matthews was blown off his feet, his insides shredded by the hollowed out 9mm Parabellum round that hit him. The other man climbed painfully to his feet and took a step towards the dead body. The Kevlar vest had done its job. Hunter knew the man was bruised, probably with a cracked rib or two, but he was very much alive. He died about two seconds later when Hunter's bullet hit him in the back of the head, the shot a quiet belch in contrast to the noise created so far.

The man Hunter had seen taking the stairs didn't reappear. Hunter guessed the man thought his back was covered.

Upstairs, chaos reigned. There were more shots. A woman screamed. The scream was abruptly cut off. Hunter crossed the room to remove the NVGs from the corpse but saw they were saturated with blood. He reached the stairs and went up two steps at a time, moving as quickly as he dared. At the top he stopped, knelt down low and looked carefully along the corridor to his room.

He saw two men, one either side of the corridor. Both were wearing NVGs. Hunter had recognised them as the old fashioned kind. Heavy, a little slow to warm up when first switched on and with a slight blurring around the edges. As a result, the person wearing them had lousy peripheral vision. Hunter knew the goggles were another reason for using silencers as any muzzle flash was blocked by the silencer. Without the silencers the flash could cause the retina to react by creating a bright orange spot that prevented sight for anything up to sixty seconds - more than enough time in which to die. A glance to his left showed the short corridor was empty though he could hear yells and screams and an occasional shot.

There was a man outside the Blue Room with his hand on the doorknob. He turned the knob and pushed the door with his shoulder. It was locked. He stumbled slightly, stepped back, aimed his gun at the lock and fired three silenced rounds. They made an eerie sound, spitting out quiet death - coughs in the night.

Hunter reached up and turned on the lights just as the man was about to shoulder the door again. The man let out a yell and reached for the goggles. As he did, Hunter shot him in the side of the head. The bullet, blood, brains and bone blew out the other side. The other gunman had been firing into the Brown Room when the lights had come on. As Hunter switched his aim, he saw the man reach for his NVGs but before Hunter could shoot, the second man was blown off his feet and smashed into the door opposite.

Silence cloaked the house. It came as no surprise to Hunter. During such an attack one of two things happened. Either it was all over in minutes or there was a hiatus while the attackers took stock. The defenders did what they always did. They defended. They had no plan to carry out an attack. They were reactive, not proactive. Hunter reckoned he had maybe two minutes before anything else happened.

He slowly and carefully walked along the corridor, looking in each room. The first room on his left showed two corpses. From the amount of blood on the bed, it looked as though they had been riddled with bullets. A girl lay alongside one of the men off the boat. The room on the right also contained two bodies.

Hunter recognised the other boatman and one of the girls.

Hunter stepped around the body of the man he had just shot and stopped outside the Brown Room, by the door. He looked at the man on the floor. He wasn't breathing, though Hunter couldn't see any blood.

'Don't shoot,' he called out. 'It's me, Hughes. Are you alright?'

There was no answer so he repeated the message. Then he added, 'I'm coming in. Don't shoot.'

He dropped to his knees and looked carefully into the room. Boris lay with his feet pointing at the door, naked, blood seeping through the bullet holes in his chest. It looked as though he had been approaching the door when his attacker opened it and started firing. Boris had been flung back but even as he'd been dying the tough son of a bitch had managed to shoot his killer. Hunter was about to step away when he saw another body on the other side of the bed, half hidden. It was the natural blonde girl, Cindy. She'd been shot once in the head.

Hunter turned to the assassin and checked him. The bullets had hit him in the chest but there was no blood. Although old in military equipment terms, the Kevlar vest was still an efficient bit of kit. However, the energy of the bullets needed to be expended and that was usually achieved by the target being thrown off its feet. The result was an occasional broken rib and a bruised coccyx. In this case, the impact had thrown the man against the wall and crushed his sternum. That alone wouldn't necessarily have killed him. However, with such an injury, every rib would have been broken and the man would have been in agony. His death should have been long and slow. As it was, his head had hit the wall so hard that the back of his skull had been crushed and he had died almost instantly.

Darting back along the corridor, Hunter headed for the other side of the house. At the corner, he stopped. He dropped to his knees and looked around the side of the wall. There were two men, each still wearing their night vision goggles. Though with the loom of the light from the corridor behind him, Hunter was surprised they still found them effective.

Only three doors remained closed. The two at the end of the corridor and the one facing him. The smell of cordite hung in the air. The two remaining attackers stood next to the door on the left. One man had his hand on the doorknob. They were hesitant. Hunter didn't blame them. They had lost the impetus. The surprise. It had all gone wrong. Why didn't they just cut their losses and make a run for it? Live to fight another day was a good motto to live by.

There was a shot, loud and clear. The man standing next to the door screamed and put his left hand to the top of his right arm. He fell to the floor screaming. His colleague didn't hesitate. He stepped up to him and put the man out of his misery with a bullet in the brain. Even Hunter was shocked at the callous way it had been done. Then, the man stepped to one side of the door and fired his gun on fully automatic so that the wood shredded and a large hole appeared in the door. He stopped when the gun clicked empty. He then pulled the pin on a grenade, threw it into the room and flung himself onto the floor up against the wall. The explosion was virtually instantaneous. What was left of the door blew open, the wall shook, dust blossomed out of the doorway and the man climbed cautiously to his feet.

Hunter made his play. The attacker had his hand on the doorknob of the door on the left when Hunter switched on the lights and simultaneously opened fire. The gun opened up on fully automatic. The target staggered backwards trying to stay on his feet instead of hitting the deck. It was a fatal error. Hunter's third and fourth shot was through the middle of the man's neck. His fifth and sixth shots hit the target in the face and his seventh and eighth shots missed. He let go of the trigger.

Hunter stayed where he was for a few minutes, listening. He could hear nothing. That left the room on the right and the one at the end of the corridor still intact. As he moved down the corridor, Hunter checked each room. In the first room on the left was the body of Yassin, lying in a pool of blood at the foot of his bed. Curiously, he was dressed and not in bed. The next two rooms left and right were empty. There were two bathrooms, one each side of the corridor and they were also empty.

In the room where the grenade had been lobbed were two bodies - one of the girls and Oscar. The girl was lying on the floor while what was left of Oscar had been thrown back into the open wardrobe. He paused outside the last door on the right and knocked using the end of his gun. There was no response. He tried again, harder this time.

'It's me. Hughes,' he said, loudly. 'Is there anybody there?'

There was no reply. Hunter couldn't blame them, if there was anyone left alive in there. He did a mental calculation. Rabbani and one of the girls were still unaccounted for. Staying against the wall, he reached over, twisted the doorknob and pushed. The door swung open. Nothing happened. He waited a few seconds, dropped to his knees and carefully looked into the room. There was a body on the bed. He stepped into the room, switching on the light as he did. It was one of the girls. There was no one else there and there was no sign of blood. She lay with her eyes shut and for a second or two Hunter thought she was merely unconscious. However, a touch to her neck confirmed she was dead. She was naked. There were needle marks down her arm and he wondered if she had died from a drugs overdose.

He returned to the corridor and stepped up to the door at the end. He was about to hammer on the door when he thought better of it. Instead, he went across to the room where the grenade had gone off and found a busted up chair. He pulled a leg off and stepped back into the corridor. Approaching the door, he dropped to the floor. He used the chair leg to knock on the door. The response was three well spaced bullets at chest height.

'Ashraf, it's me, Hughes. Come on, come out, we need to get away.' There was no reply. He yelled louder this time. 'Come on, Ashraf, for Christ's sake. We've got to go.'

There was silence for a short while and then Rabbani called out, 'How do I know it's not a trick? To get me to come out?'

'What the hell for?' Hunter called out. 'Everyone is dead. All your lot and the men who came to kill you. It wouldn't take much to shoot this door down and come in for you. Or throw a grenade. So get out here. Now! Otherwise, I'm leaving you to your own devices. I'm not staying, that's for sure. Are you coming?' Silence. 'Come on!'

Rabbani's response was another two bullets.

20

HUNTER COULDN'T BE bothered to wait any longer. He put on the gas mask, reached inside the knapsack, slid out the gas bottle, attached the hose and pushed it under the door. The thick pile of the carpet made it easy. He turned the valve on and heard the gas hissing out. He waited a minute before turning the valve off. About another minute passed when he heard a faint thud.

'Rabbani! Ashraf! Answer me!' He hit the door again. Nothing. Tentatively he reached up, took hold of the door handle and turned it. He paused and then pushed at the door. It didn't budge. He tried knocking again. Satisfied that Rabbani was in no state to open fire, Hunter stood a metre from the door and lashed out with his right foot. The door crashed open. Rabbani was lying face down, to the left side of the door, out of the firing line. He was breathing deeply, unconscious, but apparently unhurt. A Glock 17 was clasped tightly in his hand. Hunter removed the weapon, checked it, and put it in his bumbag.

Hunter was surprised to find him fully dressed. Grabbing Rabbani under his arms, Hunter dragged the body into the corridor and along to the far end, swerving around the blood pooling on the carpet. He let him drop to the floor and sat on the top stair, before removing his gasmask. He went through the numbers in his head. All Rabbani's guests were dead. There were six dead attackers. He sighed. He knew what he had to do. He stood up and went along the corridor to the first body. It took less than a minute to check there was nothing to identify the man. Ten minutes later, he was finished with all six bodies and had found nothing.

He sat on the stairs again and looked at Rabbani. His face was a pasty looking colour in spite of his naturally dark skin. However, he was breathing steadily so Hunter figured he'd live. Hunter became aware that a gray light was beginning to permeate the room. He took out the Glock, and removed the magazine. He then lifted the BXP, took out the magazine and thumbed out a handful of bullets. Like so many weapons they used the same 19mm Parabellum rounds. He checked the Glock had a full mag of 19 and then put it back into his bumbag.

Hunter clambered to his feet, stepped over to Rabbani and slapped his face. Both sides - hard. The response was a low moan. Exasperated, Hunter took a glass of water from the bathroom, returned and flung it in Rabbani's face. The response was slightly better than before. Repeating the process with slaps and water, Rabbani, moaning, started to come around.

'What...what happened?' he mumbled.

'Come on Ashraf, pull yourself together!'

Rabbani pushed himself up to a sitting position, groaned and put his head in his hands. This time he asked in a steadier and stronger voice, 'What happened?'

'We were attacked. Do you remember?'

'Yes.' He repeated the word with more emphasis. 'Yes.' As memory returned he asked, 'Is...Is everyone dead?' He looked around.

'Everyone. The two Russians, your two crew from the boat, Matthews, the waiter, the girls.'

'What about Mr. Yassin?'

'Him too.'

Rabbani sat with his head on his chest and gave a low grunt. Hunter doubted it was for the memory of those killed. Rabbani didn't strike him as the compassionate kind. More likely, the enormity of what had happened was beginning to sink in. When he looked up there was real fear in his eyes. This Rabbani was a great deal easier to deal with than Rabbani in control of his emotions. From Hunter's perspective, the decks had been cleared for him to go to the next phase of the operation.

'But what happened to me? I was standing in my bedroom and then the next thing I know I'm out here with you.'

'You must have fainted. How the hell should I know? What I do know is that we need to get out of here. Think! Is there anything you need to take with you? Papers? Passport? Credit cards? Other documents?'

Rabbani shook his head. 'I don't know. I...I'm not sure.'

'Then you'd better get sure, because we're gone in minutes,

not hours.'

'I suppose I need my laptop, my mobile, my passport, yes and credit cards and money as well.'

'Where is all this stuff?'

'In a safe in my office. Downstairs.' Rabbani stood up unsteadily, tottered and put his hand out to steady himself against the wall. Colour was beginning to come back to his cheeks. He flexed his shoulders and stepped across to the stairs, gripped the banister and started down. With each step he was regaining his strength and composure. Until he reached the bottom. The dead man at the bottom of the stairs and the body of Matthews unnerved him and he sat down on the lower steps with a bump.

Rabbani's voice shook. 'What happened? How is everybody dead while you're alive?' The thought seemed to give him strength. He asked the question again, this time with menace seeping into his voice. 'How is it you're still alive?'

'I was in the bathroom when the attack started. One of the men looked in and I dealt with him.' Hunter hefted the machine gun in his hand. 'I took this off him.'

Rabbani didn't ask how but glanced at the weapon. 'A BXP. That's a serious gun. One of the best on the market.'

Hunter raised his eyebrows.

Rabbani's eyes slitted. 'I sell them.' Then he expanded, 'My men also use them when they are on guard duty.' He paused then stared at Hunter. 'How is it you're still alive?'

Hunter said nothing, just looked at the other man. 'It's because I know what I'm doing and I'm good at it. We're alive. So let's move. Now.'

Rabbani hauled himself to his feet and started across the foyer without a word. Hunter followed him to his study. Rabbani crossed to the safe, put the palm of his hand on the reader, there was a click and he grasped the handle to twist it down and pull the door open.

It was instinct more than anything else. As Rabbani reached inside, Hunter shifted the BXP to be pointing straight at him. The other man put his hand inside the safe, and was withdrawing it with a pistol gripped in it when Hunter put a single shot into the desk.

'The next one will be into your head.'

Rabbani started and looked over his shoulder at Hunter. 'I wasn't going to do anything,' he said flatly. 'I was just removing it so I could get at the rest of my papers.'

Hunter nodded. 'I'm delighted to hear that, Ashraf, but I'd hate there to be any misunderstandings. They can get you killed. Carefully place the gun on the desk and keep it pointing away from me.'

Rabbani did as he was told and Hunter reached over and lifted it up. He smiled. 'My Pocketlite with silencer. How kind of you to give it back to me.'

In return, he got a scowl.

'Come on, Ashraf, let's get out of here. We don't know who else could be out there. I'd be surprised if this lot didn't have someone they were meant to report to.'

Rabbani grabbed a bag and pulled it out of the safe. 'Everything I need is in here.'

'Always ready to skip, is that it?'

'Yes. Only a fool doesn't prepare. Let's go.'

'Open the bag first.'

'Why?'

'I want to see what's inside. I don't like surprises.'

Rabbani shrugged and unzipped the bag. A quick glance showed there was no weapon just a few jiffy bags. Hunter didn't bother examining their contents. There would be time for that later.

'Okay. But first, I need something from my room. Incidentally, I wouldn't try making a run for it. Together we have a chance of getting away. On your own that becomes more problematic. We don't know who else there may be.'

Rabbani nodded.

Hunter took the stairs two at a time. He picked up his bag from his room before using his mobile to photograph the faces of the dead attackers. He dashed back downstairs. 'Let's go.'

Rabbani shook his head and walked away. 'I must go to the kitchen. I must have something to drink. Some water.'

Hunter nodded. He was also very thirsty. The sort of action they had been engaged in could do that. It also reminded Hunter that Rabbani was one tough son-of-a-bitch and not to be underestimated. The deaths of his men, the women and his enemies didn't appear to have affected him one iota.

In the kitchen, Rabbani filled a glass with water and drank it in one long swallow. He sighed, wiped his mouth with the back of his hand and said, 'That's better.' Rabbani reached into a drawer and removed a packet of cigarettes. He lit one and drew deeply, filling his lungs with smoke, satisfying his craving for nicotine.

Hunter helped himself to some water. 'Right. We're going to the boat.'

'The Talisman? Why?'

Because it suits me, thought Hunter. Instead, he said, 'Do you have a better idea? I don't. What are we going to do? We can't stay here, it's too dangerous. I suppose we could send for the police. Explain what happened. Spend months on remand being questioned with the inevitable trial that will follow. That, of course, will be followed by life imprisonment. Get real, Ashraf. Do you have any better ideas?'

The Pakistani shook his head. 'No. No, my friend, you are right. I cannot think of a better place to hide than the Talisman.' He paused and then added, 'But what will we do then? These bodies? They will be found.' Now that there was time to think, realisation dawned on him. 'We will be arrested. It is inevitable.'

Hunter shook his head. 'Now think, Ashraf. We came and spent a few hours here before going down to the boat. Just you and me. You're keen to sell her and I'm in the market to buy. We can both swear to that. It was sheer luck that we weren't here. We have no idea who the attackers are. We'll put out to sea, ditch the guns and our clothes, spend a few hours cruising then return to the marina. You will phone the house. There will be no reply. It will give you cause for concern and so you will phone the local police station and ask them, as a favour, to check on the place. This is such a mess; I doubt the police will be able to unravel what's happened with any degree of accuracy. If we stick to our story there shouldn't be any problems, except for a few difficult hours which our solicitors can deal with.'

Rabbani nodded eagerly. It was what he wanted to believe. It didn't dawn on him that the British police were painstaking in their investigations. However long it took, they would ferret away, looking for the truth. Especially as there had been young British girls murdered.

'Apart from the gun you were using, are there any others that are likely to have your fingerprints on them?'

Without hesitation, Rabbani shook his head. 'No. I am sure of that.'

'Good. That means you can deny all knowledge of where the guns came from, what happened and, most importantly, why it happened.' Hunter glanced at his watch. The time was coming up to 05.45. 'What about keys for the boat?'

'They are hidden in a locker on the Talisman.'

'What about provisions? Fuel, water, food?'

'The fuel and water tanks are kept topped up. There is normally plenty of food, both tinned and frozen. If we want bread and milk then we buy it at the marina.'

'Right, let's get going.' He crossed to the back door and said, 'Wait a second. Let's make sure the coast is clear.' He stood there for a few minutes, Rabbani becoming impatient by the moment. Sensing the man's agitation, Hunter said, 'Just wait, Ashraf. We can't be too careful in a situation like this.' Another couple of minutes passed, as the sun came over the horizon with the promise of another fine and beautiful June day.

'Okay, let's go. Straight to the garage. We'll take the Range Rover.' Opening the door, the two men walked towards the garage, Rabbani alongside Hunter who was carrying the BXP in his right hand, pointed at the ground. His grip was in his left hand and the small rucksack with the gas and knockout drugs was slung over his shoulders.

It came as a shock when a blonde, white man stepped out from the garage and immediately took up a firing stance with his gun, held in a two-handed grip, pointing at Hunter. The gun fired and Hunter was thrown backwards.

21

MACNAIR SWUNG HIS feet to the floor and yawned. Sleep was a precious commodity. Prepared for the possibility he would be sleeping in his office, he had a wardrobe of clothes. He was aware that to get a good night's rest, particularly during an operation, being comfortable was important. Hence he was wearing pyjamas and had a dressing gown to hand. He put fresh coffee beans in the machine, topped up the water and switched it on. Next, he went along the corridor to the bathroom where he shaved, showered and brushed his teeth. Back in his office, he changed into his uniform before pouring himself a cup of coffee. In spite of only 4 hours sleep he was beginning to feel human again. It was a few minutes before 05.40 and breakfast wouldn't be available until 07.30.

He logged on to his e-mails. Nothing from Hunter, but that was no surprise. Next he logged on to Operation Mosaic. This was a police operation instigated by the Home Office. Macnair was kept in the loop out of a combination of courtesy and acknowledgement that he often had access to information the other services didn't have.

Searches and raids had been going on all night and had revealed nothing. Mosques and houses were being hit by teams of policemen who had been briefed to act with courtesy and consideration. Macnair knew the story being given out by the authorities was that they were looking for one person in particular. Or merely information about that individual. He was also aware how the searches were being conducted. Apologies were as profuse as it was humanly possible to shower on anyone. Most of those questioned and who had their premises searched were law abiding, decent people but the visits made them resentful and angry. Some attitudes were inflamed by a few Imams and solicitors who were known for causing deep divisions between the Muslim and secular societies. There were also known fundamentalist sympathisers who were on the fringes of terrorism or possibly even more involved. Those people were the subject of particular attention by the police.

Some solicitors were making threats, but in reality, there was little they could do. The authority to carry out such searches had been laid down in statute following 7/7 though it had never been used to such an extent.

Sitting at his desk, his fingers drumming a military tattoo, he wondered what they could do next. Macnair had never been one to underestimate the enemy. He knew they were tough, often well trained and pretty much fearless.

IN SPITE oF the shock, the breath being knocked out of him and landing with a heavy thud on his butt, Hunter still had the presence of mind to sweep his left leg across the back of Rabbani's legs, knocking him off his feet.

Which was just as well, as the gunman's second shot passed over Rabbani's head. The man didn't have time for a third. Hunter pointed the sub-machine gun in the general direction of his target and pulled the trigger. Hard. The weapon coughed bullets. The first few missed but then one hit the target in his right shoulder, two hit him in the chest where the Kevlar vest did its job, and one hit him in his left shoulder. The man went flying backwards and landed heavily on the ground. He wasn't dead but he lay still for a few seconds, before he began to groan.

Rabbani scrambled to his feet, gasping for breath. A low moan, almost a growl, escaped his lips. He'd landed hard, though not as hard as Hunter who lay still for a few seconds collecting his strength. Hunter propped himself up on his elbows, twisted to the right, put his left hand on the ground and pushed himself up. Rabbani hurried across to the gunman. As Hunter straightened his back, flexing his spine, his arms and his legs, checking nothing was seriously damaged; Rabbani smashed his foot down hard on the man's gun hand.

It must have hurt like hell but the man barely flinched.

'Who sent you?' Rabbani screeched. 'Why did you come to kill me?'

In reply the man smiled, ground his teeth together and said, '*Alluha...*' he didn't complete the phrase before his head lolled to one side and he gazed sightlessly at Rabbani.

'Swine! Filthy swine!' Rabbani kicked the man in the side of the head, continuing his ranting, venting his anger and his hatred.

'Shut up, Ashraf! Shut up!' Hunter roared. 'He's dead. He had some sort of poison. It looks like cyanide.'

The Pakistani fell silent, confusion on his face, like he had just woken up and was wondering what was happening.

'Drag the body into the garage out of sight. It's time we got the hell out of here.' Hunter scanned the ground around him. He saw the flattened dollop of lead of the spent bullet lying on the ground. He wasn't surprised to see it was a hollow-point. The vest had done its job, but the flattening of the bullet had spread the impact while at the same time its momentum had been expended when Hunter went flying backwards. These were the reasons he was still alive. He walked over to the body and picked up the man's gun.

'Come on, Ashraf, stop hanging about. Drag the body into the garage.'

'There is too much blood.'

Rather than argue, Hunter grabbed the body's coat collar and dragged it across the few metres to the garage. He dumped it unceremoniously in a corner and threw the man's gun alongside. It was a Glock 17 with silencer. He took out the mag and placed it in his bumbag. The extra bullets may prove useful. The amount of hardware around the estate was enough to start a small war. Which, in some ways, was what had happened. He checked the corpse's pockets. Empty. No ID, which came as no surprise. What was surprising was the fact that the dead man was a Caucasian, unlike the others. He took a photograph of the man's face.

'Okay,' said Hunter, 'into the Range Rover. I'll drive.' He opened the door to the backseat and put the rucksack and grip on the floor. He climbed into the driver's seat and put the BXP in the side pocket, quickly and easily accessible. He had thought about ditching the gun but decided against it. It was too soon. There could be more attackers outside the grounds, a kind of fail-safe, though somehow, Hunter doubted it. None of the men had been carrying so much as a mobile phone, so they could not have kept in contact. If your forces were split, contact was of supreme importance, yet there had been no contact between the men in the house and the guard in the garage.

Rabbani climbed in beside him.

Hunter turned the key in the ignition and rubbed the middle of his chest. It hurt like hell.

'Thank you,' said Rabbani.

'What for?'

'For saving my life. If you hadn't acted so quickly, I would have been killed.'

'Yeah, well we're some sort of partnership. So I figured I'd better take care of you.'

'You did say there were others you could do business with.'

'That's true, but we have a saying here in England. Better the devil you know. Now listen, Ashraf. I'm going to hit the driveway fast. You look left, I'll look right. If you see anything, anything at all, yell and point.'

'Give me the BXP and I will shoot anyone who gets in the way.'

'I trust you Ashraf, but only up to a point.'

The Pakistani didn't reply.

'Let's go,' said Hunter.

The car was an automatic. Hunter put it in drive and slammed the accelerator to the floor. The vehicle shot out of the garage and had barely started down the driveway when it was passing 50mph.

There was no sign of anyone as they neared the gates. Hunter slammed the brakes on and brought the car to a skidding halt. The lane was empty in both directions. He hit the accelerator again and spun the wheel to the left. They accelerated down the lane.

'What if there are more men on the boat? Waiting for us?' Rabbani called, his left hand gripping the handle above the passenger's door, his right hand wrapped around the steadying handle in front of him.

'One thing at a time. Here, take a look at this.' Hunter handed over his phone.

'What am I looking at?'

'Press the middle button. Look closely at the photographs.'

Rabbani looked at the photos Hunter had taken. He paused at the fifth.

Hunter noticed and asked, 'Do you know him?'

'Let me think. Let me think,' he repeated. There were a few seconds of silence. 'It is possible I have seen this man before, but it makes no sense.'

'Why not? Who is he? Where did you see him?'

Rabbani replied, 'I cannot be certain.' He shook his head before repeating, 'It makes no sense whatsoever.'

'What doesn't?' The frustration was evident in Hunter's voice.

'I think he is the aide to a man by the name of Pervez Khan.'

Hunter hadn't expected the reply. 'You mean General Khan?'

'Yes.'

'Look, let's get this straight. You're telling me that this man is the aide to General Pervez Khan, Chief of Army Staff, Pakistan?' Hunter persisted.

'I am not telling that is a fact. I am saying I think he is.'

'How is that possible? How do you know him? Have you met the General?'

Rabbani didn't answer. Instead, he said, 'I do not understand any of this. If they had been Russian, or Eastern European I could possibly understand, but these men are Pakistani. I would stake my life on it.'

'You have. What do you mean about the Russians and Eastern Europeans?'

'You must know we have a truce,' Rabbani replied. 'We have reached an agreement where we do not interfere in each other's territories. Of course, there are mistakes. But apologies are accepted and we all continue with business as usual. You must know this!'

'Of course I do. Did you notice anything special about those men?' Hunter asked.

'Such as?'

'Let's not play games. Apart from two of the men, they were young with straggly beards. I would guess barely out of their teens and had no ID.' Hunter paused.

'It's not much but what does that add up to?'

'I think they may be Jihadists.'

'That is the conclusion I have come to also,' said Rabbani, 'but that does not make any sense.'

'Are you connected to any fundamentalist group?'

'No!' The reply was vehement. 'They are all misguided fools. All that rubbish about virgins and paradise. You have to be a moron to believe it. Do women arrive in Paradise to be greeted by seventy-two men who are still virgins?'

As far as Hunter could tell, there was no doubting Rabbani's words, or the passion in which he had said them. So what about Barzakh? 'Religion isn't meant to make sense. Not in an analytical way. It is all about belief and belief is a powerful thing. Especially when it is turned into a weapon like it has been and aimed at the West. Those men defeated your alarm system. I presume it's not connected to a police station?'

Rabbani shook his head. 'No. What would I want with the police? Any problems and we would deal with them ourselves.'

'Like last night, you mean?'

'What has happened I never thought was possible. Never. We are in rural Essex. This is a place of peace and tranquillity. People don't attack others with automatic weapons and grenades.'

'Where were the controls to the alarm?'

'In a cupboard in the kitchen.

'Did this alarm only sound in Matthews' room?'

'No, of course not. What would be the point? If there was an intruder I wanted the whole house to know about it.'

'So why didn't it work?'

'I have no idea.'

'Do you test it?'

'Yes. Without fail.'

'While you're there?'

'No. It's always done on the day I'm arriving. Matthews then reported to me as a matter of course when I arrived. It was part of...of the ritual. Like we would discuss the menu, the wines, the rooms to be used.'

'Was it Matthews who set the alarm?'

'Yes. Always.'

'Nobody else knew the code?'

'No one except me. Why do you ask?'

'You had a traitor in your midst. And if it wasn't Matthews, it was one of your entourage.'

Rabbani said, 'I don't believe it.'

'Believe what you like.'

'Who would have done such a thing? Besides, they are all dead.'

'Perhaps the traitor was killed by mistake, or more likely, deliberately so that there were no loose ends. Whichever it was, we'll not find out.'

The other man made no reply. He appeared to relax a little as he removed his hand from above the door and felt in his jacket pocket. He took out a packet of cigarettes.

'Don't! Wait until we get to the marina. I'm not sitting here inhaling your smoke. The sodding car smells enough of dog ends as it is.'

Rabbani looked sideways at Hunter, was about to say something, thought better of it and put the cigarettes back in his pocket. He handed the mobile back to Hunter.

It was only minutes later when they were approaching the outskirts of Burnham-on-Crouch. Rabbani gave directions and Hunter pulled up in the car park of the marina. Switching off the engine, they sat in silence, neither having the inclination to get out. For Rabbani, it was due to exhaustion, for Hunter, it was natural caution. He carefully and methodically looked around. If the attackers knew about the boat then there could easily be a welcoming committee. Hunter reached into the side pocket and lifted out the BXP, placing it on his lap.

There was a peace cloaking the area that was soporific. The loudest sounds were the raucous calls of the seagulls and the rhythmic tapping of loose rigging along the masts of the yachts as the morning breeze began to die down.

Rabbani was leaning forward and reaching for the door handle when Hunter placed a hand on his shoulder. 'Don't get out. Stay where you are and look around. We can't be too careful.'

'Who are you really? How do you know so much? How did you manage to kill all those men?' There was menace in his tone.

Hunter looked calmly back at him. 'Who am I really? You know who I am. How do I know so much? Easy. I spent years in the military. I've also spent too much time watching too many action films with ludicrous heroes and more ludicrous plots. How did I manage to kill those men? For a start I was very good at my job. Also, Matthews killed two, and two of them were shot by Boris and Oscar. But the reality is we succeeded only because they were amateurs. As it is, all your people were killed, you nearly bought it, and I was shot. We were damned lucky Ashraf. Don't kid yourself otherwise. If it hadn't been for my vest I'd be dead right now and so would you.'

Rabbani looked at him for a few seconds longer. 'I need a cigarette,' was all he said.

'It looks quiet enough. Is there a shop in that building across the way?' Hunter gestured with his head.

'Yes. There are also a chandlers and a boat hire office.'

'What time does the shop open?'

'I don't know. Early, I think. Look at the boats already going to sea.'

Two 10m yachts were leaving their berths. Hunter looked at the smiling faces of the people heading for a day or more sailing and wished he was doing the same. Sighing, he said, 'Go and get some bread and milk.'

'What are you going to do?'

'I'll stay here and keep watch. If I see anything strange, anything that's not right, I'll drive over and blow the horn once. If I do, you stop whatever you're doing and get back in here as quick as you can. And I mean whatever. Handing over money, taking change, I don't care. Drop everything and shift it. Do you understand?'

Rabbani nodded his nervousness returning and evident in the way his eyes flickered around the marina and his tongue was darting out to moisten his lips.

Already, a few more people were appearing. Men, women and children popping up from below and climbing on deck, getting ready for sea. There was a buzz about the place that was beginning to vibrate through the air. Hunter could see the visitors' pontoon with yachts displaying Swiss, French and German flags flapping languidly at their sterns.

'There's someone coming around that building with a bag of stuff. Looks like groceries. I'll go and park over there,' Hunter pointed, 'and I'll be able to see you go in and come out. OK?'

Rabbani was highly nervous. He nodded but sat there, immobile.

Hunter looked at him. 'Move it, Ashraf, we don't have all day. The sooner we get away from here the better.' He still didn't move. Hunter added, 'Okay. Let's go to the boat. I'll park up over there.' He nodded at the serried ranks of cars 100m away. 'If we want to, we can get anything we need later. In some other marina somewhere along the coast.'

Licking his lips again, Rabbani looked across at Hunter and said, 'I need more cigarettes.'

'Then you'd better move it because you've three choices. We go to the boat now, you get what we need first then we go to the boat, or I leave you and drive away. If I do, you won't be coming with me. I'll dump the car somewhere and grab a train. You can do what you like. What's it to be?'

'Alright. I cannot go without my cigarettes. I will go and get them.'

'In that case, don't forget bread and milk.' He looked at his watch. 'It's just seven o'clock. Now hurry!'

Climbing down, Rabbani walked towards the building, nervously looking around. Hunter started the car and drove to the parking space where he could see the door to the shop. He saw three people, a young boy and two women. They were coming out of the building that housed the toilets and showers.

A woman walked across the car park and went into the shop. She had a basket over her arm. Moments later, Rabbani reappeared; Hunter climbed out of the car, opened the back door, reached in and grabbed his bags. He slung the knapsack over his left shoulder and put the grip on the floor underneath the steering wheel. He slipped the BXP into the bag, grabbed its handles in his left hand and lifted it out. He stood with his right hand under his jacket, in the bumbag, the Pocketlite in his grasp. He flexed his shoulders. His chest hurt though he was sure nothing was broken. If there had been, he would be having sharp attacks of pain whenever he moved, as opposed to a dull ache.

Rabbani reached the car. He was sucking deeply on a cigarette, his head turning in all directions as he tried to look everywhere at once.

'Take it easy, Ashraf. Settle down. Don't look so worried. Get your bag.'

Opening the back nearside door, Rabbani took out his bag. He slammed the door shut and Hunter aimed and pressed the fob key, locking the doors.

'Lead on,' said Hunter. 'Go in front while I walk just behind.'

Rabbani hesitated.

Hunter said, 'I'm armed. I have a pistol on my hand. Trust me; I will be at your right shoulder. That will give me a clear view ahead and let me look behind without you being in the way. It also means I have a clear shot at any target that pops up in front of us. Understood?'

Nodding, Rabbani started towards the gate, Hunter at his heels. Hunter hadn't added that anyone firing from the boat would probably hit Rabbani first, giving Hunter time to shoot back or throw himself into the water.

22

THERE WAS A gate to the pontoon that was standing open. The Talisman was easy to spot, halfway along the wooden walkway, on the left, a queen amongst peasants.

He and Rabbani reached the boat. She was berthed stern to the pontoon with the bows aimed at the marina entrance.

'Wait a moment,' said Hunter, stepping alongside the other man. The boat looked empty. 'Where are the keys?'

'Under that seat,' Rabbani motioned with his head at the cushions on the starboard side of the boat. 'It is where the lifejackets are kept. There is a wooden box underneath the jackets. The keys are in there.'

'Door and ignition keys?'

'No, just door keys. The ignition key is kept in the cockpit.'

Hunter slung his grip into the aft well of the boat and stepped over the gunwale. Rabbani flicked his cigarette into the water, threw his bag after Hunter's and quickly followed.

Lifting up the seat, Hunter rummaged under the lifejackets, felt the box and took it out. He found the key and opened the door to the saloon. To say the interior was opulent was like describing the Taj Mahal as just another building. Hunter stepped along a short corridor, past a couple of cabin doors and into the main sitting area. There was a C-shaped leather settee with a collapsible table in front of it and two easy chairs on the port side. The galley was better laid out than any kitchen to be found in the most modern and well built house. In front of the galley was the enclosed helm position. Another steering position was on the deck above, in the open.

'Where are the ignition keys?'

Lighting a cigarette before replying, Rabbani said, 'In the drawer on the right.'

Hunter opened the drawer and found the key with a small polystyrene float tied to it. 'Do you know how to drive this thing?'

'No. I do not. I would order Jamil or Mady to do whatever was necessary. I would sometimes sit in the chair on deck and drive it once we were at sea. But that is all. Jamil was by way of being the Captain, Mady the dogsbody. He was also the cook.'

Hunter wasn't surprised. He stood looking at the console. 'Okay. It's not a problem. I'll start the engines. You go onto the pontoon and be ready to remove the ropes when I tell you. While the engines warm through, I'll figure out the controls and what the dials mean.'

Rabbani stood where he was.

'What's the matter? Come on, get a move on.' Hunter inserted the ignition key, turned it on, waited for a few seconds as the needles on dials flickered and then pressed the buttons to start the engines. The MAN 1360hp diesel engines sprang into life with a gentle background purr, making less noise than a first class limousine. A glance at the dials showed the diesel and water tanks were full. He looked over his shoulder and saw that Rabbani still hadn't moved.

'What, in God's name, is wrong with you?'

Rabbani looked at Hunter with his usual contempt mixed with anger. Now that he felt safe his normal character was coming back into play. 'I don't do what you tell me. I tell you what to do. No! I order you what to do. On my boat.'

Hunter stepped back into the galley area and took hold of Rabbani by the lapels of his jacket. Unused to such treatment, Rabbani's look turned to fear.

'Now listen,' Hunter shook him back and forth. 'I saved your life. I don't want thanks. I don't want anything. What I do want is to get away from here to somewhere safe. If the men who tried to kill you knew about the house, you can be sure they know about this boat. I'm certain they aren't after me. I can walk away and leave you to sort out this mess. You take the boat. You escape.' Hunter pushed Rabbani away, causing him to stumble backwards, coming up against the table. 'I'll go my own way. What's it to be? Ten seconds and I'm gone.'

Rabbani licked his lips. His arrogance had evaporated faster than it had materialised. 'Alright. Alright. I will do as you say.'

'Good. Look, Ashraf I can drive this thing. You can't. We can decide where to go later but right now let's get away.'

Rabbani still didn't move.

'What now?' There was no hiding the exasperation in Hunter's voice.

'I will be a target outside. I need a weapon. Give me your gun.'

'What are you going to do? Hold it in your hand for everyone to see? Maybe hide it under your jacket? So when do you pull it out and shoot somebody? As they walk along the pontoon? Innocent people going about their business? Explain it to me Ashraf. What will you do with the gun?'

The Pakistani stood silently, glaring at Hunter.

'As I thought. Our best bet is to get out of here. I'll be on the fly bridge and I can cover you from there.'

Rabbani looked puzzled.

'You do know what the fly bridge is, don't you?'

Rabbani shook his head.

'For God's sake, Ashraf, how often have you been on this boat.'

Rabbani looked sheepish, shrugged and then said, 'Less than ten times.'

Hunter worked out that probably meant half-a-dozen times at the most, so he nodded and raised a finger, pointing at the overhead bulkhead. 'I'll be at the upper position. I'll be able to see everything and tell you precisely what to do. Okay?'

'Yes.'

'Good. Let's go.' Hunter took a pace to the stairs and quickly went up to the open air position. He checked that the dials were in the correct range for temperature and pressure. He identified two buttons that started bow and stern thrusters as well as the controls to operate them. He wouldn't be needing them for their departure. A quick look around showed that no-one was paying attention to them. Rabbani was standing in the stern, still to step off the boat.

There was a rope either side of the stern, one either side of midships and one either side of the bow to the pontoon. He called across to Rabbani. 'Take the head ropes off, then the midships ropes and the port side stern rope. He saw Rabbani hesitate and realised the man hadn't a clue what he was talking about.

Hunter pointed forward. 'Untie those ropes there, get back onboard and pull them into the boat. Hurry up.'

Rabbani took the two bow ropes off their cleats and climbed

back onto the Talisman. He quickly hauled the two bow ropes in and dropped them on the deck.

'Now do the same thing with those two.' Hunter pointed at the midships ropes. Rabbani quickly did as he was told. Now untie the port rope, that one,' he pointed. 'Good. Now untie the starboard rope and leave it around the cleat. Step back onboard holding the end so that we are still attached to the pontoon.'

Rabbani hesitated. Hunter was about to yell at him again when footsteps on the pontoon caused both men to look towards the gate. Two men were walking towards them. Hunter slipped his hand into his bumbag. He removed the Pocketlite and placed it near his right hand.

'Leave the cleat alone. Undo the rope and just step back onboard.'

Rabbani moved with alacrity while Hunter surreptitiously watched the two men approaching. They were still a little way off when he engaged the engines, eased the boat away from the pontoon and took her into the departure lane. Once clear of the pontoon and the bow of the yacht berthed on their port side he increased speed by a couple of knots. The speed indicator showed they were travelling at 5 knots through the water, exactly as the large sign at the marina entrance displayed. The men on the pontoon watched as the Talisman crept forward, her beauty impossible to ignore.

The entrance to the marina was on the starboard side and Hunter turned the wheel to ease her into the channel. As the Talisman moved majestically through the water and her bows reached the marina entrance, Hunter could feel the eyes of the other owners fixed on her. The stares of envy were unmistakable, although he couldn't understand the feeling. Give him a yacht anytime - a boat that required real skill and real knowledge to sail. Driving Talisman was like driving a car - something to be done without thought or real ability. Once clear of the entrance, Hunter turned the boat hard to port and started down the River Crouch, keeping to the starboard side.

Looking over his shoulder, Hunter called out, 'How about making a cup of coffee?' He needed the caffeine to stay awake.

Rabbani stepped up alongside Hunter, the ubiquitous cigarette in his hand. Fatigue and stress were etched deeply on his face. He took a lungful of smoke then said, 'I have never used the galley. I don't know where anything is.' His voice was barely above a whisper.

Hunter managed to keep the contempt he was feeling from showing. How had Rabbani built an international criminal organisation while at the same time supporting a terrorist operation in Pakistan and Afghanistan yet couldn't even make a cup of coffee? It beggared belief.

'Ashraf, you are not a child. Use some initiative and look.'

With obvious reluctance Rabbani went below.

Hunter increased speed, the electronic controls responding instantly as the Talisman accelerated smoothly to 10kts.

Twenty minutes later they arrived at Foulness Point and Hunter turned the boat gradually until she was headed south. Slowly increasing speed, the turbos kicked in and just for the sheer exhilaration of it, Hunter kept accelerating. Within a couple of minutes the boat was flying along over a flat calm sea at an indicated speed of 35kts although the manufacturer's top speed was supposed to be 31kts.

After a few minutes, with no destination and no time-scale, Hunter slowed her down to 8kts and engaged the autopilot. He studied the compass as the autopilot took over and steered a steadier course than he could maintain.

There was still no sign of his coffee.

'It's a total abomination. There is no other word for it.' The speaker, Frederick Ogilvie, Conservative MP for Warwickshire North, sat on one side of the table, with Nigel Goldsmith, Liberal Democrat MP for Birmingham Yardley, next to him. Opposite them sat Stan Harrow, Labour MP for Bootle, and alongside him Judge Alistair Parker, now Lord Parker, sent to the House of Lords as an independent peer.

The four men were a special sub-committee of the all-important, very powerful Intelligence and Security Committee. The ISC had been established in 1994 by an act of Parliament. Its remit was to examine the expenditure, administration and policy of the three intelligence agencies, SIS - The Secret Intelligence Service or MI6, The Security Service - better known as MI5 and GCHQ - The Government Communications Headquarters based at Cheltenham. It also took evidence from the Home Secretary, The Foreign Secretary, and the Chairman of the Joint Intelligence Committee as well as others involved in intelligence work in the UK. The ISC, like all government committees was expanding it's sphere of influence if not downright power. It argued that in order to scrutinise policy it needed to have a knowledge of actual operations and how they were being carried out. Although the heads of the Security Services had so far complied with their requests it had been done against a background of reluctance and argument. The ISC counter argued that the information was not for Parliament but for the Prime Minister and the members were all subject to The Officials Secret Act (OSA), section 1 (1)(b) and therefore they had the highest security clearance possible. The Act as it applied to them stated:-

A person who is notified that he is subject to the provisions of the sub-section, is guilty of an offence if without lawful authority he discloses any information, document or other article relating to security or intelligence which is or has been in his possession as a member of any of those services or in the course of his work while the notification is or was in force.

Although ISC members were Members of Parliament, ordinary MPs and Members of the Lords were not subject to the OSA as they were not exposed to secret information. The requirement for secrecy was for life and not just during the time they were members. Hence the reason memoirs were vetted if written by ex-members. It was a controversy that raised its ugly head from time to time though not often. Members of the ISC took their work very seriously. They also basked in the spotlight before their peers by refusing to answer questions due to national security.

After a great deal of pressure, the Prime Minister had agreed to the formation of the sub-committee. He had also given in on who should be members and the mandate under which it would conduct the enquiry. The sub-committee had been established to investigate the methods used by TIFAT when carrying out its operations and to report its findings back to the ISC.

'It's nothing of the sort,' replied the Judge in his measured tone, the anger in his eyes in stark contrast to his words. 'We are at war. It's undeclared, but it's war nevertheless. In order to fight that war we need an organisation like The International Force Against Terrorism. We must give them as free a rein as possible to take the fight to the enemy.' The Judge appeared to be an insignificant soul, of little importance, with his medium height, average build and unprepossessing manner. At the age of 58 he was a widower with no intention of remarrying. His three children, all boys, along with their families, were close to him and held him in high regard and a great deal of affection. They had been nagging him for the last few years to find a woman and get remarried. After all, his wife had been dead for nearly eight years. He always argued that no one could ever replace her and besides, what did he want with another woman and worse, the baggage of the family that would probably come with her? He wanted time with his grandchildren, not someone else's. Although he was vehement about not dating other women, his family never stopped trying to fix him up.

'Mr. Parker,' Goldsmith deliberately refused to use the more appropriate Judge Parker, or Lord Parker, 'as a Member of Parliament I work within the letter of the law.' His blue eyes, rugged good looks and well proportioned body made him look like a film star. In contrast, the man was a physical coward though with a sharp brain and an even sharper tongue.

'Hear, hear,' said Ogilvie. 'That is why we were set up in the first place.' Ogilvie was the opposite of Goldsmith. An effete looking man, delicate of features, polite and likeable in public, in private he was a vicious backstabber of the worst kind - especially when it came to those he perceived as his enemies. He had never achieved anything of significance in his life. He had inherited a substantial trust when his parents died in a car crash when he was 16 years old. He didn't shed any tears over their deaths. They had been too enamoured of each other to take much notice of their son. A succession of nannies had looked after his welfare, none of them lasting more than 18 months. At the age of 12 he had been shipped off to a minor boarding school in Northern England which he had hated. The inferior educational standards had been mixed with bullying. It was there he discovered he was homosexual. In his final year, threatened with expulsion for cheating in his exams, he embarked on a relationship with one of the masters at the school. He stayed the course, got the necessary exam results and somehow managed to get a place at Oxford. He scraped a degree in history and politics. That was followed by a dead end job working for a small news agency. The pay was lousy, his trust fund a godsend. It enabled him to enjoy the sort of life style to which he thought he was entitled. He joined the Liberal Democrats, worked for peanuts as a researcher, contributed generously to party funds and was eventually rewarded with what was deemed a safe seat for Birmingham Yardley. That was after he had purchased a small flat in the constituency proving he intended being an important member of the community. He opened an office, paid a couple of Birmingham University students the minimum wage to run the place and allowed them to use the flat. He rarely set foot in the area apart from when election time came round. The arrangement with the students rolled along, those graduating handing over the keys to newcomers. It suited everyone.

Stan Harrow was a blunt northerner well known for his outspokenness. He was a passionate advocate of socialism and the rights of the working classes. He believed the rich should be taxed until the pips squeaked and that all education should be free. He was anti-European, wanted the UK to trade with Europe but not be governed by Brussels. Now at the age of sixty-two, he intended to stay in Parliament either until the party or his local constituents no longer wanted him, or until they carried him out in a box. Behind the bluntness was a warm-hearted, caring man who was determined to fight for what was best for his country. He believed terrorists should be shot without a second chance. He often argued that sleep deprivation, overwhelming noise and other methods of torture were nothing by comparison to a bomb going off, killing and maiming innocent men, women and children.

A smoker since the age of 14, Harrow's hands were clasped around the bowl of his favourite pipe, an item of solace he found he particularly needed when attending these meetings. His florid face and heavy gut were testament to his liking of real ale. 'The International Force Against Terrorism is vital to the safety of our citizens and the rest of the civilised world.' Then he added, 'By which I mean the Western world. We all know its record.

That organisation has saved countless lives and prevented many attacks by taking the fight to the enemy. That hasn't been without loss of their own people. We must do all in our power to ensure they continue operating as they are and protect them from the more idiotic aspects of the law. Sorry, Judge.' He smiled at Parker next to him.

'You're right to say so, Bert. The law can often be an ass. I would like to add that they haven't saved merely countless lives, but hundreds of thousands of lives. A few months ago, if those bombs stuffed with nerve agent had gone off, London would have become a ghost town. We would have been blasted back to the stone ages.'

'That may be so,' Ogilvie was almost hissing with anger, 'but the law is all we have. Therefore, we must enforce it to the letter. To the absolute letter. Or else we are no better than the terrorists themselves.'

'That's clichéd rubbish,' retorted Parker, 'as you well know.'

Stan Harrow said, 'If those bombs had exploded here we wouldn't be talking now. It was only thanks to Macnair and his lot that the bombs didn't go off. They put their lives on the line, again, I might add, without a thought for their own safety.'

'I do not recognise the application of the law as clichéd rubbish. I take offence at such a notion,' Ogilvie retorted.

'Frederick is quite right, you know,' said Goldsmith, in his sanctimonious voice, as he stared at the two men opposite. 'We are no better than the terrorists we are condemning if we sink down to their level.'

'What if we can prevent an attack if we take out a terrorist who is planning to explode a bomb in the UK or blow a plane out of the sky?' Harrow asked.

'Then,' said Goldsmith, in the same manner, 'we should arrest him or her and put him on trial.'

'I take it by the euphemism "take out a terrorist" you mean murder him,' said Ogilvie.

'You use your words and I'll use mine,' retorted the Northern MP. 'But I will make it clear. Yes, I do mean kill him,' then he added, 'or her. Or you can call it murder if you want, or assassination, or elimination, or any other word, because I don't care. If the death of one terrorist or a hundred, saves the life of just one innocent person, then good riddance.'

The committee's coffee break was conducted in silence, animosity heavy in the air. The Judge tried to get the conversation going on a more personal basis but he finally gave up. This was already their third meeting in four weeks during which time their dislike for one another had grown exponentially, in spite of the Judge's efforts to foster harmony and good working relations.

Sitting back at the table, Ogilvie began, 'we don't know if the person who is killed is a terrorist or not. That's why we have courts. To establish a person's innocence or guilt.'

Judge Parker leant forward and stabbed the table with his right forefinger. 'Frederick, as a member of the legal profession you know better than that. Sometimes, a court can prove guilt or innocence one way or the other, but many other times it's a game. Barristers play against barristers like a professional tennis match. An off-day and one side can lose. Or the jury has misplaced sympathy for the accused. Or they don't fully understand what's going on or understand the issues involved. Or a host of other things of which you're fully aware. So less of the rubbish. We need to keep the people of the world and not just this country, safe. TIFAT is an integral and important part of the way we achieve that.'

'I totally disagree,' Ogilvie shot back. 'It must be by arrest and trial. It is the only way.'

'Listen, Ogilvie,' said Stan Harrow, unwilling to speak to the man with any sign of friendliness. 'Many operations have been carried out abroad. We've prevented terrorists from actually coming into Britain and other parts of Europe. What should we have done then? Arrested them? Asked whichever country they're hiding in to arrest them while we apply for extradition?'

'Yes,' said Goldsmith, a note of triumph in his voice as though the other man had finally understood his message.

The Labour man shifted his gaze and looked steadily at the Liberal Democrat. 'You're more stupid than I thought and that's saying a lot.'

'Now, gentlemen, gentlemen,' said the Judge, 'let's keep this on a professional basis and not sink to insulting one another. Nigel, the report we did receive was given to us out of courtesy to the Prime Minister. General Macnair has no obligation to tell us what he is doing. That was made clear when we established TIFAT and don't forget, though it was agreed in secret, all of our allies supported the idea.'

'The role of that disgusting organisation,' began Ogilvie, 'is known throughout the world. Its very existence ensures we cannot take the high ground. It detracts from our moral superiority when it comes to discussing the issues with other countries.'

Judge Parker shrugged. 'We are here to examine the implications if TIFAT ceased to exist. I suggest we concentrate on that alone.'

'The world would be a better place,' said Ogilvie. 'We will be able to hold our heads up high as champions of the law where justice is served and seen to be served.'

Stan Harrow shook his head in real anguish and then spoke. 'The EU Arrest Warrant is a farce and you know it. Bribery and corruption is rife in most of the non-western EU countries. You've seen the reports about judges, juries and witnesses being regularly and easily coerced, bribed, threatened and killed.'

'No individual and no organisation,' said Ogilvie, 'has the right to take the law into its own hands and be judge, jury and, in the case of Macnair and his thugs, executioner.'

'For crying out loud Ogilvie,' the exasperation clear in Harrow's tone, 'halt or I fire means getting killed. This isn't bobby on the beat, evening all and it's a fair cop, guv. Now the criminals will shoot first and argue their case in court, assuming they ever get to court which most don't. You've read the reports from MI5 and MI6 and the rest of the alphabet soup. We are barely able to keep ahead of the threat and we should expect another atrocity at anytime.'

'That is why we have such close surveillance on those we suspect of being involved in terrorism,' said Goldsmith.

'I expect that sort of answer from a Lib Dem,' said Harrow, 'even from some of my own side, but not from a Conservative.'

'You'll be surprised how civilised we have become since the days of Margaret Thatcher.'

'I didn't agree with much of her politics,' said the Labour MP, 'but I admired her for her stance on things such as law and order and our fight against terrorism.'

'There is no issue here as far as I am concerned,' said

Goldsmith. 'TIFAT should be shut down with immediate effect and Macnair and his senior officers should be arrested and tried.'

'What for?' Harrow asked.

'Murder, sedition, corruption, theft, blackmail and anything else I can think of,' replied Goldsmith.

'You cannot be serious,' said Harrow.

'I do not make jokes when it comes to a question of the law and natural justice.'

Harrow slammed his left fist onto the table with such force that the glasses around the water jug rattled. 'Don't be so stupid. You cannot mean it.'

Judge Parker spoke. 'TIFAT does an exemplary job of intelligence gathering and passing information to the appropriate authorities in whatever country it is needed.'

'But that's equally as bad,' said Goldsmith. 'You know as well as I do that other countries will often arrest a man they suspect of terrorism and put a bullet in his head without a second thought and certainly without a trial. There is no room for such action in a modern, civilised society. Besides which, the information collected is illegal.'

Harrow shook his head in despair. 'You mean like GCHQ?'

'Of course not. The oversight committee ensures they act in a legal fashion.'

Stan Harrow leant forward, the stem of his pipe clasped in one hand, the bowl in the other. As he spoke, he broke the pipe in half. 'You fools. Even you two must see how ludicrous it would be if we forced TIFAT to close down. We'll be more vulnerable than ever. As it is, the Taliban and al-Qaeda laugh at us. They think we're weak. Pathetic. Cowards. We can barely contain the terrorism that's happening inside our borders. You know that. So what the hell's the matter with you two?'

'I would appreciate,' said Ogilvie, shooting the cuffs of his shirt and adjusting his cufflinks in a manner the Judge had seen on numerous occasions in court, 'if you did not speak to myself or to Nigel in that tone.'

Harrow's eyes narrowed. 'If we close down TIFAT they will merely relocate. Probably to the USA.'

'That would be very difficult if, as we said, the senior officers were arrested, tried and sentenced,' replied the barrister.

23

AS HE DISMANTLED the BXP, Hunter threw it piece-by-piece into the Channel. He still had to find the other weapons on the boat and get rid of them. He'd feel safer if Rabbani didn't have access to any guns. He was sitting in the Captain's chair with his feet on the ledge under the starboard window, next to the mug holder. He made himself comfortable, adjusting the bumbag around his waist. Rabbani hadn't bothered with the coffee. He had simply gone to bed. When Hunter had checked on him he was fast asleep. Hunter had guessed there might be a residual effect from the gas. He had removed the key from Rabbani's door and locked it. He found the coffee, made himself a mug and then phoned Macnair.

'Hello, sir.'

'Nick, where are you?'

'At anchor just off Foulness.'

'Where's Rabbani?'

'Asleep.' Hunter then brought Macnair up to date with the events of the night.

The General listened without interrupting. When Hunter was finished, Macnair's first question was, 'How are you feeling?'

'Fine. Just a bruise.' He rubbed his chest. 'I took a couple of painkillers. I've sent you photographs of the attackers a few minutes ago.'

'Good. I'll get Isobel working on them asap.'

Hunter took a mouthful of coffee. 'Of course, Rabbani could have made a mistake but if the man is Khan's aide, he could have gone rogue. That's happened more times than we can count in the last ten years. Fundamentalists hiding their true colours whilst plotting against the government.'

'That's true.'

'Let me run this past you. This aide, if that's who he was, knows what's going down. What if Khan gets hold of Rabbani and Rabbani is made to talk? The attack by the Taliban is not only put in jeopardy, that's understating things, but it could be an out and out disaster. So the aide is sent to kill Rabbani, courtesy of the Taliban.'

'What about Barzakh?' Macnair asked.

'When compared to a major offensive, Rabbani and Barzakh are irrelevant. The bigger picture takes precedence.'

'That's one possibility. I have to speak to Five. We need a team in there sooner, rather than later.' Five was a highly capable woman by the name of Elspeth Coolidge, the boss of MI5. Though she was new to the job she was already proving to be tough minded and highly thought of by her contemporaries.

'Will you be able to keep a lid on things?' Hunter asked. 'At least for a while?'

'I doubt it. The most we can hope for is that we won't be connected with the mess.'

'What will you tell Elspeth? She'll want to know how we know.'

'I'll tell her it was an anonymous tip off. Good source, good info. Worth checking and so on. It shouldn't be a problem. However you stack it up, we have what we wanted. I'll see about contacting Khan and getting Rabbani lifted. The sooner we hand him over, the better.'

'Sir, hold fire for awhile, will you?'

'Oh? Why?'

'He's not going anywhere and I'd like to see if I can get some more answers. There's also the question of his family. I'm positive he wasn't lying.'

'Somebody is, that's for sure. Okay. I'll delay contacting Khan and I'll speak to you later.'

The connection was broken. Hunter sat quietly for a little while longer, the mug of coffee going cold in his hand. Shaking himself, he placed the mug in the holder next to the starboard throttle, set the alarm on the radar and went below. If any vessel came within 2 miles of their position the alarm would wake him. He lay down on the settee, shoved a cushion under his head, the Pocketlite under the cushion and promptly fell asleep. It was coming up to 10.30 and he'd been awake for over 27 hours.

Macnair dialled the direct line. A number known to very few

people. 'Elspeth?'

'Malcolm!' There was no need to identify himself. The phone did it for her. 'Always a pleasure, but I suspect its business.'

Macnair knew Elspeth to be an attractive woman in her early fifties, who had earned her promotion to be the head of MI5. A promotion that had only taken place in the previous six months. As Director General she was also a Dame, a title she rarely used. She had paid for her success with two failed marriages and a daughter in her early twenties whom she rarely saw.

'It's business.'

'I don't suppose its good news?'

Macnair's chuckle was merely tinged with humour. 'Maybe. Let me ask you something. How many Islamic groups are you keeping a close watch on?'

'We have close surveillance on six and intermittently, a further seven organisations as well as dozens of individuals. They are mainly Nigerians and Somalis but all are Islamic fundamentalists.'

'Is that it?'

'For now. You know as well as I do that there's more we'd like to be doing but can't due to lack of manpower, budget constraints and the biggest obstacle of the lot, the human rights of the terrorist.'

'Are you missing any?'

'What?' There was no mistaking the incredulity in Elspeth's voice.

'Are you missing any of them?'

Warily she asked, 'That's an unusual question. Why are you asking?'

'Elspeth, let's not fence around. I'll explain but can you tell me if you're missing any of them.'

With a heavy sigh, she said, 'Yes. Two lots. Why? How did you know?'

'I didn't. I just put two and two together and come up with my usual cynical five. How did you lose two?'

'We're looking in to it right now. We've no idea where they are but they're out there somewhere. We'll find them but I just hope it's in time. One thing we're sure of and that is they're plotting something. We had a tip off about a house in Hackney which we hit last night.' She yawned. 'Sorry, I only managed a few hours here on the couch. I'm now much more appreciative of my predecessor and what he had to put up with!'

'You should do what I do. Get yourself a bed settee, it's more comfortable and you can get a better night's rest.'

'You're right. I've been promising myself that very thing ever since I took up the post. I'll get around to it one day.'

'You were saying about Hackney.'

'Oh, yes. When we got there it was empty. It was two houses with a connecting door. Looked like six, maybe eight people had been there.'

'Did you find anything?'

'The usual traces. Gun oil, a tiny amount of plastic, oh, and a 9mm round we found under the floorboards.'

'Fingerprints? DNA?'

'Loads. We're processing it even as we speak. To save time as much analysis as feasible is being done on site. So what's this all about, Malcolm?'

'I've no idea if this has any connection with what you have on your plate, but I've a group of seven you may like to examine.'

'Examine? Not interrogate?'

'You can't question the dead,' was the laconic reply.

'I take it, it's your doing?' Even Elspeth was shocked with the numbers and couldn't keep the fact out of her voice.

'No, certainly not.' Then he added, 'If questioned you can answer with a clear conscience.'

'Thank you, Malcolm, I much appreciate it.' There was no mistaking the irony in her voice.

Macnair grinned. 'When are you next before the ISC?'

'Next week. If what you say is true then this will be top of the list. Along with about another two dozen incidents and operations we have been and are involved in.' She paused and then added, 'do you know who is on the sub-committee?'

'Yes. Stan Harrow and Lord Judge Alistair Parker on our side and those pair of idiots Frederick Ogilvie and Nigel Goldsmith on the other. What are they trying to do? Shut us down?'

'That's the bottom line. However, I understand that if they cannot achieve that then they want the same operational briefings as they get from us, Six and GCHQ.'

'Not a dog's chance in hell.'

'That's what I told the Prime Minister.'

'They're only entitled to sanitised after-action reports and we tell them only what we want to.'

'I take it that's the royal we?'

'Correct. Let me share something with you in the strictest confidence.'

'You know me well enough, it'll go no further.'

'No, I want it to go further. I want it to go to the PM.'

'What?' Elspeth sounded surprised.

'The Americans approached me a couple of weeks ago. They knew about this sub-committee and they were not happy. They've offered us a station on the East Coast, near Norfolk, Virginia. They've sent me the details. It's like an estate agent's brochure. Airport attached, all the mod cons, bungalows instead of a barracks, off base housing for married personnel, details on schools and so on and so on. Also, an absolute guarantee that they will stick to the letter of the original mandate.'

'You can't be sure they'll stick to that. You know what their Congress is like.'

'You're right. But we'll get a few years without interference and that will make life a damned sight easier.'

'You're forgetting one thing.'

'No, I'm not.'

'You don't know what I am going to say.'

'I do. Relatively speaking, the USA is far safer from terrorist attack than we are in Europe. Hence the reason why we are here. We have porous borders; we're a magnet for every scumbag in the world who thinks they are safe in Europe in general and in the UK in particular. The fundamentalists hate our guts and we have home-grown Muslim terrorists by the score. And so have the rest of Europe. It's a no brainer why we are and should be in Europe.'

'That's more or less what I was going to say,' said Elspeth, 'which is why it is imperative that TIFAT stays operational in the UK.'

'I agree. I'm not going without a fight. But I will go if I have to. Did you know that Ogilvie and Goldsmith want me and some of my senior officers arrested and tried for murder?'

Elspeth gasped. 'You have to be kidding!'

They said so at their meeting today.'

'How do you know?'

'Just some inside information I picked up.'

'What? Stan? Alistair?'

'Neither. My own sources.'

'What...?' She laughed. 'My God, Malcolm, you've got the place bugged.'

Macnair's reply was a chuckle. 'That's for me to know. What you don't know you can't tell. Especially under oath.'

Macnair stood up, cordless receiver to his ear and went across to the coffee machine.

There was silence for a few seconds and then Elspeth asked, 'Back to the reason for this call. Where did it happen?'

While he was answering, Macnair poured a mug of coffee, took a sip, grimaced and poured the contents down the sink. 'Near Burnham-on-Crouch.' He returned to his desk.

'Essex?'

'That's the only place I know with that name. Sorry, I didn't mean to be so tetchy.'

'That's okay. Like I told you, we're stretched to breaking point and so why not ask CO19? Let them deal with it.'

'First of all, it's outside their territory. That'll mean using local plod.'

'Sorry, I'm not thinking straight. Of course it does,' said Elspeth.

'In turn, you know what that would mean. I'd like to keep the lid on this for a day, maybe two. If any locals get involved then the BBC will be broadcasting a full report by this evening while every newspaper in the country will be leading with the story tomorrow.'

'Point taken.' She sat tapping her fingers on her desk. If the dead men were one of the groups they'd lost then finding them again was of vital importance.

'What was TIFAT doing there?'

'I told you, this is from an informer.'

'In a pig's ear. Okay, I'll play along. Let's say that's the case, what's your interest?'

'We were asked to do a job. For the Pakistanis.'

'Doing what?'

'To lift and shift Ashraf Rabbani and deliver him to them.'

'We know about him. We've been keeping an eye on him but nothing too closely. We put him down as a criminal rather than a terrorist and so anything we learnt we passed to SOCA, which wasn't much in reality.'

'Ever heard of Barzakh?'

'No. Should I have?'

'According to General Khan it's a particularly vile terrorist organisation, already here in the West, funded and run by Rabbani.'

There was no hesitation to Elspeth's reply. 'I don't believe it.'

Macnair sighed. 'Neither do we. I wanted to check a few things before getting on to you but the more we look the less likely it seems. I'm as sure as I can be that Rabbani is not involved in anything to do with terrorism.'

'Of could, we could just be wrong. You know what it's like. If every story that crossed my desk was true then we'd have terrorist bombs exploding twice a day. By the same token, there's a lot going on out there we don't have a clue about. So what happened at the house? Do you know?'

'According to my informant, the place is a fair sized mansion. Apparently, it was a blood bath.'

'I suppose seven dead can be described as a blood bath.'

'They were doing the attacking. There are another eleven bodies.'

'What!' She couldn't keep the shock out of her voice. 'Eleven? Eighteen deaths? What nationalities are we talking about?'

Macnair gave her the details.

'Wait a second. Let me just check something.' Elspeth tapped on her keyboard and said, 'Yes, I thought so. One of the men at the house in Hackney was blonde.'

'I'm going down to Burnham. I want to see for myself what happened. See if we can learn anything. Care to meet me there?'

'I'm not sure. I really don't have the time. I don't think you should go either. On the face of it, it isn't a TIFAT Operation. It might be better if you stay out of it. We don't want to upset the sub-committee.'

'Yes, we do,' contradicted Macnair. 'Unless we deal with the idiots now, it'll be hanging over our heads. It's a distraction. One I can do without. If I force the issue then I can get rid of it. I have to be honest and say that Virginia looks very attractive from all points of view. Including quality of life.'

Elspeth sighed. 'I can't argue with that.'

'Besides, I think we need to talk.'

'Okay Malcolm, you win. When will you get there?'

Looking at his watch, he replied, 'About sixteen hundred.'

'I'll do the same. I'll send some of my people as soon as we hang up. On reflection, I think it would be a good idea to keep the local plod out of it. I'll do my best to ensure a news blackout. I'll get an injunction just in case anything slips out.'

'I was going to suggest it.' Macnair couldn't suggest sending her the photographs Hunter had taken. It would mean more explanations.

They said their goodbyes and the connection was broken.

24

ELSPETH TRIED WORKING in the car as she was driven towards Burnham-on-Crouch. However, once they were out of London, she gave up. She looked out of the window, the scenery passing in a blur. She sat alone, the divide between her and her bodyguard and driver closed. She found even when out of the office she was rarely left in peace. Either her mobile rang or the car's satphone was in action. She switched both off.

At times like this, she often wondered if it had all been worth it. With a first class honours degree in European and Islamic studies, she had been approached by a member of MI5 just days after she had graduated from Merton College, Oxford. The woman who had approached her had been tasked with finding suitable female candidates for the service. She often thought her invitation to join the company was proof that most employees who reached the top were originally a part of the Oxbridge scene. Of course, Oxford and Cambridge universities were also the establishments that supplied the most traitors during the Cold War.

When first invited to apply, she had been doubtful, but the more she learnt what would be required of her, the more she liked the idea. She had joined a team whose main task was to analyse information supplied from many sources, including other intelligence agencies, the police, as well as informers. She would take the information, analyse it and present it in a report. What the reports were used for she found out years later once she was promoted to a senior position. Sometimes, the reports had led to arrests in the UK or other parts of Europe, but often as not the information had been passed to governments overseas. There, the distinction between the legal and human rights of those acknowledged to be either criminals or terrorists was blurred and as a result, justice was often fast and final.

Some operations were conducted within MI5 but these began to reduce as more constraints were placed on the service.

Eventually, a description of their work was promulgated in a single sentence:- *MI5's values were to protect national security and economic well-being, and to support the law enforcement agencies in preventing and detecting serious crime, collect and disseminate intelligence, investigate and assess threats and work with others to counter them, advise on protection and provide effective support for those tasks.*

The problem was, MI5 was not trusted. Hence, it was overseen in three different ways - judicial oversight, ministerial oversight and parliamentary oversight. The net result was that a fine and honourable service was virtually emasculated and often found itself spending more time and effort defending any decisions taken by the service than actually doing its job. Elspeth was fighting their corner but knew she was engaged in a losing battle. Politicians, she thought, were either politically correct or anal retentives. Or sometimes both. Though she had to admit there were some good ones such as Stan Harrow in the Commons and Judge Alistair Parker in the Lords.

At least the position of head of MI5 was still held in high esteem by other agencies. As a result, her views were listened to and even acted upon.

At the highest levels of the intelligence agencies, there was one fact that they mostly agreed on - thank the Lord for TIFAT.

Her thoughts wandered into the current political scene. With the new Prime Minister she was aware she was skating on thin ice. The man hated anything to do with the military, or the security services and took political correctness to new levels of disaster. It was a fact known by few outside his inner circle, but she knew - it was her job to know. The PM made all the political noises of support while working to emasculate the Security Services. Hence the sub-committee with Stan Harrow, Judge Parker, Frederick Ogilvie and Nigel Goldsmith. It had been put about that Harrow and Parker were there to counterbalance the activities of Ogilvie and Goldsmith. In point of fact, it was the other way round. The Prime Minister was certain that Ogilvie and Goldsmith would succeed in their objective - the destruction of TIFAT one way or another.

The military and security cutbacks had been more than merely significant - they had been horrendous. The Middle East was a basket case, Afghanistan was going from bad to worse and North Africa was blowing up quite literally. In spite of there being yet more cuts the PM claimed it wouldn't affect the Armed Forces' ability to carry out the operations required of them. They fought with lousy equipment and were paid even lousier salaries. Yet they had more loyalty to their country in their little fingers than most of the Cabinet had in their whole bodies - with one or two possible exceptions.

She knew that a key ally was the current Home Secretary, Morris Samuels. He was a pillar of the Party and too highly regarded for the PM to get rid of for the time being. Another ally was Janice Clitheroe, Foreign Secretary. For how long, it was difficult to tell. Westminster, the host to the biggest back-stabbing, lying, gossipmongers in Britain, was forever suggesting the FS was about to be sacked. So far, it hadn't happened. Elspeth grimaced. Few knew it was mainly thanks to her. One person who did know was the Chancellor of the Exchequer.

As the Prime Minister's closest political ally and best friend, Douglas Bell had a great deal of influence over the PM. But, she smiled; she in turn had the Chancellor where she wanted him.

When would politicians learn to keep it in their trousers? Especially if they were high up the totem pole of government. He hadn't been Chancellor when it had happened, merely Douglas Bell MP. Her predecessor had acquired the information. His motto had been "just in case". He had said that one of the most important lessons he had ever learnt had been when he'd been in the Boy Scouts - Be Prepared. It had been her predecessor who had been instrumental in Elspeth becoming the head of MI5. She was still uncertain whether to be grateful or not.

She thought about the day she was given the position and she'd thanked him. He'd smiled and said, 'Thank me in a year or two.'

'Why?'

'You'll understand. Come with me. I want to show you something.' What he showed her was a disc of the most sensitive and at the same time, explosive information, accumulated over a couple of decades. Men and women now in power, having great sway across the country. The names of people known for their decency, their incorruptibility, their downright honesty were contained on the disc. What she had learnt had shocked her to the core. Repelled her even.

'I can see the horror on your face.'

'Why? Why do you have this...this stuff? And who else has it?'

'In answer to who is nobody. The why is because there is nobody to protect your back, nobody to cover for you. You're on your own. Believe me, no matter how good a job you do to keep this country safe, to protect its citizens, somebody out there will want to cut you off at the knees. To bring you crashing down.'

To date, she had used the information three times. The third occasion had been with the Chancellor. The arrogance of the man, demanding she go to his office. She didn't report to him but to the Home Secretary and the Prime Minister. However, once she had armed herself, she had gone with what can only be described as alacrity.

She was aware that to show his superiority she had been kept waiting for 20 minutes but not even the Chancellor dared keep her waiting any longer. The insincere way he had greeted her, standing up behind his desk and offering his hand still made her smile. He was of medium height, medium weight and developing a paunch due to inactivity and too much rich food and wine. His round, baby face did not inspire confidence in Elspeth. He had, she thought, all the charisma of a cold rice pudding.

He didn't so much as offer her a cup of coffee. Instead he had begun, 'Now, we are both busy people so I won't beat about the bush.'

'Good. Thank you Chancellor. Thank you very much for asking me over as I wanted to see you on a matter of great urgency.'

That had taken the wind out of his sails and he had mumbled. 'Em. Yes. Em. Never mind,' anger tinged his voice. 'I called you here for...'

She never did learn what he wanted because she had cut him off in mid sentence as she opened her briefcase. 'I think you will find this of interest. I am in a dilemma you see, whether to show it to the PM. In case the press gets hold of it.' She had looked into the man's eyes. 'At the party conference four years ago you had a late night.'

'There are always late nights at party conferences.'

'Ah, yes, but this one was different. You see, your wife didn't accompany you, which was highly unusual. Two of your colleagues had too much to drink and went to bed. Their wives were at the conference but did not retire at the same time. They were both in a party mood. You and your, what? Political advisor? Suggested a party up in your room.'

By the way the blood had drained from his face she knew he was remembering. That was when the bluster had started.

'Now look here. You can't prove any of this. I'll deny it. I'll have your job. I'll...' It had been so pathetic.

'Please be quiet, Chancellor.' She had spoken in an even tone, not raising her voice by a single decibel, but getting through to him for all that. 'Of course I can prove it. What do you think is in this document?'

The bluster had vanished like a pricked balloon deflating. 'What is it you want me to do? Resign?'

'Chancellor, let us understand one another. You leave me to do my job and I'll leave you to do yours. Nobody need ever learn what happened, at least not from me and that includes your wife. From one of the others? Who knows? I understand Betty Greyson is suing for divorce. Adultery, so I believe.'

'Yes.' He had spoken in a strained voice. 'Greyson won't be standing in the next election. Not that it matters to him. He's filthy rich. Politics was just a hobby.'

'I see. Be that as it may, we'll leave things as they are. I wish to stay in post, Chancellor. I hope I make myself clear.'

With bad grace and a sour look, he had replied, 'Yes, damn you. Yes, alright.'

She had said goodbye and left the room. It had been an interview, she acknowledged to herself, that she had enjoyed.

They were approaching Burnham when the driver pressed a button and spoke. 'We're there ma'am. This is the turning.'

The car swept into the drive and headed towards the house. Off to one side she could see the helicopter Macnair had used to bring him south. The house was indeed a mansion of imposing size.

25

THE HOUSE WAS in a rundown part of Stepney. Three dilapidated bedrooms, an unhygienic kitchen and a sitting room with three easy chairs with their springs showing through. The whole street was due for demolition, though the houses needed to be emptied first. Court order had followed court order but people had either refused to leave or when they did others had taken their place. Finally, the property developer had resorted to the only method left to him. He got a court order house by house, forced out the occupiers and demolished the house with just a few swipes from a crane and heavy ball.

Basel slipped the waistcoat of explosives over his shoulders, did up the straps, adjusted it to fit more comfortably and slipped on a black kagool. It easily hid the waistcoat. Faakhir and Muhsin did the same. They looked at each other.

'Can you see anything?' Muhsin asked nervously.

'Nothing is showing.' Faakhir licked dry lips. As the day approached, all three were becoming more nervous. The reality of their deaths was no longer something mythical, something in the future. It was real. It was soon.

'Do we know when we will be...be attacking?' Muhsin asked.

Basel shook his head. 'Not yet.' His eyes gleamed with the anticipation and excitement of the fanatic. 'But it will be soon. We will be texted when we must carry out our attack. It will be a glorious day. Many infidels will die. *Allahu Akbar.*'

The other two replied, '*Allahu Akbar.*' Though they did not say the words with quite as much enthusiasm.

'My God,' said Elspeth, 'this is...is horrendous. Like you said a real bloodbath.'

They were standing outside the house, in the shade of the portico. Macnair had given Elspeth a tour of the carnage. She was white faced from what she had seen. Although she had been warned what to expect knowing and seeing were two entirely different things.

A team of people from MI5 had been working there for a few hours already, trying to identify the dead bodies. So far all they'd managed was to ID the people who were already in the house from the paperwork they each carried. Be that driving licences, passports or, in the case of two of the girls, university identity cards. They still had no idea who the attackers were. They had found the two cars the men had arrived in, parked along a track about half-a-mile from the front gate, hidden behind a hedge. Their fingerprints and photos had been sent to HQ.

One of the men from MI5 approached. 'Ma'am, we just had confirmation that the dead men who attacked the house are the same people who were in Hackney.'

'Thanks, Chris. That's no surprise but it doesn't get us very far.'

'Why not?' asked Macnair.

'Because the house was sterile of any identity papers of any description. No passports, no driving licences, nothing. They were highly professional.'

'No,' said Macnair, 'I don't think so. I think they were led by a professional but I don't think they were. They're too young for a start and what's more this was a gun battle. Professionals would have been in and out in no time, leaving not a rack behind, never mind their bodies.'

Elspeth managed a grin in spite of herself. Not to be outdone, she said, 'We are such stuff as dreams are made on, and our little life is rounded with a sleep. Sir, I am vexed. Prospero in The Tempest, Act 4 Scene 1.'

'I'm impressed,' said Macnair.

'Not as impressed as I am,' said Elspeth. 'A soldier able to quote Shakespeare! Whatever next?'

The banter, they both knew, was a way of dealing with what they'd seen. The gruesome slaughtering of people, even those who deserved to die, was unpleasant in the extreme and one thing was for certain - the young girls in the house had not deserved to die.

'The fact is, vexed doesn't come near to it,' said Elspeth. 'This is going to be more difficult than I'd hoped. Or even expected.

I'll have to phone the Chief Constable for Essex and let him take over.'

'That's what I figured. I think it would be best if you told him you think it was a drug related gangland killing. What I don't understand is why attack Rabbani,' asked the General, 'and why now?'

'You said something about the Pakistanis wanting him.'

'The PM was told by the Pakistanis that a request for Rabbani's extradition to Pakistan would be with us in days and that they would appreciate it if we expedited the matter. In the meantime, I received a backchannel request from General Khan, their head of the army.'

'I know who he is. And what I know I don't like.'

'Oh? Why is that?'

'Six have had their eye on Khan for quite awhile. He popped up on the radar a few years ago. Nothing specific, just the way he had been handling a number of operations.'

'What happened?'

Elspeth shrugged. 'You need to ask Six for the details but as I understand it, a number of anti-terrorist ops that should have been plain sailing went pear shaped. Our lot were on the periphery of events and didn't like what they saw.'

'Interesting,' said Macnair, thoughtfully.

'So what else do you have?'

'Khan said that Pakistani Intelligence had learnt that there's going to be a major Taliban attack coming out of Afghanistan and into Pakistan. In the Tribal Areas.'

'That's nothing new,' said Elspeth.

'He said that Rabbani was involved with terrorism through this group of his called Barzakh.'

'I checked the files to make sure but we've never come across them before. That's nothing new of course. These groups come and go. But I did phone Six and he checked and said the same thing.'

'Not according to Khan. Curiouser and curiouser.'

'It may have been a mistake. These things can happen.'

'I suppose so. But I keep coming back to the same thing. Based on what I know, none of it makes sense. If one of the dead men is an aide to Khan then he isn't showing up. There again, an aide to a foreign general is hardly worth our attention. So there's no surprise there.'

'Malcolm, changing the subject completely. With Goldsmith and Ogilvie gunning for you, will you seriously consider moving TIFAT out of the UK?'

Macnair shrugged. 'I'll deal with it. But if push comes to shove we'll up sticks and debunk to the States.'

'Malcolm, that won't be a disaster, that's too strong a word, but it will affect your operational capability. If you go to the States, the operational timeline will be extended quite considerably. Support will be more difficult to mobilise and reaction times will be stretched to such an extent that you could find you'd be too late in responding to a serious situation.'

'I'm aware of that.'

'Of course you are. Sorry. I didn't mean to sound patronising.'

'You didn't. You were stating the obvious.'

Elspeth sighed, looking as though she was contemplating the future then she stood up straight and said, 'I know you. You aren't going anywhere. You have other plans.'

Macnair smiled. 'Let's just say the need to move isn't overwhelming.'

'Fair enough. I thought you'd have something up your sleeve.'

Macnair's phone rang. He looked at the screen. 'I'll just take this. I won't be a minute.'

'Shall I go?'

'What? No, it's okay.' Macnair spoke into the phone. 'Stan? Thanks for the info.'

'My pleasure. They are a pair of idiots but that's not why I'm phoning. I want to thank you.'

'What for?'

'The money. I told you I didn't want payment. I'm doing what I am to save this country from the forces of evil that are ganging up on us. That may be fanciful, but I think it's an accurate description.'

'So do I. And besides, I didn't pay you anything.'

'Yeah right. Like the two million quid you paid to the Sara House Trust. I know it was you and I just wanted to say thanks. Where did the money come from?'

'Better not to ask. Let's just say it hasn't cost the taxpayer a penny.'

'I worked that one out for myself.' There was a catch in the normally gruff voice of the Yorkshire man when he added, 'Thanks again. And anything you need just let me or Alistair know. We'll keep you in the picture.'

'Thanks, Stan. All the best.' He broke the connection.

'Stan Harrow?' Elspeth queried.

'The same.'

'What was that all about?'

'Stan has a seriously handicapped daughter. Her name is Sara. She's in her mid-twenties and lives in a home near Hull. She'll never leave it and she could live well into old age. Stan visits her regularly and spends every penny he has looking after her. Sara's House has half-a-dozen young people living there all with the same prognosis. Their families do their best but they are always needing money. We gave them two million yesterday. We paid the money into the trust that runs the place. It was an anonymous donation but Stan knew it was me.'

'That was very generous of you.'

'We collected the money from generous benefactors.'

'No, you didn't,' Elspeth smiled. 'I know you liberate funds and assets from the criminals and terrorists where you can. That you spend it on good causes.'

Macnair said nothing, neither admitting it nor denying it.

'Don't worry, Malcolm, I won't be saying anything. As far as I'm concerned, good on you. The two million should help the Trust a good deal.'

'It will.' He didn't add that a portfolio of shares amounting to a further four million pounds was being placed in a separate trust, the dividends from the investments being paid to the Sara House Trust. Macnair hoped it would be enough to keep the place going in perpetuity.

'What are you going to do about Ogilvie and Goldsmith?'

'What would you do?' Macnair countered.

Elspeth shrugged and then said, 'I would want them to stay on the committee. However, I would want them under my influence and I would ensure we had the outcome we desire. To be left alone to do our job.'

Macnair nodded. 'That is precisely what will happen.'

26

HUNTER HAD MANAGED to sleep for a few hours. He lay still, eyes shut, listening. There was only the sound of the sea lapping gently against the hull. He opened his eyes, stretched, stifled a yawn and stood up. He looked at his watch. Coming up to 17:00. He rubbed his chest lightly. The bruise hurt like hell.

First, he went up to the fly bridge, looked around to see there were no other vessels nearby and then down to the galley where he poured himself a glass of orange juice. A shave and a shower were followed by scrambled eggs laced with smoked salmon. He had to admit to himself that Rabbani knew how to live well. The variety and quality of the food in the fridge would have done a 5 star restaurant proud. He swallowed more painkillers, washed down with a fresh cup of coffee.

Finally, he looked in on Rabbani who was still asleep and snoring like a pig. So far, Rabbani's rest had been natural. It was time to change that. Hunter took the needle loaded with Benedrone and stabbed Rabbani in the upper arm with it, pressing down on the plunger as he did. He wasn't gentle. Rabbani awoke, stared, started to say something and fell unconscious. The single dose would be good for at least 6 hours, maybe longer.

Next, Hunter lifted Rabbani's bag, exited the cabin and locked the door. He took the jiffy bags out and laid them on the table. He began to examine them. He found numerous passports, a memory stick as well as two computer discs. There were other papers but they were written in Urdu.

Back up top, sitting at the helm, he called Macnair. 'Sir? I have a memory stick as well as a couple of computer discs. There are five passports in different names each with Rabbani's face and some papers written in what I'm sure is Urdu. The passports are Pakistani, British, Iranian, American and Spanish.'

'An interesting combination. Okay. I'll get the helo out to you though it may be a couple of hours. How's the chest?'

'Fine, thanks.'

'The men who attacked the house were already known to Five.'

'How come?'

Macnair explained about the house in Hackney, they said their goodbyes and Hunter continued his search of the yacht. Cupboards and drawers yielded nothing but clothes and various accoutrements.

Hunter went back to Rabbani's cabin and stood in the doorway, thoughtfully looking around. The luxury of the boat was truly astounding. The workmanship that had gone into building her was of the highest level.

Assuming there were guns onboard, where were they likely to be stashed? In Rabbani's situation, any weapons would be wanted for protection. Easy access was therefore required. Weighed against that was the possibility of a customs search.

He dragged Rabbani off the bunk. Rabbani didn't as much as groan. Hunter looked under the mattress. Nothing. He put the mattress back and threw Rabbani on top. The deck was teak. Access to the bilges was achieved by pulling up a hinged brass ring opening a hatch of about a metre square. He began checking the bilges but found nothing. He then had the idea of sliding out the drawers from under the bunk where he saw another hatch.

Under it he found a loaded, automatic pistol he recognised as an Austrian Glock, Model 22. He pressed the magazine catch on the left side of the butt behind the trigger and removed the magazine. True to the maxim that a weapon without bullets was a lump of metal, he emptied the mag of all 15 rounds before replacing it in the stock.

He continued with a detailed and careful search of the yacht. In the engine room he found another Glock hidden behind a drawer in a well stocked tool cupboard. None of the tools looked as though they had ever been used. In a plastic box about 12cms square and 12cms deep, he lifted out a tray of different sized screws to find a layer of ammunition. It took him the best part of an hour, but finally he was satisfied that he had looked just about everywhere. Hot and sticky, he went topside. He took a glance around, saw no other vessels anywhere near and went down to the galley to get a drink. He was gratified to find bottles of non-alcoholic lager in the fridge.

Bottle in hand, Hunter sat at the upper helm position, with a panoramic view around the Talisman. He was frowning, deep in thought. He looked at his watch. Just coming up to 19.00. He turned on the radio and tuned it from a music station to BBC Radio 4. The pips sounded and he listened to the news with half an ear. As the famous tune announcing The Archers started he turned off the radio. Just then his mobile phone rang. 'Hello, sir.'

'Do you have anything for me?'

'Nothing except I've found a couple of Glocks and some ammo. Is there anything your end?'

'Not here. No weapons, no explosives, none of the paraphernalia we associate with terrorists and suicide bombers.'

'What about his place in London?'

'Ah, that's different. Elspeth's people found a two roomed cellar. One of the rooms is smaller than it should have been. They found a concealed entrance to a third room which was stuffed full of cash as well as a load of heroin.'

'How much are we talking about?'

'A few million pounds, euros and dollars. And about ten kilos of heroin. There were also a number of Glocks and some ammunition.'

'If Barzakh is going to be operational in Europe, where's the plastic, dets, vests and all the rest of the equipment they would need? A few Glocks don't amount to much.'

'True,' said Macnair. 'But Rabbani isn't stupid enough to keep that sort of gear lying around his house. With the organisation he runs he could have gear stored practically anywhere in the UK.'

'I don't believe for one minute that Rabbani is a fundamentalist. Which means we keep coming back to the fact that this doesn't make any sense.'

'Agreed. But we've no choice. We have to play it out and see where it leads. Question Rabbani and don't be too polite about it. We need to know what's going on.'

'It'll be my pleasure, sir.'

'That's the helo on its way now. They'll be ten minutes max.'

'Right, sir.'

They broke contact. Down below, Hunter found a canvas bag. He stuffed the memory stick and computer disks into the bag and used a piece of rope to tie the handles together. He then made a loop in the end of the rope.

Hearing the clatter of the helicopter he stepped outside and looked to the north. An EC120B Colibri, a light, 5-seat single engine helo was in sight. It hovered 100ft above him and lowered a hook on the starboard side and about 10ft away. Hunter indicated to the helo and the pilot moved closer to the boat. He slipped the rope over the hook and signalled to the helo. It swept away, turning back to the north, reeling in the line as it went.

Hunter sat back at the console and put his feet up, enjoying the feel of the evening sun on his face. After a while, he slid off the high seat, went below and checked on Rabbani. He was still out for the count.

Then, he went into one of the guest cabins, took out a bathing costume he'd found earlier and changed into it. He looked down at his chest. The bruise looked worse than it felt. He shrugged his shoulders and wind milled his arms. There was a dull ache but it was hardly debilitating. He'd suffered a lot worse in the past.

He went up on deck and dived cleanly into the water.

Macnair and Elspeth sat down where the b-b-q had taken place. Elspeth let out a sigh of relief. 'That's better. It's been a long day and a long week.'

Waving a hand at the bottles on the table he said, 'Care for a drink? There's everything imaginable.'

Elspeth shook her head. 'Better not. Not if my guys are working. You?'

'No. Same reason.'

Elspeth's phone rang and she answered it with a grimace. After a few moments she thanked the caller and broke the connection. 'That was interesting.'

'Oh? What?'

'One of my people recognised a photograph of one of the dead men. One of the attackers. They've double checked and are sure his name is Mirza Nawaz.'

'General Khan's aide?'

'The same,' said Elspeth.

'If that's the case, what's going on?' He didn't let on he already suspected, as she would have wanted to know how he knew and why he hadn't told her. 'I need to speak to Khan. Rabbani has a large, criminal organisation as well as a number of legitimate businesses. What's going to happen to it all?'

'The criminal end will be a vacuum that will be filled naturally and quickly,' Elspeth shrugged. 'The legitimate side? Who knows? I understand he has family.'

'Quite possibly.'

Elspeth smiled in spite of the situation. 'Malcolm, you know a lot more than you're letting on.'

'Why on earth should you think that?'

'You've made a big mistake which surprises me.'

'That is?'

'You've not mentioned the whereabouts of Rabbani. Or questioned his whereabouts.'

'That's because I know where he is.'

'You do?' Elspeth sat up straight. 'Where? Why didn't you tell me?'

'The contrite answer to why is you didn't ask.'

'That is contrite so stop playing games.'

'I'm not. Elspeth, we come back to you being questioned by the Intelligence and Security Committee. If you don't know anything about Rabbani you can say so with a clear conscience. More importantly, you cannot be accused of lying.'

'They'll accuse me anyway,' she said dryly. 'So how do you know where he is?' She looked around and then held up her hand. 'Don't tell me. I definitely don't want to know. However, I'll bet my pension Nick Hunter is involved.'

'I cannot possibly comment but I will say that Rabbani is in good hands and will be back home in the bosom of his countrymen very soon.'

'Let's cut to the chase. What has Nick found out?'

'Rabbani said he has three wives as well as a few offspring. Yet Khan says Rabbani's only wife and family were wiped out by an allied attack some years ago, hence his hatred of all things Western.'

'Someone is telling lies,' Elspeth mused, 'and I wonder who it is?'

'I'm beginning to have my suspicions.'

'I take it the Pakistanis didn't want to do it themselves because of the inevitable fallout if our political lords and masters discovered what they'd done.'

'That's the way I read it,' said Macnair. 'Invasion of air space, operating in a friendly country without authorisation. Worst of all, no arrest, no court hearing and no extradition. The political fallout would have gone on for months, relations with the Pakistani government would have been at an all time low which is saying something, and the human rights people would have a field day.'

'Like you said, an official request and arrest would mean the timescale was working against them. Rabbani would never have been shipped back to Pakistan in time to be persuaded to tell them about the mass terrorist attack.'

'So we come back to who attacked Rabbani and why.'

'It could be another criminal gang.' Then she shook her head. 'No. The people upstairs are Pakistani. There's no doubt about that. I only know of one other serious criminal organisation in the UK that's of Pakistani origin and they operate in Manchester. From Birmingham south they're nearly all Eastern European with a couple of British gangs thrown in for good measure. Oh, and let's not forget the Somalis. They're becoming serious players in the business of organised crime under the guise of political asylum. Is it possible that General Khan jumped the gun and did come for Rabbani?'

'I don't see it. Why tell us about him in the first place if that's what they were going to do? And let's not forget, Khan wants to interrogate Rabbani.'

'I hadn't forgotten. Have you spoken to the good General Khan?'

'Not yet. He's up country somewhere. He should be back and contactable later today or tomorrow.'

One of Elspeth's team joined them. He was in his mid thirties, of average height, premature grey hair, with a beer gut beginning to show.

'Malcolm, meet Stuart Campbell. Stuart this is General Macnair.'

Macnair stood and the two men shook hands.

'Take a seat. What do you have for us?' Elspeth asked.

As Campbell sat next to Elspeth, he switched his gaze back and forth between his two superiors. 'Every one of the attackers had been at the house in Hackney.'

'Any ID?' Elspeth enquired.

'We're beginning to get somewhere. One of the men is Imaad Hossain and the blonde man is Iain McVicar.'

Elspeth said, 'McVicar. Late of Glasgow and Pakistan where he converted to Islam. He also took the name of Mustafa Hameed although he hadn't officially changed it. What about the others?'

'Nothing yet. We're still working on it. However, now we've identified two of them, the rest should follow easily enough. We'll do the usual with family and friends. It shouldn't take too long.'

27

'THE DAY IS coming,' Abrar said, speaking quietly to herself. She raised her hands up and said *'Allahu Akbar.'*

Her bedroom was large. It held a double bed, a wardrobe, a chest of eight drawers and underneath the bay window was a desk and leather chair. The bookcases held books about Islam and the history of her faith. There were no novels, no magazines, no CDs by modern artists, in fact, nothing that suggested the kind of childhood a teenager should be enjoying at her age. What music there was was all based around Islam. She had many CDs of Islamic Pakistani chanting, Songs of Praises about the Prophet Mohammed, and Quranic recitals and classical duas. She had two laptop computers. One for her studies, the other to listen to the radio. She listened to the Salawat Station, the live Hadrah Station, the Naats Station and most of all, the Quranic Station and Duas. The Duas she found particularly therapeutic. An extension of her own beliefs and desires. She could not, would not, see that her beliefs were at odds with her religion nor that the path she was walking down would lead to heartache and suffering for many people.

Abrar crossed her arms over her chest and, from memory, recited the whole of the first chapter of the Qur'an in Arabic. She then went on to quote other verses from memory. After 10 minutes she raised her arms again, saying *'Allahu Akbar.'* She then bowed, reciting three times, *'Subhana rabbiyal adheem.'* Glory be to my Lord Almighty.

She stood straight again and said, *'Sam'i Allahu liman hamidah, Rabbana wa lakal hamd.'* God hears those who call upon Him; Our Lord, praise be to You.

She stood, kneeled, prostrated herself along the ground, spoke to God, recited numerous more verses from the Qur'an and turned her body to the left and right. She repeated the ritual.

This was the fourth prayer of the day, the Maghreb. It was

recited just after sunset, reminding her of God as the day begins to end. That would leave her with one more prayer, the Isha, to be said just before retiring to bed. That was the time to remember God's presence and to ask for his forgiveness, mercy and guidance.

As she turned to go to the kitchen to make tea, she looked into the corner of the room. The three waistcoats of explosives sat waiting to be used. Excitement coursed through her veins like an elixir.

The sun had set. It was glorious sitting at the upper helm position watching the grey blanket of dusk turn to night. Hunter mused on the power of the sea. Gentle, undulating and peaceful it could change so quickly to a force of significant brutality.

He got to his feet and went down aft. From one of the lockers, he took out a three metre length of extra flexible steel wire rope, a quarter inch thick and with spliced eyes about three inches in diameter in both ends. In the tool cupboard in the engine room he found plastic tie wraps. He chose a couple that were about 12ins long and half an inch wide.

Using a shackle, he fitted one end of the wire rope to a deck connection above a porthole to Rabbani's stateroom and dropped the wire over the side. He then went into the galley, put on the coffee and while it was brewing crossed the deck to where Rabbani was still asleep.

Tying Rabbani up had been an option but that would have meant keeping him trussed up like a turkey ready for the oven. Simple tasks like feeding, drinking and using the heads would have been onerous.

Reaching through the porthole, he grabbed the wire rope and pulled it into the cabin. Then, he put a cable tie around Rabbani's left wrist, tight but not so tight as to affect his circulation, and used the second cable tie to secure the first one to the wire rope. If Rabbani stretched his arm out far enough he would just be able to use the heads.

Hunter returned up top. It was quiet. Dusk had turned to nightfall. White masthead steaming lights were becoming more distinctive against the gathering gloom, as were the red port lights and the green starboard lights.

His mobile rang. 'Hello, sir.'

'Commander. I finally managed to speak to a member of General Khan's staff.'

'What did he say?'

'That Khan will call tomorrow. I explained the situation and told him it was urgent I speak to the General but the man was adamant that it was impossible.'

'What should I do in the meantime? What about the merchant ships with their helos that are supposed to be around here somewhere? Surely someone at Khan's HQ can give us a rendezvous position? I can deliver Rabbani anywhere reasonable in less than twelve hours. Simple. Job done.'

'I couldn't agree with you more. But there's nothing we can do for the present.'

'Khan should be doing everything in his power to get his hands on Rabbani. Not procrastinating like this. It can only mean something is going on that we know nothing about.'

'Agreed. Elspeth Coolidge phoned a few minutes ago. We've identified another of the seven men. They found his passport under some floorboards in the house along with some other documents which we're getting translated even as we speak.'

'Was he Pakistani?'

'Yes. He came into the country a week ago, as did Nawaz. It seems Nawaz received three texted words from Pakistan. Essex, Underground and Heathrow.'

'Essex could have been an instruction to attack Rabbani in Essex.'

'Elspeth and I think the same thing. Which means...' Macnair let his voice trail off.

Hunter finished the sentence for him. 'Which means possible attacks on the Underground and at Heathrow.'

'There's more. Nawaz didn't destroy his sim card, and we found two mobile phone numbers on it. He had texted the words Underground and Heathrow to each number. Both were pay-as-you-go. We're monitoring the numbers but don't hold out much hope.'

'So what are we going to do?'

'Right now Five is really shaking the trees to see what falls out. She has every resource working on it. Ourselves as well as

Six are also co-operating fully. GCHQ have brought all assets to focus on the UK and Pakistan. ECHELON has the biggest job to do. All mobiles are being put through the system and trigger words have been increased fourfold.' Macnair was referring to certain words picked up by the huge bank of computers at GCHQ and ECHELON. The recordings of the transmissions were enormous. Only the very tiniest fraction could be listened to by trained operators. Certain words would bring a conversation to the attention of the operators. That in turn would allow the phone numbers to be identified and tracked. With the perceived threat so high the trigger words had been quadrupled. All it had taken was the press of a button and the computers did the rest. Information was flooding in. More personnel were put on overtime. They didn't mind. They could always use the money.

'Whatever happens, we must prevent another 7/7.' The Muslim terrorist cell that had blown up parts of London Underground on the 7th July 2005 had injured over 700 men, women and children and killed a further 52 people. The 4 terrorists had died as well. They had used knapsacks stuffed with homemade peroxide based explosives which they set off in Aldgate, Edgware Road, King's Cross and Tavistock Square. It had been a well planned and well organised attack that had left the nation traumatised. It had also caused huge distrust by the majority of the British people for Muslims coupled with a vast resentment for their religion and their way of life in the Western world.

'What about stop and search? Searching mosques? Lifting known trouble makers for questioning?'

'According to Five they are doing what they can. They've been instructed not to go in mob handed. And also to show respect. The majority of Muslims are law abiding. Upsetting them in their place of worship doesn't help ongoing relations. Everything must be done to ensure the public don't hear about it. I suspect in the next few hours things will be stepped up significantly. You can imagine the bedlam that will follow if it does get out.'

'I can. How difficult will it be to keep things secret?'

'Five has told me that apart from senior management the staff at GCHQ think the whole thing is an exercise.'

'That makes sense. What about MI5 and MI6?'

'Different situation. There are far more personnel in the know, but they're more used to keeping secrets. Even so, they're being ultra careful. There's another very interesting fact. One of the phones we found was used to make a call to Yassin.'

'Yassin? He was working against Rabbani?'

'It looks like it.'

'That explains the alarm system. Sir, what's the Bikini State?'

The Bikini State was an alert state that told the UK authorities of the likelihood of a terrorist attack. It had been in use since 1st August 2006 and consisted of five States. White meant situation stable, Black that there was a possibility of an attack, Black Special that there was an increased likelihood of an attack with no defined target, Amber that specific information had been received and that there was a substantial threat, and finally Red, which meant information had been received about an attack on a specific target. Bikini State White had never been used.

'Red, as you'd expect.'

'There's something that's also been bugging me. I know the most pleasant and jolly of people can be a murdering tyrant and I can see Rabbani as a drug smuggler and even ordering somebody to be killed in the line of business, but somehow I don't see him ordering the blowing up of innocent people. Also, this business about a family. Does he have three wives and eight children? Is he living in a fantasy world of the past? Or is it merely some sort of ludicrous cover story? Which of itself doesn't make sense because all he has to say is that he's not married. He also wasn't indulging himself with any of the girls back at his place and neither did he take an interest in any of them when we were in his club. All of that makes a mockery of the story that his family was killed during a raid on their village. If Rabbani is telling the truth then that makes the Pakistanis liars. But to what end? What are they after? I can't see President Zardarim orchestrating something like this.'

'From what I know of him, no, I can't either.'

'I don't trust the Pakistanis,' said Hunter.

'Neither do I, but I can't see their President involving our Prime Minister and doing anything underhand. At government level the relationship between the two countries is far too important.'

While they'd been talking Hunter was flashing up the engines, watching the dials flicker and settle down. He pressed a button and heard the windlass cough into life. He moved a lever and the cable started to lift. The boat was beginning to swing to the pull as the bows came round to face the cable and creep forward. The cable was up and down, the boat was stationary and then the cable broke free of the seabed and the Talisman was drifting in the gentle tide. Hunter eased the engines into gear, put on the autopilot and dialled in the course he wanted. He switched on the boats' lights, still talking to Macnair.

'General, when Rabbani comes to, I'm going to have a chat with him. Maybe he can throw some light as to what's going on.'

'I wouldn't have thought he'd talk to you.'

'There is that. But he can either talk to me, talk to Khan's people or he can go for a swim. I'm not in the mood to care either way.'

'Where are you going?'

'I'll head west.'

'Okay. While you do, I'll try and find out what's happening about the Pakistani ships.'

With the connection broken, Hunter concentrated on the sea around him. He set the radar and the warning buzzer in the event of another vessel getting too close and took one last look around to satisfy himself there was nothing coming his way. He then went below to make a sandwich and a cup of instant soup.

28

GENERAL PERVEZ KHAN was a big man in every respect. He was 6ft 5ins tall and weighed 18st 6lbs as was attested to by the size of his stomach which wasn't well hidden in spite of the excellent tailoring of his uniform. He had a large round head, ears that stuck out too much and a bulbous nose. His dark brown eyes were almost black, his eyebrows were bushy, his pate completely bald. He wore the almost obligatory bushy moustache that had more grey in it than black. Now 56 years old, he had come from a wealthy family joining the army straight from school instead of going to university. After one year, as expected, he was sent to Sandhurst to complete his training, one of the few officers in the Pakistani army who was so highly privileged. His sojourn at Sandhurst, combined with his family connections, virtually guaranteed he would reach high rank. He had surpassed all expectations when he finally reached the top job - Chief of Staff of the Pakistan Army - a four-star General.

His family was from Peshawar, the capital of The North-West Frontier Province (NWFP) created in 1902 by Lord Curzon, the first Chief Executive of the province. The NWFP was formed from areas annexed from the Emirate of Afghanistan who deemed it to be a temporary measure. Many people in Afghanistan still thought so, as did some of those living in the NWFP.

He spoke English with the accent of the English upper classes, as well as Urdu, Hindi and Pashto, the majority language in the area of the NWFP. Hindi/Urdu was spoken in Afghanistan as well as Western Pakistan. It helped to create a bond between the two countries.

During his career, two men had stood in the way of his advancement. One a politician, the other a senior officer in the army who threatened to halt his career. Both had died after unforeseen and tragic accidents. He smiled to himself, mirthlessly. Both operations had gone better than he'd planned.

Neither event had been attributed to him although rumours as to who'd been responsible abounded. After that, his rise through the ranks had continued at a meteoric rate until he was finally at the peak in terms of his military ambition. That only left politics.

His meeting with the President had gone exactly as planned. It would have gone even better if the retard hadn't contacted the British Prime Minister. He snorted. They were both fools who had risen to the top in politics in their respective countries, without knowing what they were doing.

If Zardarim hadn't spoken to the British Prime Minister, Rabbani could have been dealt with quietly. As it was, as soon as he had learnt what had happened, Khan had been forced to make other plans. He hadn't trusted having Rabbani killed in the city itself. To carry out a successful assassination required planning and knowledge. Hence the target needed to be watched so that his habits, movements and security arrangements could be known. There was also the danger that the British Government, knowing a request for Rabbani's arrest and extradition was on the cards, would put him under surveillance. Assuming the target didn't realise somebody was watching him, it wouldn't take long for Britain's security services to know. Two surveillance teams from opposite camps watching the same target was the stuff of Hollywood. Arrests would follow, questioning would probably mean revelations that the General didn't want known which in turn would be followed by information getting back to his President and the resultant mess was something he could do without.

Hence the attack on the house in Essex.

Standing up, he crossed to the drinks tray. It was after 20.00 and a whisky and soda around that time of day was a habit he had picked up from his Sandhurst years. He poured his second one, easy on the soda. He looked at the bottle of 20 year old Pakistani malt, produced by the Murree Brewery in Rawalpindi, brewers since 1860. It had been founded for the British Raj and was the only producer of beer and whisky in a constitutionally Muslim country.

His fellow countrymen were such hypocrites. Neither the whisky nor the beer could be drunk by Muslim communities. Hence, the brewery was forced by law to supply only 3% of the

population - those who practised Christianity, Hinduism and
Zoroastrianism, the religion of the Parsees. The fact was, the
actual figure was closer to 97% of the country. He used the word
hypocrites again before dragging his mind back to the issue at
hand.

It was vital there was nothing under any circumstances that
could be traced to him. No matter how remote. He had to admit
to himself that there was one thing he had learnt and learnt well
during his sojourn in Britain. The other side of British tolerance.
In effect, the breaking of the law by the security services. Don't
ask, don't tell was the establishment's motto. Beneath their
veneer of civilisation and diplomatic words the British still had
an iron fist in a velvet glove. The fist might by rusting and with
this government rusting rapidly, but it still had a ruthless punch
when it was thrown. No, he would never underestimate the actual
British Establishment. The politicians, yes. They were a lily-
livered bunch of idiots, easily fooled into believing in the best
of people. What was it the American President had said when
he'd made that speech in Turkey? Oh, yes. All Muslims are not
terrorists but all terrorists are Muslims and it was time for Europe
to wake up to the fact. That was about as angry as anybody had
ever seen the man, at least in public. But, the General admitted
to himself, his statement could easily be justified.

In the last 24 hours his own anger had welled up and threatened
to engulf him. He had been doing his best to keep his anger at
bay, knowing it wasn't good for his blood pressure nor his heart
as his personal physician had told him often enough. His anger
was an emotion he was finding more difficult to control and
woe betide anyone who was on its receiving end. It had led to
the death of more than one individual and the ruination of the
careers and lives of dozens.

The operation had been so simple. That idiot Nawaz. The
General wished the man was still alive so that he could have him
killed in a slow and painful manner. The only plus side to the
whole affair was the fact that the British had no idea who they
were dealing with nor did they know that Nawaz was his aide.
Although it wasn't a problem if they did find out. He could claim
that Nawaz had gone bad. Who wouldn't take the word of the
Chief of Staff of the Pakistani Army? Whether they believed him

or not was irrelevant. Nobody was going to accuse him of lying.

If only that idiot Zardarim had kept out of it. He could never think of the Pakistani President without the word idiot in front of his name. It had only been by luck that he had learnt what was happening. If the Attorney General hadn't been so far into his cups at that cocktail party given by Zardarim he wouldn't have discovered what was going on until it was too late. As it was, he barely had time to put things right.

He had met with the President the morning following the party. The conversation played in his head.

He had arrived at the President's residence, Aiwan-e-Sadr on Constitution Avenue, in north-eastern Islamabad at 10.00. He had flown in by helicopter from the Army House in Rawalpindi the official home of the Army Chief.

When the General was shown into the huge and imposing office, the President had stood and leant forward, holding out his hand. He had walked across the room, his own hand outstretched, a smile plastered on his face.

'Sir, it's good to see you so soon. I am sorry I had to rush away after the party last night but a couple of things had come up that I felt needed my personal attention.'

'Anything I need to know about?' The President asked as they shook hands. 'Come. Let us sit in the more comfortable seats and you can bring me up to date.'

They sat opposite each other, in leather Chesterfield chairs, manufactured in Pakistan, a low oak table between them. Coffee, tea and bite-sized sweet cakes were already laid out, the drinks in flasks to keep warm. The President, Khan knew, liked to show the common touch by pouring the tea and coffee himself.

'Coffee?' President Zardarim asked, holding up the flask.

'Please. Thank you.'

'Cakes?'

'No, thanks. I'm trying to watch my weight.' The General chuckled.

'So am I.'

Which Khan thought was a stupid thing to say. The man was thin, short, and prematurely grey, had hawk-like features and could be lost in a crowd of three. However, he was a brilliant orator, which was why he had made it to the top of Pakistani politics. Also, beneath the veneer of civilised behaviour existed the heart of a man who was as ruthless as the General and just as ambitious.

Khan added three sugars to his cup of coffee and stirred the contents. Next, he opened his briefcase and took out a file, handing it across the table. 'The details are all in the file, but let me sum up.' He began to brief the President on what was happening around the country, paying particular attention to the stand-off with India and the unrest around the border between Pakistan and Afghanistan. Both reports had been grossly exaggerated - they usually were. It was a means of ensuring maximum funding for the army in particular and the three services in general.

Zardarim merely nodded, asking an occasional question, sipping his own sugarless, black coffee, refilling the cup when necessary. Khan refused all offers of a refill.

Then, when he finished, he said, 'I understand from the Attorney General that he is going to request the extradition of some criminal from Britain, is that right?'

'Correct. His name is Rabbani. He appears to be heavily involved in drug smuggling activities which has involved a number of unexplained deaths in various parts of the country. The matter was brought to my attention by the Attorney General after he received detailed information from the Federal Investigation Agency. Have you heard of the man?' The FIA was the Pakistani equivalent of the American FBI and operated nationally.

Khan frowned before shaking his head. 'No, I can't say I have.'

'I'm surprised to hear that as his main activities seem to be centred around the Afghanistan border.'

'With all due respect, criminal activity isn't part of my remit as Army Chief.'

'No,' Zardarim inclined his head graciously, 'I agree. Why do you want to know?'

'No particular reason. But if we want him as a matter of some urgency then arrest and extradition won't work. You know as well as I do that by the time the whole thing has meandered its way via the Court of Human Rights in Strasbourg you and I will be old men.'

The President nodded his head in genuine sorrow, sighed and then said, 'I know. The AG and I have discussed the matter and we have decided that I should phone the British Prime Minister and ask if he can circumvent the process. Though I do not hold out much hope.'

'I have a better idea,' said Khan.

'Oh?' The President looked keenly at his guest. 'What better idea?'

'Keep everything legal and above board while I take a different route.'

'What route? You can't kidnap the man.'

'Of course not. I can't. But TIFAT can.'

The President looked at Khan in some surprise. 'But this is a criminal matter. TIFAT won't get involved.'

'They will, I can assure you. I will explain how this man Rabbani is involved with terrorist activities here, possibly in Europe and that he is somehow involved with a plan to carry out a large scale attack across our borders.' He smiled. 'You can leave the details to me.'

The President narrowed his eyes for a moment before he also smiled and nodded. 'Yes. That could work. Spare me the details,' he held up his left hand, palm outwards, 'I don't need to know. Oh, and Pervez, nobody else needs to know either. That especially applies to the Attorney General. He is such a stickler for the rule of law. You have to move fast. I understand the request will be made in only a few days from now.'

'You can count on me.'

Yes, he could be counted on but not that fool Nawaz. Perhaps he had over-egged the pudding, but the fact was he had panicked. It wasn't something of which he was proud. He had spoken to Macnair, explained what was happening, reached an agreement to act and should have left it at that. As always, hindsight was a wonderful thing. His biggest fear was if Rabbani talked before he was handed over. Macnair might decide to give Rabbani to the British authorities. Khan wanted to ensure the man never stood trial. The more he had thought about it, the more he realised that he needed Rabbani dead before anyone got hold of him and that included TIFAT.

Hence the reason he had despatched Nawaz to kill Rabbani.

For some time he had been planning terrorist atrocities in Europe, particularly in Britain. He hated the British with a passion. He hated them for what they had done to his country, for the partitioning of India and Pakistan and the arbitrary way it was done that had resulted in decades of war, acrimony and hatred between the two countries. As far as he was concerned, there could never be peace between them, ever. And for that he blamed the British. He knew if there were enough terrorist attacks in Europe, all shown to be Muslim based and Pakistani supported, there would be yells across the world for the President of Pakistan to take action. Khan would then ferment trouble in the country against the weak leadership of the President. He was sure he could force early elections in which he would stand and win. Then the attacks would stop. He'd stop them. But it needed one thing. Money. And lots of it. Which was why he had started in business with Rabbani knowing that one day he would take over the whole organisation. Rabbani's empire, both legal and illegal, was a cash cow waiting to be milked.

He had known that Rabbani never went anywhere without Yassin. The man was indispensable to the organisation in no uncertain terms Khan had made it clear that Yassin was not to be killed. He had emphasised the fact with promises of dire retribution if anything happened to Yassin. Yassin had been his inside man, keeping the General informed of everything that was going on. It had been Yassin who had told him about the visit to Essex, giving him just enough time to organise a hit.

The General had known about Hughes. He had thought it was merely a business transaction but it was now obvious that Hughes must have been from TIFAT. Thanks to Yassin, the General had a broad overview of Rabbani's operations, but it was a highly complex organisation. Which was why he had needed Yassin alive. Damn that incompetent fool Nawaz, he thought again. The death of Yassin could mean the loss of a fortune in assets.

Yassin had kept a meticulous record of all Rabbani's activities both in his head and digitally. The loss of both was a serious setback though not insurmountable. During the previous 12 months, Yassin had drip fed the General but had made it clear that he would bring the majority of the information with him when Rabbani was no longer a threat. When he was either dead or in the General's hands. Yassin had wanted to run the organisation on behalf of the General for the simple reason he was a believer.

A true believer. He wanted to work for his God and for Islam. It was a powerful weapon to use and the General used it ruthlessly. Yassin did not believe in the trappings of wealth or power. He believed solely in his version of Islam.

The General took a mouthful of his drink, saw with surprise that the glass was empty, poured himself more whisky then added too much soda for his liking and some ice. He took a long swallow and then topped up the whisky, before taking a sip, sighing with satisfaction. He knew some of Rabbani's people. Taking control would involve time and effort, the former in short supply, the latter no problem. Ruthless efficiency was what was called for and he had both in abundant supply. One thing played into his hands. On the illegal side, Rabbani's trusted lieutenants were Pakistani and had close ties to the home country. Coercion or assurances of a future within the organisation would work either way. Of course, eventually, his own people would replace the existing leadership.

There was another problem to be taken into account. What if the Security Services in the guise of MI5 or MI6 had got their hands on the information? Or worse still, TIFAT? The former would be pretty much powerless to do much about the international infrastructure of Rabbani's business, hamstrung as they were by the law. TIFAT on the other hand was an entirely different problem. They tended to shoot first and ask questions afterwards. An exaggeration perhaps, but he did not underestimate Macnair and his organisation.

As the permutations swirled through his head, General Khan came to the conclusion that Rabbani needed to die. Any information he did have would be extracted first either voluntarily or by other means. Threats to Rabbani's family would probably be enough.

He had informed TIFAT that there were a number of ships around the coast of Britain that could take Rabbani off their hands. It helped to give the impression that the Pakistani Government was backing the whole project. That wasn't the case. The Pashni, was heading for Southampton and was currently about 150 nautical miles south-west of Lands End. The Pashni was owned by a shell company in the Seychelles. That in turn was owned by a dummy company registered in the Bahamas, a haven for shipping companies who wanted to avoid their tax liabilities. The ship took goods to Europe and on its return journey picked up large quantities of weapons and explosives from countries en-route. These were stowed in cleverly hidden containers around the ship and delivered to Pakistan. Customs and Excise in certain Pakistani ports presented no problems - they were supporters of the General and his ambitions. He was careful not to risk using the same port on a regular basis.

He picked up the phone. He'd made his decision. Himself plus three of his most trusted people would be more than sufficient. Their passports were legal; the names were fictitious.

Then he thought about the reporter. She needed to be taken care of. Along with that weasel who was passing her the information. The man was a traitor to Islam he thought, as he took a mouthful of whisky. As always, he didn't acknowledge his hypocrisy when it came to his religion.

At least that imbecile Nawaz had delivered the vests.

29

THE AUTOPILOT WAS set to take them down to North Foreland. From there, Hunter intended heading for Deal. The water in the immediate vicinity wasn't very busy. The yachts and boats had mainly parked up for the night, either at anchor or in the many marinas that proliferated around Britain's coast. Out at sea, numerous merchant ships were in convoy, heading towards Tilbury Docks, each under the control of a local pilot.

Standing in the open so high above the water was exhilarating. There was nothing directly ahead or likely to come within a mile or two of his position so Hunter switched off the autopilot and rammed the throttles wide open. The Talisman responded immediately, lifting up on the plane, accelerating to 35kts. The wind was warm through his hair and a feeling of exhilaration swept through him. Childish, he knew, but what the hell!

With other things to think about, he reluctantly reduced speed to a more reasonable 15kts and switched the autopilot back on. He watched to see the compass needle settle on a heading of 160 degrees and checked the horizon and the radar. Satisfied that there were no vessels in the vicinity or likely to come near him he went below to make coffee.

Kathleen sat at her desk contemplating the screen of her computer. The more Omar told her, the more frightening it became.

Of course, she knew there were pockets of Islamic terrorists all across the UK. In the past, they had used homemade explosives but now it seemed that they were being supplied with plastic explosives and more sophisticated detonators. According to Omar the gear was coming from Pakistan, though he had not yet discovered how it was getting to GB. Omar had told her there was no shortage of martyrs. There were more than enough home-grown terrorists, both male and female, who were taking up the cudgels on behalf of their perverted ideology.

She knew that there was an Imam at a mosque in the East End who knew a great deal about what was going on. Omar was trying to find out more. She had pleaded with him to be careful. In reply he had e-mailed a smiley face and promised her that he would.

The latest e-mail from Omar caused her grave concern. There were a number of groups planning suicide bombings within the week - possibly even the next few days. Some of the bombers were thought to be young women from good families. Not just good families but families considered pillars of their community.

She put her head in her hands in despair.

Assuming the information was correct, what should she do? Tell the police? They'd laugh at her. Even if they took her seriously, what action would they take? Arresting Omar would probably be their first move. She sighed. 'What a lousy cynic I'm becoming,' she muttered. There was one person she believed would know what to do. Should she, shouldn't she? She picked up her mobile and found his phone number. She looked at it, sighed, changed her mind and cancelled the call. But what else could she do? Who would take her seriously? She pressed the buttons again, swithered, switched the phone off and made herself a cup of peppermint tea. It had a soothing effect on her agitation and cooled her down in the cloying, summer heat.

Damn him! She was acting like a child. Worse. A teenager. She picked up the phone, switched it on, watched as it hooked up to the supplier and pressed the buttons.

There was silence for a few seconds and for a moment she wondered if he'd changed his number. With relief she heard it ringing. Much to her chagrin, she couldn't help feeling a little excited at the thought of speaking to him. Disappointment welled up within her when it went to answering machine.

'Nick. It's me. Kathleen. I need to talk to you. Something's come up and it's urgent.' She was about to say it was something to do with a terrorist attack but thought better of it. Instead, she added, 'Please call.'

She had no way of knowing that Hunter wasn't using the phone. It was in his cabin back at TIFAT HQ in Rosyth. The one he was using for the operation had a unique feature. It couldn't be traced, nor any conversation picked up by the security services.

The conversations he and Macnair were having would have the authorities manning the listening stations going berserk - and they had enough to contend with.

The five red and white flashes every twenty seconds from the North Foreland point were clearly visible. A beacon of safety to seamen since 1499.

Once around the headland he was only 5nm from the white cliffs where he was going to anchor for the night. Twenty minutes later, he eased back on the throttles, put the engines in reverse, took the way off the boat and released the anchor. He sat there for a few minutes as the Talisman swung to the tide and then settled down for the night. Provided the weather didn't deteriorate she would sit there in perfect peace until the morning. He turned on the radio to the weather station and checked the forecast. Calm, sunny and warm, as it had been all month.

In the galley, he found a cupboard in which was a bottle of Islay malt whisky. He poured himself a generous tot, added soda and ice then returned to the upper helm position. Sitting in the Captain's chair, his feet on the console, he sipped the drink with a great deal of appreciation. However, it wasn't long before he found himself drifting off to sleep. His chin hit his chest and his eyes closed. He jerked awake, clutching his glass as it began to slip through his fingers. A final mouthful and he went below. It seemed to him that he had barely laid his head on the pillow when he was woken up by a lot of banging and yelling.

Rabbani had come to his senses. It was just after 07.30.

Macnair's phone rang. He glanced at the clock on the wall. It was 07.33. 'Macnair.'

'Malcolm, it's Elspeth.'

'Morning. Though from the look of the messages I've received during the night there doesn't seem to be much that's good about it.'

'You're right. There isn't. As of now, I'm battling to stay out of a potential question and answers session with the Intelligence and Security Committee.'

'What the hell are they doing contacting you at this hour?'

'To be fair, it was via an e-mail late last night from their

Chairman, Adam Rutledge.'

'I thought Rutledge was one of the better MPs we have in that House of Babel.'

'Careful Malcolm, your cynicism is showing through. You're right though, he is one of the better ones. Perhaps because he's in opposition he feels he can treat us more kindly.' There was no mistaking the fatigue in Elspeth's voice. 'Whatever the reason, he's not harassing me *per se* but he has politely asked if it would be convenient for me to attend an emergency meeting in the House.'

'What have you said?'

'Nothing just yet. I'll ignore the message for a few more hours which is about as long as I dare and then I'll give him a ring.'

'What will you tell him?'

Elspeth let out a deep sigh. 'I'm going to tell him about the two expected attacks. I'll make it clear to him that he should not tell anyone else because if this got out there'd be pandemonium and panic in the streets. Not,' she added heavily, 'to mention the run on the pound that will inevitably result.'

'Will he keep quiet?'

'I think so,' she said slowly.

'You don't sound so sure.'

'I'm not. You never can be with these self-serving...' She abruptly stopped speaking. 'Bloody hell, don't start me off again. The bottom line is, I'm going to ask him to keep the committee off my back until I'm ready. That I need a few more days.'

'Will he succeed?'

There was silence for a few seconds. 'I think so. I've met him on quite a few occasions. He's a tough minded sod, but then he's been a politician for the better part of thirty years. He was a minister in the last government and hopes to be one again. He keeps the committee in check when it's needed and we're only asking for a few days so, yes, I think so. Hang on a sec. Morning Abi, what do you have for me?' Elspeth's voice was distant.

Macnair waited patiently.

'Malcolm? This has just come in from GCHQ. One of the phones we've been tracking has been used. It's been triangulated by Wandsworth, Kingston and Merton transmitters. It's somewhere in a two mile radius.'

'They can't pin it down any more than that?'

'They say not yet. But they'll focus on the area which should help a lot if another call is made.'

'What was said?'

'It was two women. The one making the call said, "I have everything". The other one replied, "Good. We'll meet later at". She was cut off by the first speaker who said, "I know where" and broke the connection. That was it.'

'They sound cagey.'

'According to Cheltenham they were extremely nervous. They're carrying out an analysis of the voices, though the preliminary report says they're pretty sure the girls are Pakistani ethnically.'

'There's no surprise about them being Pakistani, but women?'

'I know,' Elspeth sighed. 'But the involvement of women is becoming more prevalent by the week, especially in places like Afghanistan, Pakistan and Israel.'

'Is there anything else? No? Then I'll be in touch if we learn anything.'

He went down for breakfast. He helped himself to fresh orange juice, bacon and scrambled eggs, toast and coffee.

30

RABBANI WAS SHOUTING loudly when Hunter opened the door to the man's cabin. 'Shut up or I'll leave you like that. You're making enough noise to wake the dead.'

Rabbani looked at Hunter in something close to shock.

'I'll bring you a coffee shortly and we can have a friendly chat.'

'I have a headache. I need an Aspirin.'

'Tough. It'll pass. Anything else?'

Rabbani let loose with more profanity but made no reference to Hunter jabbing him with the needle. Either he had forgotten the incident or hadn't been aware of what was happening.

Hunter closed the door and ignored the noise. He went onto the stern deck and looked around. There were no other vessels anywhere near. The sky was cloudless, there was no wind, the day was heating up nicely and the sea was flat calm.

Technically, midsummer would be the following day. Saturday. The longest day of the year. A day, he acknowledged to himself, that the pagan in him relished even if there was no such day. The so-called longest day lasted 7 days. The 3rd day of the period was described as the longest although there were another 4 days to follow. For those 7 days the sun would shine for 16 hours and 45 minutes in that part of the world.

He lay down on the deck, clasped his hands behind his head and did 50 sit-ups, then 50 press-ups and a further 50 sit-ups.

Rabbani fell silent.

Hunter then dived overboard and did a fast crawl five minutes away from the Talisman and back again. He did it twice more. Climbing onboard, he was gratified to find he was barely breathing hard. He examined his chest. The bruise was fading from blue to yellow. He put his fingers on it and pushed. The resulting twinge was hardly noticeable. He went below and switched on the coffee maker. While it was warming up he shaved and showered and dressed in a fresh white t-shirt and his black trousers. He fitted the Pocketlite and holster under his left arm, butt forward and then put on a lightweight, grey, fishing waistcoat.

He poured two mugs of coffee. His was white, no sugar. Rabbani's he made with sugar and milk, the way he had seen Rabbani take it.

Opening the door to Rabbani's cabin with a mug of coffee in his hand, he stood in the doorway and offered it to him. 'Do you want this?'

Rabbani glowered at him. Hatred shone in his eyes. 'Lying here, I thought that perhaps you had been taken prisoner as well and were in another cabin. Or even killed. But you are a traitor.' He spat on the deck. 'Swine! Filth!'

'Less of the melodramatics, Ashraf. Do you want this coffee or not?'

'What I want is for you to release me. What I want is to be able to use the toilet. So cut me free.'

Hunter shook his head. 'If you try hard enough you can reach the heads.' He bent over and placed the mug just inside the door. 'I'll leave it here.'

He went up top. There were more noises coming from Rabbani's cabin. Hunter wanted him demoralised. If Hunter let Rabbani think that he had an opportunity to escape, then had that opportunity taken away, the man's resistance would be significantly reduced. That in turn meant control over Rabbani would be easier. Hunter wondered what Rabbani would do with the Glock.

In the galley, he opened a drawer and lifted out a sharp vegetable knife. He placed it blade down in the top, left pocket of his waistcoat where the handle could be seen.

He slid the Pocketlite out of its holster and flicked off the safety. The weapon was already cocked and loaded. At the door to the cabin, he twisted the knob with his left hand, and pushed it open while standing slightly side on with his right shoulder resting against the doorjamb. His right hand with the automatic was out of sight. He didn't want to put Rabbani off from taking action.

The man was sitting on the bed, about two and a half, maybe three metres away, glowering at Hunter. 'Swine,' was his opening greeting.

Hunter merely shrugged.

'Why are you doing this? Money?'

There was no reply.

'Tell me! Whatever you are being paid I will double it! Treble it!'

Hunter noted the way Rabbani was sitting. Slightly side on to the door, his left hand was on his knee while his right hand was out of sight by his side, pressing on the mattress.

Still Hunter said nothing, merely stared at him. He knew it would unnerve the other man and make him react sooner than if Hunter said anything.

Rabbani glared at Hunter and then raised his right hand, the Glock was pointing at him.

'If you shoot me,' said Hunter reasonably, 'I will be thrown backwards and away from you. There is no chance of you reaching me.' In spite of the relative distance between them, Hunter figured Rabbani would shoot first and try and solve the problem after. His next words showed that to be the case.

'I do not care. If you don't tell me why you have done this I will shoot you and wait for somebody to find me, wherever we are.'

'Did you look through the porthole? You can't really miss those cliffs.' Hunter nodded in the direction of the bulkhead.

Although he had already looked out, Rabbani turned his head that way also. Towering above them were the White Cliffs and in the background the loud and raucous call of seagulls, a discordant noise in the tranquillity of the morning.

'Don't you recognise them?'

Rabbani looked at Hunter with contempt. 'How should I know where we are? They are merely cliffs, just like every other cliff to be found around the coast.'

Hunter shook his head in mock sadness. 'Such ignorance. They are the White Cliffs of Dover and we're at anchor in the shadow of their towering splendour. Although, it is true to say, there is no shadow as we'll be in sunlight for most of the day if we stay here.'

'Hughes, I am warning you. Cut me free or I will shoot.'

'Go ahead. There's no way I can stop you and I have no intention of letting you go free.' He touched the handle of the knife. 'You need this to cut the cable tie.' He wondered if Rabbani had it in him to pull the trigger.

The click of the automatic hammer hitting an empty chamber was loud in the quiet and peace of the boat. So were the next half-a-dozen clicks.

'No bullets,' said Hunter by way of a wasted explanation.

With a snarl, Rabbani drew back his hand and threw the gun at Hunter's head. Hunter ducked and it easily missed, bouncing off the bulkhead behind him. 'Temper, temper, Ashraf.' Hunter brought his gun to bear and pointed it at Rabbani's leg. He knelt down on one knee and as he pulled the trigger moved his aim to the right. The bullet just missed Rabbani's knee and embedded into the bulkhead. If he had fired from any other angle there had been the danger that the bullet could have passed through the mattress, through the deck and through the hull. There was no telling how much damage could have resulted.

In a reasonable, even pleasant voice, Hunter said, 'I can just as easily shoot you. I can aim to wound or aim to kill, either doesn't bother me. If you behave, you won't be hurt. If you don't, then it will be very unpleasant for you. I hope I make myself clear.' Although this type of action was anathema to Hunter, he knew he had no choice. He also reminded himself that the man sitting on the bed dealt in misery and death on a vast scale through his crime empire and possibly his terrorist activities.

'Who are you?' Rabbani asked in a croaking voice, his face ashen beneath his natural colour. Now that he had no gun what little bravado he'd had was gone.

Hunter shook his head. 'Who I am is of no importance. We'll be travelling for a few hours and afterwards,' he shrugged, not having any answers himself as to what afterwards would bring, 'we shall have to see.' Hunter nodded at the mug on the deck where he had placed it. 'I see you haven't drunk your coffee. Do you want a fresh cup, or a cup of tea?'

Rabbani nodded.

'Which?'

'Tea.'

'Milk? Sugar?'

'Both. Three sugars.'

'If you try anything, if you make a noise or try to attract any attention, please be assured, I will kill you. Do you understand?' There was no reply. 'Do you?' Hunter's tone was harsher, his voice louder.

'Yes.' Rabbani's voice was barely above a croak.

'I can't hear you. Speak up!'

'Yes! Yes! Yes! I understand!' He shouted, glaring at Hunter, a flicker of defiance in his voice. Then he looked down at the deck, avoiding eye contact.

'Good.' Hunter left him. He was sure Rabbani was under control but he wouldn't be making any assumptions. He would assume Rabbani was play acting. It was safer.

Returning with a mug of tea and a plate of biscuits, he placed them just inside the door and in easy reach of Rabbani.

'We'll be leaving in a few minutes. Is there anything that I can get you? I'm going to be busy for a few hours.'

'Cigarettes.'

Hunter went into the main saloon and picked up the carton of 200 cigarettes Rabbani had bought from the marina shop. He returned to the cabin and tossed them to Rabbani. Catching them, Rabbani eagerly opened a packet, his hands shaking. He placed a cigarette in his mouth and reached into a pocket to take out his gold lighter. He flicked the lighter a number of times before it lit, placed the flame to the end of the cigarette and inhaled deeply, a look of relief flooded his face.

'By the way,' said Hunter, 'don't try anything. Look up at the overhead bulkhead.'

'The what?' Rabbani looked at Hunter stupidly.

'The ceiling.' Hunter pointed. 'Those are smoke detectors and those are sprinklers. Smoking a cigarette doesn't set them off. Lighting a fire will set the alarm ringing and the sprinklers raining on you. If it happens, you will sit in the cold shower for as long as you are here. Don't think the water tanks will eventually empty as the sprinklers use sea water and the bilge pumps keep us from sinking. Understood?'

'Tell me, I must know. Why are you doing this?'

Hunter looked at the man for a few seconds before he decided that there was no reason not to tell him. 'Because you're a terrorist. Because you know about the coming Taliban attack on Pakistan.'

Hunter didn't wait for a response but stepped outside and closed the door.

31

FREDERICK OGILVIE SAT at the breakfast bar in his townhouse. The house was in the fashionable end of Wandsworth, a terraced three storey affair, with four bedrooms, all ensuite, two large rooms at ground level and a kitchen/diner at the rear. The room he was in was large, like the rest of the house. Although it was approaching 10.00 he was still dressed in his pyjamas and dressing gown. The pyjamas were bright blue cotton with his initials embroidered on the breast pocket, the dressing gown was maroon with tiny, yellow hearts dotted all over it. The gown had been a present from Algernon, his partner for nearly 12 years.

He sat there with his hands cupped around a mug of herbal tea, an uneaten bowl of muesli on the bar in front of him. Algernon was the love of his life. He had known it the minute they had met at the club in Bloomsbury. The club was exclusive which was another way of saying expensive. He had been there on numerous occasions, made casual acquaintances, had casual sex and stayed on good terms with the men he had met. It was that sort of place. It was populated by the good and the great, the sons of the gentry and wealthy, the married and divorced. The unwritten rule meant no long term relationships with other members. The system worked. Those people who ended up in lasting relationships were required to resign and if they didn't do it voluntarily they were politely asked.

Algernon Fitzgerald was tall, brown haired, with strong features, a hooked nose from his rugby playing days when it was broken by an elbow in the face and, as far as Ogilvie was concerned, oozed masculinity. Ogilvie had been led to believe that Fitzgerald, or Fitzie as he liked to be known, was between jobs but in no hurry to find employment unless it was something suited to his talents and ability. He didn't specify what they were. Ogilvie had believed that Fitzgerald was either well connected or well heeled - otherwise he couldn't have been a member of the club.

They dated the day after they met and went to bed on their second date a week later. They went out together for the next three months. By now Ogilvie was a Member of Parliament. He pestered Fitzgerald with texts and e-mails and showered gifts on him, everything from cufflinks and a gold tie pin with a diamond in the centre to books and CDs that Fitzgerald claimed he wanted to read. Expensive dinners with expensive wines and vintage cognac were the norm at least twice a week. Occasionally, the evening ended when they went to bed together, other times Fitzgerald made excuses to leave. Although he was sure Fitzgerald was going to meet someone else, Ogilvie didn't want to know if it was true, he was happy to accept the excuses doled out to him.

What he did do was hire a private detective to look into Fitzgerald's background. It turned out his boyfriend had a degree in geography and was teaching in a third-rate secondary school in Acton. He had no money and lived in a decrepit bedsit a mile from the school and walked to work. He came from a poor area of Wapping, where his mother still lived, and as near as the PI could discover, his nose had been broken when he was attacked by a gang of homophobes. That had been according to the police report filed as near as dammit three years before they had met. In essence, the whole of Fitzgerald's life, past and present, was a tissue of lies.

Ogilvie didn't care. He was in love. He was torn whether to say anything to Fitzgerald but on balance decided it was better not to. His boyfriend was touchy about his past and cagey about his living arrangements. Ogilvie had learnt early on not to say anything. If he tried, Fitzgerald would go off in a huff that could last for days or until he was given an expensive gift. The MP was also aware that Fitzgerald was unfaithful and though he tried to accept the fact, Ogilvie was riddled with jealousy.

Three months after they met Fitzgerald moved in with Ogilvie. They occupied separate bedrooms at Fitzgerald's insistence but on the whole got on well together. Fitzgerald was like a cuckoo in the nest. He gradually came to dominate Ogilvie and to make all the decisions. He gave up work. He controlled the main bank account, though he was unable to get his hands on the money in the trust. Ogilvie claimed the trust was set up in perpetuity and the capital couldn't be touched. Fitzgerald had gone into another huff but this time Ogilvie stuck to his guns. A very expensive night out solved the problem.

Fitzgerald came in. He too was still in pyjamas only he wasn't wearing a dressing gown. It was a sunny June day in London and already stifling hot. His pyjamas were black silk, the top open to his waist. His hairy chest was turning grey and his paunch was beginning to show. He was still reasonably fit looking and when dressed in his made-to-measure, expensive clothes his paunch was well hidden. Not only was he still an attractive man but he knew it and he played on Ogilvie's insecurities to get his own way.

'Fitzie, good morning!'

In reply, he received a half smile and something close to a grunt. Fitzgerald claimed he wasn't a morning person, more a night owl.

Ogilvie slid off his stool. 'Let me get you some cereal and your coffee.' He had everything ready to hand. He poured out the All-Bran, added milk and sprinkled sugar. He poured the coffee, added milk, spooned in two sugars and stirred. He carried the simple meal on a tray and placed it in front of Fitzgerald. It was a ritual they followed whenever they were together at breakfast. It was also a ritual that was becoming rarer. Ogilvie was a jealous man and was petrified of losing his boyfriend. But he consoled himself with the thought that Fitzgerald had nowhere to go.

Once Fitzgerald had taken a few sips of coffee, Ogilvie tried to open a conversation. 'Are you doing anything interesting today?'

'Hopefully. David and I are meeting for lunch and then going to the Tate Modern for the afternoon. They are showing a new exhibition by Matisse.'

Ogilvie's hands clasped more tightly around his coffee mug. Fitzgerald's interest in modern art was something new and was always coupled with the name of David. The MP swallowed as fear surged into his throat.

'You,' he croaked and then cleared his throat. 'You're seeing a lot of this David man, aren't you?'

'David? Oh, yes. He is such an interesting person. You must meet him someday.'

Both men knew it was an empty suggestion. David was Fitzgerald's latest fling. His latest bit on the side, as Ogilvie had heard Fitzgerald say once to a friend. Then he had added that it helped to keep living with Ogilvie at least bearable. The MP decided it was best if he said nothing.

However, in his heart of hearts, Ogilvie knew he was losing Fitzgerald. That it was only a question of time. When the other man found somebody as rich and generous and as easily manipulated, then he would be gone. Ogilvie couldn't stand the idea. Age was against him. He was fifty-eight, Fitzgerald was forty-two.

'I must tell you,' said Ogilvie, injecting enthusiasm into his voice. 'You know that attack that was on the news last night?'

'What attack?' Fitzgerald looked through partially slitted eyes at Ogilvie.

'You saw it on the ten o'clock news. That house in Southminster. All those dead people.'

Fitzgerald frowned as though trying to remember and just as Ogilvie was getting exasperated enough to explain further, he said, 'Oh, that one. Frederick, you know I don't take any notice of the news. It is far too depressing.'

It used to be Freddy, now it was Frederick. It was as though the formal address was indicative of a wall building between them.

'You know that twenty people were killed? Murdered in a gun battle.'

Fitzgerald yawned in an affected show of boredom and said, 'Yes. There was something, but I wasn't listening very closely.'

'I have it on good authority that TIFAT was involved. That they were responsible.'

'Who or what is TIFAT?'

It was coming up to noon and Hunter had taken the Talisman around the corner of Cap Gris Nez, literally Grey Nose Cape and was heading south.

Just north of Octeville Hunter brought the Talisman to a halt in about 8m of water and dropped the anchor. Then, he cut the engines and total peace descended over the boat like a cloak. He had decided that the other side of the Channel was a good place to hide.

Going below to make a mug of coffee, he thought about talking to Rabbani but decided to let him stew a bit longer. Mug in hand, he went back up top and phoned Macnair.

'Where are you?'

'At anchor just north of Le Havre near a place called Octeville.'

'What about Rabbani? Is he behaving himself?'

'No problem.' Then he added, 'One small thing puzzles me. I left an empty Glock for him to find. He didn't even check to see if it was loaded. He just pointed it at me and pulled the trigger.'

'I suspect it's been a long time since he's done his own dirty work.'

'Possibly. But even so, checking a weapon is practically an automatic reaction whenever you pick one up.'

'I don't disagree. Maybe he was still too befuddled. Too traumatised to think straight.'

'It could be. Or it could be that he's rarely used one which makes no sense in view of what's he's supposed to be doing. A drug smuggler not using guns isn't that surprising, particularly if he operates in Western Europe and not in the drug producing areas. But someone supposedly involved in terrorism?' Hunter couldn't keep the incredulity out of his voice.

'I see your point.'

'Paraphrasing Winston Churchill, this is turning out to be a riddle, wrapped in a mystery, inside an enigma.'

'Be that as it may, I've spoken to General Khan. He's apologised for the delay in getting back to us but he was up-country. He's asked for you to rendezvous with a Pakistan registered merchant ship called the Pashni.'

'Where?'

'No exact location but somewhere to the west of Plymouth. They'll take Rabbani off your hands.'

'Okay,' Hunter replied. 'Hang on a second, sir.' Talisman's latitude and longitude were showing on the console display. He typed in Plymouth, pressed a button and there it was. Distance to go - 258 nautical miles. Looking at the info on the console, I need to go to Portland and fill up with fuel. Anything more from the memory stick and discs?'

'Nothing about Barzakh but quite a lot about Rabbani's business dealings both legal and illegal. One thing is clear. He has a partner in Pakistan. Somebody high up in the government though there's no clue so far as to who it is.'

'I'll ask him.'

'I'll leave it to you. We'll speak later.' Macnair broke the connection.

32

AFTER HE CHECKED the course, Hunter adjusted it by a few degrees to starboard, made sure there were no vessels in the vicinity and went below. It was time to talk to Rabbani.

When Hunter entered the cabin he found Rabbani sitting in an easy chair, chain smoking. The cigarette was held in his right hand, his left hand hung down the side of the chair. An ashtray next to him was overflowing with butts but the air was reasonably clear due to the exceptionally effective air-conditioning. He glowered at Hunter but said nothing.

'We can do this one of two ways,' Hunter began, 'the easy way or the hard way. It's up to you.'

Still Rabbani kept quiet and merely stared.

'Tell me about Barzakh.'

Rabbani frowned. 'About what?'

'Barzakh.'

Rabbani shook his head. 'I have never heard of it. What is it?'

Maybe, Hunter thought, Rabbani had been rehearsing his reply should he ever be asked the question. Even so, he was a hell of a good actor.

'It's a terrorist organisation in Pakistan.'

'What is this? There's some terrorist organisation which has a stupid name meaning life after death and you're asking me about it? What's it to do with me?'

'You fund it.'

Rabbani's surprise was evident. 'Why should I fund a terrorist organisation in Pakistan?'

'How should I know why?' Hunter spoke harshly. 'I only know that you do.'

'Well I don't!' Rabbani yelled. 'Terrorism is bad for business.'

To Hunter it seemed there was more than a grain of truth behind the statement. 'Let's get this straight. You're saying you don't support a terrorist organisation in Pakistan known as

Barzakh because it's bad for business?'

'I don't support any terrorist organisation with any name anywhere!' Rabbani lit another cigarette from the stub of his last one, his hand shaking, though whether from fear or anger, Hunter couldn't tell.

'We were told by the Pakistani government that you did. That you were behind Barzakh.'

'I tell you I've never heard of this Barzakh. Never! I am a businessman, plain and simple.'

'You're a crook of the worst kind. You deal in drugs and prostitution. You spread misery across the world, blood-sucking on the vulnerable and the poor.'

'You mean like international bankers? Like the misery they've inflicted? Like the multi-nationals who have exploited the third world for their oil and the factories paying slave wages to children?' Rabbani sneered, 'I don't need any preaching from you.' He paused. 'Who are you? What's your real name?'

'You know me as Hughes and it'll stay like that.'

'Who do you work for?'

'Myself. I'm a freelance hired to hand you over to the Pakistanis. Back in Pakistan you'll stand trial.'

'Where are you taking me?'

'Offshore Cornwall. There we'll be met by a ship which will take you back to Pakistan.'

'I will not be held for long before I am released,' Rabbani sneered. 'I have very powerful friends in high places.'

'Like your business partner?'

'How do you know about my business partner?'

'I may be freelance but I have the contacts that can analyse any computer that exists. It costs me money, usually a great deal, but thanks to the fees I charge I usually get what I want.'

Rabbani said nothing for a minute before saying, 'My partner will have me released as soon as he hears about this.'

'Who is he?'

'Couldn't you find out from your contacts?' Rabbani sneered.

'I will, I guarantee it. Once I do, as a bonus, I'll make sure the information is given to the President as well as General Khan.'

Rabbani looked surprised for a moment or two, even shocked. 'What...what do you mean?'

'About the President and General Khan? What I say. As a bonus, I shall let them know who your partner is. Naturally, all of your business dealings are being sent to them although not all at once. They buy one segment at a time.'

Rabbani shook his head. His face was creased in a puzzled frown.

Frederick Ogilvie left the house in a bad mood. He'd had a blazing row with Algernon Fitzgerald during breakfast and had showered, dressed and left the house without saying goodbye. Fitzie was an ignoramus. Not to know about TIFAT was off the scale of ignorant. They were in the press often enough, even if they did work at not publicising themselves. They had done too much not to be noticed. Of course, the idiots of the press praised them to high heaven, while the more balanced blogs on the internet and articles in newspapers such as the Guardian were demanding they be held accountable for their actions.

His jealousy was eating him up. Fitzie's affairs over the years had been eating at him and now they were turning his love into resentment and, dare he say it, hatred? Perhaps not that. But boiling anger. That morning had erupted because Fitzie had announced that he and David were going to New York for a few days. The question of who was paying wasn't brought up, but he had his suspicions.

He, Frederick Ogilvie, could lay down and be trampled on or he could do what he had always done. Fight back. For all its pretence of liberal tolerance, the bar was a rabid den of homophobes. He knew about the snide comments that had been made behind his back. Well, he'd shown them. He had become a Conservative Member of Parliament in a safe seat and was tipped to go places. The fact that his career in politics had stalled, he either ignored or put down to dislike and jealousy by his fellow MPs. They were as bad as the legal profession. He'd heard what they said about him. How he was an embittered gay man of mediocre talents who should not have been given the seat in the first place. That he had been given Warwickshire North for the simple reason that the Conservatives needed more women and more gay people in the party to prove what a tolerant and all inclusive party they had become.

Very few people knew him well enough to know that he had a vicious streak in him. That he could, and did, bear a grudge for years.

Fitzie wasn't on his enemy list but Ogilvie had come to realise that they could not go on. It was time to move on. The question was, how? Revenge is a dish best served cold wasn't true. It was best served white hot with a great deal of anger and hatred. His flames were being stoked even as he hurried along the pavement.

He took the Underground to Westminster. It was hot and stuffy and there were too many people on the train, as a result, he was forced to stand. London, as was often the case at that time of the year, was overrun with tourists who, as far as Ogilvie was concerned, made life a misery. When he got off, he nimbly made his way up the steps, dodging past people milling around, reading maps and guides. He wished they'd all stay away, though it wasn't a sentiment he'd voice in public. Tourist pounds were too important.

He swiped his card at security and made his way to one of the meeting rooms on the second floor. Nigel Goldsmith was already there waiting for him.

'What you're telling me, about the President and General Khan,' Rabbani shook his head, 'I don't understand.'

'Why don't you? I'd like to know.'

'You may wish to know, but I have no intention of telling you.'

'Who is your partner in Pakistan?'

Rabbani shook his head. 'You will learn soon enough and then it will be the worst for you.'

'What do you mean by that?'

Rabbani shook his head and stubbornly repeated, 'You will find out.'

'As you wish.' Hunter stepped back and closed the cabin door. A few minutes later he had switched off the air-conditioning and slipped the gas tube under the door. He turned the gas on for a few seconds and waited 5 minutes. He turned on the air-conditioning again but even so, he took the precaution of fitting the oxygen mask before re-opening the door. As he'd expected, Rabbani was out for the count.

He cut the cable tie and dragged the inert body out of the cabin.

He removed his oxygen mask and then dragged Rabbani out on to the main deck.

Using rope he had found in a locker, he tied Rabbani's feet together and then his wrists in front of him. He attached a further length of rope to the wrist binding and attached the other end to a nearby cleat. He went to the upper helm position and after ensuring there were no other ships or boats to endanger them, he throttled back to 5kts. Returning to the stern, he filled a bucket with seawater and threw it over Rabbani. In view of how potent the gas was, he wasn't sure it would be of any use in bringing him around. After the third bucket it was obvious he would just have to wait.

Hunter had increased speed again and was sitting at the helm when he heard Rabbani yelling. He throttled back and went to the bench seat at the stern. Kneeling on the cushions, he looked down. 'I told you it can be the hard way or the easy way. Which is it to be?'

In reply he received a mouthful of abuse.

Hunter didn't say another word. He went straight down, opened the aft guard-rail, grabbed Rabbani by the scruff of his shirt collar and dragged him down the steps to the lower deck. He shoved him over the stern.

Still without saying a word, while Rabbani came to the surface spluttering and screaming, Hunter went back to the helm position and eased the throttles forward. He looked over his shoulder and watched as the rope paid out, took the strain and began to drag Rabbani through the water. The man's yells were cut off as the necessity to breath became paramount. After a minute or so, Hunter pushed the throttles forward and the boat accelerated to 20kts. After just 10 seconds he slowed the boat right down, put the engines into neutral and went aft.

Taking hold of the rope he dragged Rabbani to the stern and held him there while the Pakistani gasped for breath. Already his wrists were rubbed raw while his breathing was in painful, harsh gasps. Hunter said nothing, merely stood looking at him. Finally Rabbani looked up. The hatred in his eyes had been replaced by fear.

'Are you ready to talk? Because I can keep this up for as long as you like or until you die. Which is it to be?'

Rabbani nodded and then gasped out the word, 'Talk.'

Hunter pulled him over the stern and onto the deck. Rabbani lay still, gasping for breath. Hunter knelt down and cut the ropes around his legs. He stepped up onto the main deck and looked down.

'Get up and come here,' he ordered.

Rabbani wearily looked up, his face devoid of any reaction. He pushed himself up to his knees and then climbed to his feet. He tottered up the steps to the main deck.

'Sit.'

Rabbani sat on the deck and Hunter used a series of tie wraps to secure the man's right leg to a stanchion. Hunter went below and returned with a bottle of cold water. He thrust it at Rabbani. 'Here, drink this,' he said, unscrewing the top and shoving it into the other man's hands. Rabbani cupped the bottle between his hands, put it to his mouth and swallowed quickly, washing away the taste of the salt.

'You can stay here until you dry off. It shouldn't take long in this weather. You say you know nothing about Barzakh.'

Rabbani nodded.

'I want to hear you say it.'

'I know nothing I tell you.' There was some venom, a spark of resistance, in his tone.

Hunter believed him. He asked his next question, suddenly convinced that he already knew the answer. 'Who's your partner in Pakistan?'

Rabbani said nothing for nearly a minute, merely looked up at Hunter. Shrugging, Hunter said, 'Ashraf, it's entirely up to you. You can go back in the water or you can tell me what I want to know.

'General...General Khan.'

With that simple answer so much slotted into place. So much became obvious.

Taking his mobile from his pocket he speed dialled Macnair while going to the upper helm position, out of earshot. He stood at the stern bench looking down on Rabbani. The man was lying flat on the deck, his face to the sun, unmoving. 'General?'

'Commander. What's up?'

'I've been questioning Rabbani.'

'He talked without too much persuasion, I hope.'

'It wasn't a problem. He told me the name of his partner in Pakistan.'

'Who is it?'

'General Khan.'

Macnair was silent for a few seconds. 'Why am I not surprised? When you think about it, it makes sense. Everything fits when you have the name.'

'What are we going to do?'

'I've no answer right now. I'll need to give it some serious thought. A lot of thought.'

'What do you want me to do with Rabbani?'

'Ask him about the attack and then take him to the r/v. There's nothing else we can do short of shooting him. Let the Pakistanis deal with him.'

'It must have been Khan's lot who attacked the house. But why?'

'I suspect,' said Macnair, 'it was greed. Pure and simple.'

'You're probably right, but why? Being in the position he is in, Khan wants for nothing. Why put it all at risk? He is highly respected, even revered across much of Pakistan. According to what I've read about him he could easily be Pakistan's next President. Now with Rabbani out of the way...' Hunter fell silent.

'Nick? Are you there?'

'Sir, something's just occurred to me. What if Khan was making Rabbani a scapegoat, as well as taking his business away from him?'

'A scapegoat for what?'

'Barzakh.'

Macnair said nothing. Then, after a few seconds, he spoke. 'Would you care to elaborate?'

'Sir, what if Khan is the boss of Barzakh? What if he has some political objective in mind? Or what if he's an out and out Islamist?'

The questions were greeted with silence for a few seconds. Then, slowly, 'Anything is possible, I suppose.'

'Okay, sir, let me ask you this. Are there any rumours about a Taliban attack out of Afghanistan?'

'There are always rumours. The rumour mill keeps the allies

on their toes.'

'What if it's fed by Khan?'

'Then you know as well as I do that helps the Taliban. They are credited for events that have nothing to do with them. It makes for good propaganda. It also puts the fear of God into the villagers and townsfolk in the region. That gives the Taliban a stronger hold and ensures the obedience of the local population wherever the Taliban are operating.'

'Here's another idea. What if there's going to be an attack and the Pakistanis are led to believe it's to be at a different time and place? Their forces are deployed where they will do no good. The Taliban could have a significant victory which, as we know, adds to their credibility and strength. Another step, as far as they are concerned, to getting what they want and that is a substantial area to rule and control with impunity from retribution by government forces. We know that is part of their objective which they believe will lead to them creating a fundamentalist state in Pakistan.' Hunter paused and then added, 'Also, Khan can kill two birds with one stone. He has a credible scapegoat in the form of Rabbani who's arrested and killed, probably by a staged accident, or just disappears, while Khan takes over the organisation. The result of that is a large increase in the funds Khan wants and needs to finance Barzakh.'

'What that all boils down to is General Khan being an Islamic fundamentalist. Is that likely?'

'I don't know,' said Hunter.

'You could be right. I'll see what I can find on Khan. I'll get back to you.' Macnair broke the connection.

Hunter returned to his prisoner. 'Ashraf, how much does General Khan know about your operation?'

'What?' Rabbani glanced up from the deck with a bewildered look on his face.

'You heard. How much?'

'A lot. Not the details, of course. Just enough to keep him satisfied. I reported to him once a week by e-mail.'

33

RABBANI WAS SITTING on the deck, his knees bent up to his chest, his head hanging forward. 'Lay back and put your feet out straight this way.'

Rabbani looked bewildered.

'I'll untie them. You can walk to the cabin. Or I can drag you. Which would you prefer?'

Rabbani shoved his feet over and Hunter untied the knot.

'Now kneel and hold out your wrists.'

Rabbani did as he was told and held out his arms. Hunter untied the rope.

'Come on. Get up.'

Rabbani stayed where he was for a few seconds, his head bent, and his hands on the deck. He then pushed down, his arms straight but seemed too exhausted to move. Hunter looked on, saying nothing. After a few seconds he reached under his left arm and took out the Pocketlite. 'Ashraf, I wasn't born yesterday. Either you stand up or I'll put a bullet in you and throw you overboard.'

Rabbani scrambled to his feet and stood glaring at the other man.

'Now move it.'

Taking the couple of paces towards the main saloon, Rabbani stepped inside and went forward, flexing his fingers, getting the circulation moving. He paused outside the cabin door.

'Get in.' Hunter gestured with the pistol which he then slid into its holster.

Rabbani stepped over the coaming and turned to face Hunter. What came next was predictable. Rabbani took a swing at Hunter's head which Hunter easily blocked. It wasn't much of a swing and didn't pack much of a punch. Hunter hit Rabbani none too gently in the guts and as Rabbani bent over, gasping in agony, Hunter connected tie wraps to Rabbani's wrist and to the extra flexible steel wire rope.

'Don't be stupid again.'

'Who are you?' Rabbani gasped. 'What are you going to do with me?' The question was asked with real fear in his voice.

'I told you. I'm an independent contractor. What I am going to do with you is hand you over to some of your fellow compatriots. They will take you back to Pakistan to stand trial in accordance with the warrant that's about to be issued for your arrest. This way the appeals system is circumvented and you end up where you belong.'

Rabbani said nothing but slumped back against the bed. 'I don't understand. You know what I do. I am a criminal, I admit it, but I am not a terrorist. My business is in Europe. If I am to be arrested I should be put on trial here.'

'That's not going to happen. Not under any circumstances. Besides, it's too late for that.'

'I won't stand trial.'

'One thing I will tell you. President Zardarim assured the British Prime Minister that you will stand trial and if you are found guilty you will go to prison.'

'Yes, that is what he says. I have no doubt he believes it. It is what the British also want to believe will happen. I will lay odds that the President knows nothing about this operation. All he knows is that the legal option was taken and I died when being interrogated. Of course, that will all be a sham. Khan will want to keep me alive.'

'What for?'

'To wring every ounce of information about my business out of me as he can.

I may last a month. I doubt it will be any longer. Then I will really be dead.'

Hunter was about to say that Rabbani was wrong, when he thought better of it. Rabbani might have been a criminal, and a vile one at that, but he wasn't stupid. His organisation, built with ruthless efficiency, showed a keen mind and an ability to plan in detail. They stared at each other. Rabbani reached for a cigarette and with a shaking hand placed one between his lips and sucked the nicotine and tar deep down into his lungs. His hand stopped shaking.

'Why were you involved with Khan?'

Rabbani looked down at the deck and then raised his head. 'For my family. The good General has threatened my family. Not to arrest them. Not to kill them. But to hand them over to the Taliban with instructions to treat them especially badly. Can you imagine what that would be like?'

In truth, Hunter couldn't. Not really. His imagination couldn't sink that low. But he was aware that it would be dreadful beyond belief. The Taliban were well known for the way they treated their prisoners - especially women. Hunter nodded and then stepped out of the cabin, closing the door behind him.

'Sorry I'm late,' said Ogilvie. 'The sodding Underground was heaving.'

'There's coffee on the sideboard,' said Goldsmith, lifting his gold ringed cup and taking a mouthful.

Ogilvie helped himself, added milk and sugar and sat opposite the LibDem MP for Birmingham Yardley. He slowly stirred the mixture and smiled. 'We have them,' he said.

'Have who?'

'TIFAT. Macnair and the rest of the murdering swine.'

'What are you talking about?'

'You know about the attack at Southminster?' Ogilvie asked.

'Some. The news reports are saying it was a criminal gang affair. Thieves falling out and all that sort of thing.'

Ogilvie snorted. 'Huh, hardly. I have it on good authority that there are twenty dead and that Macnair's people were involved.'

The Conservative MP for Warwickshire North sat up and placed his cup in its saucer. Ogilvie could see the excitement in the other man's eyes. 'You're sure?'

'As sure as I am sitting here.'

'Where did you get this from?'

'One of my contacts at SO19.'

'Who?'

'Never mind who.' He waved his hand in front of his face as though swatting away a fly. 'Just rest assured I have had it on very good authority.'

'What do you want to do?'

'This is the golden opportunity we've been waiting for. If we get witnesses in front of our committee they'll have to tell the truth.'

'Nobody from TIFAT will show. You can be sure of that.'

'But that's the point, don't you see?' said Ogilvie. 'We don't need them. I was also told that Elspeth Coolidge was there. We can get that bitch as well. We'll force her to testify. If TIFAT was involved she won't be able to hide it. She'll have to come clean. We can force the issue at long last and have the lot of them arrested, tried and sent to prison for the rest of their lives.'

'Wait a moment, how can we be certain that TIFAT had anything to do with the attack?'

Ogilvie looked bewildered and then shook his head. 'Of course they're involved. The whole rotten rats' nest of them, led by that murderer Macnair.'

'Frederick, be careful with the rhetoric. You can't go round making assertions like that without definitive proof. You're a barrister. You know better than anyone what the burden of proof means. Before we do anything we will need a cast iron case to take to Harrow and Parker. Then we need to make the two of them acknowledge the facts and then take it to the Intelligence and Security Committee. Harrow and Parker won't admit to anything. They'll disagree. They'll argue. They'll lie!'

Ogilvie was outraged. 'They won't dare. Parker is a high court judge for God's sake. He has to tell the truth. He has no choice.'

'Frederick, it's because of his views and the fact that he is a judge is why he's on our committee. He believes TIFAT is needed in the war against terrorism. That's the way he sees it along with the rest of the Neanderthals in Parliament, the media and amongst the general public. It takes truly enlightened men and women like us, with the intelligence to see right from wrong, to understand what we need to save civilisation. We who have the moral fibre and courage to stand up for what's right. Otherwise we will regress to a barbaric age we thought was long past.'

'You don't need to lecture me, Nigel. I agree with you. Somehow we need to turn the attack at the house to our advantage. If we can force the issue, then the ISC will have to investigate and we can effectively start the ball rolling. We'll get rid of TIFAT yet.'

Goldsmith shook his head. 'It won't be that easy. In fact, I don't think it will be possible.'

'What if we leak the information to the press? Let them do our work for us.'

'Frederick, you know as well as I do that TIFAT are the blue-eyed boys on the block. As far as the general population is concerned, they can do no wrong. The bigger consideration is the crime we will be committing if we do leak the information. The official secrets act and all that.'

'Huh,' Ogilvie replied, 'they wouldn't dare.'

'Don't be so sure. I for one am not going to risk it.'

Ogilvie managed to keep the contempt on his face from showing by looking down and turning the cup round and round in its saucer. Why was it he felt so alone when it came to battles like this? Was he the only person to see it? He knew the only way to force the issue was via the press. However, for all his bravado, the official secrets act did, in reality, scare him.

It was like a bolt from the blue. The more he thought about it the more excited he became. He could do precisely what he wanted on two fronts while simultaneously coming out of it in a reasonable and statesmanlike way.

'Leave it to me, Nigel; I know precisely what to do.' He looked at his watch. 'I'd better get home. I have a lot of work to do.'

'What are you planning?'

'Never you mind. What you don't know can't hurt you. Just be assured that we'll get what we want. Starting with public opinion.'

General Khan arrived at Heathrow on a Pakistan International Airlines flight at terminal 3. He was travelling light so did not have to wait for luggage. Outside, he stood in the warmth of the evening sun. It was a pleasant, dry heat, not like the weather in Pakistan. There it was 38 degrees centigrade and the humidity sufficient to make you sweat as though you were standing under a shower.

It took about 15 minutes for three other men to join him. One waved some paperwork in his hand. The three men could have been mistaken for brothers. With black hair, swarthy complexions, moustaches, slim, average height, there was no questioning their ethnicity. They wore crumpled black suits with waistcoats and continuously looked around, assessing people, dismissing them as potential threats, noting the number of two-man, armed police patrols who in turn were taking notice of them.

'Sir, I went to Avis. It had the shortest queue.'

'Good.' The General said nothing more. He wasn't in a good mood. He hadn't slept on the plane even though he'd had three large brandies after his dinner. The men with him had been instructed not to drink any alcohol.

'Sir,' said one of the others, we should go. Two police officers are looking our way.'

The General turned to one of the men. 'You know what you must do.'

'Yes, sir. I have the photographs. I will deal with both of them.' He lifted his hand in a half salute and remembered where he was just in time. He nodded his back ramrod stiff. He couldn't help himself. General Khan instilled loyalty liberally sprinkled with a dose of fear. With his small suitcase clutched in his left hand, the man headed towards the Underground.

'Let's go,' said Khan, to the others.

Outside, they found the shuttle bus to the Avis compound. The road was jam packed and it took nearly 20 minutes to get there much to the General's annoyance and frustration.

From their arrival to being in an Audi A4 had taken over an hour and a half.

'Have you found a place?' The General looked at the man sitting beside the driver. The man had spent the last 20 minutes on his mobile and had just broken the connection.

'Yes, sir. A Travelodge near Exeter. It is at the Moto Service Area. We should be there by twenty-one thirty or thereabouts.'

'Good.' The General settled back in his seat, yawned and closed his eyes. 'Now, I think I will try and have a sleep.'

The two men said nothing. They didn't even exchange knowing glances. When it came to dealing with the General they were punctilious to a fault. Prudence was always the watchword.

All good things came to an end. In this case it was the weather. Hunter had adjusted the Talisman's speed to arrive at Portland at 08.00. The autopilot was set, the boat was travelling at a comfortable 20kts and he was asleep in the saloon. At about 03.15 a chop started, a swell and a few gentle waves swept under the keel from the west. Lightning flashed across the sky like a bolt from heaven followed seconds later by a thunderous crash which brought Hunter wide awake.

He'd been expecting a storm and so had foul weather gear ready. He went forward into the comfort and safety of the lower helm position.

He checked the radar. There were a couple of contacts but they were passing clear. Next, he checked his position. The Talisman was on track, on course and on time. She began to roll a few degrees more. He heard a banging behind him and realised it was Rabbani wanting attention.

As he went through the galley, Hunter slipped a mug under the nozzle of the coffee making machine and pressed the requisite buttons.

Rabbani had a light on.

'What do you want?'

Rabbani was groaning. 'I need a bucket. I feel sick.' He gagged, heaved and looked close to throwing up.

'Wait a minute and don't puke.' Hunter collected a plastic bowl from the galley and the knockout drug from his bag. He returned to the cabin, crossed to Rabbani and held the bowl out to him. As Rabbani grabbed it, Hunter jabbed the needle into Rabbani's upper arm and pressed the plunger. Rabbani looked at him in surprise, opened his mouth to speak, closed his eyes and fell back, unconscious.

Hunter returned to the galley, lifted his mug of coffee, added milk and went for'ard to the helm position. He stifled a yawn. In the old days, he would have needed an almanac to check the time of sunrise. Like everything else, all that was required was the press of a few buttons. Sunrise was at 03.46 GMT. Just then it was 03.52 BST – British Summer Time.

There came another bolt of lightning, turning the pitch dark into a bright yellow seascape followed by a roll of thunder that lasted a minute or more. The waves had turned to white caps and had shifted slightly to be coming from the port quarter. Although the sea was rougher than it had been earlier, the boat wasn't rocking so much.

The day was getting lighter. There was thunder but it was receding as the storm passed, drifting further up the Channel.

The water was choppier than ever, but still not uncomfortable. The rain stopped just as the first rays of sunshine appeared on the horizon.

The shipping forecast said it was going to be a fine day with temperatures in the mid twenties and a light wind from the east.

34

AT 5 KNOTS the Talisman entered Portland harbour. Hunter crossed to the docks where the fuel pumps were located and adroitly placed the boat starboard side to.

'Morning,' he greeted the young man standing at the water's edge.

'Morning. You want her filled?'

'Please. Here, catch.' Hunter threw the bow rope which the youth snatched from the air and then quickly wrapped around a cleat. Hunter went aft. He picked up the stern rope and stepped ashore. He swayed for a second as his balance readjusted to the lack of motion and then secured the rope to a second cleat. He stepped back into the stern well and lifted up the seat covers. Underneath were the filling points for the diesel. He unscrewed the port cap and then the starboard.

'To the gunnels, please. Need a hand?'

'No. That's okay. Do you want any water?' The youth lifted down a nozzle, flicked a switch and stepped onboard. He placed the nozzle in the port tank and clipped it open. The sound and stench of the diesel permeated the air.

'May as well. The water tanks are up forward.'

The young attendant went back ashore, took a second nozzle from the other side of the pump and repeated the action, now filling the starboard tank.

Hunter had sussed-out the small shop on the other side of the security gate. 'I'm going for some supplies. I won't be long.'

'No hurry.'

'Thanks.' Hunter went ashore and wandered along the pontoon.

The shop was a mini-market and he filled a basket with fresh fruit, milk, fresh bread, orange juice, eggs and a packet of bacon.

He returned to the Talisman. 'How's it going?'

'Won't be long.'

Hunter glanced at the pump display. He wasn't surprised to see that it was reading over £200 already.

'I've done the water.'

'Thanks.'

First the port and then the starboard nozzles clicked closed. The attendant shook the nozzles free of any diesel and leapt ashore, replacing them each side of the pump.

He read the price from the display. Hunter handed over Rabbani's cash and added £20 as a tip. The youth broke into a wide grin. 'Gosh. Thanks. Thanks very much.'

'That's okay. Just as long as you waste it,' Hunter grinned back.

The youth said thanks again and walked along the pontoon. He sat down on the deckchair next to the gate, picked up a book and began to read.

Hunter went below, unpacked the groceries, poured himself a glass of orange juice and began cooking the bacon. There was no doubt that waking up at zero crack sparrow fart, as the navy called the early hours, gave you an appetite.

He left the bacon to cook on low heat, poured cereal into a bowl, added milk and went up top. He sat in the helmsman's chair, propped his feet up and contentedly looked around the harbour. Portland and Weymouth were places he knew well from his Royal Navy days. It held many happy memories.

He finished eating the cereal, stood up and went below. The bacon was turning crispy, the way he liked it. He dropped two slices of bread in the toaster and cracked two eggs into the frying pan. The toast popped, he placed them on a plate, slid each egg, sunny-side up, onto the toast, added the bacon and, balancing the plate in one hand and another mug of coffee in the other, went back up top and resumed his position. He rubbed his sternum. A few inches higher - but for the grace of God, he thought. He finished eating his breakfast.

He flashed up the engines, waited while they warmed through, and then removed the head and stern ropes. The wind was a fresh, gentle breeze from the west and it promised to be a pleasant day. He manoeuvred the boat away from the pontoon and turned the Talisman around.

General Khan and his entourage were just finishing their breakfast at the motor services. There was little conversation.

The General never encouraged talk with his underlings. He saw no reason for it.

They left the restaurant and climbed into the car. The fuel tank had been filled when they'd arrived so there was nothing to delay their departure. They hit the road a few minutes before 08.00. The day was fine, a freshness permeating the air after the storm of the night before. The sun was bright and the temperature was climbing steadily. It was a day to be at your destination, not travelling towards it.

They by-passed Exeter, reached the end of the M5 which metamorphosed into the A38. Although relatively busy, they made good progress for about the next 10 miles. The traffic built up steadily as holiday makers headed for the coast and then disaster struck. A caravan overturned a few miles ahead and all traffic ground to a halt.

After the best part of an hour the traffic began to move slowly. It was another forty-five minutes before they came to the diversion set up by the police. They were directed towards Newton Abbot and just as they hit the town, they turned onto the A383 back towards the A38. Finally, they were back on the dual carriageway and driving at the comparatively reasonable speed of 45mph.

On the outskirts of Plymouth a sign showed them the way to the airport. It was only 10 miles. It took them the best part of fifty minutes.

The helicopter was parked in the nearest of the three grass landing circles close to the runway, a few hundred metres from the terminal building.

They had returned the car to the Avis officer at Plymbridge Lane. Although they were offered a lift to the terminal building which was close by, the General declined. The walk enabled him to stretch his legs after being cooped up in the back of the car.

Walking into the terminal, they were spotted by the pilot who came nervously across to them. He drew himself up and began to throw a salute when the General hissed at him. 'Stop it, you fool. Do you want to draw attention to us? Idiot! Let's go!'

'Yes, General. I mean no, General. I mean...I...'

'Shut up and get us out to the ship.'

The pilot led the way to the helicopter and fussed about while he got his passengers seated and secured.

A flight plan back to the ship had already been filed and once the pilot had completed his pre-flight checks permission was obtained from Air Traffic Control to start the engine. Simultaneously, the aircraft marshaller standing in front of the helo raised his left arm until his hand was at head height with one finger pointing skywards. With his right hand he made circular motions from his waist to his head. The signal was a repeat instruction to the pilot to start the engine.

The marshaller then held his arms horizontally sideways and the helo went into the hover. As it did, the marshaller turned the palms of his hands up and raised them to meet above his head. He repeated the process as the helicopter lifted gracefully into the air while turning to port and heading out to sea. The helo's maximum cruising speed was 103kt, the Pashni was 60nm to the south-west. The General was in a hurry. Flying time was less than 40 minutes.

The helo's soundproofing wasn't of the best and even with earphones on, it was still noisy with a continuous shudder passing through the seats. They levelled off at 5,000ft. with its nose angled forward. The view was panoramic and breathtaking.

Merchant ships didn't carry helicopters. The Pashni was an exception. Smuggling arms and people was made easier using the helo. However, with the British, it was even easier to use container ships because they didn't berth in the UK. They went to other European countries where customs and excise weren't so vigilant. Once on land anywhere in the EU the goods could easily be transported to any destination. The General looked down at the water rushing beneath. False passports were easily obtained. Dealing in fake European Union passports was already a major industry. Not only was the business an important profit making centre for many criminals, particularly from Eastern Europe, but it was also a way of flooding Islamists into the West. A double success that gave the General a great deal of satisfaction. The British were fools. An island nation that could and should defend its borders had opened the doors, and windows, he thought, to criminals and terrorists from all over the world. It was a failing he was already taking advantage of and one he would be exploiting to the maximum.

The pilot said, 'There's the Pashni, sir.'

The helicopter moved steadily towards the bow of the ship, gradually losing height. Once alongside, the pilot adjusted their speed to parallel the vessel and hover just above the deck. He received instructions over the radio while simultaneously being waved on by a man holding two batons like table tennis racquets. He moved the helicopter sideways until they were centred above the landing space. The man held his arms out and then dropped them straight down. The helo landed with barely a bump on the specially reinforced loading hatch in the middle of the ship. Later, the hatch would be hydraulically operated and the helo taken down into the bowels of the ship and away from prying eyes.

The General climbed down onto the deck followed by the other two while the pilot carried out his post landing checks. The three men hurried forward, away from the rotor blades and the engine noise.

'General Khan,' the Master of the ship greeted his illustrious guest, pulling himself up straight while throwing a salute. Although it looked ludicrous for a man with such a heavy gut and a hat cocked to one side to make such a gesture the General didn't notice. The salute was expected.

The group of men moved aft towards the living quarters and the ship's bridge. They stepped through a door in the superstructure and into a lift that took them the 20m or so to the top deck.

On the starboard side of the bridge was the Master's chair which the General commandeered.

The Master stood nervously next to it. 'Would you like a tea or coffee? Something to eat?'

'Coffee will be enough.'

The Master passed the order to a Filipino steward who was waiting in the background. The man rushed below.

35

WHEN HE CHECKED on Rabbani, Hunter found he was still unconscious. He guessed it was due to Rabbani having some residue of the drug from the first shot. Whatever the reason, it meant a quiet life, which suited him admirably.

His mobile rang. 'Yes, sir?'

'I have the co-ordinates of the ship's position, along with her course and speed.' He gave Hunter the information. 'Any idea how long before you get there?'

'Wait a second, sir.' Loading the Pashni's position into the navigation system, along with her course and speed, he looked at the readout. 'Eighty-six miles so about two and a half hours. Is there anything else?'

'The girl whose mobile we're tracking has made two calls. In each case she said Monday at noon. That was all.'

'Do you think the target is Heathrow?'

'Yes,' was the stark reply.

'What's going to happen?'

'We aren't sure. There's nothing more we can do at the moment. Although the idea of shutting the airport is appealing, it's a damned sight more difficult to do than to say.'

Hunter knew about the dozens of exercises involving the mass evacuation of Heathrow as well as every other airport in the UK. The problem was it had only been from an official's viewpoint and what was expected of the staff. For obvious reasons, the general public had never been involved. Even those exercises had been with a seriously restricted number of personnel.

While they were talking, Hunter altered course to starboard and passed down the side of a large merchant ship travelling up Channel. As soon as he was astern of her, he set the autopilot, dialled in a new heading and adjusted the speed to 30kts. 'There must be something we can do.'

'I spoke to Five. She's having a meeting with the Prime Minister and some of his cabinet this afternoon. It'll be his decision as to what they do about Heathrow.'

'And the Underground?' Hunter asked.

'We just don't know. If we shut down the Underground how long do we do it for?'

'I take it neither Five or Six have come up with anything of any use?'

'Not a lot,' said the General, 'but it's not for the want of trying. On the international side, Six are pretty certain there's going to be a major attack by Muslim fundamentalists in the next couple of months. In the meantime, here in the UK, dozens of people have been rounded up and taken to detention centres for interrogation. The press are catching on and we're expecting the proverbial to hit the fan in the next forty-eight hours. Probably less.'

'If it does?'

'Then your guess is as good as mine.'

'Prime Minister,' Elspeth nodded her head as she entered Cabinet Office Briefing Room Alpha, or COBRA, at the appointed hour of 13.00. So much for lunch, but then the last few days had meant food and drink on the run.

'Ah, Elspeth, do come in and take a seat. I think you know everybody.'

Elspeth nodded. There were fewer people than she'd been expecting. In fact, far fewer. Walking to the seat indicated she said, 'Good afternoon, Chancellor, Home Secretary, Foreign Secretary.'

Although she was facing such an august body, Elspeth wasn't intimidated. 'Why so few of the Cabinet?' She asked as she pulled out the chair next to Janice Clitheroe, the Foreign Secretary and faced Morris Samuels, the Home Secretary, and Douglas Bell, the Chancellor of the Exchequer.

David Canton, the Prime Minister, though expecting the question, looked slightly uneasy when he replied, 'We must keep the lid on this. It's imperative nothing gets out. There'll be a level of panic that just doesn't bear thinking about.'

'You'll get no argument from me, sir,' said Elspeth. 'But with all due respect,' a phrase used when respect was the last thing on the speaker's mind, 'that still doesn't answer my question.'

She was aware that she was perilously close to overstepping the fragile boundaries between herself and her political masters, but fatigue was taking its toll.

The Prime Minister waved his hand and said, 'If the complete cabinet was here, half-an-hour after we adjourned the whole of the press would know what was happening.'

'You do them a disservice. Most of them are more efficient than that. I would say ten, perhaps fifteen minutes at the most.' Janice Clitheroe had the ghost of a smile. In her early fifties, she was one of the most intelligent and talented people in government. Coupled with her diplomatic manner and an ability to make anyone she met feel like a friend, she was ideal as Foreign Secretary. A slim, attractive blonde, she was happily married with two children and was loved by the press. This was especially true of the newspapers that liked stirring up mischief, normally along the lines of asking when she would be taking over as Prime Minister.

As always, Janice was dressed in a smart trouser suit, today a gray one, with a fetching dark blue blouse. Elspeth felt dowdy by comparison but, she reminded herself, she hadn't been to bed for the best part of 48 hours and had only managed to get home and change into her black skirt and white blouse in time to make the meeting.

Mentally, she shook herself. She had far more important things to think about than how she was looking.

The Prime Minister sat at the head of the table. Being a Saturday afternoon, he was dressed casually in a green cotton, short-sleeved shirt and dark gray trousers. He appeared as youthful as ever. Elspeth knew that the man never bothered himself with detail, nor worried about what was really happening in the world. As far as she could ascertain, he wanted to be PM so that his name would go down in history. After all, he was rich enough, even if the money was his wife's. Politics had always been a game to him and as a result of not taking it seriously he had sailed through the ranks of the Conservative Party. He had been in politics since leaving university, first as a researcher and then, following the 2001 general election, as a backbencher. A Daily Telegraph reporter said of him, "I wouldn't trust him with my daughter's pocket money", and a Sun reporter wrote, "He is a poisonous, slippery individual." To date, very few people who knew him disagreed with either statement.

'Elspeth, may I offer you a coffee?' The Home Secretary was leaning forward in his chair, his tie, as was so often the case, slightly askew. He had a genuine smile of welcome as he pointed a finger at the coffee machine at the end of the table.

'Thank you, Morris. I'll get it.' She made to push back her chair and offer a cup to anyone else when Janice Clitheroe intervened.

'No, you stay where you are, Elspeth. From what we've heard you haven't stopped in the last three days. I'll get it.'

'Why, thank you, Janice. Thank you very much.' There was a genuine warmth between the two women which under different circumstances could have easily blossomed into friendship. However, with the stresses and strains involved with both of their jobs, that hadn't happened.

'How do you take it?'

'Black, two sugars.'

'Anyone else?'

The others shook their heads.

The CVs of the others flickered through her mind. The Home Secretary leant back in his chair. In his late fifties, he was the oldest person at the table. Divorced with two grown-up children, it was rumoured that he and his ex-wife were getting on so well together that there was talk of reconciliation. He was tall, slim, with brown hair going gray. His accent was Welsh valleys, and his education Pontypridd Grammar School followed by Cardiff University where he had read electronic engineering. He had started his own business manufacturing mobile phones, which he sold to a Chinese company at the start of the new millennium. He'd pocketed ten million pounds and went into politics, eventually getting himself the safe seat of Witney. Morris Williams went through life as though he enjoyed every minute of it, irrespective of what it brought to his door. Which was why he was both highly respected and liked. A combination that made the Prime Minister very jittery.

Of the three senior politicians, she knew that the PM trusted only the Chancellor. It was well known that he wanted rid of Janice Clitheroe, but that was something Elspeth knew would be difficult for him to justify. What was worse, from the Prime

Minister's point of view, without the Chancellor's support, it was probably impossible. But the rumour was the Chancellor wouldn't do it. No explanation. Just no. Not a good idea. Or words to that effect. Elspeth knew the Prime Minister was reasonably astute and must have been beginning to wonder who was pulling Bell's chain. He would never know it was her. Neither would Janice. It was a secret between Elspeth and the Chancellor.

Elspeth kept the hostility she felt towards Bell masked behind a straight face. She picked up her coffee cup and took a sip, glancing towards the man. His hatred of her was almost palpable. 'What we know and what we believe are, frankly, far apart. That is nearly always the situation with intelligence matters.'

'Yes, yes,' the Prime Minister interrupted testily, 'we don't need the homily. Get on with it.'

Elspeth took another sip of coffee. She was surprised. Normally, the PM was indifferent to the problems that surrounded him. He let others take the strain and, more significantly, the blame in the event of anything going wrong. She replaced her coffee cup and thought wearily it would be a long meeting.

36

ELSPETH PURSED HER lips and opened the buff coloured file with the red cross extending from corner to corner. The action enabled her to get her emotions under control. She had to acknowledge to herself how very tired she was feeling. Her eyes felt gritty, her brain not firing on all cylinders. Power up, she told herself, a trick she had learnt from previous stressful and demanding occasions. But then, she acknowledged, most things that landed on her desk were precisely that - stressful and demanding.

'I will not bother you with the details of how we acquired the information I am about to divulge. However, I will say we are fairly confident of its accuracy.' She looked from the PM to the other four. 'Two days ago, we changed the Bikini state to Red. I know the Prime Minister and the Home Secretary were aware of the fact, but what about you Chancellor and you Foreign Secretary?'

'I didn't know,' said the Chancellor, petulance in his thin and reedy voice.

'I knew,' said Janice Clitheroe. 'Morris and I discussed it yesterday. I'd assumed it wasn't just an exercise.'

'You're right. It's far from that,' said Elspeth. 'Sorry, Chancellor, you wanted to say something?'

'Em, no. No. Do carry on.'

Elspeth was fairly certain that what he wanted to say was what in hell is Bikini Red? If he kept his mouth shut he might find out.

'For those of you who may not be certain and, I don't mean this in any patronising way whatsoever, Bikini State Red means we have information about a terrorist attack on a specific target. In this case there are two. One is Heathrow. The other is the Underground.'

There were exclamations of shock from the Foreign Secretary and the Chancellor. The Home Secretary and the Prime Minister had been briefed on an ongoing basis, in case decisions needed to be taken quickly.

'We are fairly certain that the Heathrow attack is due Monday at twelve noon. We can't be sure about the Underground or where it is going to be.'

'What sort of attack. Do we know the details?' Janice Clitheroe asked.

Elspeth shook her head. 'We don't know. Automatic weapons? Suicide bombers? Parcels or suitcases left unattended?' She shook her head. 'We just don't know.'

'That's a fat lot of use,' the Chancellor snorted. 'What are we supposed to do? Close the airport? Close the Underground?' Both questions were asked with derision in his voice.

'As things stand at the moment, that is one course of action we could take,' said Five.

'That's ludicrous,' the Chancellor's voice dripped disdain. 'The cost to the economy would be huge. Huge,' he repeated.

'Considering our current fiscal deficit I don't see that it matters,' said the Home Secretary.

As always, the Prime Minister said very little. Elspeth knew he liked to listen and watch as the other members of his cabinet argued and pontificated before stepping in. Usually it was to call the meeting to an end with no decision taken and allow events to take their course until he had no choice other than to decide one way or another. She guessed it was a strategy he would be following that day. Just in case fingers had to be pointed if the wrong decisions were made. He was as unlike certain Prime Ministers as chalk from cheese. She had read Margaret Thatcher's autobiography. She may not have made all the right decisions, but by God, she made them and wasn't afraid to do so.

The Chancellor didn't reply to the Home Secretary. Instead, he sighed and said to them all, looking around the table, 'Stopping the Underground is...well...it's unthinkable.'

Perversely, Elspeth had enjoyed suggesting closure as one option but knew it was unrealistic. 'I agree with the Chancellor, though not for the same reasons.'

'What reasons?' Samuels asked, though Elspeth suspected he already knew the answer.

'It's pointless. If we shutdown the airport or the Underground, then the terrorists need only postpone what they intend doing and come back another day.'

The FS nodded. 'So we need to keep them open in the hope of catching the perpetrators before they can do whatever it is they're planning.'

Elspeth glanced at her and then looked at the three men before replying. 'That's it in a nutshell. An explosion on the Underground will affect only a section of the network and a relatively small one at that. There will be some deaths and a lot of injuries. A bomb exploding at Heathrow will equally result in death and injuries, some destruction but a large part of the airport will either continue to run or very quickly be back in operation. All that will be needed is to shut down the terminal where the explosion occurs. Economic loss will be at a minimum compared to shutting the whole of Heathrow. In essence, we let events take their course.'

'You are very cavalier,' said Bell, 'with other people's lives.'

Elspeth wanted to retort that she dealt with life and death situations on a regular basis. Instead, she kept her peace and hid her frustration.

'What do you mean by letting events take their course?' asked the Foreign Secretary.

Elspeth shrugged. 'We shut the airport and the Underground and these people will attack another day. How long could both places be out of use? One day would be a financial problem, to say the least; two days would be a disaster. Bikini Red means that we have knowledge of a specific target. However, in this case, I have issued the warning on a country wide basis with over twenty potential targets named. The actual targets are known only to a very select few.'

'Why?' asked the Chancellor. 'Surely all personnel involved should know the details.'

It was a stupid question under the circumstances and the other politicians in the room exchanged glances. Elspeth wondered how an idiot like Bell became Chancellor of the Exchequer.

'If too many people know what is really happening then the information will, I can assure you, get out. A leak to a newspaper for cash or a member of staff having family and friends at the airport. What would you do?' She looked pointedly at Bell. 'I can honestly say that I would warn family and friends and anyone saying differently is lying.' She had decided not to mince her words. No niceties of language. She was fed up to her back teeth having to deal with idiotic politicians.

It was Canton who asked, 'So what do you think we should do?'

'At present, the actual targets are known to very few. The extra police patrols at Heathrow are replicated at the other airports so that the whole thing is seen more as an exercise than anything. If we get firmer intelligence we can reassess the situation then. So for now we sit on our hands.'

'What sort of further intelligence?' asked the PM.

'I don't know. Leave it to me to act on it should we learn anything new.'

'I've never heard anything so preposterous.' There was indignation in Bell's voice.

Elspeth frowned and looked at the man. 'What do you mean?'

'What I mean...' he floundered and said again, 'What I mean is that we cannot close the Underground, nor Heathrow, but we can't put passengers lives at risk to...to catch these people.'

'What do you suggest?' Samuels asked. There was real puzzlement in his Welsh brogue.

'Well...Well...I suggest the security forces do their job and stop these people. Find them,' his voice grew stronger and more confident, 'arrest them and bring them to trial. Yes,' he nodded. 'that's the thing to do.'

'What,' Elspeth asked in a soft voice, 'do you think we're doing? We have every officer available working on the problem. People are being called back from leave even as we speak. Even those who are off sick are coming in to man desks and computers.'

The Chancellor was too thick skinned to look particularly put out. He said, 'Well, all I'm saying is that more has to be done to ensure lives are not put at risk.' He then said what Elspeth was sure they were all thinking. 'The political repercussions could be devastating. Devastating.'

It was Janice Clitheroe, her voice dripping with contempt who said, 'Political repercussions are not relevant. The lives of innocent people is paramount. We have no choice other than to go along with the recommendations made by the security services.'

The Prime Minister spoke. 'Douglas, we have to take all the advice we can before we decide what is best. On the one hand I agree with Elspeth, but on the other, I don't like it either. The thought of putting innocent lives at risk fills me with great horror.'

More like the effect it would have on votes, thought Elspeth, keeping her face straight. Her job was tough, she often thought, and dealing with politicians was the toughest part. Except for a few. People like Janice Clitheroe and Morris Samuels for instance.

Samuels said, 'If we did close both the Underground and Heathrow for say twenty-four hours, we'd probably delay the attacks and you would have more time to find them.'

'I'm sorry, but you aren't going to like the answer I am about to give. It's a politician's answer,' said Five.

'What's that?' The Chancellor asked in a waspish tone.

'Yes and no.'

'What do you mean by that?' asked Bell.

'We are doing everything in our power to find these people. The difficulty is, the longer we take there is more likelihood that the press will find out what's happening. As well as that, there is serious unrest building up in the Muslim communities. Which, under the circumstances, is something we can't blame them for. The raids that are taking place are already being reported. It's only dribs and drabs at present but that's going to escalate rapidly. Questions are beginning to be asked. Why are we carrying them out, who are we looking for and what is going on? Press involvement is escalating and will soon be out of control. So far we've kept a lid on things. But the fact is, we could easily have an explosion of riots across the country with serious, long term consequences.'

The implications were clear to all of them. She might not have liked the Chancellor or the PM but she knew that they were both relatively astute when it came to political matters.

The Prime Minister actually shuddered. Elspeth recognised it was a reflex action. However, she was sure he wasn't thinking about the public and the prospect of deaths and injuries, but for himself and his political future.

'Of course, there's something else.' The enormous stress she was under, coupled with a lack of sleep, made her sound tired, which she was. Very tired. But it went with the job. Never in its history had MI5 been so busy and so stretched. Financial cuts made her feel as though she was fighting with one hand tied behind her back. That, coupled with the Court of Human Rights in Strasbourg, or the Court of Human Wrongs as she often thought of it, made her job near impossible. But one thing she acknowledged about herself, and that was she was a bloody minded sod who would never give up.

The FS asked, 'What is it?'

'Right now, we know the targets. What if they change them? What if they have a contingency plan, worked out to the last detail, just in case we did find out what they were intending to do?'

Samuels nodded. 'It's a fair point.'

The Prime Minister added, 'So what then?'

'Operation Mosaic is already underway.'

The Chancellor interrupted her. 'What's Operation Mosaic?'

Elspeth didn't need to answer. Morris Samuels did it for her.

'For God's sake, Douglas, have you no idea what's going on? Don't you read the information you're given? Don't you listen? We were all briefed on Operation Mosaic when we came to office. We were told the trigger points that would automatically set the whole operation going so that there would be no dithering by us. No hesitation. No arguing over the politics. Just a need to move fast to save peoples' lives. It happened in this room. Elspeth,' he nodded at Five, 'was here along with senior management from SIS.'

'Oh, yes,' the Chancellor nodded slowly, 'I remember now.'

To Elspeth it was evident the man didn't remember. She glanced at the others. She didn't think they did either. She experienced some heart-burn. If she wasn't careful she'd be getting an ulcer.

'For the sake of clarification, let me spell it out.' She paused marshalling her thoughts. 'As you know we have over two thousand individuals on our radar. Either we believe them to be active supporters of Islamic fundamentalists or they are passive supporters. These are the people who help to raise funds, write letters to the newspapers and put out blogs on Facebook and Twitter extolling the Muslim way of life while denouncing the West. It's mainly rhetoric that strikes home with a lot of people, especially when they go on about segregation in schools, homosexuality and education for girls. Gay marriages have a lot of people incensed, particularly in the Muslim communities but also, as we know, amongst Christians and even amongst agnostics and atheists. So that issue isn't all one way.'

The Home Secretary said, 'I believe that the hard-core of Islamic fundamentalists who wish us harm, blaming us for the problems in Muslim countries, are far fewer than that.'

Elspeth nodded. She knew that Samuels was aware of the facts. He had mastered his brief when he came to office and had stayed on top of it ever since. 'When it comes to those figures there is, of course, good news and bad news.'

'Give us the good news first,' said Janice Clitheroe.

'Those who we think would be prepared to commit a crime in the name of Islam, and by that I mean setting off bombs or killing individuals, is less than a hundred.'

The PM shook his head and looked at the Home Secretary. 'Why don't we deport them?'

'I'll answer the first part,' said Elspeth. 'It's because half of them are British citizens. Born and brought up in the UK but subsequently radicalised, often by the Imams.'

'And the second part?' asked the Prime Minister, looking at the Home Secretary.

Elspeth despaired as she listened to the political leader of the United Kingdom asking such a ludicrous question.

'It's because of the Court of Human Rights in Strasbourg,' said Morris Samuels. 'We cannot deport known terrorists, those inciting violence in *our* country, nor known criminals who have committed horrendous crimes back in their own countries. David, you know all this. So why ask?'

'I am just clarifying one or two things, that's all. Something should be done about it.'

'You know what we need to do. And I've been telling you for years. Along with many other members of the party. We get out of Europe, control our own borders and tell the Court of Human Rights to go and stuff itself.' There was real anger in Janice Clitheroe's voice.

'That won't happen under my watch,' said the Prime Minister, in the sanctimonious voice Elspeth had come to detest.

'In that case,' said Five, 'we have no choice but to fight with both hands tied behind our backs.'

'And both feet tied together,' said Samuels.

'Yes, yes,' said the PM, 'let's move on. So what are we doing?'

'Operation Mosaic is in full swing. We are moving as fast and hard as we can. We have also called in MI6.'

Douglas Bell interrupted. 'They do not operate within our national borders,' he said in his censorious tone of voice, as though he was announcing some new and important fact.

The FS answered, her anger barely contained. 'For crying out loud, just shut up, will you? You've been told that when Operation Mosaic kicks in all SIS personnel are mobilised. Irrespective of their mandate. What's more, if push comes to shove then the army will also be used.'

The Prime Minister blanched. 'We daren't have the army on the streets of Britain. It will be political suicide.'

Morris Samuels said, 'The only people who would be used are military police and they won't be in uniform. At present we have no need of them but that can change if things escalate.' He looked at Elspeth. 'Is that likely?'

She shrugged. 'We've no way of telling. The longer it goes on the worse it will be. There is no doubt the tension will escalate and the propensity for violence will increase dramatically. We're hoping to keep a lid on things by arresting the known trouble makers and holding them incommunicado until this whole thing blows over.'

'How long will that be?' asked Douglas Bell, trying to sound reasonable.

'We've no way of telling. At least, not for sure. We have played out this scenario on numerous occasions and we've examined it from every angle. Two things will defuse the situation in the immediate term, though not in the long term. The first is the bombs go off, people are killed and injured, we clean up, blame a few radicals, make it clear the majority of Muslims in this country are decent and law abiding and we move on with our lives. That is, except for the families of those killed and the injured themselves.'

'And the other?' asked the PM.

'We stop the whole thing in its tracks. That's the best outcome, obviously.'

'What can we do?' asked Canton.

'Continue what we're doing. We've no choice. I've told you, we are raiding every house we have on our radar looking for the smallest clue to help us identify the terrorists. The airport is saturated with armed officers patrolling the public areas as well as glued to the surveillance monitors. In the airports and on the Underground, we are classifying each operation as a training exercise. We carry out such exercises on a regular but ad hoc basis, so the troops on the ground won't think it unusual. We can quickly and easily bring everyone into the picture when the time comes. GCHQ is concentrating all its resources on the area, listening to and analysing everything they can. Trigger words have been increased a total of tenfold.'

'What are trigger words?' Bell interrupted.

Elspeth looked across the table at the man. 'They are words that trigger the computer to record conversations that have been intercepted. They are needed because it's impossible to listen to more than the tiniest percentage of phone calls. When this whole thing started GCHQ quadrupled the trigger words and now have increased them tenfold. We've highlighted Heathrow Airport, the Underground in general and the name of any Underground station. Cryptic messages have also been ear-marked for particular attention. I am sure that we can all agree there are very few short phone calls made on mobiles nowadays.'

'Are we having any success?' Janice Clitheroe asked.

'It depends on how you define success. If you mean has it taken us any closer to finding the terrorists then the answer is no. Once we are satisfied that whoever is using the mobile is not one of the people we are looking for then we are able to block the number so that the system doesn't waste its time listening and recording any more message from or to that phone. We are eliminating numbers at the rate of about ten thousand an hour but, even so, it's a Herculean task, as I am sure you can appreciate. We have had a great deal of active assistance from TIFAT.'

The Foreign and Home Secretaries sat up with interest. Both were keen supporters of the organisation and had made that clear often enough in the past. They exchanged nods of satisfaction.

The Home Secretary said, 'That's only to be expected.'

The Chancellor and the Prime Minister exchanged frowns. Neither was missed by Elspeth.

'How are you using them?' Samuels asked.

'Thanks to TIFAT,' said Elspeth, 'we know that the organisation behind the attacks is called Barzakh.'

'Who are they?' The PM interrupted.

'I am just coming to that. They are a Pakistan based organisation dedicated to the spreading of Islam across the world though presently concentrating its energies on enforcing fundamentalism in both Afghanistan and Pakistan. They are active supporters of the Taliban and supply a great deal of weapons to them.'

'If we know all this, why can't we stop them?' The PM asked.

'There are any number of reasons. The first is that we have only just learnt of their existence. You may be aware that these groups come and go regularly. They use different names though often with the same leadership. It adds to the confusion surrounding their activities. This is compounded, as you know, by support and involvement of senior personnel in both Afghanistan and Pakistan.' She was not surprised at the interruption.

'Preposterous,' spluttered Bell. 'The Pakistanis are fighting terrorism on every front and at every level. Preposterous,' he repeated.

Elspeth bit her tongue before replying. 'There is nobody in the Western security services that would argue with that. But,' she emphasised the word by tapping her forefinger on the file in front of her, 'there are also many supporters of the Taliban and al-Qaeda. Many are in important positions in both countries.'

'Such as?' It was the PM who asked the question. 'Do we know?'

'If you don't mind, sir, I would like to wait another twenty-four hours before I answer that question. That is only because we must make certain of our facts. It would not be right to blacken a man's name without substantial proof.'

The Foreign Secretary nodded, 'You're quite right, Elspeth. We can wait a day.'

Elspeth knew that this also suited the Prime Minister. It meant that decisions could wait.

37

EASING BACK ON the throttles, Hunter turned the Talisman to parallel the Pashni. He was on the ship's port beam, approximately 100m away, travelling at 15kts. The hull of the ship was painted a dull maroon with a green plimsoll line about 1/2 a metre above the surface, the sea washing over it from time to time. The ship, to Hunter's experienced eyes, looked to be well maintained. There were half-a-dozen men lining the guard-rail, looking down at him.

A man with a loudhailer announced, 'We will slow down to just a few knots and launch the seaboat. We will come across and take the prisoner away.'

Hunter waved acknowledgement. Rabbani was awake and in the stern well, trussed up securely, protesting about his human rights and his right to a fair trial. Hunter found it easy to ignore him.

The ship began to lose momentum as did the Talisman. The two vessels moved slowly closer until they were less than 50m apart. As the seaboat was being lowered, Hunter went down to the well-deck.

'Shut up Rabbani,' he said, 'unless you want me to gag you.'

In reply he received a torrent of abuse. Then he added, 'you think I will be well looked after until we get to Pakistan?' He nodded in the direction of the Pashni as the boat chugged towards them.

'I don't know and I don't care. Now shut up.'

The boat came alongside and a bowman threw a rope which Hunter grabbed and used to pull the boats alongside one another. There were three other men in the boat, the driver and two others, all of whom carried automatic pistols holstered at their sides.

'Give me a hand,' Hunter said to one of the men, grabbing hold of Rabbani under the arms and dragging him to the boat's side.

The man he'd spoken to said something to the bowman who

climbed into the Talisman and took Rabbani by the feet. The crime boss was wriggling like crazy but to no avail. He seemed to come to his senses because he suddenly stopped as utter defeat gripped him. He looked across at the Pashni and back at Hunter.

'May God curse you and your family for all eternity,' he said in what was a reasonable tone of voice.

'Go to hell, Rabbani, which I have no doubt you will.'

Hunter exchanged waves with the men in the boat and watched as they headed towards the ship. He looked up. Men were still at the guard-rail. Somebody approached one of the men and did something very strange. He saluted. Hunter frowned and lifted a pair of binoculars to take a closer look. The man who had done the saluting was wearing a jacket with four gold stripes on the sleeves. The Master was saluting somebody not in uniform? He focused on the other man. They were talking together. Or more precisely, the man was talking and the Master was listening. The man had a dignified look about him.

The boat arrived back alongside the ship, and as it did, the Master saluted again and walked away. The boat had been hooked onto its hoist and was being lifted out of the water. Rabbani was sitting athwart ships, his head bowed, seemingly oblivious of what was happening to him.

The boat reached deck level and stopped. Rabbani was pushed out and the four men clambered on to the deck after him. The seaboat then continued upwards to fit snugly into its cradle.

At the stern of the Pashni, the sea began to churn as the engines engaged and the propellers began turning. Slowly but steadily, the ship began to pick up speed.

Hunter was ignored as the distance between them increased. Rabbani, with a man either side of him, walked aft along the deck to where the military looking man was standing. Hunter picked up his mobile and telephoned Macnair. 'Sir?'

'You got rid of him?'

'Yes.'

'Any problems?'

'No, but I just saw something strange,' Hunter replied.

'What was that?'

'I saw the Master of the ship salute somebody not in uniform.'

'Are you sure it was the Master?'

'He had four stripes on his sleeves.'

'So who's the other man?'

'No idea. Sir, send me whatever photographs you have of Khan, can you?'

'You think it could be him?'

'No idea. But it's worth checking.'

'I'll do it now. Hang on a moment.' The line went dead and then Macnair came back a few seconds later. 'Isobel will have a few with you in a minute or two. The big question is, if it is Khan, what's he up to?'

'Come to take care of Rabbani himself? There can't be any other explanation.'

'He has minions who could have done that. There has to be something else. Something more.'

'My phone's just bleeped. It must be the photos. Let me take a look.' There was a pause. 'It's him alright.'

'Commander, let me run this past you,' Macnair spoke thoughtfully. 'Rabbani's disappearance can't be kept quiet for long. To all intents and purposes, let's suppose you're the new boy and you're now in charge. After all, you've been very much in the background and unknown to anyone in the organisation except a very few. You and you alone have control of the manufacture and the supply of the drugs. With Rabbani no longer in the picture, you need to meet with the men at the top of the distribution ladder to establish your position. In no uncertain terms. Would you leave it to someone else? Here's another thought. You were the one who arranged to have Rabbani taken out. Hence, you are able to show how easy it was for you to make it happen.'

'In effect,' said Hunter, 'how powerful you are.'

'Precisely. Greed and fear are two very strong emotions when it comes to establishing and cementing loyalty.'

'Also when enforcing secrecy, ' added Hunter.

'Agreed. What if you have plans to expand the business?'

'He'd need the men at the top of the distribution chain to agree to it.'

'What better way than with a personal visit? In fact, a personal visit would be mandatory.'

'I see what you're getting at,' said Hunter. 'There's also the legal end of the business. Will Khan take over that as well?'

'I don't see how he can. Not straightaway. However, let's assume someone in Rabbani's family inherits the business. Using threats and coercion, there will be nothing to stop Khan taking control. However you slice it,' concluded Macnair, 'Khan will be in the driving seat and will be in a position to generate a great deal of money.'

Sitting in the Master's cabin, General Khan was well satisfied with the way things were working out. Rabbani had resisted his questions for about five minutes. When a pair of bolt cutters were used to cut off the little finger of Rabbani's left hand no more threats had been necessary. When there was no escape, nowhere to go, only limitless agony in front of you, the decision to talk wasn't a difficult one. The General had watched Rabbani closely. He was used to interrogating prisoners and had developed a sixth sense when people lied. Rabbani had tried to do so once only. The loss of his right index finger ensured Rabbani didn't tell any more lies. Of that, the General was positive.

Yassin had not been telling the truth when he had said that Rabbani was an ignoramus when it came to the detail of his organisation. Rabbani had all the facts in his head, down to the smallest detail. The General wasn't surprised that Yassin had lied. After all, making himself indispensable to the General had been a good move, albeit an obvious one. It was designed to ensure the General kept him alive, maybe even make him the General's right-hand man. That had never been on the cards, of course. Once he had finished with Yassin, Yassin would have gone the way of many others. Khan liked to ensure there was no trail behind him, something that became more important the closer he was to his ultimate goal.

He licked his lips. President of Pakistan. With Sharia law and Islam the only religion in the whole of the country. It would take time, but he would achieve it. Of that he had no doubt whatsoever. Barzakh was his secret weapon. Not because of what they could achieve. They were dogs. Animals to be used as cannon fodder. But because they would strike fear into the hearts of the Pakistani people. And fear was a very powerful weapon when used correctly and he knew precisely how to use it.

The General had expected the interrogation to last days if not weeks. It had barely lasted 6 hours. Rabbani had been answering questions one minute, gasping for breath the next and dead the next. It was a heart attack. Khan recognised it. He had seen more than a few under similar circumstances. He was pretty sure he had most of what he needed. In particular, the names and contact details of key people who supplied and distributed the heroin.

Now, Rabbani's body was lying in about 50m of water, wrapped in chains and unlikely ever to be found. It meant that he could put into place his plans to take control of the organisation. He chuckled, an unpleasant sound in the quiet of the cabin.

There was a knock on the door.

'Enter!'

The Master opened the door, closed it behind him and stood respectfully in front of the desk. The cabin was large, tastefully decorated with leather seats and a settee, a table big enough to sit 6 people, and a sideboard containing soft drinks and chocolate. The Master, being a good Muslim, had no alcohol on board. Apart, that was, for brandy that was kept strictly for medicinal purposes. A door led to sleeping quarters with a separate shower and toilet. While the General was onboard the Master would be sleeping in the First Mate's cabin a deck down.

'I trust you are comfortable, sir?'

Khan nodded. 'Yes. Thank you. When will we be at Tilbury?'

'We are due to arrive at fourteen hundred hours tomorrow, sir. It has been confirmed with the relevant authorities.'

'Take a seat, Humam, after all, this is your cabin. I am merely borrowing it for a day or two.'

Thank you, sir. As I have said, it is not only a great honour to have you with us but a great pleasure also.'

'Have the arrangements to pick up the consignment of arms been confirmed?'

'Yes, sir. I received a signal not ten minutes ago. It is what I have come to tell you.'

'Good. The Saudis are true friends of Islam.' He didn't add that the price he was paying was negligible when compared to the goods that they were receiving.

'A barge will meet us just off the coast south of Jiddah in fifteen days.'

'Does that give you sufficient time to dock in Tilbury, unload and then get to Saudi?'

'Yes, sir. We shall leave on the evening tide on Monday. It is less than eleven days to Jiddah and from there to Port Qasim is a further six days.'

'Excellent. That gives us enough time to deliver the arms and ammunition to the territory.' He rubbed his hands together in glee. 'Plenty of time, in fact. Then, my dear Humam, we shall light a fire that will not be extinguished until we say so and that will be when Islam and the word of Allah rules our country.'

The Master smiled broadly. Khan knew it was something Humam had always wished for, prayed for. Just like the rest of the crew and their supporters that numbered in the millions. President Zardarim and his effete government would soon know what it was like to face the wrath of the true believers of Islam. At last, the day was coming. 'Come and join me. It is time to say the asr.' Muslims all over the world would be pausing at the end of their busy day to remember God.

'My General, I shall be greatly honoured.'

Khan walked around the desk, stood next to the other man, bowed towards where they thought Mecca to be and began.

The General was aware that the Quran could be interpreted in many ways as the mullahs and scholars showed with their endless discussions and arguments. He chose to interpret the book as hatred of all things non-Islamic. It was a choice that suited his objectives and desires.

Afterwards, Khan went back around the desk, sat down and said, 'I feel refreshed. When we get to Tilbury we will have a number of people coming to visit us. I want them shown here immediately.'

'Yes, sir. How many are coming?'

'Six. Two at a time. I have a great deal to discuss and many arrangements to make. Leave me. I have a lot of work to do.' So saying, he switched on his laptop and logged on. Taking over such a complex organisation as the one he and Rabbani owned was not as simple as it sounded. Furthermore, he had many more attacks on the West to plan and arrange. God, he thought, was truly great.

38

HUNTER ABSENTMINDEDLY RUBBED the fading bruise on his chest. It was now irritating, not painful. The Talisman - what to do with her? There was no one to claim title to her. What was more, he didn't want the thing. He could return to the marina and dump her there. The police could then deal with the matter - eventually. What would they do? Sell her? Auction her? What would happen to the money? In the next few weeks and months a feeding frenzy would be erupting around Rabbani's estate. The Pakistani government would be wanting it all, the lawyers would be wanting their slice of the action and the Rabbani family would be demanding their share. The fact that the wealth created by Rabbani was built on crime would be treated, on the whole, as irrelevant. Of course there was the legitimate side to Rabbani's business empire to consider which Hunter guessed was worth a good deal - unless it was mortgaged to the hilt. He would have to get Isobel to check it out.

A lot of people would make a lot of money while keeping the legal profession busy for years to come. Of course, there was an alternative.

In the past, TIFAT had lifted its fair share of ill-gotten gains and spent the money on the organisation and various charities. Technically, it was theft, morally it was a good way of spending the assets of criminals. With so many organisations involved, from Britain's security and police forces to Pakistan's government it should prove relatively simple for TIFAT to lift a large part of Rabbani's wealth without being detected. Isobel and her team were very good at that.

He had an idea. Why not take the boat to Scotland and TIFAT HQ? She could be available for pleasure jaunts around Scotland by everyone at the base. He had found the ownership papers in a drawer in the main saloon. They were in the name of an off-shore company registered in the Bahamas. He smiled. What the hell, why not?

The memory stick he had passed to Macnair had been loaded with business information which appeared to be legitimate. They were still unable to tell whether the legit businesses were connected to Rabbani's illegal activities. Hunter knew it was going to take quite some time to take the organisation apart. SOCA would be the ones dealing with it and that would involve search warrants and arrest warrants.

TIFAT wasn't geared up for such niceties and so had effectively bowed out. Its involvement was at an end. What now happened on the international scale with regards to Khan and Pakistan was nothing to do with them. At least, not for the foreseeable future. There was still a possibility that General Khan was innocent of any wrongdoing. After all, they didn't know for certain that Khan was the senior Pakistani official involved with Rabbani's business. Rabbani could have been lying.

Hunter's phone burped. 'Sir?'

'The ship is headed for Tilbury Docks, arriving tomorrow afternoon.'

'What's her manifest, sir?'

'Textiles.'

'That's a pretty useful cargo to have if you want to hide a load of heroin. Even explosives.'

'True. Except I doubt there's anything like that onboard. Not with Khan there. If customs found even a trace of anything illegal, drugs, weapons explosives they'd all be arrested. Khan wouldn't risk that,' said Macnair. 'I just spoke to somebody in President Zardarim's office asking if they knew where Khan was. I told them something had come up on our radar that the General might be interested in. That it was nothing very important and certainly there was no need to disturb the President. Just a matter of courtesy, senior officer to senior officer. They told me Khan was in border country, carrying out an important reconnaissance. That he wasn't due back for at least four days. Apparently, he uses video conferencing to stay in touch with the President hence convincing his illustrious leader that he's doing his duty. Which is interesting.'

'Sir, I've thought of a scenario that covers all the bases and makes sense.'

'I'll be delighted to hear it.'

'We know that Pakistan is going to make an official request for the arrest and extradition of Rabbani. We know that it will take so long to happen we'll all be drawing our pensions before he leaves Britain.'

'That's usually the case.'

'However, Rabbani has a very powerful bargaining tool.'

'Khan.'

'Precisely. If Rabbani can prove the General's involvement in Rabbani's criminal activities then the General is finished. He could exchange that information for an amnesty. Prison would be the least of Khan's worries. So Khan needs to get his hands on Rabbani quickly. Also, it needs to be done in such a way as to ensure there is no arrest and official questioning. No lawyers and court appearances. Khan can't allow it. So Khan goes to Zardarim and explains the urgency in questioning Rabbani. Zardarim talks to our PM who, in turn, dumps the problem in our lap. Rabbani is taken back to Pakistan in secret where Khan can control anything Rabbani says.'

'In reality,' said Macnair, 'Khan wants the details of Rabbani's criminal empire. He's not asking about Barzakh because he knows Rabbani knows nothing about it. Khan gets what he wants and kills Rabbani. Khan then has control of a large and very lucrative crime organisation that can be used to finance Barzakh.'

'I've figured out the Barzakh angle,' said Hunter, 'or at least I've come up with two answers that make sense.'

'Go on.'

'First, Barzakh exists and Khan is using it to make trouble. A big attack by the Taliban and Barzakh in some part of Pakistan that he puts down will win him huge support. He'll probably be a shoe-in for the next Presidential elections which are next year. So the timing is perfect. That scenario is acceptable.'

'To whom?'

'Us, here in the West,' said Hunter. 'A strong President willing to attack the Taliban is what we want.'

'Agreed.'

'And let's face it; Zardarim hasn't done much in that direction practically since he gained office.'

'Because Khan hasn't been effective at his job.'

'Precisely. That leads me to another conclusion,' said Hunter.

'Khan supports the insurgents.'

'That fits. Suppose Khan supports a caliphate with himself as the supreme leader?'

'Everything that's happened slots into place. He ferments an attack, he puts it down and sacrifices a few hundred lives,' said Macnair.

'More likely it will be a few thousand. It makes no difference to him but it has to be convincing. A massive triumph. Once he's the President, he moves to create the caliphate taking his time about it.'

'It's incredibly ambitious,' said Macnair thoughtfully. 'The question is, is it doable?'

'Look what happened to Iran once the Shah was deposed. Nobody expected the country to be taken back to the stone ages by Muslim fundamentalists but it happened. It's only now, thirty six or more years later, that Iran is coming back into the modern world. And that's very slowly. An iron grip mixed with brain washing from an early age can achieve wonders. Again, look at North Korea.'

'You can't possibly compare North Korea with Pakistan!'

'Of course not, sir, I'm just saying what can be done. Khan doesn't need to take it that far just far enough.'

'A nuclear power caliphate is the stuff of nightmares.'

'I could be wrong,' said Hunter.

'You could be. I hope you are. I think you're not.'

'So what do we do?'

'I don't see what we can do at the moment. We can't arrest Khan. We have no proof of anything.'

'We can prove he's got Rabbani.'

'How?'

'We search the ship.'

'We need just cause and a warrant. Also, it's all too easy to hide a single person on a large ship and never find them. It's an impossible task. Hell's teeth, this is ludicrous. We've only just got rid of the man and now we're talking about getting him back. It's just not on.'

'So Khan leaves with Rabbani and then what?'

'Then we come at the problem from a different direction

entirely.'

Hunter knew better than to ask what direction. 'That brings us back to the question as to why Khan is still on the ship heading for Tilbury.'

'To meet people in Rabbani's organisation. When better? He needs to stamp his authority or else the organisation could splinter and Khan could lose the lot. In a perverse way it makes sense. Khan can hardly travel back and forth from Pakistan to England on a regular basis. It's not feasible. He needs to tell the key people that the organisation is under a new regime. That nothing changes. He might even do something to sweeten the pill, like give them a bigger cut of the profits.' The General contradicted himself. 'No. He wouldn't do that. He's too greedy.'

'I agree.'

'Also, taking Rabbani into Tilbury isn't a problem. Customs are looking for contraband, not people. If nobody tries to leave the ship they aren't interested. So there's no danger there.'

Hunter spoke slowly, thoughtfully. 'If Khan leaves by helicopter then the chances are he has Rabbani with him and he'll head for France. It'll probably mean he is going back to Pakistan as quickly as possible. Probably using a private plane.'

'Okay, I can go along with that,' said Macnair.

'If he doesn't leave but goes on to Tilbury my bet is he will meet with the leaders in Rabbani's organisation. Nothing else makes sense.'

'Any preferences as to which is most likely?'

'Yes. The latter. Otherwise the Pashni would be hightailing it south as fast as she can steam. Clear of territorial water and answerable to nobody.'

'I concur.'

'If Khan docks in Tilbury what are we going to do?'

'Nothing,' said Macnair. 'It's not our problem. In the meantime, sit tight. I'll let Five know what's going on and leave it to her. She can tell the PM who in turn can tell President Zardarim. If she hasn't already, she can also explain the Barzakh problem.' With that, they broke contact.

Checking the radar, Hunter saw he was a couple of cables closer to the Pashni and adjusted the speed on the autopilot to compensate. He watched the radar closely, making small adjustments until he was dead astern at 3nm doing 15.8kts. He set parameters around the system. If he went closer than 2.8nm or opened to more than 3.2nm an alarm would sound.

One last look around and he went below to make himself something to eat. In the freezer he found a few steaks one of which he took out and put in the microwave to defrost. Then he found a packet of oven chips as well as tins of baked beans. It wasn't gourmet eating but it would fill a hole. Once it was cooked, he took the food up top. The steak was tough and the chips soggy, which meant the beans were the best part of the meal. His initial assessment of gourmet eating onboard had been wrong.

The autopilot bleeped and he took a look at the radar. The Pashni had gone ten degrees to port and closed to 2.8nm. He made the necessary adjustments and sat listening to the Friday night edition of *Any Question*" on the internet. As always, the politicians spouted more fiction than fact.

While he did so, he got rid of the hypodermic needles, sleeping gas and the weapons over the side. He broke up the former and took apart the latter. He kept the Pocketlite.

Frederick Ogilvie was someone who was able to justify to himself any action he took or anything he said. It was a self delusional trait that meant he made decisions without seriously thinking about the consequences. He knew this about himself, which was why he had done reasonably well in politics. The fact that the very same traits had stalled his career because few people trusted him was lost on him.

He now believed he would be happier if his partner was no longer in his life. He believed that if he could get the media to report the facts about TIFAT the clamour for its removal from Britain, or even better yet, its closure would be loud and insistent. Then it would be easy to go one step further and have Macnair and others arrested, tried and imprisoned. Public opinion was changing. With the convictions in the phone hacking scandal no-one was above the law. TIFAT operatives deserved whatever happened to them. He savoured the thought as he planned the first steps.

He sat in his kitchen, at the bar, on a high stool, a bottle of expensive Champagne open and a flute glass in front of him. He held the stem between his thumb and forefinger and rubbed it back and forth. He stared at the light amber liquid and watched as the bubbles rose in the glass. Now he was on the verge of carrying out his plan he was having doubts. Maybe it wasn't such a good idea. Maybe Algernon wouldn't fall for it. Maybe he had read things all wrong. Maybe David wasn't a new lover, just an acquaintance. Maybe...Maybe any number of things. He put all doubts aside and decided that the die was cast. It would be the start of a new adventure. It would clear the decks for him to find a new partner. It would also put him in the limelight. Once the genie was out of the bottle he could take the moral high ground and point an accusatory finger at TIFAT. He would demand arrests, trials and the closure of the base in Scotland. It would be easy to orchestrate a media frenzy. He would create an ideological objective that the left press particularly liked. Where would it lead? He would be on every chat show in Britain, probably in other countries as well. America would want him. Speeches and perhaps even a book would follow. Attendance at events, denouncing the cancer that was growing in the West where the rule of law no longer applied. He'd get an agent to take care of the grubby details.

He paused. What about his political career? What about it, a small voice asked? He had got this far thanks to his abilities. He was stopped dead in his tracks by people who weren't fit to clean his shoes. Who were jealous of him. Like those idiots Stan Harrow and Alistair Parker. No, he shook his head, raising his glass. Politics had taken him this far - now it would take him even further. An idea occurred to him. The Commissioners in the European Union were all rabid left wingers, of that there was no doubt. He would become a Commissioner and from there it was only a stepping stone to one of the four Presidential positions in the European Parliament. His fame would almost guarantee it. Not almost, he told himself. It was a certainty. He would then be in a position of greater influence, which was another way of saying power, than the Prime Minister and also able to help to steer the EU to have an actual President with the powers of the President of the United States of America. He might be the first one. He would go down in history.

He savoured the thoughts, each one building on the last as his imagination soared.

The sound of the front door opening brought him back to earth. He plastered a smile on his face and turned to greet his lover.

'Fitzie! You're back!'

Fitzgerald nodded. He had a sparkle about him and a spring in his step. It was obvious to Ogilvie that he had been drinking. It was also obvious that he had been having sex. Dear Fitzie always had that look about him afterwards.

'Yes, I'm back.'

'Did you enjoy yourself?'

'What?' Fitzgerald looked confused for a moment.

'At the gallery.'

'Oh, yes. Yes.' Quickly changing the subject he said, 'Champagne! How delightful! Let me join you in a glass.'

Fitzgerald took a flute glass from a cupboard, placed it on the bar, lifted the bottle and filled the glass, pausing as the wine bubbled to the rim and threatened to spill over. He topped up Ogilvie's glass. 'Is this a special occasion? Something to celebrate?'

Ogilvie's laugh was forced, his eyes weren't smiling. He picked up a memory stick and waved it in the air. 'Do you know what this is?'

Fitzgerald looked confused for a second and said, 'A memory stick.'

'No, Fitzie. Not what it is. What's on it.'

'No. How can I possibly know?' His irritation showed.

'This contains all the information I need to bring TIFAT to its knees. To expose them for the lying, murdering swine they are. To have the place closed down, the officers arrested, to have such a scandal that whoever releases this information will be lionised the world over. Think of it Fitzie! On the world stage. The chat shows. The serious political debates that will result. The lectures. The worldwide tours. The articles written about the person who exposes the whole rotten edifice. The book deal. My God, Fitzie, the rewards will be enormous.' His smile widened as he watched the implications of the picture he was painting take hold, the excitement building up in his partner. Soon to be ex, he thought.

'I can see it. We'll,' he quickly changed it to, 'you'll be famous,' said Fitzgerald.

'The Sunday Observer has already offered me £250,000 for an exclusive. They asked to see me tomorrow. I told them I would have to think about it.

'Think about what? All that money? A quarter of a million! Think what we could do with so much.'

'We, Fitzie? We?' Then, just as his partner began to look uncomfortable, he said, with a forced laugh, 'Of course, we.'

Fitzie's relief was obvious.

Now for the bombshell, Ogilvie thought. 'There is a problem of course. The amount of prestige, fame, wealth will be huge. You can see that, can't you? The money to be earned will run into many, many millions.'

Fitzgerald licked his lips. 'Yes. Of course I can.'

'The problem is, tempted though I am to release it, I cannot due to Parliamentary rules. So as I sat here daydreaming, drinking the Champers I came down to earth a few minutes ago. It's a quandary but I don't see how I can risk it. I have to go out. I'll be about an hour.' He slid off his stool, then added, 'Enjoy the Champagne. I won't be long.'

He placed the memory stick on the bar. It was in the centre, the computer end facing him, aimed at the middle of his stomach. At the front door he put on his lightweight jacket and stepped outside. He'd give Fitzie an hour. That was all the time he would need.

The computations of what was possible and what was not possible pounded through Fitzgerald's brain. Ogilvie would not release the information. He was a coward. All bluster. He could talk the talk but he didn't have the guts to walk the walk. But if he did it? The fame and fortune would be his. The world would be his oyster. He would be able to pick his own friends, not be forced to endure Frederick's. He would be able to openly enjoy the company of other men, not sneak around like a thief in the night. He had already had a lot to drink, the Champagne merely added to his euphoric courage. As soon as the door closed he acted.

He swept up the memory stick and, his glass in his hand,

hurried into the study. It was book lined, had a coal fire with an ornate marble surround, a sideboard laden with drinks and a large ornate desk on which sat a computer. He pressed the right buttons, flashed it up, shoved in the memory stick and e-mailed the files to himself. When the last file was sent, he deleted all traces of the e-mail and returned the memory stick to the kitchen.

He went up to his room and on his computer began to trawl through the information. It was hot stuff. TIFAT was doomed. Fame and fortune was his to be had.

Ogilvie arrived home less than forty minutes later. He hadn't been able to contain his eagerness. He looked at the bar and smiled. The memory stick had been moved. It was at right angles to how he had left it and no longer in the centre. Neither the bottle of Champagne nor his glass had been touched.

He debated with himself for a moment whether or not to call Fitzgerald to have something to eat or even go out but decided against it. He wasn't too sure he could carry off the appropriate demeanour. Anyway, he was positive Fitzie wouldn't want to. He would be like a cat on a hot tin roof. No. It was better to leave him to himself. Let him dream his dreams. A nightmare would follow and follow soon.

39

'MALCOLM?'

'Hello Elspeth. How did your meeting go?'

'Sorry I'm so late getting back to you but I had a myriad of things to attend to after I left Downing St. How did it go? Exactly as we expected. Two idiots at the wheel and two astute and committed people following behind.'

Knowing who was who, Macnair asked, 'Did they advocate shutting the Underground as well as Heathrow?'

'Just as we expected. I finally talked some sense into the PM and the moron Bell. Morris and Janice understood the implications of any action we take and didn't need it spelt out. My orders are to arrest the swine. However, I did explain the difficulty in recognising the terrorists before we could make an arrest.'

'Only arrest?'

'I tried the notion of killing them but was shot down in flames. Pardon the pun.'

Macnair said nothing, his silence louder than words.

'Yes, I know,' Elspeth sighed. 'A committed suicide bomber will take no notice whatsoever. The chances of stopping him or her from setting off their bombs are negligible.'

'I take it you told them all this?'

'Of course I did.' She spoke sharply, her irritation and anger showing. 'Sorry, Malcolm, but it was one hell of a meeting.'

'I can imagine. So what orders are you going to give?'

'I have no choice. SOPs means freedom to shoot only if other lives are in danger.'

'But surely, Standing Operational Procedures cover this very situation.'

'Malcolm, you should have heard the Chancellor going on about the moral high ground and other claptrap. The PM kept nodding, the Home Sec and Foreign Sec argued with them and I was on the sidelines.'

'That makes things extremely difficult. More to the point, dangerous.'

'Which is why I want Nick Hunter close by. He's been in the kind of situations that makes him practically unique when it comes to responding to this sort of thing. You know what it's like. SO19 and Special Branch may be highly trained but very few of them have fired a gun in anger. Look how many times our police have been in a position that requires extreme measures but they hesitate for those fateful few seconds that make all the difference between life and death.'

Macnair sighed. He knew only too well. 'The fear of an enquiry, a wrecked career and even a jail sentence for possible murder or, at best, manslaughter is a powerful incentive not to act.'

'Precisely. The Tottenham case and the riots afterwards are a prime example.' Elspeth was talking about the death of a known criminal who was also known to handle firearms. When he was shot by a policeman, it was found that he had discarded his weapon. A coroner's inquest resulted and 8 out of 10 of the jurors found it to be a lawful killing, with 2 jurors undecided. No concern was shown for the well-being of the policemen involved in the traumatic events.

'Is there any chance of getting more of your men down here? Even one more could make all the difference.'

Macnair was about to say no. They were stretched to the limit. Hardly an operative available between on-going operations and those on well earned leave. Besides which, recalling them would take too long.

Before he could reply, Elspeth added, 'At least then we'd have somebody who could shoot to kill without waiting for permission.'

She was referring to TIFAT's mandate. That mandate meant that there was no need to hesitate. No need to wonder if the warrior would be in trouble afterwards. There might be hell to pay but no one would be arrested.

'I have nobody I can send. I'm sorry.'

Then she surprised him. 'What about you?'

'Me?'

'You do remember one end of a gun from another, don't you?' she teased.

There was silence for a few seconds. 'Okay. I'll be there. Somewhere. Available.'

'Armed?' Elspeth queried.

'Of course armed. Otherwise there'd be no point in me coming. Has anything changed? I take it the only timing we have so far is for Heathrow.'

'Correct.'

'Twelve noon on Monday when all the terminals are packed to the gunwales.' He didn't need to spell it out. 'Will you be implementing Operation Standfast?'

Operation Standfast, in spite of its name, was designed for the mass evacuation of personnel from Heathrow Airport. Similar operations, worked out to the finest detail, were in place for just about every place in the country where crowds gathered, from Land's End to John o'Groats.

'They wanted the op to kick-off at eleven hundred,' Elspeth said.

'That's ludicrous. Far too early. At least you need a chance to identify the perpetrators and,' he was about to say, 'take them down,' when he changed the words to, 'arrest them.'

Elspeth's sighed. 'Yeah, right. Arrest them, my foot. You know that will never work.'

They both knew that if a determined suicide bomber was willing to kill him or herself then carrying out an arrest was not only stupid it was suicidal - for the police officers. There were four ways to detonate an IED. One was by timer. The second was remotely. The third was by pressing a switch which took the bomber with it. The fourth and, in reality, the most dangerous, was the release switch. It was usually held in one hand, a thumb press switch holding the circuit open. Let it go and the bomb exploded, either voluntarily or when the terrorist was shot. The first three held the possibility of the bomb not exploding; the fourth was a foregone conclusion. The only action the security services could take was one of containment. Minimum lives lost and minimum damage to property. It wasn't much of an option.

Elspeth sighed. 'You know all the arguments about stopping the terrorists. If we don't stop them when we have pretty good intel then what chance do we have if we have no idea where and when they are going to attack.'

'I take it you explained all this?'

'Of course I did!' She paused. 'Sorry.' Then, in a more reasonable tone, she repeated, 'Of course I did. But the fact is, I was wasting my breath. They already know it all. It's interesting that in the abstract they say one thing, and in reality something else entirely.'

'So what's going to happen?'

'I got them to agree a compromise. Steadfast will be implemented at eleven forty-five.'

'It means the attackers could still escape and come back another time.'

'It was the best I could get. You aren't going to believe me when I say this, but I almost felt sorry for Bell and the PM. The PM in particular is between a rock and a hard place. If we evacuate and we don't catch the terrorists, and there is no bomb, then the attack will take place later. If we don't do anything to save the passengers and the bomb goes off, killing people, then he and his government will be roasted alive for not giving a warning.'

The operation meant stopping all traffic on the M4, the cancellation of the Underground and the diversion of all planes coming into Heathrow. It was a mammoth task of almost inconceivable proportions but one that had been put together over the years. Aircraft departures would continue. It was one way of getting people safely away. Passengers would also be herded into the departure lounges after going through security. The process would be speeded up. After all, the departures side of the airport should be another safe place.

Elspeth added, 'You know, when the paper exercises are carried out it seems feasible. When you look at it in the cold light of day, what's involved makes the task awesome. Frightening, really. It's been giving me sleepless nights.'

'Have you arranged to have the Underground camera recordings transmitted to the right people?'

'Yes,' Elspeth replied. 'I've also sorted out Heathrow as well. We'll get them onto the monitors here, and also at Six, with yourselves and GCHQ. Somebody might spot something.' There was little conviction in her voice.

'I've had a long talk with Commander Hunter and I want to run a few things past you.'

Macnair explained the conclusions he and Hunter had arrived at.

'So you want me to tell the PM who in turn tells Zardarim.'

'That was what I thought but then I realised a serious flaw.'

'No proof.'

'Exactly. We can't run around making wild accusations against the Chief of Army Staff of a friendly power without proof. And substantial proof at that.'

'So will you tell the Prime Minister?'

'No. The decision of what we do is too important to leave to politicians.'

Macnair chuckled. It was an old joke amongst the security services around the world.

'Incidentally, since Khan arrived on our radar we've put him through photo rec and he's been in and out of the country at least twice in the past eighteen months.'

Elspeth was referring to the fact that any person landing at an airport in the UK from overseas had his or her photograph taken as they moved through the roped arrival queues. Even if there was nobody else in front, there was still a requirement to follow the roped pathway. By the time a passenger reached the immigration officer, their photograph had been put through a photo comparison and recognition computer programme. If known to the authorities, then that person could be stopped, arrested, deported, whichever was appropriate.

'I assume he was using a false name?'

'Correct. He's been using a passport in the name of Abdul-Nasser Hoda. Hang on a sec. I've another call. I'll come straight back.' A few minutes later she was back talking to Macnair. 'Malcolm? I've just received what could be good news.'

'Good news? I could use some.'

'Maybe that's pitching it a bit strong but the girl has used her phone again.'

'What did she say?'

'Starbucks ten o'clock. That was all.'

'That could be anywhere.'

'We can but hope it also means a Starbucks at Heathrow.'

'How many are there?' asked Macnair.

'Three. One at Terminal Three, another at Four and another

at Five.'

'So what do you think? They, whoever they are, get to meet at Starbucks at one of the terminals on Monday at ten o'clock?'

'Possibly. It's time we had some luck with this case,' Elspeth couldn't help the note of wishful thinking in her voice. She and every other person working against terrorists were aware that for all the hard, painstaking work they did, no matter how meticulous, a lump of luck was needed. Usually a lot of luck.

'I take it you'll be using dogs?'

'And how. Every mutt available from every force is being drafted in. Refreshers are running so that they are right up to date. We're looking at least ten possibly twenty dogs per terminal.'

Refresher courses were a regular requirement so that the dogs would remain in-date and alert. The problem was, the terrorists were aware of all that and were careful to pack IEDs - Improvised Explosive Devices - in airtight containers. As ever in the world of terrorism, as soon as a solution was found to one particular problem, the terrorists found a way around it.

'What are you proposing to do about the Underground?'

She sighed. 'I argued that closing down the whole network wouldn't work. How long would we shut it for? A couple of hours would be disastrous and cost the country millions of pounds, as people need to be able to go about their business. Also, we can't keep staff on high alert, the stress is too great. Understandably, attention wanders, people miss things. How do we recognise suicide bombers?'

'The problem is compounded,' said Macnair, 'if they are Muslim women wearing the burqa.' Macnair was referring to the black veil worn by some Muslim women which included a gauze across their eyes, completely covering their heads and faces. To Macnair, it was an affront to a modern, open society. Macnair detested what the burqa represented. He thought of the women in the burqa as walking scarecrows who added nothing to the colour and diversity of Britain's society. They also presented a security threat. This was shown to be the case when on the 7th July 2005 the Underground and bus bombers were reported as wearing the burqa. They were young men.

'Nobody can see what is underneath a billowing black shroud.' continued Macnair. 'If the terrorists are planting bombs and trying to escape, then we do have an opportunity to spot the unmanned package and deal with it. The knowledge that suicide bombers are expected in London, on the Underground, can only be kept quiet for a short period of time. If the Government denies there is a threat and a bomb goes off then politically it will be a disaster.'

'I agree.'

'So what's going to happen?' asked Macnair.

'Let's assume the bombers are going to strike at twelve hundred on Monday.'

'They won't want to be loitering around a station or on a platform for too long in case somebody becomes suspicious.'

'Knowing that, I've agreed with the PM that we will evacuate the Underground at eleven fifty and not a minute before.'

'Too early by five minutes,' said Macnair.

'I said I've agreed, I didn't say I would order it. I have also agreed with SO19, Special Branch and the Commissioner that I would be the one to give the order to proceed.'

'So any fallout falls on you.'

'To be honest, Malcolm, I don't care. I could quit tomorrow and not miss a damned minute.'

'I think you'd miss it very much.'

'What? The eighteen hour days? On-call twenty-four hours a day, seven days a week? Lousy home life, continuous stress and so on. As you know only too well.'

'Delegate more.'

'You're right. But this is one operation I need to control.'

'We aren't in control,' said Macnair, 'we react. The terrorists are in control.'

'True.'

There were a few seconds of silence and then Macnair asked, 'So what are you going to do?'

'I'm taking full responsibility for ordering the evacuation of the Underground and I will decide the actual time. Systems are in place, as you know all too well, but the exercises we have carried out show that we need at least five minutes for the orders to disseminate to the level where anything is done. So the order will be given at eleven fifty..'

'Makes sense, I guess. Timing is vital. What else are you

doing?'

'We are shaking the trees, kicking down doors and interrogating a lot of people.'

'Public relations?'

'I have decided to ignore public relations, race relations, religious relations and every other relations you can think of. Saving lives is more important, coupled with catching and stopping these people.'

'When it comes to evacuating the stations what excuse are you going to use? You can't very well say because of a potential bomb threat. If you do, panic will set in and people will be injured, even killed.'

'We know. Because each station is isolated, we can make the same announcement from Cockfosters to Morden. We'll say that tunnel works have uncovered a Second World War bomb. There is no danger and so on and so forth.'

'That should do it. The bomb's been there long enough, no danger, just a precaution. Don't panic, move in an orderly fashion.'

'Precisely. In the meantime, I really could do with some help.'

40

AFTER A DISTURBED night with the alarm waking him 3 times by 08.00 Hunter was at the helm when he phoned Macnair.

'Morning, sir.'

'Morning, Nick. I take it nothing's happened?'

'Doesn't appear to have.'

'Where are you?'

'Just off Folkestone. They'll be making their ETA without any problems.'

'How far behind are you?'

'Three miles.'

'Drop back to five. We don't want anything to spook him at this late stage.'

'Is there something happening I need to know about?'

'I need you in Central London.'

'What for? What can I do that CO19 can't?'

'Remember the mess when that Brazilian Jean Charles de Menezes was killed in July 2005?' asked the General.

'Yeah, poor sod. Talk about being at the wrong place at the wrong time. Wasn't it something to do with getting those who had been planning another bombing attack on London? Didn't they try to set off a bomb but it failed to detonate or something?'

'That was basically it. The detonators worked but the explosives failed to go off. If they had, the loss of life and injuries would have been horrendous. There would also have been massive disruption to the Underground where three of the explosions were planned as well as the one on a bus at Shoreditch. There were four terrorists involved. Two were Somalis and one was Ethiopian. They had applied for political asylum which had been granted. The fourth was an Eritrean and the son of two people who had been granted political asylum fifteen years earlier. All four were Muslim, which came as no surprise. CCTV showed the men to be brown skinned, slim with dark hair. Menezes fitted

Paul Henke

the description of one of them fairly accurately. Also, don't forget as well, this was only two weeks after 7/7. Tension and feelings were running high. Anyway, Menezes was wrongly identified as one of them and followed from a high rise block of flats in Tulse Hill to Brixton tube station by bus. The station was closed and so he took another bus to Stockwell. Armed officers were sent to Stockwell tube station where Menezes was shot dead with seven rounds to the head and one in the shoulder.'

'Isn't that overkill?'

'Probably. Following the incident there have been two major enquiries. I have a transcript of both as well as having seen some of the official papers not shown in court. Nick, if I had been the commander on the spot I would have ordered the shooting and if I had been the cop I wouldn't have hesitated. That's my reading of it. However, due to the blame culture we're living in, a real mess has resulted. Although none of CO19 were arrested or charged, and rightly so in my judgement, careers were wrecked and good men were either shifted out of CO19 and back to ordinary duties or they left the force.'

'I still don't see why I'm needed,' said Hunter.

'We now have a system of control that virtually paralyses CO19. Permission to act at every stage passes up the line to a Senior Officer. Nowadays, it's a man by the name of Peter Hargreaves. The message I got from Elspeth at MI5 is that he's a jobsworth terrified of making a decision. As a result, on more than one occasion, we've been lucky to avoid a significant number of deaths and massive destruction due to terrorist attacks.'

'So the best trained, dedicated and competent anti-terrorist police force in the Western world is not allowed to do its job properly because of the idiot at the top. But, on the other hand, it's a huge dilemma. No officer wants to put at risk an innocent life.'

'That's it in a nutshell. If CO19 are dealing with it and they end up in the Underground there's another big problem,' said Macnair.

'No comms to get instructions. As a result, the guys on the ground are unwilling to risk what happened following the Stockwell inquiries and so the prospect of bombs being set off is much higher.'

'Quite. We have more freedom to operate, so we're going to be there.'

'Who's we? Are some of the others back?'

'No. It'll just be you and I.'

'Where shall we meet?'

'Take the boat back to Burnham. Dump it there and go up to London. I've booked us into the Naval Club on Hill Street. It's convenient.'

Hunter was a member and knew the club well.

'Once the Pashni docks what happens then?'

'Elspeth and the rest know what they're doing. We're finished with that end. Our concern is helping to stop any attacks.'

'Roger that, sir. Have you spoken to President Zardarim?'

'No. I did e-mail General Khan who sent a polite e-mail back thanking me and telling me that he was looking forward to interrogating Rabbani when he arrived in Pakistan.'

'So he doesn't know that we know he's on the Pashni.'

'It looks that way.'

'Why not talk to Zardarim?'

'And say what? General Khan is taking over a crime syndicate and financing a terrorist organisation called Barzakh? That it's all part of a plan to become President and maybe establish a caliphate in Pakistan?'

'It sounds ludicrous when you put it like that.'

'Isobel has been digging. The stuff you took from Rabbani has enabled her to identify bank accounts belonging to quite a number of people, the biggest beneficiary being Khan. The money went via the Cayman Islands. According to Isobel, it's all very amateurish.'

'So why not dump the information into Zardarim's lap? He can take care of Khan.'

'Khan is too powerful. No, like I've already said, we'll have to find some other way.'

Hunter rubbed the bruise on his chest. The bruise was itching, a sign it was fading fast. 'Understood. Anything else, sir?'

'No. That's it. I'll see you in London. We're going to be kitted out in CO19 uniforms. We can't very well be armed and in civvies. Someone might shoot us.'

'Weapons?'

'Hecklers.'

'Which one?'

'MP5SD.'

'Good. If I get a chance to use it I may get more than one target.'

The Heckler and Koch MP5 was the ubiquitous weapon of choice by many of the armed police forces around the world, as well as specialist army regiments such as the SAS and SBS. The MP5SD with its integrated suppressor coupled with sub-sonic ammunition made it extra quiet. Hollow tipped, 9mm rounds prevented over-penetration which very importantly reduced the likelihood of a bullet passing through the target and hitting an innocent bystander.

They said their goodbyes and Hunter went below, his coffee mug in hand. It was time for a refill.

Kathleen opened the Sunday Times and began to glance through the articles. The stories were detailed as well as accurate. Or at least, she thought, for the main part. She'd finished writing her own story about the terrorist plot the country was facing and sent it to various editors she knew. Two had already come back wanting more information which she was happy to supply.

She looked at her watch. A few minutes after 09.00 and still nothing from Hunter. Damn him, she thought. She put the paper down and went into the kitchen to make a cheese sandwich and a mug of soup. She had to cut the mouldy bits off the cheese before cutting it up into slithers and putting them between two slices of bread that was just beginning to turn stale. As always, when working on an important story, the thought of food came way down her list of priorities.

She went back to her desk and logged on to check her e-mails. Not a word. Not only had she left three messages so far on Nick's mobile, she had also sent two e-mails.

Where are you, Nick?

Turning a page of the newspaper, she stared at the photograph. It was a rotten shot and it took a few seconds for her to recognise him. Omar Sylla was found dead on a rubbish dump in the East End of London. It appeared he had been tortured to death.

Kathleen made it to the sink before she vomited up her cheese sandwich and her breakfast of Corn Flakes.

When she stopped heaving she began thinking. She needed to get out and get some fresh air. She couldn't stay in the flat. She was feeling claustrophobic. She poured a glass of water and washed out her mouth. She refilled the glass and drank thirstily. It took the vile taste away but it didn't help her feel better.

Omar! My God, Omar? What did they do to you? Much more importantly, why did they do it? Was it because of the information he was passing to her? She'd told him to be careful on more than one occasion. So how had they got to him? Why torture him? Did they know about her? Was she in danger? The thoughts swirled around her head as she pulled on her shoes, grabbed her handbag and let herself out of the flat.

She passed the lift and headed for the stairs. It was one of her feeble attempts to try and keep fit.

Outside, it was warm and sunny. She hurried away, towards King George's Park. It was a place she frequently visited when she needed to think and have some quality time. She didn't see the man across the road, nor did she realise he was following her.

41

GENERAL KHAN LOOKED through the information contained on his computer. He was a meticulous and methodical man. When it came to himself, he was also honest. He knew he was overwhelmingly ambitious, ruthless, egocentric and loathed everybody who wasn't a Muslim. This last trait was one he had kept secret for decades, though it had become more difficult as the years went by. Now, he felt, he was close, so very close, to fulfilling his ambitions as well as being able to let the West and other non-Muslim countries know the contempt he felt for them. This was particularly so when it came to dealing with India. It was a country he would like to wipe off the face of the earth using Pakistan's atomic weapons. It wouldn't happen, of course, but he could dream.

If all went well, he would unite the North West Frontier Province with Afghanistan and from there a Jihad would be launched that would ignite the Islamic world against the West. The thought sent a thrill through his veins. A holy war with God on their side against Satan.

The Qur'an stated clearly that Allah required Muslims to fight against those fighting against them. There was no option.

He knew that once he had control of the area and incorporated it with Afghanistan, he would become their leader and thousands, no, hundreds of thousands, would flock to his cause. It would become a great time for Islam and all true followers.

In the meantime, pressure had to be kept up on the West. Relentless pressure caused by death and destruction. Now with control of Rabbani's criminal organisation and the money it brought he could arm his warriors so that nothing would be able to stand in their way. He smiled with satisfaction. He had spent the last 10 years moving senior officers around his command until he had a hierarchy that supported his objectives and were utterly loyal to him. They in turn, had identified more junior officers and so on down the line to the humble squaddie. He had a veritable army at his beck and call.

There was a knock on the door. 'Come in,' he called.

'Sir, Master's compliments, but he said to tell you that we are two hours sailing from Tilbury Docks and that lunch is ready in the canteen.'

'Thank you. I will be there shortly.' As the man nodded and closed the door, Khan moved to a different file. It was encrypted, like all the files on his computer. He went through each operation. There were a total of eight. Two were progressing nicely; the other six needed both co-ordination and some recruitment. Each cell consisted of three people. Experience had taught him as well as the other Jihadists that a single location attack could easily fail due to a combination of factors. One was the infiltration of the Muslim communities around the UK by people who either worked for the security services or who were traitors to their faith.

Then there was the sheer ability of the security services and the British police, which should never be played down. Their resources were amazing, their ability to track down holy warriors awesome and their ruthlessness something that was often underestimated.

He looked at the screen. The operation in Heathrow and on the Underground would happen the next day at twelve noon. Perfect. Death and destruction caused by the bomb and the bullet, misery and unhappiness fermented by drugs and crime.

Lunch was a subdued affair. They were, after all, going into the lair of the enemy.

The meal was quickly over and they returned to their duties. The Master was on the bridge and the General joined him.

The Master pointed to starboard. 'That, sir, is known as Canvey Island. You can see ahead how the river turns sharply to the left. Once we are there we are less than 3 miles from the docks.

'Good. Very good,' the General rubbed his hands together. He sat in the Master's chair and looked as the land seemed to flow serenely past. The water had become a muddy brown, a big difference to the blue/green of the Channel. The sun was shining and there wasn't a cloud in the sky which, he told himself, was proof that Allah was smiling down on them.

Instructions were radioed to the ship and a short while later the Pashni was dead in the water with a tug alongside.

The tug gently pushed the Pashni starboard side to. Eager hands took the heaving lines, ropes were pulled ashore and the eyes of the hawsers were dropped over bollards. The ship was secured safely alongside; the order was given to finish with main engines and peace descended throughout the ship.

A gangway was placed near the bows and ship's officers met the customs and immigration people and took them below. It wouldn't be long before the cranes started the task of emptying the hold of the ship's containers, stacking them on the docks ready to be transported to their destinations. Extra care was taken searching them but nothing out of the ordinary or contrary to the manifest was found.

Hunter arrived at the marina and slowly reversed the Talisman up to the floating pontoon. He grabbed the port stern rope, stepped ashore and secured it to a cleat. He took the starboard rope and did the same. He followed this with the two midships ropes and the bow ropes. The Talisman was now berthed securely alongside. He switched off the engines. Then, he checked the gas and diesel were turned off before grabbing his grip, locking the boat and placing the keys under the upper starboard bench seat.

He took Rabbani's car. Although it was Sunday and roads weren't too busy it still took him the best part of two hours to get to Hill Street.

He dumped the car at the Audley Street car park but didn't bother buying a parking ticket even if it was pay and display. The car park owners could deal with the car.

Crossing the road, he wandered along Hill Street. The Naval Club was just ahead. After he signed in and dumped his bag in his cabin, he went down to the bar. An alcohol free beer helped to quench his thirst.

Kathleen spent most of the afternoon in the park. She wandered from bench to bench, unable to settle in any one place for very long. She was scared witless. What was she to do? Go to the nearest police station? She took out her mobile and speed dialled Hunter once more. It went straight to answering machine which was also beginning to worry her. In view of what he did, what if something had happened to him? Her imagination, vivid at the best of times, was in overdrive.

She went to the toilets in the middle of the park, stood and watched a game being played on the bowling green and finally bought herself an ice-cream from a van parked near the gates. She managed two licks before she threw it into the nearest rubbish bin.

At one point she bought a cup of tea, and though it tasted foul, she drank it and managed to keep it down.

It was with a start she noticed the time. She headed home across the park. Throughout the time she'd been wandering around, she hadn't noticed the man following her. Once she was back in her flat she sent Hunter yet another e-mail.

Feeling restless, Hunter decided to wander the streets. Window shopping had never appealed to him and he quickly became bored. He turned towards Hyde Park and strolled around its grounds for a while. Hunter was a throw back. He would have been happy to have sailed in the sailing ships of the 18th and 19th centuries. He appreciated nature on land but loved the sea. He enjoyed reading books about the sea, like those written by Patrick O'Brian and his eponymous hero, Jack Aubrey. Hunter had one complaint about the books. Just as Aubrey made Admiral, the author died! There had been groans across the sea-faring world, as avid fans were cheated by the unfortunate death of the author.

Hunter left the Park and eventually found himself outside a coffee shop. He bought an Americano with milk. Taking out his mobile, he decided to check his personal e-mails. When on an operation it was something he did very rarely but he figured the op was virtually over and it was time to get back to his own affairs. He was reading a long newsy message from his sister, Louise, when he saw a new message in his in-box - Kathleen XXX. He then noticed another 2 from her. The message was the same. *Nick, please call. Urgent. XXX.* He thought of ringing but decided he'd just turn up. He liked the notion of surprising her. He grabbed a taxi. All the way there he wondered what could be so urgent that she had sent 3 messages. It made no sense no matter how he looked at it.

He climbed out of the taxi, gave the driver £10 and told him to keep the change. He went through the front door and took the stairs two at a time.

The door to the flat was ajar. He could hear noises coming from inside and saw that the lock was broken and hanging off. He slipped out his Pocketlite. He didn't need to check it. It was ready to fire, with a round up the spout.

He darted through the small hall and into the lounge. He took it all in with one glance. Kathleen was on the floor, a man was sitting on her, his hands were around her neck and he was choking her to death.

Hunter took two paces to reach them, the man looked up at him and Hunter tried to kick him in the face. The man was incredibly fast. Hunter missed as the man swung away and leapt to his feet.

Kathleen groaned, put a hand to her throat and gasped for air. She watched the tableau in front of her before she pushed herself backwards, away from the men.

Hunter concentrated on the man. He was a good 6ins shorter than Hunter, swarthy, with a moustache, his belly hanging over his belt. He was crouched forward, his eyes darting back and forth. It appeared to Hunter that he was looking for a way out.

Hunter didn't crouch. He stood and contemplated his opponent. The Pocketlite hung down his right side, partly obscured. If he shot the man the noise could bring nosey neighbours or reports made to the police about gunfire. He didn't want SO19 coming in armed to the teeth, taking control and removing him to a police station. Explanations and check-ups would take too long.

The man was two paces away when Kathleen threw her laptop and hit the man just above his left ear. As he staggered backwards, Hunter stepped forward and in one swift movement brought the sole of his right foot crashing down just above the man's right knee. He put all his weight and strength behind the move.

Hunter understood the science of such an attack. The blow tore the ligaments, stretching those behind the knee to breaking point and beyond. The menisci shattered, like broken crackers, and the bursae or fluid sacs burst. Agony shot through the man's body like an electric charge.

The man stood there for a second before collapsing with a crash to the floor. He went down, screaming. He held his knee, his leg sticking out at right angles, tears streaming down his face.

Hunter glanced at Kathleen. She walked over, picked up the laptop and looked at the man.

'Help me! Please! Help me!' He was gasping.

Kathleen said, 'Certainly.' She swung her laptop over her shoulder and brought it down with a resounding crash across the man's head. Immediately his screams and pleadings stopped.

'Have...Have I killed him?'

Hunter could see that the man was still breathing raggedly. He shook his head. 'No.'

'Pity,' was Kathleen's reply before her tears started.

Hunter put his arm around her shoulders while she sobbed. After a couple of minutes or so she stopped crying and pushed herself away. 'Thanks, Nick. Thanks very much.'

'What for?'

'For saving my life.'

'It was nothing. Do you have any rope?'

Kathleen shook her head. She still had her computer in her hands and she looked at it. 'It's broken,' she said inanely.

'I'll use the electric cable.' Hunter crossed to the desk, got down on his hands and knees and pulled out the plug. He tied the unconscious man's hands behind his back. He made sure the binding was tight - very tight.

Kathleen summoned up a wry smile. 'At least I keep backups of everything I do.'

To Hunter, the man looked Pakistani or at least Middle Eastern. He felt in his pockets and recovered the man's wallet, a mobile phone and a passport. A flick through told him just about all he needed to know.

Taking out his mobile, he pressed the speed dial button. 'Sir? Where are you?'

'Just arrived at the club. Where are you? I thought you'd be here by now.'

Hunter briefly told him what had happened.

'Okay. I'll contact the police.'

'Nick!' Kathleen said. 'Nick!'

'Hang on a second, sir. Yes?'

'I think this could be the man who killed Omar. Omar is the man who's been feeding me information. I've been investigating

Muslim terrorism.'

'What!' exclaimed Hunter. 'Sir, did you catch that?'

'No. What?'

Hunter repeated what Kathleen had said.

'Find out what she knows as a matter of urgency. I'll let the police know what's happened and get somebody senior over to you. Is the man armed?'

'No, sir.'

'Pity.'

'Why's that, sir?'

'Minimum force and all that nonsense. I'll call you back.'

Hunter broke the connection and smiled at Kathleen. 'You okay?'

'I...I think so,' she rubbed her throat. 'My God, I've never been so scared.'

'That's not surprising. I know it's easy to say but try not to dwell on it. You're not hurt, at least, not badly and you're safe.' Hunter's phone rang. 'Sir?'

'The police will be there in ten. A Detective Chief Inspector Sam Outhwaite is in charge. I've spoken to the Commissioner. He's told the DCI to take a brief statement and to leave it at that. Any follow up action can come later.'

'Okay, sir.' Hunter broke the connection and told Kathleen what Macnair had said.

'Nick, I don't want to stay here. What if there's somebody else out there waiting for me?'

Hunter nodded. 'I'll speak to the police. See if I can get someone to stay with you. Or better still, there's a boat berthed at Burnham. She's called the Talisman and I have access to her. Go there and wait for me. I'll come down as soon as I can.'

'You want me to go there alone?'

'No. I'll see about a police escort.'

'What about keys?' Kathleen asked, as pragmatic as ever.

'I've left them under the starboard seat in the upper helm position.'

'Is the boat yours?'

Hunter was about to shake his head when he said, 'Yes. You okay with this?'

Kathleen nodded wearily. 'Yes.' She spoke with a croak and

put her hand to her throat. It was obvious she was in pain.

The police arrived mob handed. They were led by a man in his fifties, stocky, clean shaven, a few inches shorter than Hunter with a no-nonsense air about him.

He walked over to Hunter with his hand outstretched. 'Commander Hunter?' His grip was firm and dry. 'Sam Outhwaite. SO15.' He was a senior officer in the Metropolitan Police Service Counter Terrorism Command with a national brief to keep the country safe from all forms of terrorist activities, whether that was Islamic fundamentalism or the Real IRA.

'That's me. Call me Nick.'

'I'm Sam. It's a great pleasure to meet you, Nick. We know all about TIFAT, of course.'

'All good, I hope.'

'All good, Nick. Believe me.'

There were two other people with him, a man and a woman. The man was nondescript, the kind of individual described as lost in a crowd of two. Everything about him was average, from his height, weight, looks, brown hair and ordinary clothes. She, on the other hand, was extremely attractive. She was tall, a couple of inches shorter than Hunter, fit looking, a trim figure, blonde hair tied back in a ponytail, an oval face with high cheekbones and blue eyes. Hunter shook hands with both of them. Both were detective sergeants, his name Hunter forgot, her's was Rosemary Young. He looked her in the eyes and smiled. She smiled back.

Outhwaite looked at the terrorist. 'I hate the scum. Not very professional, I know, but I'd like to shoot each and every one of them.'

'You're a man after my own heart, Sam.'

'What's to happen to him?'

'Nobody's told you?'

'Not a word. I took a call from the Commissioner himself. Told me to get over here as soon as possible. Told me about the threat. There are four of my men outside looking around, making sure there are no unpleasant surprises waiting for us. The sniffer dogs will be here in a couple of minutes, just to double check.'

'I don't think you'll need them.'

'I don't either. But it's SOPs nowadays.' Standard Operating Procedures took away the need for decision making and covered all the bases, ensuring, as near as dammit, that nothing was missed. 'So what about him?'

'You'll need to speak to the Commissioner, I guess. Arrest, hospital, and loving tender care is what I suspect. He's a Pakistani. Here's his passport and wallet.' Hunter handed them over.

'God,' moaned Outhwaite, 'the paperwork on this one.'

'I sympathise. This is Kathleen Summers,' said Hunter. 'The man on the floor was strangling her when I came in.'

'Lucky you got here when you did,' said Sergeant Young.

Hunter nodded. 'Sam, Kath could still be in danger.'

'I figured that as well.'

Hunter told them about the Talisman. 'If somebody could go with Kath just for a day or so I'll see what we can do after that.'

'Rosemary? You up for a bit of babysitting?'

'On a luxury boat?' Rosemary Young smiled. 'You bet.'

The DCI nodded approval. 'Good.'

'Sam,' Hunter looked at his watch, 'I need to get going. Is there anything else you need from me?'

'No. I can take it from here.'

'Thanks. Kath, you okay?'

'I'll be fine. Only hurry back, won't you?'

Hunter grinned. 'I'll do my best. Don't forget the keys are under the upper starboard seat.'

'I won't.'

'Thanks, sergeant,' Hunter smiled at Rosemary. 'Take care of her.'

'I will, sir.'

'I need to get going.'

'We're done,' said Outhwaite.

Hunter said, 'Kath we need to talk. Sam, is it okay if they come with me for a chat?'

'Is it anything I should know about?'

'No. It's not about the man on the floor.'

As if in acknowledgement, the man groaned.

'Okay. You go. I know where to get hold of you if I need you.'

'Shall we go and find a coffee somewhere?'

Kathleen led them to an independent coffee house around the corner from her flat. The coffee was excellent. Kathleen was still badly shaken from her experience but, as the minutes went by and she gave Hunter the details that she had received from Omar, she began to regain her composure. After a few minutes, she paused to rub her throat?

'You okay?' Hunter asked.

Kathleen nodded. 'Yes. I'll live.'

'Glad to hear it.'

Hunter asked pertinent questions that Kathleen did her best to answer. The bottom line of it was she didn't have much more to tell than they already knew.

At one point, Rosemary said, 'So tomorrow isn't an exercise?'

'Pardon?' said Hunter.

'Tomorrow. Leave cancelled, unlimited overtime announced, those on leave recalled. We aren't stupid. Tomorrow is more than an exercise. And Kathleen's information confirms it.'

Hunter nodded. After all, Rosemary was a sergeant in SO15. If he couldn't trust her to keep quiet, who could he trust? 'That's about it.'

'Who was the man who tried to kill Kath? Do you know?'

'No idea. I only know what you know and that's the man's name. If his passport isn't a fake, that is.'

Once he was satisfied that he had everything he could get out of Kathleen he stood up and said, 'See you on the Talisman.'

42

ABRAR HAD BEEN awake most of the night. Her last on earth. Excitement had coursed through her since she had gone to bed. At last, the day had come. Monday. That day she would prove her devotion to Allah and Muhammad, peace be upon him.

Her parents had arrived back from Pakistan the previous evening on a delayed flight. She had greeted them with due respect.

Her mother had called, 'Abrar, darling, we're home!'

Abrar had stepped out of the kitchen and bowed her head to them both, 'Ahlan wa sahlan, Ummu, ahlan wa sahlan, Abbun.' Welcome Mother, welcome Father. The correct form of address showing respect. Not using Ummi, my Mom, or Abbi, my Dad.

Her mother had held her arms out to her, 'Come, my Darling,' she had said, 'it's been too long.'

Abrar had chosen to ignore her and returned to the kitchen where she had been preparing a meal.

They sat at the table in the dining room, her parents attempting to make small talk. To ask about how she had been, what she had been doing. They tried to involve her in their time in Pakistan, the work they had done amongst the sick, the photographs they had taken and loaded onto their laptop. She had not been interested in any of it.

Finally, they had given up and a gloomy silence had settled over them. Abrar had loaded the dirty dishes in the dishwasher and bade them goodnight even though it was only just nine o'clock. She had a great deal of praying to do.

She hadn't noticed the despair on the faces of her parents, or more to the point, chose to ignore it.

In her room she had began the Isha, the evening prayer said before bedtime. She had been extra devout, extra pious, as she spoke with her God and with his prophet.

Now she was on her knees, bowing as one should, towards the

east, reciting the Fajr, the pre-dawn prayer. The light outside was just turning gray, lighting the room enough for her to see her waistcoat of explosives she had taken from the wardrobe. She prayed for her friends. For their courage and devotion.

Basel had been at his prayers all night. He had tried to sleep but had finally given up around midnight. Since then he had been on his knees. He had read the Qur'an, the word of God as revealed to mankind through his prophet, Muhammad in the year 610 CE.

They had received their instructions. They had been explicit. The detonations were to occur at exactly 12.00. The stations chosen were Piccadilly Circus, Westminster and Marble Arch.

They had agreed to leave at around 10.00 which would give them plenty of time. He looked around his bedroom and at the sagging bed in the corner. He would be glad to leave that accursed world, to arrive in Paradise, to prostrate himself before Allah and his prophet. It was a great day. The greatest that any man could have.

Elspeth spoke at the phone on her desk. It was on loudspeaker. 'Customs checked the manifest and ship's papers. They're pristine. We've searched all the containers that have been unloaded and found nothing.' Wearily she lifted a cup of coffee to her mouth, sipped and grimaced. It was cold and if there was one thing she heartily disliked it was cold coffee. She pushed a strand of hair behind her left ear. Even though she had changed into a fresh white blouse and dark blue business suit with trousers and a waist length jacket, she felt dowdy.

'Only to be expected. Any visitors?' Macnair enquired.

'Not so far. Incidentally, the info that journalist gave us proved useful. It's enabled GCHQ to tie-in that mobile we were tracking to Wimbledon. Close to the Common. The mobile was used just after eight o'clock this morning.'

'What was said?'

'A girl said - They arrived home last night. They will be surprised when they find what I have done. What we have done.'

'Arrived home from where?'

'It doesn't matter. We have something to go on. At that time in the morning the girl was probably at home. The Met are saturating the whole of the Wimbledon area, knocking on doors, asking if anyone there has just returned from a trip. Checking nationalities and names.'

'What about house deeds? The Land Registry Office can supply names.'

'Already on it. We've downloaded a file of all Pakistani surnames and are putting it through the Registry computer for Wimbledon and Wimbledon Common. The name might not be a common Pakistani name. The father might be non-Pakistani with a name like Smith. The Devil alone knows. The permutations are endless. Hence the door knocking. Where are you?'

'I'm about to leave the club and take the underground to Heathrow.'

'Where's Commander Hunter?'

'He's already at King's Cross.'

'Good. Armed teams have been brought in from all over the country and are being deployed. I've had the PM on my back, wanting to know what time we'd be shutting down the Underground.'

'Again?'

'Yes, again. Malcolm, if I wasn't a lady I'd use some extra strong language.'

'By all means feel free. Don't mind me. What did you tell him?'

'That it would be in plenty of time and left it at that. He seemed satisfied.'

'He is, as long as he can deny all events if anything goes wrong. Let's hope we identify the terrorists before it's too late.'

'Amen to that,' said Elspeth.

'What has the Met done with the man Hunter stopped yesterday?'

'We offered to take him off the Met's hands and they were happy to hand him over.'

'What have you done with him?'

'Our cousins want to talk to him. We'll fix him up and then send him to Gitmo.'

Elspeth was referring to Guantanamo Bay Naval Base on the south-eastern corner of Cuba. Leased by the Americans from the Cubans since 1903 it was now a military prison with an infamous reputation. The prisoners held there were from Iraq, Afghanistan and other places. They were considered highly dangerous but there was nothing to try them for and no way of putting them behind bars for any length of time.

'Good. Did he say anything to you?'

'Not a word, I'm afraid.'

'Anything else happening with the ship?'

'There have been six visitors. Entourages, really. They came at half hourly intervals. Three times there were two car loads of eight men and each time only two men were allowed onto the ship. We photographed everything and everybody. Number plates and IDs are being checked. One thing I can tell you. None of them are Pakistani, of that there is no doubt.'

'What did you do when they left?'

'Ah, I have good news and bad news.'

'The good?'

'We had them followed.'

'The bad?'

'We lost one of them.'

Macnair didn't insult her by making any comment. Tailing somebody was difficult at best. 'Were the tails spotted?'

'They assure me not. That's probably why they lost one of them. The balance between being ultra careful and not losing the target is a fine one and a mistake can easily be made. Anyway, spilt milk and all that. We have enough to get on with. Serious crime has taken it over and we'll just have to leave it to them.'

'What are you doing to keep this quiet?'

'We've requested a DA-Notice 05 be sent to all editors and UK newsrooms, both TV and radio.'

'What's the Secretary saying?' Macnair was referring to the Secretary of the Defence, Press and Broadcasting Advisory Committee or DPBAC. The Secretary was always a two star military officer, in this case Major General Hacker. There were five senior civil servants, plus representatives from all the UK's newspapers and media. This ranged from TV and radio broadcasters to Google. Until 1993 it was known as a Defence Notice more commonly called a D-Notice. If one was requested by the different agencies that request was sent to a long list of recipients. Usually, the request was honoured at least until matters could be cleared up, but sometimes they weren't, depending on the subject.

The DA Notices covered five different and wide ranging categories. They started with Military Operations, then Nuclear Weapons, followed by Communications, then Sensitive Addresses and finally to the UK's Security and Intelligence Special Services. The request was being made under the fifth category.

'He's put the call out but isn't too hopeful,' said Elspeth.

'Why doesn't that surprise me? Bad news mixed with fear starts panic and riots which in turn lead to more fear and more panic and more riots and great TV.'

'What a cynic you are, Malcolm.'

Kathleen woke up in bed and wondered for a few seconds where she was. As she became more compos mentis, rational thought and the memories came flooding back.

She lay still, savouring the opulence of her surroundings.

They had stopped on the way at a supermarket and stocked up on food, white wine for her and herbal teas for the policewoman, Rosemary. They had also found a shopping mall with a Marks and Spencer and kitted themselves out with clean underclothes, jeans and blouses.

The two women had hit it off and, as the night had been pleasantly warm, they had sat in the upper helm position, she sipping her wine, Rosemary sipping her spearmint tea.

'Thanks for coming with me,' said Kathleen, 'I appreciate it.'

Rosemary smiled. 'Are you kidding? Look at this place. It's a floating palace. I've never seen anything like it. Does it belong to that dishy man you were with? Oh, sorry. Is he your boyfriend?'

'Nick? No, not really. Not at all, actually. Though we did date for a while but that was a long time ago and it was only for a few months off and on.'

'And you let him get away?'

'Trust me when I say that Nick Hunter goes where Nick Hunter wants to. He's a male chauvinist pig with all the grace of a...of a...hyena.'

Rosemary burst out laughing. 'A hyena? That's a new one. So you did fall for him. Not that I blame you. What did he do?'

Kathleen sighed. 'The fact is he's a gentleman. Kind, considerate. You know the type. Opens the door for you, steps aside. I'm sure if there was a puddle he'd throw his cloak on the ground for a lady to walk over.'

'Sounds too good to be true.'

'I don't know about that.'

'So what was the problem?'

'He would never talk about himself. I did do a bit of digging. Have you heard of the Griffiths family? They own shipping lines, banks and God alone knows what else.'

'I've heard of them, of course. Who hasn't? Why?'

'His mother is a Griffiths. She married a journalist by the name of Tim Hunter. The family is filthy rich. So is Nick, though you wouldn't believe it if you knew him.'

'Why didn't he go into the family business?'

'I asked him that. He just shrugged and mumbled something about it being too boring. You know, there's something about him. Almost...I don't know. Almost feral.'

'So what does he do? I take it he isn't a banker. Not the way he dealt with that man back at your place. The kick he gave, doing that to the knee, takes training. I know. I've tried it. Only when training you understand.'

'That was part of the problem. He wouldn't tell me. He works for that mob in Scotland. TIFAT.'

'What!' Rosemary sat up suddenly, spilling her tea. 'He's *that* Nick Hunter?'

'What do you mean, *that* Nick Hunter? I told you, he said practically nothing about his work. He'd just take off without so much as a by your leave and come back days if not weeks later and expect to just take up where we'd left off.'

'Kath, Nick Hunter is practically a legend in SIS.'

'SIS?'

'The Secret Intelligence Service.'

'*He* is? Rosemary you've got to be kidding.'

'No, honestly. You name it and he's been in the thick of it. We know he stopped a nuclear device exploding in Switzerland. He also prevented some sort of deadly disease being let loose in London. What else? Oh, yes. Remember a couple of years ago when those bigwigs were taken prisoner in Scotland? Out in the islands, somewhere.'

'I remember. I wrote an article about it.'

'Nick was the leader that saved them. Trust me when I say he's highly regarded.' She scowled.

'What is it?'

'He is highly regarded but not by everybody. There are a few people who would like to see TIFAT in general brought to heel and some of its officers in particular.'

'Is Nick one of them?'

'He's top of the list. Though from what I hear he couldn't care less.'

'From what I can tell, he doesn't.'

'He has the reputation for not taking prisoners.'

'What's that supposed to mean?' Kathleen asked.

'Just that. Though it's mainly hearsay. I suppose we're envious.'

'Of what?'

'TIFAT's freedom to act. Shoot the terrs first, question them after.'

'Sounds barbaric,' said Kathleen, taking a gulp of her wine.

'It is. But when you're fighting barbarians you have no choice.'

'I don't agree.'

'After what happened to you?'

'In spite of what happened to me. I believe completely in the rule of law.'

Rosemary frowned. 'Let me ask you something. A man comes along this walkway with a gun in his hand. He is going to kill you. He aims it at you. Do you want me to yell halt or I fire or do you want me to shoot him? Bearing in mind the man is an Islamic fanatic and is not only prepared to die in his warped perception of Islam but is happy to die. I have one second to decide whether you live or die.'

'I don't know. I have to think about it.'

'You don't have time to think.' Rosemary slapped the table with the palm of her hand, the noise a loud bank in the silence.

Kathleen jumped. 'You scared me.'

'Sorry. But come on. What shall I do? What do you want me to do? Do I give the terrorist a chance when there is a likelihood that you will die or do I kill him?'

'You could...you could wound him.'

'Forget that rubbish. That's for films only. I'm an excellent shot and I couldn't be sure of just wounding the man unless I was within a few metres. He could start blasting and empty at least a dozen rounds in our direction. We'd be dead. What do you want me to do?'

Kathleen shook her head and then said, 'I suppose I want you to shoot.'

'But I've hesitated. It's too late. You, me, we're dead.'

'What's your point?'

'A number of them. Nick does what he needs to do to keep people safe from terrorists. It isn't pretty but it's effective. If he was faced with the situation I just described he wouldn't hesitate. He'd shoot. Twice.'

'Why twice?'

'To make sure the terrorist doesn't get up.'

'Would you hesitate?'

There was no reply.

'Have you ever shot anyone?'

'No. I haven't,' Rosemary said softly. 'And the irony is, I hope I never do. So would I hesitate? Probably. And if I do? Then it will be in the lap of the gods.'

That had been last night. They had finally gone to bed after 02.00, Kathleen being too wound up to try to sleep any earlier. As it was, she had put her head on the pillow and gone out like a light.

Her mobile rang. 'Yes?'

'It's me,' said Hunter. 'You okay?'

'We're fine.'

'I thought I'd tell you that the man in your flat is sort of known to us.'

'Sort of?'

'Yes. Not on the radar as a terrorist but as an aide to someone.'

'Who?'

'Can't say. Sorry.'

'What's happened to him?'

'He's been treated. His knee has been operated on. Apparently it took the surgeons all night. They said he'll walk again, always limp and always with some degree of pain.'

'I'm glad,' Kathleen said fiercely.

'You surprise me. I thought you were a pacifist. Though from the way you hit him over the head with your computer your pacifism has certainly diminished somewhat.'

'That was in the heat of the moment,' she retorted. 'What's going to happen to him? What will happen when he gets to court?'

'He won't be going to court for a long time.'

'Why ever not?'

'It's too complicated to explain. He's yelling blue murder for a lawyer. Screaming about his rights but he can forget it. In half-an-hour he'll be on his way to Gitmo on Cuba.'

'Guantanamo Bay? Why?'

Hunter sighed. 'Let's just say we have nowhere else to put him. There are important questions he needs to answer and that's the only place to ask them.'

'By ask you mean torture,' she said bitterly.

'Kath, I don't care what you call it. This man probably has information about terrorist cells operating in the UK. We need to find out about them.'

'But you just said it yourself. Probably. He should be treated like a prisoner and given all the rights he's entitled to under the law.'

'You are absolutely right.'

'What? What did you say?'

'You are absolutely right. We'll let him have his day in court. We'll let you be a witness. That'll put your name into the public domain. That will allow every fundamentalist to target you and finish the job. After all, what's your life compared to the rights of an individual to be treated in accordance with the law? Shall I suggest that to General Macnair? I'm sure he'll be able to stop the man being taken away. So we can either send him to Guantanamo or put him in a cell, with a solicitor, a preliminary hearing and a court case in a few weeks. What do you say?'

Kathleen found her hand shaking. 'I...I...I see,' she said in a whisper.

'That's reality Kath. Armchair do-gooders can talk in the abstract as much as they like. But when it comes down to it, when they are in the firing line, it's all a new ball game. They don't feel or sound so righteous, believe me. That's the time when they are shown to be hypocrites. I've seen it often enough.'

'Has the man said anything?'

'No. He's still sedated. He'll come to somewhere over the Atlantic. Hopefully, the threat of a few decades at Gitmo will loosen his tongue. Incidentally, forensics have connected him to the killing of your friend.'

'Omar? Oh my God!' She couldn't keep the bitterness out of her voice when she said, 'I shouldn't have continued with the story. I should have dropped it. Omar might be alive if I had.'

Hunter spoke with an edge to his voice. 'Get a grip Kath. That sort of thinking is total bunkum and you know it. There's no need to feel guilty. Omar knew what he was doing and your information has helped us a great deal in finding the other terrorists. Look, I'll come down in a day or two so try and relax and don't worry. I've got to go.' He broke the connection.

Kathleen slowly climbed out of bed. Her mind was in a whirl. Having Rosemary with her for a few days was one thing, being a target for weeks even months was something else. She showered, dressed in her new jeans and a short-sleeved blouse and went into the galley.

Rosemary was already there, coffee in hand. 'I heard your phone. Anything important?'

'It was Nick. He said that the man who tried to kill me is on his way to Guantanamo Bay.'

Rosemary smiled. 'Excellent. Just the place to dump scumbags like him. Maybe we'll get a few answers.'

Kathleen stood pouring coffee into a mug, in need of the caffeine for a change. She sighed. 'I just don't know. It goes against all my principles. The humanitarian and logical side of me says we should adhere strictly to the letter of the law, my instinct is to want to kill him with my bare hands.'

'You did a pretty good job with your computer.'

'I was angry as well as scared. If I'd had a gun I would have shot him.'

'That's natural.'

'But that was the heat of the moment. I was scared. Desperate. It's not the same as killing somebody in cold blood.'

'You're right. It takes someone with a great deal of courage to do that.'

'And Nick has that courage?'

'I don't know him at all, only what I've heard. And I've told you, he has one heck of a reputation.'

Kathleen merely nodded and switched on her BlackBerry to check her e-mails. It was a different address to her normal one, given to friends and special contacts only. That meant there was very little spam inundating her with the kind of rubbish thrown around the internet.

There was one message. She read it in shock. Her hand was shaking. She phoned Hunter.

'Nick?' She couldn't keep the fear out of her voice.

'Kath? What's the matter? Are you okay?'

'I've just received an e-mail from Omar.'

'He's dead.' Hunter stated the obvious.

'Shut up and listen. He says that the leader of the team of women who are going to attack Heathrow is named Shaban.'

'Is that her first name?'

'No, her family name. She lives out Wimbledon way somewhere.'

'I'll call the General. Thanks.'

43

THE HAMMERING ON the door and the continuous ringing of their door bell had both Mr. and Dr. Shaban hurrying to see what was the trouble. Dr. Shaban opened the door and froze in horror. The street outside the house appeared filled with police cars with flashing lights, policemen looking grim and two plain-clothed men both of whom waved identity cards. Two dogs were being let out from a van.

'Is it...is it Abrar?' The doctor asked, her hand to her throat. The Shabans' initial fear for their daughter was short lived.

'Madam, not that we know of. My name is Detective Chief Inspector Lane and I am from CO19. We are looking for a terrorist gang that we believe to be in the area.'

'What has that to do with us?' Shaban asked, a certain amount of belligerence in his voice.

'Sir, we're not saying this is anything to do with you. But we must check everyone.'

Shaban stepped to the front of the door and looked up and down the street. 'I see you are only picking on us because we are Muslim.'

'Sir, please, this is important. We have no time.'

'Show me your warrant.'

'I don't have one.'

'Then you cannot come in.' Shaban stepped backwards into the house and began to close the door.

The Chief Inspector didn't wait. He stepped forward, barged into the door with his shoulder and shoved it open causing Mr. Shaban to totter backwards.

'How dare you! How dare you!' Shaban shouted while his wife started to yell at them to get out.

DCI Lane looked behind him. 'Get the dogs in here. Search everywhere. Come on, move it.' His voice was grim. The importance of the next few minutes was not to be underestimated.

If they were at the wrong address then God alone knew what would happen. Human rights, racism, Islamophobia and every other accusation would be levelled at them. However, his orders had been explicit. There was little time left and so no time for the niceties.

Shaban was yelling, trying to stop the invasion of his house. It was like trying to stop an avalanche. The DCI knew that he could apologise later and ask for forgiveness if they were wrong. He would grovel, the Commissioner would grovel, the Home Secretary would grovel and the press would get hold of the story and all the grovelling in the world wouldn't help one iota.

As soon as the dog handlers entered the house Lane knew their information had been correct. Both dogs, spaniels, were excitedly sniffing the air, pulling at their handlers. Heading for the stairs. The two plain-clothes coppers exchanged knowing looks and followed the dogs up. The dogs stopped at a door on the right and began pawing at it. They were whinnying, excited, scratching the paintwork.

Lane tried the door. He couldn't open it. 'Why is it locked?'

'What is this? How dare...' Shaban began to bluster. The terror he was feeling was showing on his face.

'Shut up!' The DCI yelled. 'Answer me!'

'It's our daughter's room.' Shaban's wife answered for them. 'She likes to keep it that way. She has done for some time. She says...she says it's her private space. That we should respect her desire for privacy. What...what is this all about?'

Lane ignored the question. 'Is she in there?' From the way the dogs were behaving it probably meant that they had sniffed explosives. If the girl was inside, she could easily set them off. Lane needed to make a decision immediately. Break the door down or get the hell out of there. The road had already been blocked off as a precaution but now the houses either side and opposite would need to be vacated.

'No...No. She's gone to meet friends,' Dr. Shaban replied.

Lane pointed at his Sergeant and nodded at the door. No words were needed. The Sergeant threw his shoulder at the door and easily burst the lock, smashing the door open. The dogs went straight to a corner of the room. They were sniffing, pawing at the carpet, excited.

The dog handlers exchanged looks and nods. One of them said, 'There's no doubt about it.' Even as they spoke, both men were reaching into their pockets and taking out biscuits, feeding them to the dogs, petting them and stroking them. Both dogs basked in the attention they were receiving.

'No doubt of what?' It was Dr. Shaban who asked the question. Though ashen white, she had regained some of her composure.

'There's been explosives in here and recently,' replied the DCI. 'Where is your daughter? Do you know?'

'Explosives? What are you talking about?' Mr. Shaban was also recovering his normal dignity. 'I must ask you to leave our house immediately.'

'I don't have time for this.' Lane put his radio to his mouth. 'Base? We're at the Shabans. The dogs have sniffed explosives but there are none here. We're getting very little co-operation from Mr and Mrs Shaban.'

'Tell the Shabans that they will be charged with accessory to murder if they don't co-operate. Make it clear that they'll spend the rest of their lives in jail.'

'Yes, sir.' He looked at the couple. 'You heard. Now tell us, where is your daughter?'

'We don't know,' Dr. Shaban faltered. 'Oh, God. Please tell us what's happening.'

'We believe your daughter is involved in a terrorist attack on Heathrow Airport. Do you have a photograph of her?'

The Shabans exchanged devastated looks. Dr. Shaban's eyes filled with tears which began to roll down her cheeks. She broke into sobs, hid her face in her hands, as her shoulders began to heave.

Mr. Shaban said, 'She will be wearing the burqa as well as the veil. A photograph will be of no use, but I will get you one.' The man seemed to age before their very eyes. His shoulders slumped, tears formed and then he too was sobbing, his arms wrapped around his wife.

Lane called it in. One of the constables scanned the photo from the car. In seconds, all personnel at Heathrow had been told to look for a woman wearing a burqa with a full face veil. A caveat was added. There was a likelihood that there would be three of them. They also received a head and shoulders shot of a beautiful young lady, with black lustrous hair down to her shoulders, a half smile and a shy expression. The photo was five years old.

'Implement OperationStandfast,' the Home Secretary ordered. The orders went out. It was the first stage and was effectively carried out in secret. The objective was to reduce the number of people in the airport's terminals.

Aircraft were immediately diverted and the roads to the airport were closed to all vehicles heading that way. The result was the M4 motorway was quickly grinding to a halt. All trains on the Piccadilly line were being stopped and emptied before continuing on to Heathrow's terminals. They were backing up ready to complete the journey to the terminals when the evacuation of Heathrow would begin. That would be in approximately fifteen minutes.

Morris Samuels sat at his desk, clenching and unclenching his fists. The strain was showing in his face and in his hunched posture. He was desperate for a cigarette but controlled his craving. His mobile phone rang. He saw the call was from No.10. He switched the phone off. Sod the Prime Minister. He knew how it would work out politically. The PM was safe in his metaphoric bunker in No.10 waiting results. Everything successful? Aren't I a great PM and leader! Anything gone wrong? It's nothing to do with me. Those in charge of implementing policy and controlling events give the orders. I cannot be responsible for every little detail. He could hear the man as though he was holding a press conference right there and then.

Of course, there was another dangerous result of the operation. If fear and panic took hold, it would be very difficult to control the crowds. Possible death and certainly injuries would result if the people stampeded like a herd of elephants.

Morris Samuels shuddered. It scared the Bejesus out of him.

Hunter was at King's Cross and stood looking at the underground surveillance monitors. He knew that every camera in operation was being closely monitored locally. Furthermore, they were all connected to banks of screens in MI5, MI6, GCHQ and TIFAT. In each establishment, operators were flicking from one camera to the next; hoping to spot something, anything, out of the ordinary. There were 270 stations served by the Tube and 260 of them were manned. Some of them, like Baker Street had 10 platforms. There were over 2,000 platforms some with 3 or more cameras. The numbers bounced around his head. It meant that those operators in the security forces could see only a relatively few platforms at a time. To say the least, masses of luck was needed.

Hunter knew that Isobel had called in all her team who were still in the UK, whether they were on leave or not. TIFAT would be using new state-of-the-art face recognition software developed at Rosyth. Even so, it was still needles in a haystack.

He looked at his watch. In ten minutes the Underground would be shut down. Every entrance would be manned by armed officers but to what avail? Hunter knew that the scenario playing out at that moment was one that had been exercised, debated and argued over for years. Even since the Islamic threat mushroomed in the UK following the 9/11 attacks. In many respects the 11th of September changed the lives of the people who lived in the West irrevocably.

To start with, there was a vast amount of distrust generated by non-Muslims towards the Muslim communities wherever they existed in the world. No matter how hard the politicians worked to eradicate the distrust it existed and, as far as Hunter and those involved with keeping people of all faiths safe, the distrust was widening and deepening. Previous attacks had been brilliantly planned and executed. That was one reason the Western Security Services were so paranoid about the possibility of further attacks. They had every right to be.

The 9/11 attacks in 2001 were textbook operations. Nineteen al-Qaeda terrorists hijacked four aircraft and forced the pilots to crash them into different targets. American Airlines Flight 11 and United Airlines Flight 175 crashed into the North and South towers, respectively, of the World Trade Centre in New York. American Airlines Flight 77 was crashed into the Pentagon, while the fourth plane, United Airlines Flight 93 was targeted at Washington. However, the passengers attacked the terrorists and the plane crashed near Shanksville, Pennsylvania. Almost 3,000 people died in the attacks, including 227 civilians and 19 hijackers onboard the aircraft.

The rejoicing in the Islamic world was sickening and still brought a knot to Hunter's stomach when he thought about it. TV footage had been broadcast around the world, day after day, week after week, month after month by the Islamists.

Now they were facing a threat at least as great as 7/7, 2005.

The dilemma faced by the security services flashed across Hunter's mind. If they evacuated the stations and Heathrow too early, the terrorists could vanish from whence they came and attack some other time. If there was some significance to 12.00 on that Monday then the terrorists could get amongst the crowds and detonate their bombs. Death, injury and destruction would be horrific and the martyrs would have achieved their objectives - panic, fear and anarchy that would fester in the minds of the British for years to come.

Everything depended, as it often did, on a number of factors. The first was the announcement over the stations' tannoy systems. Hopefully, telling the passengers that there was a technical fault and that they should leave the station would be enough to make the attackers pause, even if only for a few minutes. Should they leave the platform? Should they detonate their bombs even though it was still a few minutes to midday? Should they follow the rest and blow themselves up outside, at 12.00?

Would the indecisiveness created be enough?'

Portable explosive detectors had been erected at some of the main Tube stations. But there were few of them and using them held up the evacuation to a dangerous degree. These dilemmas had been debated, argued and actions agreed. However, in the end, it all came down to the officers in the front line. Identifying a suicide bomber was a job that made even the bravest officer fearful.

Hunter cleared his head of the frightening thoughts and concentrated on the screen in front of him.

The radio burst into life and the operators in the room paid attention. Was this it? Had a target been identified?

'This is Chief Superintendent Hargreaves. On no account are shots to be fired without my express permission. I repeat. No firing without my authority. That's all.'

The armed officers in the room exchanged looks. The looks said it all. The man was a self-important moron who should never have been given the job of senior officer of SO19.

Hunter was staring at the screen in front of him and frowned. Something wasn't right. What was it? Something. He stared more closely at the monitor. The realisation came as a shock. How the hell hadn't they been noticed earlier? The weather was continuing hot and dry. Typically, London was baking with the atmosphere of a sauna. Yet there were three men wearing kagools.

There was only one explanation. He shot out of his chair, ran for the door and yelled, 'Listen up. Main concourse. Three men wearing black kagools. They look Asian. It's probably them.' He pressed the transmit button on his radio and made the same announcement. Next he flicked the fire mode selector on his MP5 from "S" or Sicher position which denoted safe, to "E" standing for Einzelfeuer, or single shot. The next position, was marked "F" for Feuerstoss, or continuous fire. He hoped to avoid having to use "F".

Immediately a voice came over his earpiece. 'Who is this? Identify yourself. This is Commander Hargreaves. Did you hear me? Do not fire. I say again. Do not open fire. Identify yourself.'

Another voice came back to him. 'We've locked in on them. They are heading for the Underground. One is going for the Piccadilly line, one for the Victoria line and one for the Northern line. Correction. Two for the Piccadilly line but they've drifted apart. The one is still heading for the Northern line.'

Hunter was running virtually flat out. He barged through people, jumped over luggage and yelled at others to get out of the way. A uniformed policeman carrying a firearm like the Heckler & Koch MP5SD, running and yelling at them, had people scattering in panic.

'Do not open fire. This is a direct order. Do not open fire, whoever you are. This is Commander Hargreaves.'

Hunter wrenched the earpiece out and let it dangle by his side. Two other CO19 officers joined up with him.

'You two take the Northern Line. I'll take the Piccadilly.'

One of them gasped, 'There's two on the Piccadilly Line, only one on the Northern.'

'Just do as I say,' Hunter said. Whereas Hunter wasn't even breathing hard the two policemen were panting and wheezing.

However, in the humid heat, all three were sweating.

Macnair had taken the precaution of issuing Hunter and himself with the uniforms of a Chief Superintendent. It helped to ensure orders were obeyed.

'Right you are, sir,' one of the men replied.

Hunter leapt the turnstile and reached the corner to the platform. He paused before stepping out. It was busy but not packed. One of the men was only a dozen paces away, nervous, sweating, looking around. The other man was about 50m along the platform also nervous, also sweating, though he was staring at the track.

Hunter didn't hesitate. He could see that the closer man was skinny yet his kagool billowed out around him. The man shifted. He lifted his kagool slightly and pulled it away from his body, trying to cool himself down. He turned and looked straight at Hunter. His face registered shock as Hunter raised the gun to his shoulder and fired two rounds at point blank range. The man's head exploded. The gun barely made the sound of a loud burp.

Two girls who had seen what had happened looked in shocked horror and then both drew in deep breaths to scream. A couple stepped in between the second target and Hunter. He did the only thing he could do. He sprinted along the platform. Behind him the screaming had started. The second target was about 20m away when he looked around to see what was going on. He looked at Hunter. Hunter fired on the run. Twice. Both were head shots. Again, the target's head exploded in an eruption of brains, blood and skull.

Behind the screams came the rumble and sound of an explosion.

44

THERE WERE SIX patrols, each consisting of two CO19 officers, as well as five dogs with their handlers. The patrols were strolling at random, looking relaxed, as though it was like any other day. The dogs were sniffing at people and bags, their tails wagging excitedly. Due to the fact that no further passengers were now arriving at the airport and others were going through to departures, the terminal was thinning out. Most people were on the move, going somewhere, doing something. But not all.

One of the officers transmitted, 'Starbucks. Three women covered head to foot in black. At least, I think they're female. I can't see their faces properly.'

It was a reasonable comment. The perpetrators who survived the 7/7 attacks had tried to make their escape wearing niqabs so that their faces were also covered. They had been men.

'Are they wearing veils?' his superior officer asked.

'Wait a moment. I can't tell.' There was a pause. 'No. I can see their faces now. I can't tell what age they are.'

'Is one of them Abrar Shaban?'

Both men looked at their mobiles. Abrar's photograph had been sent to every officer involved with the operation. One of them looked at the girls, at the photograph and at the girls again.

'I'm...I'm not sure. I don't think so.'

'You don't think so?' The voice on the other end repeated incredulously.

The officer looked at his companion who shook his head.

'Sir,' there was desperation in the young officer's voice, 'neither of us is sure. It's too difficult to tell.'

'What's wrong?'

'One of them is looking at us.'

'Turn away. Don't look at them. I'll call it in.'

The men in the patrols moved in different directions, the dogs ecstatically sniffing everything they could get their noses to, their tales wagging.

The order came over their radios. 'This comes from on high. Hold your fire. Do not shoot them. I repeat, do not shoot.'

Knowing Superintendent Hargreaves' position on the shooting of the terrorists, Macnair had hurriedly left the control room as soon as the sighting had been radioed in. He didn't look at the women but headed towards the two officers who had made the report. Both men were constables.

'Sir,' one of the officers nodded to Macnair.

'Gentlemen,' Macnair nodded. 'What are your names?'

'I'm Constable Smith and he's Jones.'

Smith was 6ft tall; broad shouldered and carried the mass of gear needed to perform his duties with little effort. He cradled his MP5 like a new born baby, his right index finger resting on the outside of the trigger guard. Macnair glanced at the weapon and saw that the selector was pointing at "E".

Jones was about 5ft 8ins tall, thin, with eyes that never stopped roaming. He looked swamped by his gear but Macnair could see he carried it with ease. His finger was also on the outside of the trigger guard and Macnair assumed it was also ready to fire on single shot.

'Did you get the information about the explosion at King's Cross?' Macnair enquired.

'Yes, sir,' said Smith, 'a few minutes ago. Quite a few dead and injured.'

'Correct. Including two CO19 officers.'

'Yes, sir.'

'They died because they didn't shoot the bombers first. You heard about the other two being shot?'

'Yes, sir,' the second officer replied. 'Two killed. Both wearing explosive vests.'

The General said, 'In a few minutes the announcement will be made that there is an emergency and that the terminal is to be evacuated.'

'We know.'

'Once we start the evacuation, they could panic and set off their bombs. The result will be catastrophic.'

The two men exchanged worried looks. 'We realise that, sir,' said Jones.

'We now know that the bombs are activated by pressing a switch attached to the middle of their waists. So no dead man triggers. Which is a relief.'

The two officers nodded.

'I want you to kill them. We'll each take one.'

'But Superintendent Hargreaves has ordered us not to fire,' said Smith. 'We are to call on them to surrender. To give them a chance.'

Macnair looked at the two men as though he felt sorry for them. Which, in fact, he did. They were damned if they fired and possibly dead if they didn't.

'I'm countermanding that order. People were killed at King's Cross because a bomber was called on to surrender. It takes a second or two for the bomber to press the button. We now know that if they are carrying the same amount of explosives as the men in King's Cross then the blast will be devastating. I have no intention of risking the life of a single innocent person. Not one. Do you understand?'

'Yes, sir. But our orders...' Smith tailed off.

'Constable, at what point do you shoot these women? When they clasp their hands to their midriffs? That will be too late. The switch is a press button affair. It takes a bit of strength to set it off to stop accidental detonation but it's not that hard to do. Are you going to risk it?'

Neither man moved.

'However, we need a positive ID,' there was urgency in Macnair's voice. If they shot the wrong women nothing would save him or the constables from long prison sentences and the demise of TIFAT. Both results, Macnair knew, would be justified. His palms were sweaty as the implications of the decisions he took in the next few minutes took root. His demeanour showed nothing of the inner turmoil he was experiencing. 'We do not go around shooting suspects just because of the clothes they wear. Also, if we shoot the wrong women the bombers will set off their explosives immediately.' He paused, then added, 'But look around. How many innocent people do you see? Those girls deserve what they get. They intend to kill innocent people indiscriminately. Men, women and children. I am not going to allow that to happen. Do you understand?'

There was no reaction as the two constables exchanged looks. 'Well, do you?'

'Yes, sir,' said Jones.

'I don't like this any more than you do. But you're professionals. We do our job. Understand?'

'Yes, sir,' Jones answered.

'Smith?'

'Yes, sir.'

'If we fire it will be at my command. I take full responsibility.' He didn't add that if he was wrong and the bombs did go off they'd be dead anyway.

'Good. I'll tell you which one is your target and you put two taps into her head. Remember, head shots. We can't risk a shot to the torso as it could set off the explosives. Do you have that?'

The two officers said nothing, merely frowned.

'Do you have that?' Macnair repeated, angrily.

'I...I'm not sure I can, sir,' Smith said.

Macnair looked at the other man. 'What about you?'

Jones licked nervous lips and nodded. 'I can. You can rely on me.'

'Good.' Macnair looked across at the three girls and quickly looked away. 'Actually, I have an idea. It might work.' Although Macnair had been insistent on the action they should take, he did not like the idea for one instant of killing a teenager, whether male or female. He had wanted to instil in the men the idea that killing the bombers was one option very close to the top of the to do list. However, he was about to opt for another course of action.

'Let's stroll across the hall, away from them.' He began walking slowly away and the two men fell in beside him. He checked his watch. Evacuation of the terminal would be starting in two minutes by an announcement over the tannoy system. A fire in another part of the building would be the reason for such a measure being taken. Merely a temporary safety precaution. Nothing more. It wouldn't be for long. That, embellished with the usual claptrap, was an effort to prevent panic from erupting amongst the passengers.

'Okay, let's see if we can do this without any loss of life. Let's keep going. We'll walk around the perimeter and head slowly towards where they're sitting. I want the pair of you to smile at people, to nod, to be non-threatening. Once the announcements start, people will begin to leave. We'll point at the normal exits as well as the emergency exits. We'll keep going. Don't look at the women at the table. When we get abreast of the table I'll point at the serving counter and say something. With luck, they'll look as well. We'll then move. Grab their hands and grab them tight. Not even fingers being able to be moved. Understood?'

'Yes, sir,' both men said in unison.

'Let's head back towards Starbucks. Switch off your mobiles and take out your earpieces.'

'Sir?' Jones looked puzzled.

'No distractions. Not for the next few minutes. Not under any circumstances.'

The three girls sat at Starbucks, mugs of untouched coffee on the table in front of them. They were holding hands. Abrar was saying the Dhuhr out loud, even though it was another 15 minutes until noon. Sofia had tears rolling down her cheeks; Maida's eyes glistened with unshed tears while Abrar's were aglow with fervour.

'It will not be long now, my sisters,' she said, once she stopped praying. 'In only a short while we will be in the presence of our God. The one true God and his servant Mohammed, peace be upon him.'

They sat staring at each other, two in fear, one in ecstasy. They were oblivious to what was happening around them, their focus being on their immediate future - or lack of it.

'Shortly, we must go our separate ways,' said Abrar. 'But we will soon be together again in Paradise. Come, let us not falter. Let us think of the great good we will do the world as we help to drive it towards Islam. What a wonderful day that will be when the world is of one faith.'

The other two nodded, albeit reluctantly. If Abrar detected any hesitation on the part of the other two she chose to ignore it. Her heart was soaring; she had never felt such ecstatic joy in her life.

Sofia's shoulders were shaking. The tears welling from a trickle to a flood. She looked around and gasped. 'I...I cannot do this. Look at the people. So happy. The children, so excited at going on a plane. Going on holiday. Visiting family. These people have never done anything to us.' She gasped, and looked angrily at her friend. 'I have been a fool. I listened to you. All your talk about Allah and the way to eternal happiness in Paradise. I was a fool. Oh, Allah, help me. I will never see my family again. I will never play with my little brother or teach him things. I will never marry, have children of my own.' She let out a low moan. 'What have I done?' She bent her head forward, covered her face with her hands and sobbed.

'Stop it, Sofia, stop it!' said Abrar harshly. 'People are looking. Stop it, I say.'

But there was no stopping her. Sofia's shoulders shook and she let out another low moan.

Maida sat up straight and glared at Sofia. 'Stop it! Stop it! We have come this far in the glory of Allah and the prophet, Mohammed, peace be upon him and it is too late to turn back now. We will be immortalised. We will be known and revered throughout the Islamic world. Our names will be uttered with great respect and love. It is a joyous day.'

'We will go to Jahannam for this,' whispered Sofia.

An image of Hell flashed through Akbar's mind. Sinners and nonbelievers inhabited Jahannam. The Quran described the treatment of its inhabitants in detail. It was a place where fire burnt off the skin, which was replaced only to be burnt away again. A process that never ended. Clothes of fire were worn, boiling water was drunk, faces caught fire, lips were burnt off, and the bodies were tied to yokes and dragged through boiling water and fire. When examined in detail it was ludicrous, but Abrar believed. As part of that belief she chose to ignore one important fact, a fact that all zealots pretended was of no consequence as the greater good outweighed the bad. On the day of judgement, a person who commits suicide will be punished by the same means used by him or her to end their lives. They would also go to Jahannam.

The Imams argued, usually successfully, that the greater good of martyrdom was more important than committing suicide and that Allah would forgive them. The actions were never referred to as suicide, always martyrdom.

Abrar felt strange being in public wearing a short skirt with a loose fitting thigh length black coat. She looked enviously at three sisters wearing the burqa at a table on the other side of Starbucks.

The constables replied with two nervous nods. They felt in their uniform pockets and took out their mobiles.

Smith switched his off and removed his earpiece. Jones removed his earpiece but took another quick glance at the photograph of Abrar. He looked at the three girls in their headscarves. Their faces were rounded slightly be the tightness of the scarf under their chins.

The announcement over the tannoy system was made only a minute later. The three men were about 30m from the women and pointing at the various exits, smiling, telling people there was no hurry. It was merely a precaution. They moved closer. They saw the three women looking around.

Jones looked again at his phone and again at the girls. 'I am sure they aren't the ones!'

Macnair stared at the three women in burqas. Their veils were unclipped and hanging down so that they could drink their coffees. He saw that they were older women. He looked around, fear stalking him as the possibility of what could happen hammered home if they didn't find the three bombers in the next minute or two.

Hunter walked along the platform towards the dead body. It hadn't taken many seconds for the place to empty of passengers but now it was filling up again with police. He stood looking thoughtfully down at the inert form and then knelt alongside it. He carefully rolled up the kagool and looked pensively at the vest.

'Did you shoot him?' An overweight Superintendent asked him. He was a member of the Met, but not CO19.

'Yes. As well as the other one.'

'Then I'll need your weapon. Drop it in this bag.' He held out an evidence bag.

Hunter knew it was SOP after a shooting. However, that didn't apply to TIFAT operatives.

'I said hand over your weapon. You were told no shooting.'

Hunter looked at the man for a couple of seconds. 'Say that again.'

'You were told no shooting by Chief Superintendent Hargreaves.'

Hunter nodded. 'Yes. But Hargreaves is an idiot. A gutless, pen pushing moron.'

The Superintendent began to get indignant. 'How dare you talk about a senior officer like that! I'll have you on report! Hand over your weapon!'

'Look, I've just killed two men and you're talking like an idiot about putting me on a report because of my comments about Hargreaves? Take a look at that PE. What was I supposed to do? Yell, halt or I fire? Is that what happened on the other platform?

The man looked uncomfortable for a moment or two.

Hunter knelt down and took a closer look at the firing mechanism. The trigger was a button on the front of a black box about the size of a cigarette packet. It was held in place by a belt strapped to the man's waist. Inside, he knew, would be the batteries to operate the detonators. The vest was thick cotton with vertical pockets running its length, about 5cms wide. One of the wires led to the back and Hunter assumed there were another four, possibly five pockets. He could see they were stuffed full. Tentatively, he touched one of the pockets and then squeezed slightly. He could feel the bumps created by ball-bearings. He wasn't surprised. They would increase the effectiveness of the explosion by a considerable factor.

It was a simple but deadly piece of gear.

He was acknowledged as being more than adept when it came to dealing with explosives - either using them or rendering them safe. He knew that experts from the Royal Engineers were standing by. These people spent their lives dealing with explosives. They would be arriving shortly. With no lives at risk, only damage to the Underground, there was no need for him to stay.

It was then that a red glow from underneath the black box caught his eye. He knelt down and put his head almost in the crotch of the body. What he saw made him curse. On an LCD screen he saw the seconds ticking down, heading inexorably to 12.00. There were 6 minutes and 13 seconds to go.

Hunter leapt up and yelled, 'Everybody out. Move it!' The policemen and policewomen stopped what they were doing and looked at him in surprise. 'Get out! There's...'

He was interrupted by the Superintendent. 'Look, I don't know who you are but you can't yell orders like that.' His anger was palpable.

'Everybody out, except this idiot. The vests are on time switches and will go off in, he looked again, 'about six minutes.'

That sent a shudder of fear through the twenty or so people there.

'There's no guarantee that's the real timescale as these things can be set to display a different time to what they are set for,' he shouted.

The platform began to empty. The Superintendent turned to go, a green look about his face.

Hunter couldn't help himself. He grabbed the Superintendent's arm. 'You stay here and look after things.'

The man tried to pull his arm free but to no avail. 'Let me go!'

'You're a sanctimonious idiot just like Hargreaves. Get lost.' Hunter took his hand away.

The man forgot all about Hunter's gun. He hurried away, puffing and panting, his size and too many cigarettes having taken their toll.

As time had passed, the bombers had become more creative when it came to designing the vests. First, there were no zips or buttons. The bombers helped each other on with the vests and then sowed them together. A change of mind at the last minute made removing the vests all the more difficult. The timer meant two things. A change of mind, and a decision not to press the button was overridden by the timer and the vest exploded anyway. But there was a further, hidden trick to the system. The timer could be set to explode earlier than the display indicated. It meant anyone trying to disarm the device could be caught out and also killed. With the platforms clear and with no danger to life, Hunter took off at a run. He shot past the gasping, waddling Superintendent and some of the others hurrying to get out.

It wasn't until he hit the pavement that he had a signal on his phone and was able to connect with Macnair.

45

'SHOULD WE GO as well?' Maida asked. 'Abrar, tell us what we must do.'

Abrar looked at her friends, unsure, indecisive. What choice did they have? What to do? They couldn't stay. Should they set the explosives off there and then? But people were already moving away from them. The explosions might damage the building but every second meant fewer people would die. Their sacrifice could be watered down to virtually nothing. To insignificance! The thought filled her with dread.

Abrar looked around. Allah, help me, she called out in her mind. Help me! She saw the police officers coming closer. They were smiling, pointing. She suddenly made up her mind. The policemen were only metres away. They were looking at them. The older one was smiling, the other two frowning.

Macnair saw that the three western looking girls were staring at them. A second later Macnair made the connection. One was Abrar. There was no doubt. Older than the photograph but definitely her.

'It's the women straight ahead!' he yelled.

Abrar suddenly stood up. The crowd was rapidly thinning. She started after them, almost running. She didn't look back. Instead, she screamed, *'Allahu Akbar*! *Allahu Akbar*!'

Macnair raised the H&C to his shoulder and fired twice into the back of Abrar's head. She was blown forward and landed on her front. The force of her dropping onto the floor could possibly set off the bomb. Macnair prayed that this wouldn't happen as he turned back to the tableau behind him. Even as Macnair was registering the fact that there was no explosion he was absorbing what was going on with the other two.

Sofia's hands were resting on the table. She was facing away from Abrar and looked in surprise over her shoulder in time to see her friend's head being blown apart. She sat unmoving, her mouth open. Jones darted forward and grabbed her hands, squeezing them so tightly Sofia's knuckles cracked and she screamed in pain.

Smith was frozen to the spot. He was looking the wrong way, staring at the body. Maida was looking at Abrar, horror and fear written on her face. Then she looked at Smith, looked at Macnair, looked back to Sofia and Jones and moved her hands to her waist.

Macnair didn't have time to direct either of the two men to shoot one of the targets. Instead he fired. His first shot hit Sofia in the forehead. As her head was thrown back, his second round smashed through her chin, the roof of her mouth and into her brain. Even from such a close distance, thanks to the hollow tipped rounds there were no exit wounds.

'Don't let her move,' Macnair ordered Jones.

Sofia was sobbing, her shoulders shaking, her head sunk down. Macnair, none too gently, ripped her jacket off her shoulders to expose the explosives vest. He tore it the rest of the way off.

'Hold her tight,' said Macnair to Jones, grabbing the back of the chair and tilting it all the way back. He stepped round and took hold of Sofia's ankles. 'Lift her off the chair.'

Sofia began to struggle, screaming and moaning at the same time.

'Smith take her ankles and both of you stretch her out. Don't let her move. '

The two officers did as they were ordered. Pandemonium was breaking out in the hall as more people saw the dead bodies of the two girls. The blood and gore was horrendous and children were beginning to cry.

Macnair had his radio to his mouth. 'All, I repeat, all officers to Terminal 3. We need the bomb squad. The three women have been dealt with.'

Already, officers were streaming in from all over the airport. Fire blankets were grabbed and thrown over the bodies hiding the blood and gore. People were pushed back and a perimeter was set up.

Macnair switched his mobile back. It rang almost instantly.

'Sir? The vests have timers. They are set for twelve hundred.'

'Thank you, Commander.'

Macnair yelled at the other officers to move away. 'The vests have a timer. Give me your cuffs,' Macnair ordered Jones who was holding Sofia's hands. The officer pulled Sofia's hands together, held them in one bone-crushing grip and handed the cuffs over. Macnair slapped them on Sofia's right wrist - tightly - grabbed a length of chain used for lane control and clipped it to the other end of the handcuffs, pulled the chain tight and tied it to the metal railing marking Starbuck's boundary.

While he did so, he said to Smith, 'Do the same to her legs.' He looked over his shoulder. 'You two,' he nodded his head at one of the patrols who had joined them, 'give us a hand. We need your cuffs.'

The two men unclipped their cuffs from their belts and knelt beside the girl. Sofia was spread-eagled, wriggling, sobbing and moaning, begging to be let loose.

'Shut up, you murdering bitch,' snarled one of the officers, 'before I shut you up.'

Sofia took no notice, tears streaming down the side of her face, her wriggling getting more frantic.

Macnair ignored the comment. He knew how the officer felt and was expressing the thoughts of many. They all knew that the danger wasn't over and fear was palpable in the air.

Macnair said, 'Right, you two, grab the other two bodies and drag them over here. Be careful the switches don't press on the floor. We don't know how delicately balanced they are.' Nobody moved for a moment. 'Come on! Move it.'

Four officers jumped to the task. They threw aside the blankets covering the bodies, grabbed arms and legs each, lifted Akbar and Maida and unceremoniously placed them alongside Sofia.

One of the men yelled, 'Look at the blood and guts and brains. Look at them!' He knelt beside Sofia, grabbed her chin and twisted her head to look at Akbar's shattered head.

Sofia screamed.

'That's what you wanted to do to the men, women and children in here. You are filth! I am a Muslim and you bring shame down on our great religion and dishonour to your family and all Muslims everywhere. Suicide means you go to Jahannam. The souls of these women are now being tortured in eternal fire and damnation. When you die you will be joining them!'

The officer stood up and faced Macnair, 'I am sorry, sir. It was unprofessional of me.'

'It's okay.' He looked at his watch. 'But time's running out. The bombs are also on timers.'

The officers quickly stepped well away, forming a cordon over 30m from the sobbing Sofia.

Two people rushed across to Macnair, an MI5 senior officer and a Chief Inspector of CO19.

The CO19 officer and Macnair shook hands. 'Chris Denning, sir. I've been informed who you are. It's a pleasure to meet you.'

'Thank you. Likewise,' said the General. 'Hello, Seb,' he shook hands with the agent from MI5.

'Hello, Malcolm.'

'What's the score?' asked Denning.

'One of my men phoned. He was at the King's Cross attack. The bombs are on a timer. The vests are packed with PE and ball bearings. We need the Sappers here now!'

The words were barely out of his mouth when three men and a woman arrived. They were in uniform and had the maroon and blue insignia of the Corps of Royal Engineers on their shoulders. Macnair knew the Regiment well, having been a guest at official dinners in Chatham, Kent. The Sappers had no battle honours but had been involved in every war, every battle and just about every skirmish since they were first formed during the time of William the Conqueror, by Bishop Gundulf of Rochester Cathedral. The regiment claimed over 900 years of unbroken service to the crown and the country. As far as Macnair was concerned, the Corps held the bravest men and women who walked the earth.

One of the men was a captain, the other three were sergeants.

Macnair said, looking at his watch, 'According to my information, we have about five minutes. The bombs have timers.'

The four Sappers exchanged looks. They knew all too well what that meant.

The Chief Inspector said, 'Now that the situation is contained we have a duty of care and assistance to the prisoner. In this case,' he nodded in the direction of Sofia who was no longer struggling but sobbing and keening loudly, 'her.'

'What do you want us to do, sir?' one of the sergeants asked.

They were already kitted out in body armour, a precaution that was a waste of time. That much PE would blow anyone into tiny pieces.

The Captain said, 'Lofty, Cecil, grab the dead bodies and drag them into the middle of the concourse. Leave them together. Sal, I'll go in. I'll try and save the girl. If we have time we'll see about the other two devices.' He looked at the others. 'I'm not risking the lives of my men to try and stop a building being damaged.'

'I agree,' said Macnair, nodding.

The Captain switched on his radio and hurried across the room. 'Okay, Sally,' he called over his shoulder.

'Yes, Sam. Loud and clear!'

Macnair had seen Sappers at work in the past. His admiration for them knew no bounds and he watched as Sergeant Sally began to repeat what the Captain said. He couldn't help wondering what a lovely looking young woman was doing in such a dangerous profession. He guessed she was barely 5ft 4ins tall, the minimum height requirement to become a Sapper. 'Roger that, sir. Basic. Cutting both wires. Timer stopped.'

The Sergeant smiled at the audience who had been staring at the Captain. All done. 'What's that?' He put his finger to his earpiece. 'All out. We have less than a minute before the two bombs go off!'

Macnair ran across the concourse to Sofia's prone body. She was moaning and wriggling. The captain was unclipping the handcuffs from the rope at her wrists while Macnair did the same for her legs. Macnair lifted the girl's legs at the knees while the captain lifted her under the arms. She continued to struggle though her efforts were becoming feebler by the second. They hurried towards the exit doors and barged through stepping to the left, putting the wall between them and the expected blast. Just as they did, there was a tremendous explosion followed a second later by another.

Ball bearings hit the walls and shattered the windows like bullets from a machine gun. Luckily, no one was hurt, though there were screams and yells. Then silence reigned for a few seconds and then a spontaneous roar went up, as the people realised how close they had come to death. Macnair wasn't sure if it was a roar of relief or anger. Probably both, he thought.

'My job is done,' Macnair said to the officers nearest him. 'I have to get back to London. By the way, Jones, you did well. I'm going to put you up for a commendation. Smith, you need to get your act together.' Macnair had never been one to pull his punches. He knew all too well that if he hadn't been there the outcome would probably have been entirely different. SO19 in particular and SIS in general couldn't afford to have officers like Smith. The man needed to be directing traffic, not prancing around places like Heathrow with a machine gun slung over his shoulder.

Thanks to Hunter killing the two terrorists and managing to clear the platform, the resultant explosions had not killed or hurt anyone. However, the initial explosion had killed two officers from CO19, as well as eighteen passengers and injured a further thirty-six. The tape from the safety cameras covering the platform showed the officers with their weapons aimed at the terrorist's head.

The voice of one of the officers ordering him to lay down, with his arms and legs outstretched was clear. Basil's face showed clearly that he was shocked at the turn of events. When the tape was slowed down it showed him moving his hand under his kagool. The explosion was devastating.

The suicide bomber was later identified as Basel Laham, born and brought up in Birmingham who had become radicalised in his teens. He had spent many months in Pakistan and, it was thought, Syria.

Somebody made a copy of the film and sent it to various news outlets. As a result, it was broadcast around the world. The shock and horror displayed by people in the West was in sharp contrast to the jubilation shown by those who lived in the Middle East. The leaders of the Muslim communities condemned what had happened in no uncertain terms, pointing out that three of the passengers killed and two injured had been British born Muslims. Politician after politician was interviewed and kept saying that a bomb was indiscriminate. That all sectors of society were at risk. The British National Party used the incident to stir up hatred of all things Islamic.

46

FITZGERALD HAD THE information he'd downloaded off Freddy's memory stick and had read through it. It was strong stuff. It was marked top secret on every page with dire warnings at the beginning and end that the information wasn't to be divulged. There were threats of fines and imprisonment. He didn't believe it. That was rubbish. In a democratic society the people had the right to know what was going on. Of that there was no doubt. His quandary was who should he take the information to? Who would pay the most? How much was it worth?

He was walking in Regent's Park, happy to get out of the house and away from Freddy's baleful looks. He was sure Freddy knew about David, but that was too bad. He was bored with Freddy and had been for a long time. He craved change and excitement. It was why he could never be faithful. His problem was he had no money and no job.

He shuddered at the thought of having to find work as a teacher in a third rate, deprived area school trying to educate morons well enough for them to pass an exam in geography. God, the thought was unbearable. That was why he had put up with Freddy all this time. But he wanted out. He had one of two ways to do it. Get his hands on a load of money or find someone as generous as Freddy. He'd noticed that Freddy was becoming more parsimonious by the day. That was why he was sure Freddy knew about David. David excited him but he was also penniless. A dropout from school he had amounted to nothing whatsoever. The most demanding job he had ever aspired to or achieved was serving in a fast food joint in Clapham.

So there was only one thing for it. He had to sell the information to the highest bidder and it had to be high. What was the minimum he could accept? A hundred thousand? Two? Three? Was it worth that much? Yes. He was sure it was. But who would pay? Those were the questions tormenting him. Then he had an idea. One that had his heart racing. Of course! Idiot! He berated himself. He looked at his watch. He'd give it another half-an-hour. Freddy would be gone and he'd have the house to himself.

Impatiently, he drifted around the park and then, after twenty minutes, headed back to the house. As he expected, when he arrived, he was alone. He flashed up his computer and started work. He took extracts of a few sentences only, tantalising whoever read them, with the thought that there was so much more to read. The scandal and political fallout had the potential to be huge. Any investigative journalist or political editor would recognise that fact.

When he was finished he sat there, indecisive. What was the best thing to do? Should he e-mail them or post them? E-mail was quickest. But there was always the danger that the message would be dumped in the spam box and never read. Or how about an e-mail plus a phone call? That should do it. Who to send it to?

It had to be the written press. To the best of his knowledge the broadcasters rarely, if ever, paid for information. No. This sort of stuff needed an article in a newspaper or serialised in a magazine, and followed up by radio and television interviews as appetisers to the full story.

This was his way to fame and fortune and freedom. He started on a list of newspapers. This stuff was weekend reading. It was ideal for the Sundays.

The Mail on Sunday
The Sun on Sunday
The Sunday Times
The Sunday Telegraph
The Sunday Express
The Sunday Mirror
The Observer
The People

He studied the list. He decided that he would contact them all. He googled their sites and found the names of their political editors, phone numbers and e-mail addresses.

Next question. Should he let them know they were in a bidding war? Or should he keep it secret? What to do? Maybe he should keep it secret to start with and, once he knew how the land lay, open it up to bids. Yes. That would be the sensible thing to do.

He personalised each e-mail and sent it. He'd give it 10 minutes before he made the calls. It was just long enough to make himself a cup of tea.

The Pashni used her own steam to draw away from the jetty. Her diesel tanks had been topped up and she had taken on the necessary provisions and fresh water. She was ready for a long voyage.

General Khan stood on the bridge wing. It was precisely midday. He smiled. Right now there should be deaths, injuries, destruction, panic, fear, and total chaos. He breathed deeply and began to say the Dhuhr. He blessed Allah and the prophet for all that they had helped him to achieve so far. The meetings with the infidels had gone well. They had accepted him as the leader of their widespread criminal empire and assured him that it would be business as usual.

He finished praying and leant on the railings on his elbows. He narrowed his eyes. Yes, it had gone well, but there was one man he didn't trust. A Somali. An avowed fundamentalist and hater of all things Western. There was something about the man he didn't like. He would have to have him investigated and he knew just the people to do it. Or was he reading too much into it? He hated all blacks. They were the dogs of the earth. They were only good to serve the true believers, the followers of Islam in countries like his own, Iran and Afghanistan. Africans were born to be their slaves - it was all they were good for.

The ship was now sedately passing through the narrow entrance and beginning to turn to port. He stepped back onto the bridge and said to the Captain, 'I shall be in my cabin. I wish to listen to the news.' He nodded to the pilot who would be leaving the ship before they reached the open sea.

In the cabin he sent for the steward to bring fresh coffee. He then tuned the radio to the all day news and sports channel, BBC Radio 5 live.

He was sitting at the desk, his feet propped up on one corner, his coffee in his hand when the interview with a minor politician was cut short.

'There has been an explosion on London Underground. The

details are sketchy but we know that a number of people have been killed. There are also reports coming in of explosions at Heathrow airport but so far there are no reports of any casualties.

The General was a happy man. It was all going to plan. The attacks would divert any attention from him. At the same time they would help to create unrest in the West and more hatred of all things Islamic.

As reporters gained access to the sites of the explosions and to official spokesmen, the full picture began to emerge. The General began to realise that the attacks had not gone according to plan. He got to his feet and began pacing the cabin. He was panting as though he had been running for miles. Growing angrier by the minute, he stopped next to the desk and looked for something on which to vent his spleen. He picked up the cup and saucer and threw them against the bulkhead where they shattered and scattered across the carpet.

He wanted to kill somebody. Anybody. Then, after a while, he had his breathing under control. He stopped pacing and he sat back to listen to the details.

Two terrorists had been killed on the platform for the Victoria Line at King's Cross. They had been shot by members of SO19. A third man had detonated a suicide vest and killed himself, two members of SO19, 18 civilians and a further 36 injured. Damage to both platforms had been extensive and the lines were expected to be closed for days if not weeks.

At Heathrow there had been two suicide bombers who had died. Both had been shot by an officer in SO19. Their bombs had exploded but no one had been injured. A third terrorist, a young woman had been taken into custody.

It could have been worse, Khan convinced himself. They could all have been stopped. So some good had come of it. The question was how had the security services got on to them so quickly? Could it have been the journalists? Where was that idiot Rind? He'd been given the simple job of killing two journalists. One he had dealt with. The second he had heard nothing about. So where was Rind?

Khan would be taking off in an hour. The helo would fly him to the airport at Calais and from there he had a small private plane ready to take him to Charles de Gaulle airport. He was booked on an evening flight back to Islamabad using a false passport. He didn't want anyone outside of his tight circle to know he had even been out of the country, never mind where he'd been and what he'd been up to.

Lots of terrorist activity in Europe, massive funding thanks to Rabbani's criminal organisation and a major attack in Pakistan. When added together this all made him a dead cert for President. He had changed his mind about the time scale. He wasn't going to wait until the next election. As soon as he quelled the attack by the Taliban he would instigate a vote of no-confidence, massive riots and demands for action.

He would be the man to save Pakistan and ferment Jihad on a worldwide footing from the security and fortress that would be Pakistan. Jihad was a religious duty of all Muslims. The word meant struggle and, in the Quran referred to the never ending struggle against those who did not believe in Allah as described in the holy book.

Khan closed his eyes and contemplated the words he had read so often in the Quran. There were two meanings to Jihad. The first was greater Jihad which meant the internal spiritual struggle to fulfil one's religious duties. It was non-violent as opposed to the lesser Jihad which meant an armed struggle against all non-believers of Islam. The General was at peace with his greater Jihad, and spent any spiritual time thinking about the lesser Jihad. As President of Pakistan he would have the greatest power at his finger tips.

He would have his hands on nuclear weapons. The sword of Islam would be his to use! It was a breathtaking thought and one that kept him awake at nights.

Hunter met Macnair back at the Naval Club.

'We're finished down here,' said the General, a cup of excellent coffee in his hand, his elbows on the table in front of him.

Hunter was leaning back, his coffee cup sitting in a saucer before him. The room was old-fashioned, wood lined, naval prints and a few original paintings all of battle scenes at sea were hung around the walls. The other tables were empty; most people were in the TV lounge watching what was happening at Heathrow and King's Cross. Both men had changed out of their

SO19 uniforms and were once more in civilian clothes. Macnair had on a light grey suit with a naval club tie while Hunter wore a dark blue blazer, grey trousers and an open-necked white dress shirt.

'What's going to happen about the men who visited the Pashni?' Hunter asked.

'Nothing to do with us. Organised crime has it all under control, so Elspeth assures me.'

'Good.'

'You've a few days owing. What are you going to do?'

Hunter smiled. 'I'm taking the Talisman to Rosyth.'

'Rabbani's yacht?'

'The very same. Why not, sir? Who else is going to claim it? It'll make a great toy for us to have. I was thinking along the lines of us paying to use her and giving the funds raised to a charity. Like Help for Heroes. You've no objection, do you, sir?'

Macnair waved his left hand in front of him as he used his right to put his cup to his mouth and take a sip. 'Not at all. We may as well. What about crew?'

Hunter merely shrugged and said, 'I'll sort something out.'

Macnair smiled and said, 'I hope she proves to be a good sailor. How long will it take to get there?'

'It's about four hundred and fifty miles. Even at ten knots I'll be in Rosyth in forty-eight hours. I'll play around with those figures. Maybe stop somewhere on the way.' Hunter finished his coffee. 'Sir, if there's nothing else, I'll get going.'

'No, that's all. Enjoy your cruise.'

Hunter went up to his room, packed his belongings, paid the bill and left for the train station. At 16.00 he was walking along the pontoon towards the Talisman.

Rosemary Young watched his approach. When he was just a few yards away she smiled and said, 'Welcome.'

Hunter stepped onboard and replied, 'Thanks. Everything okay?'

'Yes. Kath is down below watching the news. I saw some of it but figured I would be doing a better job if I came up here and kept an eye out.'

'You're right. Seen anything suspicious?'

'Not a thing. One yacht left from the other pontoon about an hour ago but apart from that it's been as quiet as the grave. Now you're back, do you have any orders for me?'

Hunter gave a half shrug. 'I guess you may as well RTB. And thanks.'

'My inspector called. I'm off for the next five days. So I'll be going home.'

Just then, Kathleen put her head out. 'Nick, you're back! I've just been watching the news. Did you have anything to do with what happened?'

'Some. Why?'

'I've been hearing about the deaths of those Muslim girls. The poor deluded things. And I feel so sorry for their families. I don't believe for a moment they couldn't have been taken prisoner. Did you shoot them?'

Hunter stared at Kathleen for a few seconds before replying, 'Suppose I did?'

'Then,' said the reporter contemptuously, 'you're a murdering thug and should be in prison.'

'Are you for real? Have you any idea what decisions had to be taken? How little time there was to respond to what was going down?'

'I don't know and I don't care.' She was stiff backed with anger.

'Okay, if that's what you believe then there's nothing further to say. You may like to know that I received a message on my way here to the effect that in view of what's happened you can, if you wish, either stay with me for a couple of days or go straightaway to a secure location until the threat to you can be removed. What do you want to do?'

'I cannot stay with you. I'm repelled by the things you've done. Like kill those girls.'

It had always been the same and it always would be. When the proverbial hit the fan it was the front-line services the public screamed to for help, whether that was the police, SIS or the military. He didn't bother replying but took out his phone, speed dialled Macnair and, looking at Kathleen, said, 'Sir? Kathleen, the journalist, is insistent she doesn't want to stay here. I'm sending her back to London with Sergeant Young. Can you arrange a safe house?' He listened for a few seconds. 'Thanks, sir.' He broke the connection. 'That's fixed.' He looked at Rosemary. 'General Macnair is talking to your boss. He'll sort out a safe house and tell you where to take her.' He turned his attention back to Kathleen. 'Are you packed?'

'It'll only take me a few minutes. I'm sorry, Nick. It's just...It's just...Oh, I don't know, I can't explain it.'

'You don't need to. Pity. I'm taking the boat north in the morning and thought you might like to come with me. I can just as easily make the journey on my own.'

Rosemary nodded. 'That's fine with me. I'll just grab my stuff.'

The two women went below and were back in a few minutes. As they climbed down on to the pontoon and turned to leave, Hunter spoke. 'Incidentally, Kath, I wasn't at Heathrow. I didn't shoot those girls.'

Kathleen hesitated.

'Goodbye,' Hunter said.

The two women walked away and Hunter watched them go. Kathleen didn't look back, Rosemary did and gave a little wave. Hunter didn't respond. It had been a long, tough day. The adrenaline rush of action had left him feeling tired and Kathleen's attitude left him angry.

He went below, poured himself a whisky and soda, opened a packet of salted peanuts and sat at the upper console, his feet up. It was a beautiful evening, there wasn't a cloud in the sky, a light breeze was coming from the south, the rigging in the yachts was rattling faintly and a pleasant calm blanketed the area.

47

ALGERNON FITZGERALD WAS in a blue funk. He had phoned the editors of the newspapers he had contacted and none of them were particularly interested in what he had to tell them. He had insisted there was a great deal more and had given each of them a few more paragraphs. Then a few more. What he hadn't realised was that he was playing poker with experts. Once they had extracted enough information for a story they would leave it there. Anything they were unsure about they would make up. After all, no reporter in any of the media ever allowed the facts to interfere with a good story. Such things as ethics and honour died out around 1950.

Finally, he got a bite. It was the Guardian. They were prepared to go as high as £10,000 and not a penny more for the full information.

Fitzgerald sat at the bar of a local pub and nursed a large gin and tonic. It was his third and the ice had barely melted when he lifted the glass and took a long swallow. He placed the glass back down on the bar and looked at the slice of lemon floating in it with a great deal of introspection. Ten thousand lousy quid. It wasn't enough. Not by a few hundred thousand. Were the editors that stupid? Self pity welled up within him. The unfairness of it was what rankled the most. Life was unfair. He deserved a far better life than the one he had. Still, ten grand would pay off his credit cards and leave him with a few hundred to spend. He would have to get his hands on more of the house-keeping. Since Freddy had taken to scrutinising the invoices so closely it was becoming more difficult by the day. He was beginning to hate the man he had been living with for so many years. If only he had started siphoning off some cash from the very beginning. He would have a very healthy bank balance by now. It had just never occurred to him. Damn, damn and damn!

He saw, with some surprise, that his glass was empty and he

gestured to the barman for a refill.

Hunter decided to go below for a nap. He left half the whisky and the uneaten peanuts and went below. He slipped off his shoes and lay down on the couch with a couple of cushions under his head. He went out like a light.

The boat rocking brought him wide awake. It wasn't a question of groggily coming to and wondering where he was. One second he was asleep, the next he was wide awake, sliding off the couch, and slipping his hand under the cushions for his Pocketlite. He stayed where he was for a few seconds. It was dusk and the clock on the bulkhead showed 22.03. He heard footsteps on the deck and moved softly across to the door. He slowly went up the steps to the upperdeck. From the sound of it, there was only one person. Even so, he wasn't going to rush anything. There could be others waiting for him standing on the pontoon.

He looked over the edge of the deck. There was someone in the well deck. A quick glance to his left showed there was nobody else on the pontoon. He stood up and then gave a sigh.

'What an unexpected pleasure,' he said.

Rosemary Young was sitting on the aft bench, a bag was at her feet. 'Hello. Oh, hell. I had it all worked out. Something clever to say. But here I am and I'm tongue tied. What am I doing here you might be wondering?'

Hunter stepped down to her and smiled. 'I'm delighted to see you. It was going to be a lonely cruise to Scotland. I take it that's why you're here? To help me man this thing?'

Rosemary smiled. 'Something like that. You don't mind?'

'Me? Mind? Good lord, no. Far from it. Let me take your bag.' He swept it up in his left hand, his right dangling down by his side, the pistol gripped in it.

'Will you put it in the guest cabin or the owner's?'

'Where would you like me to put it?'

'In the owner's cabin. It saves needing to wash a second pair of sheets.'

'That's highly practical. I'll do that. How about opening some wine? There's white in the fridge and red in a rack next to it.'

They sat out on the upper deck, a bottle of red wine on the table in front of them. It was nearly midnight. Hunter was wearing a pair of jeans and a short-sleeved shirt while Rosemary had on a flimsy dressing gown, held together by a belt tied at the waist. She had nothing on underneath.

'What time shall we leave?' she asked softly. It was an absolutely still night and voices carried across the water.

'When we're ready,' said Hunter. 'There's no hurry. Unless you have to get back?'

'No. Well, not for five days.'

'Same here. In that case we can take it easy. We'll stop off on the way north. Find some quiet little port to visit. How does that sound?'

'Lovely.'

'I'm glad you came back. It was going to be a long, lonely voyage otherwise. Or at least, a lonely couple of days.'

'Are you kidding? To spend a few days on a boat like this? The height of luxury?'

'And I thought it was all down to my magnetic charm.'

Rosemary chuckled. 'There was that as well.'

'How do you enjoy being with the Met?'

'I like it a lot. There's always something different going on. The only thing I hate is the paperwork. Of which there is far too much.'

'It was the same in the navy. However, with my lot, paperwork is kept to a bare minimum. No tedious after operation reports. Just a chat with the General. Useful information is gone over, classified and stored and that's about it. It lets us get on with our job.'

'Tell me about the bruise on your chest,' Rosemary abruptly changed the subject.

Hunter rubbed it. 'It doesn't hurt anymore.'

'How did you get it?'

'Em. Somebody hit me there with his elbow.'

'No they didn't. I've seen films of bruises like that.'

'You have? Why? What for?'

'To show us how effective a vest is. Not the stab vests, but a fully fledged, all singing, all dancing, Kevlar bullet proof job. They show us the film to give us confidence in the equipment. Is that what happened? Were you shot?'

Hunter shrugged. 'It was no big deal.'

Rosemary shook her head. 'It was. A few inches higher and we wouldn't be having this conversation.'

'True.'

'Doesn't it bother you?'

Hunter frowned, considering the question. 'Bother is the wrong word. I don't want to die until I am a ripe old age but that doesn't mean I'm going to stop what I'm doing.'

'Aren't you ever afraid?'

'Of course. Fear helps to keep you alive. I really believe that. It means you're extra careful. No gung ho and once more unto the breach. No fair play. Sneaky and deadly is the name of the game. Except, of course, it isn't a game. I know...I know, it sounds contrite, but fear with a healthy dose of paranoia helps keep you from dying. For you guys it's full kit and in the eyes of the public, very often. There's a certain safety in numbers and openness. For us it's underhand, down with the scum, scraping slime balls off the shoes of civilisation.'

'Wow! That's almost poetic.'

Hunter looked slightly sheepish. It wasn't in his nature to speak so openly about such things. He changed the subject. 'Out of interest, what was up with Kath?'

'Does it matter?'

'I suppose not. I'm just interested. I've known her for a while, though not well. Let's face it, she came running to me and now she couldn't get away fast enough.'

'I stupidly told her what I knew about some of your exploits. She asked me how many people you had killed.'

'What did you say?'

Rosemary looked guilty for a few seconds. 'I may have exaggerated the figures a little.'

'Why would you want to do that?'

'I don't like people like her. Holier than thou until she needs people like us. Well, more like you, really. I tried to remind her of that but she went on about humans being killed, not monsters. I suppose it's always the way, Nick. We just have to accept it. We don't have to like it, but we do have to accept it.'

'You're right, of course, and I do. Like you, I just occasionally get hacked off with the ingratitude of some members of society. Do you like poetry?'

'Some. Though I won't claim to be a huge fan,' said Rosemary, sipping her wine.

'I like a lot of Rudyard Kipling's stuff. Do you know the poem, *Tommy*?'

'I've heard of it.'

'My favourite lines are, *For its Tommy this, an' Tommy that, an' "Chuck him out, the brute! But its "Saviour of 'is country" when the guns begin to shoot.'*

'I suppose it was always thus.'

'That's true. The problem is it's becoming worse.' Hunter took a sip of his wine and helped himself to a handful of peanuts. 'Anyway, enough doom and gloom. What are your ambitions? Stay in and climb the slippery pole of promotion?'

'Probably. Unless I meet the right man, get married and have two point four children or one point eight or whatever it is. What about you?'

'Me? I don't know. I'll certainly stay where I am for the next few years. I won't go back to the mob. The RN and I have parted company. I guess it's too tame.'

'What about the right woman, marriage and all the attachments? Has there ever been anyone? Sorry, did I touch a nerve? Me and my big mouth.'

'No, it's okay. There was somebody. A few years ago.'

'What happened? Did she die?'

'No. Though she came close. She's an Israeli. Works for Mossad.'

'Works for? She still does?'

'As far as I know. I thought we were going to go the full hog but it didn't work out.'

'What stopped you?' Rosemary took a drink of wine, and then added, 'Sorry. It's none of my business if you don't want to talk about it.'

'Oh, no, it's nothing like that. Things just happened. The job got in the way for both of us and she walked out, all the way back to Israel.'

'Didn't you go after her?'

'As a matter of fact, I did. But I realised it was no good and moved on with my life. It was probably for the best. Anyway, I have no regrets.' He grinned. 'And here I am with a beautiful woman, on a luxury boat, about to embark on a five day cruise in near perfect weather. How can it possibly get any better?'

'Let's go below and I'll show you.'

Hunter slid his arm out from under Rosemary's head and then slipped out of bed. He put on a t-shirt, shorts, socks and running shoes. He put his bumbag around his waist, checked the Pocketlite and went up top. It was just coming up to 07.00. Stepping ashore, he headed along the pontoon towards the gate. He reached the car park and began to jog. A few minutes later he picked up his pace to a fast run. Twenty minutes after setting out he came to a quiet parking place. He dropped to the ground and did 50 fast push-ups, turned on his back and did 50 sit-ups. Then he turned over and did a further 50 push-ups before leaping to his feet. He ran, he didn't jog. He cut four minutes off the time to get back. He stopped with his hands on his knees, gasping for air. He quickly got his breath back and went into the marina shop.

He bought fresh milk, four croissants and a newspaper. He also arranged for them to move to the fuelling jetty for 09.00.

He returned to the Talisman where he found Rosemary dressed in shorts and t-shirt putting on the coffee machine.

'I needed the exercise,' he greeted her.

'You have to be kidding! Would you like some bacon and eggs, or something?'

'No, thanks. Orange juice, muesli, croissants and a coffee will do for now. After that we'll take on some diesel and water and head out. I'll have a shower and get changed.'

After breakfast, Hunter took the Talisman to the fuelling slip where the diesel tanks were filled and the water topped off. They then headed out to sea. The water was flat calm and Hunter slowly increased the speed on the boat until she was on the plane doing an indicated 30kts. They maintained that speed for twenty minutes before cutting back to 10kts on automatic pilot. They had to do some zig-zagging past Felixstowe due to the many ships and ferries entering and leaving the busy port.

At 11.00 Hunter left Rosemary to keep an eye out while he went below to make a couple of bacon sandwiches.

They spent the evening at Lowestoft Marina. They ate in a local pub, both enjoying locally caught mussels served as moules marinière. Hunter drank a pint of real ale with his, while Rosemary had a glass of white wine. He admitted that he was a sucker for a decent pint. As he put it, none of that fizzy cold stuff for him, give him a British ale anytime.

Late evening found them sitting on the boat watching the sun set.

The following morning, having paid their harbour dues, they left the marina just after 09.30. He adjusted their course and speed once they were clear of Lowestoft Ness to get to Bridlington at 21.00. He left it to the computers to work it out and just sat back and watched as the world eased by.

They approached Bridlington harbour and were directed to berth on the south side, at the end of the central pier known as Chicken Run. That evening they stayed onboard and ate fillet steak washed down with a fine red wine - courtesy of Rabbani.

In the morning, Hunter moved to another jetty to fill the diesel tanks before they headed out to sea once more.

They continued their leisurely voyage to Rosyth, enjoying each other's company immensely - both in and out of bed. They spent their last night alongside in Granton Harbour, Leith, before arriving in Rosyth at 11.00.

Macnair was there to meet them when Hunter took the boat alongside the jetty at HMS Cochrane. One look at his face told Hunter something was up.

48

The General caught the head rope and adroitly secured it to a cleat. He walked along the pontoon and did the same with the stern rope. Hunter cut the engines.

Macnair stepped onto the boat and held out his hand to Rosemary. 'Pleased to meet you sergeant.'

'Likewise, sir.'

'Good trip?'

'Yes, thank you. I don't think I've ever been surrounded by such luxury. Can I get you a coffee or a cup of tea?'

'Coffee, black, no sugar would be much appreciated.'

'What's up, sir?' Hunter asked.

'Have you been listening to the news?'

'Not much. It was too good an opportunity to get away from it all, and that included listening to the BBC.'

'In that case you won't have heard that three bombs have gone off. One was premature and the only death was the bomber himself. The other two were in shopping malls. Men dressed in burqas, veils, the lot. A total of forty-six people killed and over one hundred and twenty injured.'

'My God,' said Rosemary, 'where?'

'The Leeds Corn Exchange shopping centre and the Bullring in Birmingham.'

'Any warnings given?' asked Rosemary.

Macnair shook his head. 'Nothing.'

'I'll just be a few minutes,' said Rosemary. 'I'll get you the coffees. Nick?'

'Yes, please.'

She went below and Hunter could hear her pottering around in the galley.'

'Anyone claiming responsibility?'

'Barzakh. They announced it on Twitter, Facebook and about a hundred other social networking sites. Same message about death to non-believers, western foreign policy is to blame, unless all troops are removed from Muslim countries Jihad will continue until the end of time. So on and so on. Stuff we've all heard before.'

'Any good news?' Hunter turned as Rosemary appeared with three mugs of coffee and handed them out.

'There is, though there's a major problem as well.'

'There usually is,' said Hunter. 'What this time?'

'First of all, have you heard of a man by the name of Frederick Ogilvie?'

Hunter frowned and replied, 'I've heard the name.'

'I have,' said Rosemary, 'he's an MP who sits on the Intelligence and Security Committee.'

'Have you had any dealings with him?'

Rosemary shook her head. 'Being a mere sergeant I don't get to move in such exalted circles. Though from what I've heard of the man it's probably just as well.'

'His boyfriend is one Algernon Fitzgerald. He leaked some highly sensitive information to the press. Mainly about us and the operations we're known to have carried out.'

'I thought the committee worked under strict rules of secrecy?' Rosemary said.

'They do,' Macnair replied. 'However, Ogilvie, who is subject to strict adherence to the Official Secrets Act, said that the information was stolen by his live-in partner, unknown to him. He is arguing that he cannot be responsible for such a theft and that it could happen to anyone. Which, on the face of it, is true.'

'But?' Hunter said.

'But I don't believe him. Isobel has been digging. Phone records, e-mails, bank accounts. All the usual. It appears Fitzgerald has another boyfriend. A man by the name of David Crowther. According to Crowther, Fitzgerald wanted to get away from Ogilvie and to start a new life together. Apparently Fitzgerald told Crowther that he had a way to make a lot of money. When Crowther asked him how, Fitzgerald said it would have to remain a secret for a few days but after that they would be living in the lap of luxury. He did say that Fitzgerald mentioned TV appearances and a book deal.'

'What's Ogilvie saying to all of this?' asked Hunter. 'More

importantly, why do you think Ogilvie has something to do with it?'

'It's simple. Ogilvie made a few comments, denounced his former lover and then has spent the time screaming blue murder about our operations. He's revealing stuff that Fitzgerald hasn't.'

'Can't he be stopped?'

'How? It's impossible to get the genie in the bottle once it's out. No, we need a damage limitation strategy which is what I've been working on for the last couple of days.'

'What are you going to do?' Rosemary asked.

Macnair merely shook his head in obvious frustration and then said, 'The press are trying to get hold of me but the calls are being vetted and diverted. Although Judge Parker and Stan Harrow are arguing on our behalf, Nigel Goldsmith is now making a real nuisance of himself. He seems to think that now some information has been made public there's nothing to stop him telling the world about the rest of it. He's yelling murderers and criminals and accusing us of operating outside the law.'

'Which is what TIFAT does and why you're so successful. There are too many idiots who don't understand that. Especially amongst the chattering classes. The armchair holier than though brigade. I can tell you we at Special Operations hate their guts.'

Macnair and Hunter exchanged grins while Rosemary suddenly looked uncomfortable. 'Sorry, General, but Nick and I have already talked about this.'

'I'm sure you have. Commander, leave the boat here for now. We're getting the side jetty tidied up. We'll keep her there. What are your plans, Rosemary?'

'I'm heading south. I've work to get back to. I'll take an afternoon train.'

'You wouldn't rather fly?' Hunter asked.

'No. I've checked the timetable. There's a train at fifteen thirty-five from Rosyth getting in to London King's Cross at twenty fifty-two.'

Hunter asked Macnair, 'Are services back to normal?'

'Yes. Even the underground is running. Look, it's time for lunch. Let's go to the wardroom, and then you can take Rosemary to the station.'

As always, Macnair's suggestion was correctly interpreted as an order.

After lunch, Hunter drove them to Rosyth Station, a few minutes up the road. Neither had mentioned possibly meeting again in the future. When Hunter pulled up outside the station he turned to her and said, 'Thanks. It was fun.'

'Yes, it was.' She smiled and waited for him to speak.

'Care to do it again, sometime?'

'Are you asking me out?'

'Well, yes, I suppose I am.'

'What, drinks and the theatre next time you're in London? Or should we go hiking up Munros the next time I'm in Scotland?'

'I'm more of an underwater man myself as opposed to climbing up mountains over 3,000 feet high.'

Rosemary shook her head. 'I told you, Nick, I love being in SO19. Promotion beckons. I'm not leaving and you made it clear you won't be quitting TIFAT anytime soon. So it's been a pleasant interlude. A very pleasant interlude and one that I will remember for a long time. But that's all it was.'

Hunter could be as poker faced as a Las Vegas gambler when he needed to be and this was one of those times. 'Okay. But at least give me leave to call you should I be in London and at a loose end.'

Rosemary laughed. 'First, you're relieved. You aren't looking for any sort of commitment, are you?'

'I guess not. And second?'

'And second, my fiancée might not like it.'

'Your fiancée?' This time Hunter couldn't avoid showing his surprise.

'I'm getting married in three months. A nice man. Works in the City and earns a fortune. So I may have two point four children after all. Even manage to combine it with a career. You never know.'

'Won't he have missed you for the last few days?'

'He's quite used to it. I sent him a couple of texts but he knows that when I'm on a training course I don't want to be disturbed. I told him this course was an important stepping stone to promotion. That's something he understands. Promotion. So he hasn't been bothering me.'

'I hope you're very happy,' said Hunter.

'Thank you. More than likely I'll become part of the national statistics. Happy and long marriages don't seem to go together with SO19.' She leant over and kissed his cheek. 'Bye Nick. Have a long and happy life.' She opened the door, climbed out, opened the back door, lifted out her small suitcase, waved a hand and walked away without a backward glance.

Hunter put the car into gear and drove away. He admitted to himself he was relieved. Perhaps, though, with a slither of regret in there somewhere. For a moment he wondered why she'd done it and then put the thought to the back of his mind.

Duty called.

Algernon Fitzgerald was terrified. He was sitting in a single cell at Charing Cross Police Station. It was eight feet by six feet. It had a bunk with a thin mattress, a stainless steel sink in the corner and a toilet, the flush handle was embedded in the wall. It was stark, too warm and miserable. He had only just stopped weeping. The tears had rolled unbidden down his cheeks. He was sitting on the edge of the bunk, his feet on the concrete ground, slippers on his feet. He was wearing jeans and a short sleeved, white shirt. It was becoming grubby. His leather belt had been taken from him. That didn't matter. He didn't need it. It had been for show. His head was in his hands, his eyes covered by his fingers. He needed a shave.

The tears started again. He let loose with a low moan. What had he done? What had he done? He kept asking himself the same question over and over. How was he to know that the information was subject to the Official Secrets Act? The announcement at the beginning of the file warning anyone that opened it was breaking the law was ludicrous. It was a farce. Who read that crap nowadays and believed it? Every page with "Top Secret" written along the top in bold, red letters and every page designed to whet the appetite of anyone who read it. It was dynamite. Since his revelations more and more was exposed to the press about the activities of TIFAT.

As always, the press was polarised. The Guardian and its readership were screaming blue murder about TIFAT while the Daily Express and its readers were happy for Macnair and his organisation to continue doing their job.

On one level it was a public relations coup, on another, it was a security nightmare. The most damaging were the photographs of Hunter at the Underground and the part he played in killing the bombers. To some, he was a murderer who should have given the attackers an opportunity to surrender. To the majority, he was a hero and should be given a medal.

Fitzgerald felt the bile rise in his throat. If the people at TIFAT were arrested and tried for their crimes the spotlight would be off him. He could quietly leave and fade away into the background. He could rebuild things with Freddy. He would suggest that they start again. Make a clean break and get things back the way they were. The thought galvanised him. It lifted his spirits for a few seconds and he took his hands away from his face and looked around. His surroundings plummeted him back into despair. Tears of self pity welled up.

Freddy Ogilvie had a bounce in his step when he shaved and showered. He went down to the kitchen, poured himself a freshly squeezed orange juice from his new kitchen appliance designed for that very task, debated with himself whether or not to have scrambled eggs, decided against it and made a slice of toast instead. Another machine created the perfect cup of cappuccino while he swallowed his juice in one long gulp. That was better, he thought. It helped to alleviate the slight hangover he was feeling following the private celebration he had enjoyed the night before. A bottle of Champagne and a few large brandies were just the thing after the satisfying time he had spent with Judge Parker, Stan Harrow and Nigel Goldsmith.

Parker and Harrow were arguing that TIFAT's operations should be kept secret. That identities and names of personnel within the organisation put them and their families at risk. To which he, Frederick Ogilvie MP had replied, tough. They shouldn't have broken the law.

He left his house and went to the nearest Underground. He bought half a dozen papers whose headlines caused him to smile with excitement. There he was! His photograph all over the place. The Indi, the Guardian and Mirror all described him as a fearless champion of the law. The rags such as the Sun, Express and Mail denounced him as a friend of terrorists. The press coverage was ideal. He would be able to prove he was a man of principle and integrity. That he stood for law and order and that without it we were all barbarians. The previous evening, while channel hopping on his TV, looking for news items about him and TIFAT, he had been rehearsing what he would and could say. The sound bites necessary to make the biggest impact.

Three days ago there had been one nasty moment. Actually, it had lasted the best part of an hour. The Security Services led by a senior officer in MI5 had questioned him about the leaking of the information. They had appeared satisfied with his answers and released him with the admonition not to say anything more to the press. He had said he wouldn't and had kept his word for at least 30 minutes. A phone call, a briefing and the right questions were being put to all and sundry.

He perched himself comfortably on the throne of the righteous and threw morsels of information to the dogs to fight over. He would hold his superior position throughout.

Now there was only one more enjoyable matter to deal with. He had a spring in his step as he bounded up the steps of the Underground at Charing Cross.

He arrived at the police station.

A sergeant in uniform with a no-nonsense look about him was at the reception desk. He glared at the Member of Parliament.

'My name is Frederick Ogilvie.'

The sergeant stared back.

'The Member of Parliament.'

'And?'

It was then that he saw the newspaper on the desk with his photograph in it. It was the Daily Express and so he knew whatever was written there wouldn't be complimentary.

'I don't like your attitude. I have come for a private interview with Mr. Algernon Fitzgerald. A message was sent through earlier that I would be here,' he made a show of looking at his watch, 'right now.'

Ogilvie had fixed up the appointment by invoking his position on the sub-committee of the Intelligence and Security Committee.

The sergeant nodded his face deadpan. He waited a few seconds, staring at the MP before he reached for the phone on his desk. 'I'll tell the Superintendent that you're here.' He picked up the receiver and pressed two buttons. 'Sir? Mr. Ogilvie is here.' Somehow he managed to show the contempt he was feeling in the word mister. 'Very good, sir.' He hung up the receiver. He said nothing.

'Well? What's happening?'

'The Superintendent will escort you personally to the interview room. He is busy right now talking to somebody at the Home Office. As soon as he is free he will join you. Please take a seat over there.' He nodded at a row of hard backed chairs lined up against a wall. There were a dozen seats, all were empty. Ogilvie sat down. He couldn't help it. He felt intimidated. Now that he was here, amongst the enemy so to speak, he wasn't so sure of himself. These were the people who condoned the actions of TIFAT.

He kept glancing at his watch. Five minutes, ten, he was about to stand up and give the sergeant a piece of his mind along with a demand that the superintendent appear at once when the man did just that. He was in uniform, with the crown on each epaulette signifying his rank.

'I must protest,' said Ogilvie, 'at being kept waiting for so long. It's a disgrace. I would like to know your name.'

'Superintendent John Evans,' he spoke with a soft Welsh accent. 'You may call me Superintendent or Superintendent Evans.' He didn't offer his hand to shake and looked at Ogilvie with the same dead look as his sergeant. He was 5ft 6ins tall, slim, with the build of a marathon runner. He looked to be about forty years old, with brown hair cut short and brown eyes that stared at the MP.

Ogilvie looked distinctly uncomfortable. 'Well, let me say this is intolerable. Intolerable. However, on this occasion I won't say anything about it.'

'What would you say and to whom?'

Ogilvie could see the sergeant watching, listening and trying to hide a smile. 'I want to see the prisoner.'

'Then you had better follow me.' Evans turned and stepped to a door. He entered the security code and pushed the door open. He didn't hold it for Ogilvie who only just managed to get to the door before it closed in his face. He followed the Superintendent, his anger almost at boiling point.

Along the corridor, at the sixth, door the Superintendent stopped, turned the doorknob and pushed the door open. He gestured for Ogilvie to enter past him.

The MP entered the room. It was about 15ft square, there were no windows, a table in the middle of the room and a single, hard backed chair either side. The walls were plain cream coloured. He noticed the chairs had chains anchoring them to the floor though they could be moved a few inches in any direction.

'Where is Mr. Fitzgerald?'

'He is being brought from the cells and will be here in a few minutes.'

'This is a private meeting.'

'I know. As you can see, there are no windows and no opaque walls with anyone standing on the other side watching and listening.'

'Do you give me your word?'

'What about?'

'About the fact nobody is listening and watching?'

Evans shook his head with barely disguised disgust. 'I told you. Now that we are alone I am going to tell you something. You are a disgusting little twerp. TIFAT has saved God alone knows how many lives, stopped massive numbers being injured and prevented damage to property that would have run into probably hundreds of millions of pounds. I've read the after action report on the Underground and I've seen the footage. Commander Hunter did precisely the right thing. That's why many more people weren't killed and injured. You, Mr. Ogilvie, are going to do a great deal of damage to the lives of the people of this country because of your stupidity.'

'How dare you talk to me like that. I will have you fired.' Ogilvie was spluttering with outrage.

'What do you mean? Talk to you how? What did I say?'

'You...You...'

'There's nobody here to hear me. Furthermore, rest assured, my superiors think the same way only they are not in a position to say so.' He looked over his shoulder. 'You sit there.' He indicated the chair nearest the door. 'There's a panic button next to the door.' He indicated a red button at shoulder height. 'If you need any help in an emergency, just press it.'

'Why should I need help?'

'Why indeed?' Evans stepped aside. 'Here he is. In you go, Mr. Fitzgerald. Bear in mind,' he glanced at the two men, 'I have allowed this meeting out of courtesy. You have no right to be here Mr. Ogilvie, as much as you might think so. The power and influence of the ISC does not stretch as far as this station. You have ten minutes.'

'Freddy,' said Fitzgerald, relief in his voice, 'I am so glad you've come.'

49

MACNAIR AND HUNTER entered the intelligence room. It was a large space, the second floor of a three storey block of offices on the other side of the parade ground. The small offices that used to be there had been removed. Now the place was open plan with head height partitions separating the desks. When TIFAT was launched just a few years earlier there had been only half a dozen employees in the intelligence section, now there were 35 men and women. They were highly skilled technocrats who could do things with computers that neither Macnair nor Hunter came close to understanding. All they did know, and all they needed to know, was that the department delivered when asked.

One wall was covered with plasma screens that could be looked at individually or joined up if a much larger picture was required. The pictures were beamed in from geosynchronous satellites in the sky, orbiting the earth to appear stationary relative to the earth's rotation. At the equator the satellites were, as near as dammit, 22,258 miles high. Space was about as busy as the M25 motorway during rush hour. Since the first satellite, Sputnik 1, was launched in 1957 and started the space race, many more spacecraft had been sent up to orbit the moon, the sun and other planets. Now there were over 1,100 satellites floating around space, some were dead, others were working and some spoke to each other. The ones that spoke to each other meant that there wasn't a spot on earth that couldn't be seen from space and the pictures sent back to those organisations that had access. That included TIFAT.

The two men walked over to Isobel Sweeney, TIFAT's head of computer and intelligence operations.

'Just in time,' said Isobel.

'Can we hear them?' Macnair asked.

'Loud and clear,' said Isobel. She was 5ft 6ins tall, attractive, with fair hair and a nice figure. She was wearing a black trouser suit and a white blouse. She was 43 years old, unmarried but now with a steady boyfriend, an SAS Sergeant Major attached to TIFAT.

'How are you getting the broadcast?' Hunter asked.

'Courtesy of Superintendent John Evans. He placed a bug under the table.'

'Nice of him,' said Hunter.

'I've known John for a couple of years,' said Macnair. 'He's one of the good guys. Isobel, let's go to your office and we can listen on loudspeaker.'

The office was in a corner of the building, one side with a view to the River Forth and the railway and road bridges, the other to the open ground to the west of the establishment.

There was a large desk with a computer sitting in the middle and a comfortable looking swivel chair. There was a small conference table with 6 chairs, a wall lined with shelves full of reference books and a second wall with 4 computer screens that were slaves to the main system in the big room.

Fresh coffee was brewing, the smell of roasted beans wafting the air.

'I'll get the coffees,' said Hunter, and began pouring the coffee into mugs while Isobel crossed to her desk and pressed a couple of buttons on a console. The voices came clearly into the room.

'My God, Freddy, am I glad to see you. You have to get me out of here.'

'How?'

'Use your influence. Your power.' Hysteria and panic was building in Fitzgerald's tone. 'Your authority. I can't stand this place. Please. Please Freddy, for me.' The last few words were spoken in a petty, childish way that was cringe making to the three people listening.

Hunter handed around the coffees while he sat at the table, his mug on a coaster in front of him.

Ogilvie said. 'No can do, Fitzie, old boy. You've been very naughty. Breaking into my computer like that. Stealing all that information and then getting it published.'

'I know. I am so sorry. Freddy, please believe me that I will do all that I can to make it up to you. Honest I will.'

'How will you do that, Fitzie?'

Hunter said, 'The little creep is enjoying himself. He likes making Fitzgerald squirm. He'll have him begging in a few minutes.' Neither of the other two responded.

'I'll...I'll manage. I promise. I'll never look at your papers again. Ever. And I'll be a good boy.' The pathetic voice came again.

The three of them exchanged disgusted looks as they listened.

'What about David?' There was bitterness in Ogilvie's voice. 'What about all the other men you've slept with? Tell me that? I've kept you all these years and all you've done is repay me with deceit and lies about what you are doing, where you are going and who you are meeting. And all this time, I knew. I knew Fitzie, about the other men and the sordid things you did. The dinners, the parties when I was away on parliamentary business, even when you brought other men back to my house.'

'No, Freddy. No. It's not true. There's only ever been you. I swear. David means nothing to me. Just someone to visit the galleries with and things. Nothing more. You're always so busy. I love you, you know that.'

'You're a liar. I came to say goodbye. You will never see me again. I have arranged for Oxfam to come to the house and remove every item that belongs to you. Every stitch of clothing, your jewellery, your watches. How many is it now? Six of them? Whatever, Oxfam can have the lot. Oh, as well as your television and very expensive hi-fi system I had installed in your room. You may find when or if, I should say, you get your mobile back that it is disconnected. The phone was in my name. Your laptop is broken. Somehow I dropped it and the screen broke. Such a pity. I think that's all.' There was the sound of a chair scraping a few inches across the floor. 'By the way, thanks for doing what you did.'

'What? What do you mean?' Fitzgerald's voice was hardly more than a whisper. Before Ogilvie could answer, Fitzgerald added, with real hysteria in his voice, 'Please don't do this to me, Freddy. I beg you. We can work something out. Please, Freddy.'

'Did you hear what I just said? I said thank you.'

'What for?'

'For doing exactly what I wanted. You pathetic little man.'

'What did I do?'

'I knew about the Official Secrets Act and how it applies to me. If I had leaked that information I could have gone to jail for a very long time. Now it is out in the open I can capitalise on it. I can get TIFAT shut down using public opinion as well as the courts even if I have to take it all the way to the Court of Human Rights in the Hague. I will have the men, and the women,' he added as an afterthought, 'arrested and tried for crimes against humanity. See if I don't. But I couldn't have done it without your help, Fitzie,' the name was said with scorn. 'I have spoken to a friend of mine at the bar, who has it on good authority that they intend chucking the book at you. You'll be lucky to get out in ten years. It's more likely to be twenty. Just think of all those men you'll be able to choose from, Fitzie, aren't you the lucky one.'

They heard a yell. A chair was pushed back and Fitzgerald could be heard yelling, 'I'm going to kill you.'

Anything further was drowned out by the ringing of a bell, loud and clear.

'Interesting,' said Macnair, 'but pretty much what I thought.'

'Why was that?' asked Hunter.

'Dear Fitzie doesn't have the brains to think of doing it. The idea was planted and he went ahead with it.'

'Will he go to prison?' Hunter asked.

'Maybe,' said the General. 'Probably an open prison for a year or two at most. Ogilvie was just being spiteful, scaring Fitzgerald half to death.'

'What about the Act?' Isobel asked.

'The reality is, it's virtually worthless. It scares the honest into behaving while the dishonest take no notice. If Ogilvie had leaked the info he would probably have had a slightly harsher sentence and been forced to resign. As it is, nothing will touch him. In fact, as far as the left wing press is concerned, he's something of a hero.'

'So what are we going to do?' Isobel took a sip of coffee.

'Not we. Me. First I'll get him to change sides and then I'll get him repairing the damage.'

'How will you do that?' Hunter looked keenly at his boss.

'Its better I don't tell you. Right, I am on the evening flight to London. May as well strike while the iron is hot. Isobel, anything on the General Khan front?'

'Not a thing. He's back in Pakistan. Have you spoken to President Zardarim?'

'No. I've decided against it. I can't very well phone him up and say Mr. President, your head of the army is the boss of a large criminal organisation that is funding terrorist activities in Europe as well as your own country and we think is planning to organise an attack by Islamic extremists from Afghanistan into Pakistan. The first thing he'll ask for is proof.'

'Even if we could prove it,' said Hunter, 'what could Pakistan do? Arrest him? Such a prominent figure? I've been reading about him on the internet. Riots in the street would be the least of it.'

'Okay, you guys. Back to work. Thanks for the coffee,' he smiled at Isobel. Hunter followed his boss outside. They were walking across the parade ground when he said, 'You aren't doing it, sir. I am.'

'Doing what?'

'You know damned well. I'll take care of Ogilvie.'

'It's my problem.'

'No, it's not. It's equally mine. Sir, I've a pretty shrewd idea what you're going to do.'

'Oh? And what's that?'

'Frighten him to death. It's the only way with somebody like him.'

'But not kill him?'

'No, sir. And not because of possible comeback on TIFAT. I doubt the police would try too hard to pin his death on us even if we did it. No, the problem would be another person like him being given the job. What can we do then? Keep killing them? I wouldn't, in fact, I couldn't do that. I doubt you could either.'

'That's true. So we have the moral dilemma on the one hand and a need to ensure we can operate like we have been doing on the other.'

'That about sums it up and I'll take care of it.'

'How?'

Hunter grinned. 'Sir, wouldn't it be better if you didn't know? Open and honest denial is so much easier than having to lie.'

'Nick, I'm not sure. This is my part of ship, as you sailors say.'

'Sir, let me ask you something. What are we going to do about Khan?'

'If we find proof positive about his activities, you mean?'

'Yes. We're agreed telling the Pakistani President is not on, for obvious reasons. So if the man is fermenting trouble in Pakistan, if he is controlling Barzakh, if he is responsible for terrorist attacks then you have a more important job to do.'

'Are you presuming to tell me my job, now?' There was no rancour in the General's voice. Then, he added, 'Tell me how you see it.'

'You need to plan an operation to take out Khan. That will be the only way to stop him. You know it, I know it. It will be tough and demanding to plan and execute but there isn't any other choice.'

'Is that what you think?'

'Yes.'

'Me too.'

The two men paused in the doorway to the office block. 'Okay, Nick. You deal with Ogilvie. I'll leave it to you. Remember, don't kill him.'

'I won't, sir. Don't worry. I'd better go and talk to Isobel.' On that note, Hunter retraced his steps.

Frederick Ogilvie was in his element. His phone hardly stopped ringing as members of the press tried to get hold of him for an interview. He was in a quandary. Should he talk to the left wing press who were sympathetic, or the right wing who palpably hated him? If he played his cards right, he could show up the gutter press that supported TIFAT for what they were - anti-law and anti-human rights. Yes, he could turn the interview back on them. The idea gave him food for thought tinged with a frisson of excitement. He was sure he would be able to do it thanks to his superior intellect and fast thinking. No journalist could outwit him, of that he had no doubt.

'Ogilvie, are you listening?' Stan Harrow couldn't keep the impatience out of his voice.

'What? What did you say?' Ogilvie focused his attention on the man opposite.

The room was electric with animosity. Like vicious dogs,

Harrow and Judge Parker had been at loggerheads with Ogilvie and Goldsmith all morning. They had been snapping and snarling at each other non-stop, their tempers barely held in check.

'I said if it hadn't been for the quick thinking of General Macnair the deaths and destruction would have been far greater. He saved a lot of lives.'

Goldsmith slapped the palm of his right hand on the table with such force he winced. 'I have it on good authority that the girls were trying to surrender.'

The Judge shook his head. His exasperation was clear for all to see. 'That was why the girl ran screaming God is Great towards the crowd when General Macnair shot her.'

'It didn't mean she was going to set off the bomb. She could just have been making a point before giving herself up,' said Goldsmith obstinately.

'You can't possibly believe that,' said Harrow. 'You've seen the camera footage. It's as plain as day.'

'Then she should have been arrested,' said Ogilvie. 'Not shot like a rabid dog.'

'She was a rabid dog,' said Harrow. 'A bigoted, stupid, brainwashed woman who wanted to kill as many people as she could in the name of her religion. That's the reality and for some reason you two are unwilling to come to terms with the facts.'

'Fact one,' yelled Ogilvie, holding up the index finger of his right hand, 'she wasn't given an opportunity to give up. Fact two, she was shot in cold blood. Fact three, we have on film the man who did it. Fact four, Macnair and the rest of TIFAT have a lot more blood on their hands. Fact five, he shot the other girl in cold blood when she was just sitting at the table. Fact six, the girl arrested is claiming that they had been ready to give themselves up. Fact seven...' he faltered and then said, 'That's enough facts. He needs to be arrested and tried for murder.' He sank back into his chair as though exhausted. 'I rest my case.'

Judge Parker spoke in a reasonably calm voice that was in direct contrast to the way he was thinking. 'Fact one, the woman who ran at the crowd was going to blow herself up in the crowd. Fact two, the girl who survived did so because the army's Royal Engineers dismantled the bomb. Fact three, Macnair risked his life to grab hold of the girl and cart her to safety. Fact four, she admitted they were intending to set off the bombs but changed her testimony after a visit from you.' He glared at Ogilvie. 'A visit you had no right to make.'

'I most certainly did.' Ogilvie sat up straighter. 'Are you forgetting that I am a barrister? That I am still a barrister? I offered my services to the girl's distraught family and they accepted.'

'Don't give us that dogs' bollocks,' said Harrow. 'You went there and persuaded the girl to change her statement. You know it, we know it. Don't insult our intelligence by denying it.'

'I did no such thing,' said Ogilvie with as much dignity as he could muster.

The girl was being held in Charing Cross Police Station. Harrow and the Judge both knew what Ogilvie had said to the girl by the simple expedient of the recording forwarded to each of them from TIFAT. The problem was, they couldn't use the information.

Harrow and Parker said nothing, just stared at the other man.

Ogilvie began to look uncomfortable and blurted out, 'We also have the footage of the attacks on the Underground. That murdering thug Commander Nicholas Hunter,' the name was spoken with scorn, 'shot dead those two men in cold blood, just like his boss.'

'For crying out loud. He stopped people getting killed. The poor sods who yelled at the terrorists to surrender were killed along with a lot of other people.'

'He should still have given them the opportunity,' said Goldsmith, obstinately. 'It's murder otherwise. No matter how you look at it.'

Harrow and Parker exchanged looks. The Judge said, 'We'd better stop. We'll never agree. I'll tell the Prime Minister and let him decide.'

'I shall also speak to the PM,' said Ogilvie, stiffly.

Harrow and Parker stood and left the room. The other two stayed where they were for a few moments.

'Well?' Ogilvie looked at Goldsmith.

'I don't know. We have a strong case. Will it be strong enough for us to achieve what we want? I'm not sure. A lot will come down to public opinion. Get the public on our side and then it'll be a different kettle of fish.'

'Do you think we have enough for arrests and convictions?'

Goldsmith shook his head. 'Probably not. However, if we lowered our sights to getting TIFAT closed down then yes, we probably do have enough.'

'That's what I thought.'

50

HUNTER'S MEETING WITH Isobel went extremely well. She would put three of her people on the case. They're job would be to blitz the social media sites about the stupidity of the MPs Ogilvie and Goldsmith. They would emphasis the saving of lives and the reduction in the amount of damage that could have been done. Ogilvie was busy casting a bad light on TIFAT's activities; Isobel's department would get busy doing the opposite.

In the meantime, the General contacted everyone he knew who was sympathetic to TIFAT. It was a mixed bag. Some didn't take his calls, others said they were waiting to see which way the wind was blowing and some announced firmly they fully supported him and TIFAT.

Hunter got a lift into Dunfermline. He was in time to catch the 16.05 train to Edinburgh where he changed to the 17.00 East Coast train to London. He travelled first class. He was smartly dressed in a light grey suit with an open necked white shirt. He had his grip with clean clothes, including a pair of black jeans, black shirt and a black, single-breasted jacket. He ate the complimentary dinner and found it surprisingly tasty. He had been unable to fly. The small backpack nestling in the grip would never have got through security and neither would the contents of his bum bag.

He arrived at King's Cross at 21.50, a mere seven minutes later than advertised and took a taxi to The May Fair Hotel. It was an expensive place to stay but he was paying the tab, so what the hell. He checked in and went up to his room where he changed into his jeans, black shirt and jacket.

He left the hotel with the backpack slung over his shoulder and took a taxi to Wandsworth. The cab dropped him about a mile from Ogilvie's house. He walked until he found the street he was looking for. By now it was dark and the street lights were on. The area was smart, the houses well looked after. Ogilvie's was near the middle, a terraced, three storey affair with a tiny front garden. Hunter went round to the back. The gardens stretched back about 50ft and ended in a track wide enough to take a car. On the other side of the track were more gardens leading to the next terraced street of houses. Each garden had a 7ft high wooden boundary fence running between them. Erected for privacy between neighbours. However, the rear boundaries had low brick walls with double iron gates. Most of the gardens had cars in them. There were lights on in the houses but no street lights along the lane.

A BMW sat in the driveway in front of a garage, halfway along the garden. He could just make out the rubbish bins to the left of the backdoor. Different colours for different uses as mankind attempted to save the planet, thought Hunter, with more than a degree of cynicism. The garden was concreted over. There were no flowers or plants as far as he could see.

Hunter retraced his steps and walked briskly past the front of Ogilvie's house. There were lights on downstairs. Even as he looked they went out and a few seconds later lights appeared on the second floor. Hunter kept going. He went for a long walk around Wandsworth Common. He found a wooden bench and sat down. It was a balmy night, with a cloudless sky, the moon not yet risen. It gave him a yearning to be at sea, preferably onboard a yacht, sailing free, running before the wind. The sounds of vehicles faded as the traffic thinned. At 02.00 there was only the occasional car or lorry and Hunter decided it was time to make a move.

He returned to the back of the house. There were now no lights showing in any of the houses. He looked around and saw nobody. Even the traffic could no longer be heard. He stepped over the wall and went behind the garage. He waited patiently. If anyone had spotted him, police cars would be arriving in minutes.

Hunter waited a quarter of an hour. Nothing happened. At the kitchen door he saw that the lock was a simple Yale. He took out his lock-gun, selected a pick, inserted it into the lock and gently pressed the trigger. The pick engaged, he twisted it, the tongue slid back and the door opened.

Stepping inside, he closed the door and stood still. It was pitch dark. From his pocket he took out a black ski mask and pulled it on. Now, only his eyes and nose were showing. From his bag he took a pair of night vision goggles and put them on. The room lit up in a green glow. The kitchen was large, modern, and well equipped. He crossed the room to the door opposite. His rubber soled shoes made no sound. The door was open. Stepping into the hall, he inched his way slowly up the stairs. He stayed close to the wall to minimise the steps squeaking.

The first door on his right was a library or study. There was a second lounge next to it, and next to that a third door that led to a toilet and shower room.

He continued to the second floor. There were three doors facing him. Two were ajar, the third door, the one nearest him, was closed. First, he checked the open doors. He didn't want any nasty surprises. Both rooms were empty.

He opened the third door and hit his first snag. There were two people in the bed. He heard snoring.

He stopped in the doorway. The room was large. The bed was on his left, about 10ft away. The bed was so large Hunter reckoned it had been specially made. To his right was a wall lined with wardrobes that fitted from the ceiling to the floor. In the middle was a full length mirror.

On the bedside tables he could see glasses and two bottles, upside down sticking out of an ice bucket. He didn't think either person would be waking anytime soon. He glided across the carpeted floor.

The nearest person was young looking. He had short, fair hair, a round face and looked about 19. He was breathing silently. Hunter slid his backpack off his shoulder and took out a syringe. He placed his hand over the youth's mouth while simultaneously pushing the needle into the boy's upper arm and depressing the plunger. The youth squirmed for a moment, his eyes opened in shock and then he went limp.

Hunter withdrew the needle and placed it back in his pack.

He stepped around to the bed and stood looking down at the snoring man. Frederick Ogilvie was not a pretty sight. He was on his back, his mouth was partly open and he was twitching and jerking as though caught up in a dream.

It's about to become a nightmare, thought Hunter.

The province of Sindh is one of the four provinces that make up Pakistan. To the west it is bounded by the River Indus and Balochistan, to the south by the Arabian Sea, the east by the states of Gujarat and Rajasthan and to the north by Punjab. Its capital is Karachi. The province had been given the title of Bab-ul-Islam which translated to the Gateway of Islam. About 25mls to the west of Karachi is the headland known as Ras Muari.

Five miles short of the headland, overlooking the Arabian Sea, sat a massive house with high walls topped with razor wire with only one gate into the property. Armed guards patrolled the acres of land the wall surrounded. There were notices every few yards warning people to stay away. They were written in the provincial languages of Sindhi, Pashto, Punjabi and Balochi. Every third sign was in Urdu and English. What the punishment would be if the warnings were not heeded wasn't spelt out. However, there were plenty of rumours about people going missing, falling off the edge of the cliffs, being eaten by sharks or being taken into the property where unspeakable things happened to them before they died. Whatever the truth, the rumours kept trespassers away. The local police chief was paid a handsome amount every month, equal to 6 weeks pay, to ensure the occupants of the house were left in peace. He was happy to do so. The alternative had been spelt out in no uncertain terms as to what would happen to him and his family if he didn't comply.

General Pervez Khan liked the house. He particularly liked the round tower in the south-east corner that gave him such spectacular views of the Arabian Sea to the south and the province of Sindhi to the north. On a clear day he could see the outskirts of Karachi, the 3rd largest city in the world, and the largest city in the Muslim world. General Khan hated Karachi in spite of the fact that a great deal of his power base was to be found there. He hated the poverty, the filth, the stench, the pollution. He smiled. Green energy was a joke and when he was President, helping to drive forward the powerhouse that would be Pakistan, a country to rival India and Brazil, he would be building coal fired power stations all over the country. With the huge deposits of coal discovered in the Thar Desert in the Sindh province, Pakistan had been catapulted into being the 7th country in the world in terms of lignite deposits. It was estimated there were 175 billion tonnes of coal, sufficient to meet the country's fuel requirements for centuries. Europe and the west were fading and fading rapidly. Victims of their own stupidity.

Khan knew that his political ambition, coupled with the wealth that he would soon command, would help to drive Pakistan to its rightful place in the world. Mecca in Saudi Arabia may have been the birthplace of Muhammad, peace be upon him, but the real centre for Islamic domination in the world would be Pakistan, and he would be the leader. His name would be spoken for centuries to come in the same breath as the Holy Prophet.

The General was sitting in his tower. The diameter was 35ft, with windows all around made from the latest bullet-proof glass, the thickest manufactured at 3.5ins. Outside was a balcony, 6ft wide that encircled the tower. It had a waist high stone wall, reinforced by sheets of steel. Every door and window was alarmed, with infra-red sensors as well as hidden cameras that were monitored 24/7.

The grounds had patrols of armed guards, 6 of them at any one time, armed and fanatically loyal to him. The full contingent of guards on the property at all times was 20. The General was not a coward. He was a ruthless bully who knew where his destiny lay and that nothing should be allowed to stop him achieving it. Nothing would. However, he was no fool. He knew that as his popularity grew, so did his enemies. He had to be very careful as the penultimate move in the game of power chess that he had been playing came ever closer.

The house was the only place he fully relaxed, knowing he was safe.

The actual room was 20ft high and opulently fitted out to a garish degree of sofas, cushions, gold fittings and a well stocked, oak-made bar overlooking the southern vista.

Directly beneath was a room of equal size and opulence that was his bedroom. He spent his time at the house between the two rooms, rarely venturing into other parts of the sprawling mansion. Two trusted officers had rooms at one end of the house, along with the array of servants he had at his beck and call.

Between the tower and the servant's quarters there was a suite of 6 bedrooms and an accompanying living area. This was where his four wives and eleven children stayed when they visited. However, this had become less frequent - they were only welcome when he invited them. He had been toying with the idea of getting rid of his second wife. It was a decision he would have to take sometime in the not too distant future. In the meantime, he'd let her live, even if she was a fat cow who spent her days gorging on sweets and chocolate. Their son, now 11 years old, was no better.

The guards were housed in a barracks in the north-western corner of the grounds. Around the grounds were scattered half-a-dozen gazebos, where his children would play. He had little to do with either of the seven boys or four girls. They ranged in age from 5 years old to 16. The eldest boy, the only child he spent any time with, wanted to join the army. The eldest girl, at 15, was very smart and wanted to be a doctor. It wouldn't happen. Unknown to her, she was betrothed to an important man in the political hierarchy of Pakistan. What if he was 52 years old? She would do as her father told her and that was that.

The remainder of his children had still to show their mettle and prove if they were worthy of the name of Khan. He was glad they were at their house in Islamabad. It meant he didn't have to make an effort to be nice to them.

Now, sitting on the balcony, looking south, his feet on a stool, enjoying a glass of finest brandy and a Cuban cigar he felt extremely happy.

The house and all its fitments had taken 10 years to build. It had cost him a fortune, funded mainly by Rabbani. Now, his fortune would escalate significantly and he would make his moves. He puffed contentedly, lifted his glass, took a mouthful of brandy and looked forward to the report he expected imminently.

As Khan finished his cigar, a nervous looking man appeared at the door and looked at the General.

'Sir...'

'Ah, my good and deserving Shafiq, come and tell me what you have discovered. More, how many bank accounts and how much wealth.'

'Sir,' Shafiq Domki stepped onto the balcony. He was a slight man, in his mid-twenties, with black hair, clean shaven, with an angular face and a thin, pointed nose. His eyes were watery and he wore glasses. He spent most of his waking hours in front of a computer screen. It was acknowledged by all those who knew him that he was a computer genius. He was also an Islamic fundamentalist who believed in Sharia law and the need for a good Muslim to kill at least one unbeliever before they died.

The General saw instantly that something was wrong. 'What is it? What have you found out?'

Domki licked his lips and said, 'Sir, I have checked every bank account I could trace belonging to the crook Rabbani.' He paused and looked even more agitated. The General's bouts of white hot anger were legend.

'Out with it. What have you found?'

'Sir, I should explain. No matter what you do, if you have many bank accounts there is often a link between them of some sort. It's inevitable, unless the account lays dormant.' He took a deep breath, removed his glasses and wiped them on his shirt. His hands were shaking. He replaced his glasses.

'If you do not come to the point quickly I shall have you removed and shot. Do you understand?'

'Yes, my General. As I said, they almost inevitably have a connection. I tracked down the accounts of the legitimate businesses. They are empty.'

'Empty? What do you mean, empty?'

'Sir, please sir, just that. There is no money in them.'

'What? None?'

'That is correct, sir. In fact, nine accounts are overdrawn and one account has a single pound in it.'

'A single pound? Is this some sort of joke?' The General roared. He placed his glass on the table, threw his cigar over the side of the balcony and stood up. He towered above the computer specialist who was cowering back, terror etched in his face.

'No...No, sir. It's not a joke. Technically, I would say that Rabbani's businesses are bankrupt.'

'But how is that possible?'

'The accounts have all been emptied in the last twenty-four hours!'

Khan's mouth dropped open. He put his hand on the balcony to steady himself and then said, 'What? What did you say?'

'The accounts have been emptied in the last twenty-four hours, sir.'

'How much has gone?'

The little man referred to a sheet of paper he was holding and then stuttered, 'Twenty-eight million, three hundred and forty-seven pound, ninety-six pence exactly, sir.'

'Where did it go? Who has taken my money?' As far as the General was concerned, everything that Rabbani had owned was now his.

Shafiq Domki shook his head. 'I...I cannot tell, sir. Whoever did this are experts. I have never come across anything like it before.'

'What about his other accounts?'

The man's hands were shaking badly and he put his arms down his sides and gripped his trousers, trying to control them.

'I have traced two more. They are off-shore accounts. They contained five...five...'

'By God, Domki, get on with it! Five what?'

'Five million dollars and...'

'Never mind the and. Where is my money?'

'I cannot say. The walls surrounding the transactions are impenetrable.'

'Will you be able to get through them?'

'Eventually, sir. But it will take time. Sir, I venture one possibility.'

'What? What possibility?'

'I can think of only a number of organisations capable of doing this. The CIA is one.'

'The CIA had nothing to do with Rabbani.' The General sat back down as the answer hit him. 'TIFAT is the other organisation.'

'Yes, sir. Possibly MI6. The Chinese also. But that would make no sense.'

'You are quite right, Domki. There is only one answer. It was the swine in Scotland. It was TIFAT. They are the only ones who have been involved in this whole affair.'

'What...what do you want me to do, sir. Keep trying?'

'Of course, keep trying, you fool. There must be vast sums in accounts all over the world. Find them and find my money or I'll have you strung up and flayed alive. Do I make myself clear?'

'Yes, sir. Perfectly.' Bowing his head, Domki backed out of the General's presence.

Khan took a mouthful of brandy, gagged on it as his anger threatened to choke him and threw the glass over the balcony. He heard the tinkle as it smashed on the ground below.

They would pay. He would start immediately. His plans may have been pushed back by a few months but that was all. Rabbani's empire was intact. Khan would double the traffic in prostitutes, increase the delivery of heroin threefold and add more cocaine to the business. He had suffered a setback but that was all it was. A setback.

He picked up an internal phone. 'Colonel? I want attacks to take place in Britain as soon as possible. It does not matter if the individuals are caught. I want maximum disruption to life in Britain, many deaths and much damage. Do I make myself clear? Good. Also, I want the unrest in Punjab to be stepped up. I am going to move up the timetable.' He slammed the receiver back into its cradle.

He'd make them regret getting involved. TIFAT should have stayed out of his business.

He had conveniently forgotten that he had been the one to involve them in the first place.

51

LOOKING DOWN AT the sleeping body, Hunter pondered his next move. He'd thought of different scenarios. The objective wasn't to kill the man but to frighten the life out of him. He took his silenced Pocketlite from his bumbag, switched off the goggles but kept them in place, and turned on the bedside lamp.

Hunter leant over Ogilvie and slapped him hard on the cheek. Ogilvie moved, his eyes opened, unfocussed and Hunter slapped him on the other side of the face. Ogilvie snapped fully awake.

Seeing Hunter his mouth opened in terror and he took a deep breath. He was about to scream. Hunter put his left hand over the MP's mouth and pressed down hard. The joint between his thumb and forefinger clamped on Ogilvie's nose. The man's eyes bulged. He grabbed Hunter's arm and tried to pull it away. It didn't move. As Ogilvie's eyes bulged Hunter placed the Pocketlite against the man's temple and pushed it hard, forcing Ogilvie's head to turn and for him to look at the form lying next to him.

'See that boy there? He's out for the count. Try and wake him.'

Ogilvie didn't move. Instead, he began shaking, tears came to his eyes. Due to the hot weather, the bed cover was only a thin blanket. Hunter watched dispassionately as a damp stain spread across the sheet where Ogilvie urinated. He eased his grip on Ogilvie's nose, letting him breathe again.

'Go on. Try and wake him.'

The Member of Parliament reached across and tentatively pushed at the boy's shoulder.

'Try harder or I'll pull the trigger and splatter your brains all over the place.

Ogilvie was galvanised. He shook the boy, he thumped his arm. He did it again, harder.

'He won't be waking up anytime soon,' said Hunter. 'I'm going to remove my hand. If you make the slightest sound I'll kill you. Do I make myself clear?'

Ogilvie nodded.

Hunter removed his hand. He knew what a terrifying apparition he was and that Ogilvie would be scared out of his brains.

'Do you want to live?' Hunter's tone was conversational. Friendly even. There was no response, merely a wide eyed stare. 'Do you?' Now his tone was harsher.

The message seemed to penetrate Ogilvie's mind and he nodded. He had stopped weeping but now the tears started again.

'Say it!'

'Yes. I want to live.'

Hunter replaced his revolver in his bumbag. The relief on Ogilvie's face was short lived. Hunter took out a Ka-Bar knife. It was the knife of choice of most of the world's special operations personnel. He placed the razor sharp point on the MP's throat and drew an inch line of blood.

The man began to moan. 'Please. Please. Anything. Take whatever you want. Only please don't hurt me. Please.'

'Listen to this.' Hunter withdrew a handheld tape recorder from his pocket and pressed the play button. After a few seconds he heard, 'Freddy, I'm so glad you've come.'

Ogilvie's mouth dropped open as he was forced to listen to more of the recording. Then it shut off and Hunter put the machine back in his pocket.

'We have a recording of your meeting with dear Algernon.' He stopped speaking, letting the tension build.

After a few seconds the MP said, 'What are you going to do?'

'I've been sent here to kill you.' The matter of fact tone was more frightening than if the words had been spoken with menace. Hunter pressed harder with the knife. Unknown to his victim he had twisted the blade so that the back of the knife was pressing into Ogilvie's carotid artery.

'Oh my God. Oh my God. Please! What do you want?'

'Nothing. I just told you. I'm here to kill you.'

'Please, whatever you're being paid, I'll pay you more. Whatever it takes.'

'That's a very tempting offer, Ogilvie, but my orders are straightforward. I am to kill you unless you agree to certain conditions.'

'Anything. Anything. I swear to you. Anything.'

'You will withdraw your demands for an investigation into the activities of The International Force Against Terrorism.'

'What?' Ogilvie looked at Hunter in complete astonishment. 'What?' he repeated.

'You heard me. If you want to live to a ripe old age you will support what TIFAT does and make it clear to the world at large that TIFAT does a good job. One that is vital in this day and age.'

'I...I cannot. It goes against all my principles. Everything I've been doing for the last three years.'

'Your choice. Then you die.' Hunter pushed slightly harder on the Ka-Bar.

'No. No, wait. Alright. Damn you. Alright. I'll do it.'

'Ogilvie, let me make myself absolutely clear. If you double cross me I will be back. I will find you. I will kill you. Only next time it won't be a simple, straightforward and quick death. You'll die screaming in agony, begging me to kill you.' He paused. 'Do you understand?'

'Yes. Yes. I believe you.'

'There's nowhere for you to hide. Nobody who will be able to protect you. You've heard the tape. Our reach is long and deep. To prove it, if you check your bank accounts you will find them in debt. All three of them, including the account on the Cayman Islands. At six pm today we will return the cash in your British accounts. You can kiss goodbye to the money in the Cayman's. If you contact the police and report any of this you will be dead within a week.'

Hunter turned the knife and drew a long, shallow cut down Ogilvie's neck, making sure he did not go near the carotid artery. Even so, the cut began to seep blood that oozed down Ogilvie's neck and soaked into his pillow.

'When you turn on your computer in the House of Commons and turn on your laptop you will find that the screen saver is an innocent picture of a Thai boy. Should you do anything or say anything that is detrimental to TIFAT your computers will be flooded with filthy images of young boys proving to the world that you are a paedophile. The police will be informed and I can assure you they will investigate. You will be vilified before you die. Let me now tell you how you'll die. You will hang. It will be suicide. It helps to prove suicide when the rope tied around your neck isn't a slip knot. It will be tight but not too tight. You will be able to get your hands between the noose and your neck. You will be able to pull down and at the same time lift your body a fraction and be able to take in air. You should manage to do that for about ten minutes. Certainly not longer. It means you will die a slow and painful death. The autopsy will clearly state suicide. You will not be mourned, you will not be missed and you will be spoken about in the same way people speak about Jimmy Saville. Think on that.'

Hunter straightened, turned and walked toward the door. He stopped in the doorway. 'Incidentally, you will find a personal file of yours, headed "The future" on your computer. It outlines your thinking about the actions you now deem necessary following the atrocities on the Underground and at Heathrow. I suggest you follow them to the letter. If you don't, it will be bingo, it's all over. By the way, your young friend will wake up in a few hours. He'll have a rotten headache and will probably puke. Don't say I didn't warn you.'

With that, Hunter turned and left.

For a nano-second a thought came into his mind. It was one he'd had before.

Sed quis custodiet ipsos Custodes?

But who will guard the guards themselves?

'Stan? It's Malcolm.'

'Malcolm. What a pleasant surprise. At least I hope it's pleasant.' Before Macnair could reply, the MP for Bootle said, 'Listen. Alistair and I are doing our best, but we're losing the battle. Ogilvie and that little turd Goldsmith are really working the PR angle for all they're worth. We'll keep fighting, but we need some sort of miracle to stop them.'

'That's okay. They may have won a battle or two but we'll win the war.'

'What do you mean?'

'You said we need a miracle. Let's just say that Ogilvie has had an epiphany. He has been converted to our side and will say so loud and clear. That's why I'm phoning so early. You know I've just had a demand that I appear before your committee?'

'Yes. I told them that the most we can do is request you attend.

We have no powers to demand that you appear before us. After all, we have no jurisdiction over TIFAT.'

'I appreciate that. I ignored the demand and sent an e-mail back to Goldsmith saying that if he requests my attendance I would be happy to appear before you.'

'Are you sure you want to do this?' There was a degree of alarm in Harrow's tone.

Macnair chuckled. 'I wouldn't want to miss it for the world. I gather kick-off is at fourteen hundred tomorrow.'

'Correct. What is it you're not telling me?'

'Just wait and be pleasantly surprised. By the way, I'll have Commander Hunter with me.'

'Good. I'll make a point of congratulating him on a job well done.'

Macnair hung up and then had a similar conversation with Lord Parker.

After Macnair had explained, Parker said, 'It was J. Edgar Hoover who said that justice is incidental to law and order. He's right, of course, and we judges know that. We interpret the laws as laid down by Parliament. There is no common sense. The law says a thing so we have to do as the law says. I have argued with my peers about the way evidence is gathered. If evidence is available that is pertinent to a case it should be admitted, no matter how it is obtained. Why do we need a search warrant if the police have sufficient knowledge to require them to ask for one? The law is to protect the innocent and punish the guilty. All too often it protects the guilty and puts the innocent through a hellish process that is anathema to most right thinking people.'

Macnair was silent for a few seconds and then said, 'I agree with you entirely. It's why we do what we do.'

'I know. And it is why we need you. Of course, that is a damning indictment of where we are today.' Parker sighed. 'I apologise Malcolm. I was on my hobby horse. I'll see you tomorrow.'

52

GENERAL MACNAIR MET Hunter at the main entrance to the Houses of Parliament. They were expected. They signed in and were escorted through security. They dumped the contents of their pockets into trays that passed through an x-ray machine while they passed through a metal detector. Then they were patted down before they collected their things. In both cases that consisted of ID cards, wallets and mobile phones.

They were led to a meeting room on the first floor. At a long table, ranged on the side facing the door sat, left to right, Stan Harrow, Alistair Parker, Nigel Goldsmith and Frederick Ogilvie.

Macnair approached the table, leant across it, held out his hand and said hello to each man in turn. Hunter followed alongside him. They took seats opposite the other four.

There was no Chairman to the panel and Harrow opened the proceedings with, 'Thank you, General Macnair and you, Commander Hunter for coming in. We appreciate it.'

'Huh,' was the response from Goldsmith.

'Is there a problem, Mr. Goldsmith?' asked Macnair.

'Yes. You were summoned, not asked to come.'

'If that's the way it's going to be,' said Macnair, 'then let me make myself absolutely clear. Neither you nor anyone else has the authority to summon me or my officers anywhere. We came as a courtesy. We will answer your questions to the best of our ability and that depends upon operational requirements for secrecy. If we are to be held to account you know that a panel has to be set up under the authority of certain governments including the USA, France and Britain. The whole point of TIFAT is to stop political interference. Some is inevitable. I accept that. Some is unacceptable. You need to accept that.'

Goldsmith had the bad grace to nod curtly while looking uncomfortable. Ogilvie merely looked white, pasty and ill. There was a flesh coloured plaster on his neck. When he was asked what had happened he'd replied, 'Nothing. A silly accident,' and left it at that.

Hunter decided to pitch in. 'Mr Ogilvie, it's a pleasure to see you again.'

Ogilvie looked at Hunter, his mouth slightly agape. His hands were on the table and Hunter noticed them trembling as he slid them out of sight.

'You've met?' Goldsmith looked from Ogilvie to Hunter.

'Briefly,' said Hunter. 'At some do or other. Something to do with Thailand, if I remember correctly.'

'Never mind the pleasantries,' said Judge Parker, 'let us carry on.'

Goldsmith began by picking up a remote control and pointing it at a television in the corner of the room. A video recording started. It showed the events in the London Underground. It showed Hunter clearly shooting the terrorists and the platform emptying of civilians and the police.

'That was cold blooded murder,' said Goldsmith.

'That...' began Macnair, but Hunter placed his hand on the General's arm.

'Hang on, sir. I'll deal with this. That was an operational decision I took that saved the lives of many people and prevented injuries to dozens more.'

'You should have given those men the opportunity to surrender,' thundered Goldsmith, already working himself up into a lather.

Stan Harrow broke in. 'I expected this,' he began, standing up and stepping behind the Judge. He reached out and snatched the TV remote from Goldsmith's hand. He walked over to the TV, pressed a button, watched as a drawer opened, slid out the DVD and replaced it with a second. He aimed the remote, pressed the requisite button and the picture changed to the scene on the other platform.

It showed two policemen pointing guns at a man. They were yelling at him to lay down with his arms outstretched and feet apart. They yelled the message over and over, as they neared the terrorist. The passengers stood still, shocked into immobility. The policemen kept yelling. The terrorist yelled back, *'Allahu Akbar,'* and exploded in a bright flash and devastating noise. It was uncannily like an action thriller movie and for a brief second it was possible to believe it was fiction. A moment later the screaming and crying began.

Harrow pointed the remote and paused it on a scene of a mother cradling a dead child. There was silence in the room. In spite of their knowledge of the atrocity, seeing it like that left all six men shocked to the core. Even Hunter and Macnair, who had seen more than their fair share of deaths, injuries and destruction were silent as they turned their gazes from the screen to the four committee members.

'That's the result,' said Judge Parker, 'of trying to do things the ethical way. The right way. Any other way the politically correct like to bleat about when it isn't their lives at stake.' He looked sideways at Goldsmith and switched his gaze to Ogilvie. 'Like you two do all the time.'

'I agree,' said Frederick Ogilvie in a mumbled voice.

Hunter and Macnair both looked at the Member of Parliament with deadpan faces. The other three turned to look at the man as though he had suddenly grown a second head.

It was Goldsmith who spoke. 'What did you say, Freddy? You agree?' He croaked, the words seeming to stick in his throat.

'Yes,' Ogilvie cleared his throat, and said again, 'Yes.' This time his voice was stronger. 'I have given it much thought. Without...without TIFAT and officers such as General Macnair and Commander Hunter we would be in far greater trouble.' He faltered again, before adding, 'I think it is time we gave our full hearted support to TIFAT.'

There was shocked silence for a few seconds. Harrow and Parker looked at Macnair and Hunter, both of whom looked steadily back. Hunter watched as Goldsmith's face drained of colour and just as quickly turned bright red as anger exploded and he thumped the fist of his left hand down onto the table.

'No! Never! Have you gone insane? After all we've said and done? This is our chance. Have you seen the footage from the airport? That was cold-blooded murder and we have General,' he said the word contemptuously, 'Macnair dead to rights.'

Stan Harrow said, 'I've seen the recordings. Malcolm saved a lot of lives.'

'He killed two innocent children,' thundered Goldsmith.

'Are you insane?' Harrow yelled back. 'They were not innocent children. They were murdering, despicable individuals who should have been strangled at birth!'

'You can't talk that way about those two girls,' said Goldsmith, his face puce with anger. 'It's not their fault they were radicalised.

Looking at him, Hunter wondered if the Liberal Democrat MP was going to have apoplexy and keel over with a heart attack. It didn't happen and the man slowly calmed down.

'General,' said the Judge, 'in your opinion, what would have happened if you hadn't shot those women?'

'A lot of innocent people would have died,' was the stark reply.

'There is no doubt about that,' said Harrow. He turned his head to look at Frederick Ogilvie, 'What do you think, Freddy?'

Ogilvie looked down at his tightly clenched hands. His face was still ashen; he looked at Hunter who stared impassively back. He said, 'I agree with you. This committee must do all in its power to ensure no action is taken against any members of TIFAT and that includes the General and the Commander.'

'You cannot be serious,' Goldsmith began.

At that point, Hunter tuned out. He knew the way the argument would flow and he was pretty sure of the result. A short while later a break was called in the proceedings. Hunter was grateful. He could do with a coffee. There was a bar just along the corridor and the men decided they would adjourn and meet back in thirty minutes. Hunter politely let Goldsmith walk in front of him to the door and as the MP passed he pinched his thumb and finger on the man's coat. The transmitter immediately stuck to the cloth. It was opaque, about a centimetre in diameter and thumbnail thick. Unlike the other's he had used at Rabbani's, these had a range of only 10m or so.

When they arrived at the bar, Macnair, Hunter, Parker and Harrow sat at one table, Ogilvie and Goldsmith sat at another on the other side of the room. Of the 20 or so tables in the room, only half were in use.

He saw Ogilvie and Goldsmith with their heads bent close, arguing like mad. The recording device in his mobile was listening to every word.

'What's brought on this change of heart in Ogilvie?' asked Harrow in his blunt Northern manner.

'I told you, it's an epiphany,' said Macnair, with a straight face.

'He has seen the light!'

'Amen to that,' said Lord Parker. 'And the real reason?' His question was directed at the two TIFAT officers.

'Sir,' said Hunter, 'its better you didn't know. I...'

At that moment a door burst open and a man Hunter recognised as a Cabinet Minister said in a loud and excited voice, 'Two bombs have gone off up north! One in Leeds and one in Birmingham.'

Silence suddenly cloaked the room. 'How many dead and injured?' Macnair asked.

'We don't know.'

'What's caused them?' Somebody called out.

'They're bombs, you bloody fool. What do you think?'

'Let's take our coffees and return to the committee room,' said Harrow, 'we can see if there is anything on the TV.'

They did as suggested. They watched as the scenes of death and destruction were shown, the reporters filling in with hypotheses as to what had happened when no hard facts were available.

No more committee work was discussed and after 10 minutes Hunter and Macnair left. Hunter went to his hotel and collected his gear while Macnair did the same from the Naval Club. They caught the next train to Scotland.

The two men armed themselves with large whiskies and sodas and sat at a table next to the rear door of the carriage. There was nobody in earshot. Hunter took out his mobile and played back the recording of Goldsmith and Ogilvie.

'What the hell was that all about?' Goldsmith asked in a low voice, his anger clearly apparent.

Luckily, the bug was on the right side of Goldsmith's jacket and next to the wall. It meant that any background noise was pretty much filtered out.

'What was all what about?'

'You know damned well! You've capitulated! You're letting them get away with murder. With breaking the law. With...with everything we've argued against since day one. Why? I don't get it.'

'I told you. I've given it a lot of thought. We need TIFAT to do its job its way. We have no choice.'

'Is this anything to do with Algernon Fitzgerald? I thought him leaking the information played into our hands.'

'It had. It does. It's just I came to realise that we need an organisation like TIFAT if we are to keep people safe.'

'No, no, no! They are an abomination. It is the law that counts and nothing but the law.'

'I cannot agree. Let it drop, Nigel, for pity's sake, let it drop.'

'My God, Freddy, you're frightened. Somebody's scared you witless. Who?'

There was no answer but Hunter realised that was about the time Ogilvie had looked across at them. It was confirmed a few seconds later.

'Them?' said Goldsmith. 'They threatened you?'

'I'm not saying anything of the sort. Look, just drop it. I am going to go public with my support. I will be informing the Prime Minister and I will make it clear that TIFAT is in the front line of defence against terrorism.'

'I am so very disappointed, Freddy, you've no idea.'

There was silence for a few seconds and then they heard the near hysterical voice of Ogilvie.

'I'm telling you, Nigel, drop it and support TIFAT.' At least the MP was following the instructions given to him by Hunter to the letter. 'The fact is, they are not abusing their power. They are protecting us when we are unable to protect ourselves. I urge you, for the sake of your family, don't keep attacking them.'

'What do you mean about my family? They wouldn't threaten my family,' then as an afterthought, he added, 'would they?'

'No, of course not. And I am not suggesting it for one minute. Even I admit they wouldn't sink so low. It's just...it's just they do have the power to blacken your name. To ensure you're vilified. To destroy your reputation.'

'Huh, let them try. I'm not afraid of them.'

'Then you're more stupid than I thought, which is saying something.'

'What do you mean by that?'

'Nothing. Forget I said anything. Nigel, I will be making my views clear this afternoon. I strongly recommend you get onboard.'

At that moment the door burst open and the cabinet minister began yelling the news.

Hunter switched off the recording. 'Think Goldsmith will

keep quiet?' Hunter asked, taking a sip of his drink.

'We might need to give him some encouragement. Let's wait and see.' Macnair's phone rang. He took it out of his pocket and glanced at the screen before pressing the receive button. 'It's Isobel,' he said to Hunter.

After a few minutes he said, 'Okay. I'll call her. You get on to tracking down those calls. Let's see if we can pinpoint where they came from.' He broke the connection. 'Elspeth Coolidge wants to speak to me.' He pressed buttons. 'Elspeth? It's Malcolm. I understand you're looking for me.'

Hunter sat toying with the glass in front of him while Macnair listened to the boss of MI5. Occasionally, he made a comment. Then, he said, 'Okay, Elspeth. Thanks for that and good work. Leave it to us.' He broke the connection and placed the phone down on the table. He lifted his glass and took a large mouthful. 'It looks as though we have a job to do,' he announced.

53

THE NEXT MORNING a briefing was held in the auditorium next to the operations room. It was more a brain storming with all participants taking part.

It was a large room, with windows overlooking the river on one side, and the parade ground on the other. The room was set out in theatre style and could take 60 people in comfortable, padded seats. Each seat had a cup holder on its right arm. The stage was only 3ft high and stretched the width of the large room. The wall at the back of the stage held a huge screen which could be cut down into sections for different images.

Hunter was gratified to see the best men that TIFAT had on its books were assembled, either back from leave or returned from other operations.

He mentally ran through the team he wanted with him.

Jan Badonovitch, the Spetsnaz sergeant was back from his exploits in the Mediterranean. He greeted his boss with the question, 'What's up Nick?'

'Glad to see you, Jan,' Hunter smiled. 'Been working on the tan at tax-payer's expense, I see.'

'You know how it is, all work and no play makes for dull boys. What's up?'

'An op in Pakistan. I don't know the details but the General will fill us in. Dave, how was Wales?'

Sergeant David Hughes was Special Air Service, medium build, black hair with piercing blue eyes, he was deceptively mild mannered. He was slow to anger but if he did it was best to stay clear of him. 'You know, boss, there's only one problem.'

Hunter grinned. His family was originally from Wales and he still had many relatives living there. 'Don't tell me, it's full of Welsh people.'

'No,' Hughes shook his head and smiled, 'the English are taking over. The sods are getting everywhere.'

'Have a good time?'

'Yes, thanks. The wife's pregnant and is now nagging me to quit and get a proper job.'

'What did you say?'

'I said I had a proper job, saving the world. She's agreed at last to move up to Scotland. If I know my Peggy, she'll be busy on the internet right now looking for a place to buy.'

'Good. We'll get logistics to help out. Let her know the visitor suite is yours when she comes up.'

'Thanks, Nick. I forgot. I'll give her a call later.'

Hunter turned to the man standing next to him. Sergeant Don Masters was a Royal Engineer and acknowledged to be one of the greatest experts alive when it came to explosives and explosive devices, both manufactured and improvised. He was the same height as Hunter, with brown hair and brown eyes. He had an aquiline face with a dimple and looked at life as though it was a huge joke. He had been married and divorced twice, and made it clear he was happy there had been no children. He swore black was white that he would never remarry and to prove it he had a succession of girlfriends who never lasted more than a month or two. He was just back from a combined operation in Somalia.

'Don,' they shook hands, 'how was it?'

'Hi, Nick. A bust.'

Hunter frowned. 'How come? I thought the intel was spot on.'

'It was,' Masters shook his head, a look of disgust on his face.

'So what happened?'

'We waited over the horizon onboard HMS Daring. We shadowed the tanker all the way from the Suez. The Merlin was ready to go twenty-four seven.' He was referring to the RN helicopter carried onboard the type 45 destroyer. It could carry 24 seated passengers or 45 standing. 'We had two teams with rigids.' Rigid raiders had hulls made from glass reinforced plastic and, with the new, virtually silent engines, were capable of speeds of up to 80mh, carrying 6 to 10 men with their kit. 'The Somalis attacked at dawn, exactly when and where we were told.'

'Did we have anybody on the ship?'

Masters shook his head in disgust. 'Don't go there Nick. The ship's Master refused. The Swedish retard said some crap about peace, goodwill and being protected by the Lord. Anyway, we ID'd the pirates and we went in by helo. We dropped off a rigid five miles short and a second one three miles the other side. The helo did its job, keeping the pirates boxed in while we attacked. ROEs,' Rules of Engagement, a pain to all those fighting piracy on the high seas, 'were emphasised and when we got up close the pirates surrendered without a shot being fired. Just like that.'

'Then what happened?'

'Jesus, you aren't going to believe this. We took them back to the Daring, gave them tea and biscuits and let them go free.'

'You're kidding,' said Hunter. A few of the others had joined them.

'I kid you not. We couldn't arrest them. We couldn't shoot them, we could do nothing.'

'Why couldn't you arrest them?' asked one of the others.

'There were no charges we could bring. You see, they hadn't actually committed a crime. They hadn't shot at anybody, they hadn't tried to board the ship. Nothing. They also dropped their weapons over the side so there was nothing we could do under international law. Nick, you should have seen their faces. They made idiots of us and they were laughing themselves sick. I can tell you, any one of the lads would have shot them on the spot. But as it was a joint op, under the control of the EU, there was nothing we could do.'

Hunter knew that Masters had been the only TIFAT operative there. 'Who else was involved?'

'We had Special Boats then there were the French, Dutch and Italians. And just to keep things nice and even and ethnically balanced, we had half a dozen Kenyans who were as much use as chocolate teapots. The worst of it was we also had two UN observers. Both were real pains,' said Masters.

They all knew that the men allowed to go free would be back attacking ships, killing innocent people and taking prisoners within days. It wasn't the first time they had heard such stories. It was further proof, if it was needed, that TIFAT was a vital force when it came to living in a civilised world.

'Actually, the UN guys weren't the worst of it.'

'What was?' Hunter asked.

'Working with the French, Dutch and Italians. It was supposed to show how effective a European Military Force could be. It didn't. There was too much bickering. I reckon if we did have a combined force we'd have the British generals saying charge, the French saying retreat and we'd all be wondering where the hell the Dutch and Italians had got to.'

His comments raised a grin from the others.

'As bad as that?' asked Badonovitch.

'Pretty much,' Masters said.

'Is Peter back?' Even as Hunter spoke, Peter Weir appeared. He was a United States Ranger and an expert shot with just about any weapon ever designed. On an op like the one they were facing he was a vital member of the team. The two men shook hands.

Weir was British but his family had emigrated to America when he was just 7 years old. They had ended up in Tennessee. Weir described it as a state where, if you didn't shoot, hunt and fish you were considered a nancy boy. So he learnt all three skills and almost inevitably went into the army. He was transferred to the Rangers and ten years later found himself in TIFAT. He was happily married with three children and lived in Dunfermline. Hunter knew he was having a few issues at home. Like the rest of them, he was often away although TIFAT did their best to ensure the married personnel did as few operations as possible. After all, there were plenty of jobs on the base that needed doing. However, Weir and the other married personnel didn't want special treatment. They knew what they had signed up for. So did their wives. It was take it or leave it. Many wives left it. Hunter hoped Weir's marriage wouldn't go down a similar road. At 40 years old, he was the second oldest fully operational member of TIFAT. Hunter looked around for the oldest.

He walked in just then. He approached Hunter with an outstretched hand and a warm smile. 'Did you think you'd be going without me?'

Matt Dunston was an anomaly. He was 51 years old, a bachelor, had joined the army at 16, transferred to the SAS at 21, quit, went to college to read theology, became an ordained minister, rejoined the SAS in his vocation, joined TIFAT 15 years later, and one year after that gave up the priesthood. His belief in God had been tested to breaking and, though he still believed in a Deity, he had also come to the conclusion that turning the other cheek didn't work. He was as tough as they came, a superb hand-to-hand fighter, and could even hold his own when sparring with Hunter. He had a thin face, a hooked nose broken when playing rugby at a tough comprehensive school when he was a teenager. He also had a sharp wit. He no longer wore a uniform. He was on the TIFAT books as a consultant. Naturally, the books were never examined.

Hunter felt a tap on the shoulder and turned to see Joshua Clements, a Captain from the American Delta Force, the USA's primary anti-terrorist unit. Hunter knew he had just returned from a holiday in Miami. Like the others, he was incredibly fit, tough and skilled in the black arts of covert warfare.

As he helped himself to coffee he asked, 'What's up? I had to cut short my vacation by two days just as it was becoming both rewarding and fun.' Clements was a known womaniser and at 30 years of age and film-star good looking he was never short of female company.

'You'll find out. It may not be a goer. We're waiting for confirmation.'

'Is it anything to do with the bombings?' asked Matt Dunston. Hunter nodded.

Isobel joined them. She had in tow two of her people. She referred to them as her right and left hands. Leo was short, overweight and always on a diet of some sort while Gareth was tall, skinny and looked as though a strong wind would blow him over. They were geniuses when it came to computers and they were devoted to Isobel.

'Hello, you guys,' Hunter greeted them. 'Have you anything for us?'

'Hi, Nick,' replied Isobel, 'and hello you lot.'

The men grinned at her. Isobel was a favourite with them all. Not only was she a very nice woman but she was also brilliant at her job. More than once they owed their lives to her and the info she was able to supply. She was also responsible for liberating the crooks and terrorists of much of their ill-gotten gains. It was cash that they knew would be used to look after their loved ones should anything happen to them.

Macnair announced from the front of the stage, 'Grab your seats.'

While they were doing so, Isobel was working on a keyboard attached to a computer that was sitting on a table at the side of the stage. As she did, pictures appeared on the huge screen. Top left was Elspeth Coolidge from MI5, then came a picture of Arthur Woods, the new head of MI6. Hunter was still to make his mind up about the man. He seemed too cautious to be in such an important job. Then came Sarah Fleeting, the boss of GCHQ. A tough lady in her late fifties, she was known for her blunt speaking and disregard for the law. Her small, inner band of operatives, broke the law just about every day when it came to surveillance, phone tapping, intercepting e-mails and straight forward eavesdropping. As a result, vital information was unearthed. The info usually went to TIFAT.

'Sarah, let's start with you,' said Macnair. 'What have you found out?'

'Thanks to what we know about General Khan we've been able to focus our assets where we needed them. We've intercepted e-mails as well as phone calls. They come in two distinct categories. We followed the orders originating in Pakistan to the UK where they were disseminated to other groups. They were in code that was, quite frankly, child's play to break. We passed on the information to Elspeth.'

The audience switched their attention to the boss of MI5.

'I let the relevant forces know and this morning raids were carried out all over the country.'

'Good,' said the General. 'Has there been any feedback yet?'

'Some. We've found drugs, explosives and weapons at every site we've hit so far. Which is good news. It means the intel is first class.'

'Are there many more targets?' Macnair enquired.

Elspeth nodded. 'There have been eighteen raids so far and there are another ten in the pipeline. Some of those will already have happened but I've had nothing back yet. So we're looking at a good result. God alone knows how many bombings and attacks we've prevented.'

'Arthur? What have you got for us?'

Arthur Woods scowled. He was in his early fifties, with a round face, a fringe of grey hair, bushy eyebrows and thick lips. He was overweight and had the rasping voice of someone who smoked too much.

'We've been on to the CIA for clarification and cross referenced what they know with what we've got. There is absolutely no doubt whatsoever that Khan is orchestrating the unrest that is building up in Pakistan.'

'Sarah, you said two categories,' said Macnair.

'In the second category were a number of e-mails to the men who had met with Khan on the Pashni. It seems Khan is stepping up his illegal activities. He's going to increase the supply of heroin and prostitutes as well as move more heavily into the cocaine market. Reading between the lines I'd say he was needing a lot more money. Or he's just plain greedy.'

Macnair didn't tell them that Khan needed the funds. That TIFAT had liberated the Pakistani of much of the wealth he thought he was getting from Rabbani.

'Malcolm,' said Elspeth, 'I've just been handed a note. An update. There have been seven gun battles so far. A number of people have been killed, including a policeman though I don't know where. We've found some explosives in two houses in Luton that belong to one man. He's a well known Islamic rabble rouser who claims to be an Imam though we have been unable to find out where he did his studies.'

'Pakistani?' asked Macnair.

'Yes. Right now I expect he's screaming blue murder about his human rights, his legal rights, his Islamic rights and every other right he can come up with. These people are well versed in this sort of thing. There's going to be loud screams of xenophobia, Islamophobia and I am expecting any day now the announcement of a new phobia called Pakistaniphobia. He's denying all knowledge of the explosives and claims it's been planted there by us to discredit him.'

'There's no surprise there,' said Macnair.

'It's going to get very messy,' said Sarah Fleeting, 'politically a nightmare for Westminster. It well divide the country even further.'

There was no disputing what she said. The conference went on for another hour. It was interspersed with updates as news of operations trickled in. Most had been successful. Or at least as successful as they could be, thought Hunter. The aftermath was where the real work began. Reports, investigations, evidence gathering, disclosure, trial, defence versus prosecution and then, with a vast amount of luck, sentencing that was meaningful and not the usual slap on the wrist. In many respects, arresting people was the easy part. It was why SO19 liked it when their targets resisted arrest. Then they had an excuse to shoot the criminals. This was a fact nobody admitted to, not even to friends. You never knew who was listening.

54

DAVID HUGHES PUT up his hand. 'Sir, do we know where we are going?'

Macnair nodded. 'Yes, Sergeant, we do. We know Khan is responsible for the attacks. GCHQ are sure of Khan's whereabouts and that's been confirmed by Isobel.' Macnair stood with his hands behind his back for a few seconds. 'Telling the Pakistanis will do no good, we're pretty certain of that. Therefore, killing Khan is the only option we have. After lunch we'll meet back here and start work on the op.'

Lunch was soup and a salad for Hunter and the same for Matt Dunston who had joined him.

'What's this I heard you brought back some sort of gin palace?' Dunston asked.

'The Talisman. It belonged to Rabbani. You know all about it?'

'Only that you'd brought her up from down south.' He grinned. 'I also heard there was a second mate onboard. Or is that a first mate?'

'Just crew, Matt. Just crew. I had thought about us keeping her for jollies. Maybe charge something for her use and then give the proceeds to, say, Help for Heroes. But it goes against the grain. Proceeds of crime and all that. I think we should just sell her and give the money to one or two charities.'

'Alternatively,' said Dunston, thoughtfully, 'why don't we start a club for deprived kids in this area? A sailing club. Set it up in the marina at South Queensferry, if they'll let us. Use the Talisman as a base. Get a few dinghies and other boats. Maybe some canoes.' He shrugged. 'Heck, let the kids decide what they want to do. Get them involved. Give them a purpose.'

Hunter nodded and smiled. 'Great idea. We can get rid of some of the more opulent fittings and make room for more bunks. Make her a sort of floating HQ. I like it. I'll let the General know. I'm sure he'll agree.'

Dunston chuckled. 'It was his idea.'

'We'll need to ask for volunteers.'

'Leave it to me.'

'How was your holiday?' Hunter asked.

'Not bad. That's another one crossed off my to do list before I depart this mortal coil.'

'I didn't know you had a list.'

'Metaphorically speaking. I've always had a desire to climb to the top of Everest. At least, it's been an ambition of mine for years. Now it's done. So it's on to the next thing.'

'Which is?'

'I don't know. I'm still making up my mind.'

'What about your list?'

'I add to it as I go along.'

'What was it like? At the top.'

'No idea. The weather closed in, you couldn't see more than a hundred yards and as soon as we got there we turned around and came back down.'

Hunter laughed out loud.

'Yeah, I know.' Then Dunston started laughing as well.

They finished lunch and returned to the briefing room.

'Right, gentlemen,' General Macnair began, 'it's the usual rules. Ideas and interruptions are welcome throughout. I want this thing put to bed by eighteen hundred when we'll start the deployment.' It was a few minutes after 14.00. 'Isobel, over to you.'

Leo sat at the computer. He pressed the necessary buttons and a photograph flashed up on the screen. It showed the position of the house and the surrounding landscape, out to 5 miles. A second showed a closer look at the grounds, while a third was an even closer look at the house itself. Next, he put all three photographs up at the same time.

'Gentlemen,' said Isobel, 'we are ninety-nine percent positive that Khan is at a house about twenty miles to the west of Karachi. The problem is we don't know how long he will be there. As far as we can tell, he tends not to stay in one place for very long. At least, he hasn't since he became a posi.' A Person of Special Interest was subject to the closest scrutiny imaginable. Their lives were turned over and any maggots that crawled out were put under the microscope. 'We're sure about his movements because we have been able to track back his e-mails. The house on the screen was built three years ago. It took a year to complete. Gareth has spent the last forty-eight hours tracking down the builders and the architect. He accessed the computer holding the drawings of the building. Leo, if you please.' The photographs shrank to half size and two more appeared underneath. This time they were architects plans. Isobel used a laser pointer. 'The house is huge and must have cost a fortune to build. As far as we can gather it is Khan's retreat. According to the architect's notes, he thought he was designing and building the house for a wealthy businessman. Ownership is in the name of an off-shore company. The first drawing is the layout of the ground floor, the second is the bedroom area. There is no basement as far as we can tell. A2 copies of the drawings are on the easels along the side.'

The men glanced over to the right where a row of easels displayed the drawings.

'This area here is where Khan lives, this is where the family live when they are in residence. He has four wives and, we think, ten or so children. The good news is that they are all at Khan's place in Islamabad.'

'Are we sure?' asked Hunter.

'Yes. Satellite photos prove it.'

There were nods of relief all around. As far as they were concerned, wives and children were off limits. The problem was, it didn't stop the older children and some of the tougher wives from picking up a gun and firing at them. When all said and done, a bullet could kill you no matter who pulled the trigger.

Isobel nodded to Leo and the photographs changed. This,' she moved the pointer, 'are the guards' quarters. Compared to the rest of the house they are pretty stark. Each guard has his own room. It's hardly more than a cell, about ten feet by ten feet. This is the shower and toilet area and this is the kitchen and dining room. There are thirty rooms but as far as we can tell, only twenty guards on post. We assume each guard has his own room on a permanent basis, twenty men are on duty at any one time and ten are elsewhere. This suggests a duty roster of two weeks on, one week off.' Isobel smiled. 'That's more generous than you lot, that's for sure.'

The men grinned back.

'We'll go into more detail later. I just want to give you an overview. Okay Leo.' The drawings changed. 'These are Khan's quarters. You can see the round tower. This is his bedroom. It's huge. This is his bathroom and toilet. His living room is above the bedroom and here is what could be an office. This is the kitchen where his personal chef works.'

'What about other servants?' asked Dunston. 'Are there any?'

'I was coming to that. They are quartered here. Gareth,' she nodded in his direction, 'managed to get access to the computer Khan is using while he is there. Gareth, over to you.'

Gareth stood up and Leo changed the screen. 'This is a list of the servants. There are twelve in all. I can't tell if they work some sort of roster but it looks as though six are permanently stationed there to look after the house and grounds while six move around with the General. At present, all twelve are on the property. They also have a room each, their own kitchen and canteen and shower and toilets. From the names we found there appears to be eight men and four women.'

'No wonder Khan wanted to take over Rabbani's operation,' said Hunter, 'this estate must have cost a fortune to build and also a fortune to maintain.'

'We looked at that,' said Gareth, 'and you'd be surprised. The guards and staff are on the books as serving in the army. So most of the running costs are met by the Pakistani taxpayers. Also, consumables such as food, gas and oil for the generators are also courtesy of the army. We'll show you where that's all housed later.' Gareth continued with his briefing for another twelve minutes before he sat down.

'I want to go over the plans of the grounds,' said Isobel. The screen changed to a single photograph. 'You can see from the date time stamp that this was taken at eight thirty this morning using one of our own satellites.' Isobel began pointing out the relevant features around the grounds. 'A swimming pool, these are gazebos,' she continued pointing, 'this is the main gate here, in the north-east corner. There are no other gates to the property. This is a guard booth.'

'What's the room on the right? asked Hunter. 'It looks low and long.'

'It is,' Macnair stood up. 'I figure it's a firing range and armoury. It would make sense.'

The team nodded.

'And the one next to it?' Hunter enquired.

'Probably a garage. It's big enough to hold maybe a dozen vehicles. You can see the concrete driveway leading from the gate and ending outside the doors.'

There were more nods.

'The walls are topped with razor wire and in the corners,' she aimed the laser, 'are platforms rising about 6ft above the walls. They are also 6ft square. You can see the waist high, brick walls and the roofs. There is also a tower right next to the gate. All four have a sentry. We can assume they're armed. From the heat signatures, there appears to be two guards in the gatehouse. We have identified four guards patrolling the grounds. At first, we thought they were moving randomly but it became clear that they are following a set path.' She outlined the movements of the guards. 'It's fair to say that they will probably stick to the same paths at night. The compound walls are 500m along the seafront, and 500m in depth. This means the compound is, as near as dammit, 6 acres.'

'What about bullet proof windows?' asked Peter Weir. 'Also alarms in the house and sensors in the grounds?'

'We know the place is alarmed. We used the info held by the architect to track down the security company who installed the alarms. They are number coded. From the details Gareth found, they should be easy to dismantle.'

'How?' asked Don Masters.

Gareth replied. 'Merely cut the wires. The type and make of alarm is generations old. Cheap in other words.'

'That surprises me,' said Hunter.

'Us as well.' Gareth shrugged his skinny shoulders. 'There's no way of telling why, only what the position is.'

Isobel stepped to the podium and pointed her laser. 'This building contains the generator. We're sure of that from the heat signature. You can see it is a fair distance from the house and we suspect that is because of the noise. This thing here, outside the shed, is the oil tank. This,' she moved the pointer, 'is an open structure with a roof. We know from the architect's drawings that it holds two large tanks of gas.'

Isobel continued with her briefing. The detail was impressive. An hour later she said, 'That's all for now. If anything else comes in we'll let you know.'

'Thanks, Isobel,' said Macnair, getting to his feet. 'And thanks Leo and Gareth. Good job. Right,' he turned to look at the team arrayed in front of him, 'it's operational planning time. Everything is on the table.

'We'll start with the objective. It is to kill Khan and his guards. Also, if you find Rabbani, kill him as well.' Macnair always spoke bluntly. That way there was no misinterpreting his orders. 'Do your damnedest not to kill or injure any of the servants. However, don't put your own lives at risk. Let's start with ingress. Ideas, please gentlemen.'

Two hours later the operation had been given shape and some depth. As always, the detail couldn't be planned. There were far too many variables. Actions would be taken as events unfolded. Too much planning obscured the operation. Flexibility was vital.

The necessary signals were sent. As part of its remit TIFAT dealt directly with the forces of other countries. If help was required they usually got it. In this case, help was needed, asked for, and agreed.

The team packed their gear and were ready to depart a few minutes after 18.00. They were carrying a lot more than usual but they had a big job ahead. They drove to Edinburgh airport in Range Rovers, followed by two Transit vans crammed with equipment. They moved onto the airfield using a side gate. In one corner of the secure area was a large hangar with an office building close by. The vehicles drove into the hangar.

The C-17A Globemaster III was waiting for them. It had arrived an hour earlier from Brize Norton where the squadron was based. Standing next to the plane, looking up at the massive beast, Hunter felt tiny. He knew a few facts about the Globemaster. Such as her speed was 550kts and range 4,500 nautical miles. Crew of 3. The direct flight from Edinburgh to Karachi was 4,050nm. On a direct flight, the plane would cross Denmark, Poland, Ukraine, the southern end of Russia, Azerbaijan, the Caspian Sea, Turkmenistan, Afghanistan and then into Pakistan. Such a flight plan was a nightmare to request and follow. Instead, it was decided that the plane would stay over NATO airspace all the way to Istanbul. There they would land and refuel. From there they would rise to their maximum cruising height of 45,000ft and fly south-east to Syria and Iraq. The two countries were such basket cases of conflict there was virtually no likelihood that anyone would notice them. They would stay at that height and cross Saudi Arabia, the United Arab Emirates and Oman before turning directly east. They would get permission to cross the airspace of the three countries as they were friends of Britain - at least they were on the diplomatic circuit. The reason for the transit of the Globemaster was that it was heading to Mumbai for a joint exercise with the Indian Air Force. Not only wasn't that true but the Indians knew nothing about it. It wasn't necessary. Nobody would be checking.

The team worked fast. In minutes, the vans were empty, the cargo doors closed, the engines flashed up and the aircraft was taxiing. The time was 19.17. They took their seats and were strapped in by the time the plane lifted into the air. Ten minutes after take-off the loadmaster, an RAF Master Aircrew, announced they could take off their seatbelts and walk around. He went on to say there was no point in giving any instructions in the event of a crash as none of them would survive. That received grins all round. He showed them the galley, the packed food, the microwave and the urn for boiling water. He also showed them where cot beds were stowed and invited them to help themselves. The belly of the plane was huge and empty. The men were used to it having flown in Globemasters in the past.

Hunter made his way forward to the cockpit. He rapped on the door, opened it and went in. The pilots were sitting back relaxed, neither had a hand on a control or a foot on a peddle. Both had hot drinks in their hands.

'Welcome onboard, Commander,' said the pilot in the left hand seat. 'I'm Seb Cole and this is my co-pilot, Francis Wayne. I hope you guys are okay back there.'

Hunter shook hands with the two men, and introduced himself. 'We're fine thanks. We'll break out the cots and get our heads down. Are you taking us all the way?'

'Yep,' said Cole. 'There's no such thing as the working time directive in the RAF.'

Hunter smiled. 'It seems to have bypassed us as well.'

'Nick, care to tell us what's going on?'

'Just an exercise,' said Hunter. He and the pilot exchanged looks.

Cole burst out laughing. 'Yeah. And Santa Claus really exists.'

'Sorry, Seb, I can't say.'

'That's okay. I didn't really expect any other answer. Can I ask one thing?'

'Shoot. If I can answer it I will.'

'Is it anything to do with the bombings?'

Hunter thought for a moment. 'Let me put it this way. The people responsible are going to wish they never got involved.'

'That's good enough for me. Okay, the flight plan. We're going to land at Istanbul in about,' he looked at the digital displays laid out in front of him, 'three hours and 12 minutes, according to Gertrude here.'

'Gertrude?'

'Named after his mother,' said the co-pilot. 'He reckons she was always bossing him around as a kid.'

'She was,' said Seb Cole in a hurt tone. 'According to her,' he pointed, 'we will be landing at midnight seventeen. Refuelling and the rest of the paraphernalia and we should be back in the air around one thirty. Flight time to our destination is just over five hours. We'll be taking the long way around as instructed. Daybreak at the drop-off point is around five fifteen, sunrise is at five forty-four.'

'Good. That gives us plenty of time. If you gentlemen will excuse me, I'm going to get some sleep.'

55

THE FLIGHT WENT according to plan.

At 05.00 local time the Globemaster was circling an area of the Arabian Sea, 150nm south of Pakistan. The plane had a unique feature. Its design allowed it to carry out high-angle approaches and take-offs, which meant it could land on an airstrip 3,500ft long and only 90ft wide. As it approached, the aircraft dropped down from a cruising height of 40,000ft to a drop-off height of 3,000ft.

Hunter stood in the cockpit, kitted out and ready to go. He wore a wetsuit with a knife strapped to his right thigh. On his back was a parachute with an automatic opening device and on his chest was the emergency pull if the device failed to work. In his left hand he carried a pair of fins.

He was looking at the radar screen in the centre of the cockpit console. The blips on the screen were vanishing one by one as the horizon shrunk. Finally, there was only one, 3,500ft below the plane.

'That's her,' said Cole. 'Two minutes.'

The weather was perfect. A cloudless sky, virtually no wind and visibility out as far as the horizon'

Cole turned to Hunter and held out his hand. They shook. 'Good luck.'

'Thanks. Bye Francis.'

The co-pilot held out his hand, gripped Hunter's and said, 'Kill the swine.'

Hunter merely nodded. He turned and walked aft. The team was ready to go.

'One minute to opening,' said the Loadmaster. 'Right. That's it,' he said, as a light changed from red to amber.

The huge doors at the rear of the plane opened. The gear sat on trolleys. The Loadmaster pressed a button and the trolleys trundled aft to the edge. The light turned green. He pressed

another button and the trolleys slid out, the parachutes deployed
and the loads floated gently down. The team followed in rapid
order. Hunter was last. He assumed the flight position, arms
and legs outstretched, back arched, belly down. In seconds, the
automatic release engaged, his shoulders were jerked upwards
and he was floating through the air. A quick headcount showed
the others in the same profile, their flight paths following that
of the pallets. About half-a-mile away he could see the black
conning tower of one of Her Majesty's Submarines.

Hunter hit the water. As the weight came off the lines the
parachute was released and it floated clear of Hunter, a few
metres behind him. He pulled on his fins, turned and gathered
the 'chute into a tight bundle. A minute later he began to swim
towards where the others were congregating. The trolleys had
jettisoned on hitting the water and now all that was left were
the six reinforced plastic containers. They were each 6ft long
and 2ft wide. Their construction made them naturally buoyant
even when packed tightly with gear. If the weight was too
great, automatic pouches along the top, filled with helium, kept
them afloat. In this case, one of the containers had deployed its
floatation pouches.

'Okay?' Hunter asked.

'Couldn't be better, Boss,' said Badonovitch. 'There's nothing
like a swim in the blue, warm waters of the Arabian Sea.'

'That's for sure,' said Don Masters, 'only you ugly lot are the
wrong sex.'

They laughed. Even with their skill and experience, jumping
from an aircraft had its risks. The banter helped to lighten the
mood. They cut the parachutes free of the canisters and rolled
them up as best they could. They lazily kicked their fins, watching
as the sub approached. They could make out four men standing
in the conning tower. Two had binoculars to their eyes and were
scanning the horizon, two were looking at them.

The sub stopped about 100m away. A foghorn appeared and
one of the men broadcast, 'Want a lift?'

'Yes, please,' yelled Hunter, 'but only if you're going our way.'

The team swam towards the submarine. A hatch in the bow
of the hull flipped open, half a dozen sailors appeared and boat
hooks were held out to grab the canisters. It only took minutes

for the canisters to be hauled aboard and for the team to follow. Hunter followed his men into the guts of the beast, seconds later the hatch closed and almost immediately the sub started down to her natural environment.

One of the ratings asked, 'Which one of you is Commander Hunter?'

'I am.'

The Petty Officer saluted. 'Sir, the Captain's compliments. You're bunking in his cabin. If you would like to follow me, I'll show you the way.'

'Please don't bother. I'll come and thank the Captain as soon as I've changed into some dry clothes. I'll stay with my team. Where are we bunking?'

'The forward mess has been prepped, sir. Your equipment can stay here. Breakfast is being served in the galley. As soon as you change, just go and help yourselves.'

'Thanks,' said Hunter, 'we will.'

He lifted a nylon bag out of one of the canisters. 'Showers?'

'Over there, sir.'

'Thanks.' Hunter went into the shower, stripped off, washed away the Arabian, dried himself and put on a green t-shirt, camouflage trousers, green socks and a pair of jungle boots. He rejoined the team who had also changed into similar clothes.

'I'll go and see the Captain. I'll join you later.'

'Follow me, please, sir,' said the Petty Officer.

Hunter followed the man aft, walking the narrow corridor, stepping over the combing around the watertight doors. Finally, they arrived at the control room. He saw the Captain looking at an electronic chart of the coast of Pakistan. He turned as Hunter entered.

'Permission to come aboard, sir,' said Hunter.

'Hello, Nick. Welcome to HMS Astute.' The Captain held out his hand. The two men shook hands warmly. Scott Llewelyn was 5ft 11ins tall, with an average build, brown wavy hair and brown eyes. He had an aura of competence and leadership that inspired his men and made him popular at the same time. He was wearing his naval tropical shorts with a white short-sleeved shirt with the insignia of three gold stripes on his shoulder pads.

'I heard you had command. Congratulations, Scott.'

Llewelyn and Hunter had known each other at Dartmouth and been promoted with their third stripe at the same time. They had been friends but, as was the nature of friendships in the military, people came and went. Friendships broke off and resumed at a later date, when paths crossed again.

'Let's go to my cabin.'

Hunter followed Llewelyn who put his head into the steward's pantry and said, 'Lassimer, coffee for two, please.'

'Coming right up, sir.'

The two officers entered the cabin. It was small, had a bunk, and a desk, above which certain information was displayed on a monitor. On the desk was a photograph of a very attractive woman.

'Who's that? The wife?'

'Michelle and yes, the wife, as you so inelegantly put it. She's due to have a baby any day now.'

'Congratulations. Boy or girl?'

'A boy.' He frowned. 'I wish I was there for the birth. However, there's nothing I can do about it. Michelle knew before she signed up what being married to a sailor would mean.

Hunter sat on the bench and Llewelyn sat at the desk. The steward came in with a tray holding two mugs of coffee, milk and sugar. 'Is there anything else, sir?'

'No, thanks.'

The steward left.

'Milk? Sugar?'

'Just milk. Thanks.'

'Care to tell me what's going on?'

There were some people Hunter needed to keep in the loop and the Commanding Officer of the sub was one of them.

Hunter went through the operation in some detail. Llewelyn asked a number of pertinent questions but for the most part kept quiet.

Llewelyn picked up a phone and pressed a button. 'Officer of the Watch, turn north and head towards Pakistan. Speed 15kts. Depth 50 fathoms.'

'What are you doing out here?' Hunter asked. 'I was surprised when the General said there was a sub available.'

'We were on anti-pirate patrol. In close, trying to track the swine and passing info to the surface ships, both military and merchant. Waste of time, of course, but our idiot politicians like to stand up in Parliament and claim they're doing something to combat piracy. They really are morons.'

'Amen to that. Scott, you appreciate that this is the blackest of black ops? Not a word to anyone.'

'Don't worry. What time do you want to egress?'

'How close can you get us?' Hunter countered.

'I don't know yet. I should think we can approach to within a mile. Or is that too close?'

'I need to think about it. Is there a moon and if so, at what time?'

'Nope. No moon. If there is, it will be the smallest of slithers.'

'Good. That helps. In that case, a mile takes about thirty minutes with the gear. I want to hit at about three thirty. So say we leave at around zero three hundred?'

'Whatever you want. Is there anything you need?'

Hunter grinned. 'Breakfast.'

'Me too. Let's go to the wardroom. One thing we do rather well is serve a good plate of bacon and eggs.'

'Then lead on Macduff,' said Hunter, misquoting Shakespeare. They took their coffees with them.

The wardroom was empty. The two men helped themselves to orange juice, bacon, eggs and toast before sitting opposite one another.

'Sorry we aren't carrying a mini pod,' said the Captain.

'A what?' Hunter paused with a forkful of eggs and bacon wavering in the air.

'A mini pod.'

'Sorry, I don't know what you're talking about.'

'I thought you'd know. We now have in service a mini submarine that can be attached to the casing, behind the conning tower. It will carry eight, fully kitted men and can be launched while we're submerged.'

'I've never heard of it. Pity, it would have come in really useful. Saved us a lot of effort. This is excellent, by the way,' he waved his fork at his plate.

'Thanks. Our chefs are about the best in the mob. The mini pod is a new innovation. It used to be dropped by helo. Now that we

can carry one, we can get it in much closer to the shore without
being detected than we could by helo. We had one at Gibraltar for
trials. It worked fine. Then the powers-that-be didn't think we'd
have any use for it this trip. So we left it behind.'

'Not to worry. The exercise will do us good.'

They left the subject of the operation and exchanged stories
about their respective careers. Llewelyn made it clear he was in
for the duration. He had his sights set on rear-admiral at least.
Maybe even higher.

'You chose the right specialisation,' said Hunter. 'Whereas I
will never make it as an MCDO.' A Minewarfare and Clearance
Diving Officer rarely made it above Commander unless he was
both very lucky and had somehow landed the right jobs. 'It's one
of the reasons I'm with TIFAT.'

'You're not moving on?'

'No. I've decided I'm staying until I resign or retire.'

'Is that likely to be soon?'

'Hell, no. I like the job too much.'

'Nick, you always were an adrenaline junkie.'

'You're probably right. But I don't think that's why I'm doing
it.'

'Then why?'

'Because I think TIFAT is making a difference. We're taking
the fight to the real enemy and that's the terrorists. None of it is
possible without the work carried out by all our armed services
but in the wars we are engaged in today I think we're the sharp
end.'

'I agree. Anyway, enough about the mob. What about you
settling down? Any unfortunate filly trapped you yet?'

'No chance. I'm enjoying life too much at present.'

Eventually, their reminiscences and chat wound down. Just as
they did, the tannoy called the Captain to the control room.

'Excuse me, Nick. Duty calls.'

'Scott, can I use the comms centre?'

'Sure. No problem. It's next to the control room.'

'Thanks, and Scott, thanks for the ride.'

'It's a pleasure. I'll speak to you later.'

Hunter lingered over a final cup of coffee and then went
forward. The others had eaten and were busy stripping out their

equipment and checking it over.

'We're out around zero three hundred,' announced Hunter, 'with a mile to go.'

There were nods of acknowledgement. It was about what they had expected.

Hunter made his way to the communications centre. There were two ratings on duty, a chief petty officer and a leading hand.

'Chief, I'm Commander Hunter.'

'Yes, sir, I know who you are. Come in and sit down. The Captain said you'd be dropping by. What can we do for you?'

'I'd like to get in touch with TIFAT in Scotland.'

'Yes, sir. No problem.'

The CPO turned to the vast array of dials and buttons laid out before them. After a few seconds he picked up a telephone and handed it to Hunter. 'Here you are, sir. TIFAT.'

'Thanks, Chief, that was fast.'

'All part of the service, sir.'

Hunter took the phone. 'It's Hunter. Put me through to the General, please.' There was a few seconds delay. 'Sir?'

'Hello, Nick. Everything went smoothly?'

'Yes, sir. We're onboard and heading north. We'll be going feet wet around twenty three hundred your time. Has anything changed?'

'Nothing. I'll be in the ops room until further notice and if anything happens I'll let you know. I have the contact details for Astute.'

'Right, thanks, sir.' The connection was broken and Hunter offered the handset back. 'Thanks again. If TIFAT calls back, it will be General Macnair on the line.'

'Right, sir. We'll let you know.'

Hunter went to the forward messdeck that had been allocated to them, found an empty bunk, laid down on it, put his hands behind his head and thought over the plan.

There had been a number of options. Parachute onto land and come in from the north. Go in the way they were doing, up the cliffs, or go in by sea at the end of the promontory and yomp it. The decision had been his, and his alone, and he had settled on the route they were taking. It kept them out of sight for the longest time possible as well as allowing them to get to the compound from a direction that would be pretty much unexpected. From the satellite pictures supplied by Isobel it appeared as though defences were concentrated towards the land. That was perfectly reasonable. After all, who in their right minds would be coming from the sea, scaling 100ft high cliffs and attacking the compound?

He dozed off.

The next thing he knew he was wide awake and surprised to find it was coming up to 16.00. He'd slept the greater part of the day. From the gentle snoring that was going on around him he figured the rest of the team were also asleep. He climbed out of the bunk, pulled on his shoes and went to find the heads. After that he made his way to the wardroom where he found tea and toast available. A couple of other officers came in.

They introduced themselves as the Navigating Officer and the Communications Officer. Though they were obviously curious as to what Hunter and the team were doing on board, they managed to refrain from asking. Hunter didn't enlighten them.

The CPO from the comms centre stuck his head through the doorway. 'Sir, you've got a call. It's the General.'

'Thanks, Chief. Excuse me, guys.'

Hunter made his way to the comms centre. 'Sir?'

'Nick, bad news I'm afraid.'

Hunter gripped the receiver more tightly. He kept his voice steady when he asked, 'And what's that, sir?'

'I pile of cars have just appeared. It looks as though the family have arrived along with a contingent of guards.'

'They could be changing the guards. We know that's the way they run things.'

'Perhaps. As soon as I know more I'll get back to you. As it is, ah, thanks, Isobel. Nick? Isobel just handed me a note. We've identified an extra ten guards, the whole family appears to be there which means four women and we've confirmed eleven children.'

'Okay. Nothing we can do about it. Nothing changes. I'll let the others know.'

56

GENERAL KHAN HAD his anger back under control. The fact was, his bursts of temper, though they erupted like a volcano spewing forth vast amounts of lava, rarely lasted for long. He had given the order to attack the British and so far there had been three explosions reported on the BBC World News, that had resulted in dozens of deaths and many more injuries. He had contacted his business colleagues and told them of his plans to increase the quantity of heroin and cocaine as well as bring in more prostitutes and they had assured him they could deal with the increased traffic. So his temper was back on an even keel and he was even thinking about sending for his third wife to join him.

His feet up on the desk, he was leaning back with a feeling of reasonable contentment when there was a timid knock on the door.

'Come in!'

The door opened and one of his aides appeared. 'Sir, I am sorry to trouble you, sir.'

'I don't think I am going to like whatever it is you are about to tell me,' Khan said.

The man was literally shaking, though he did his best to hide the fact. 'Sir, we have had no confirmation but I thought you should look at the BBC World Service.'

'Why?' Khan frowned as he reached for the remote, aimed it at the wide screen TV and pressed the requisite buttons. The picture came to life and he watched as people were being led away into police vans. 'Why should this concern me?'

'Sir, some of the names have already been released. The Home Secretary of England has been on the news. She has said that the arrests are connected to organised crime as well as a terrorist organisation. She...She named the organisation, sir.' The man faltered.

'Out with it. Now!' There was icy calm in the way that the

General stared at the man, in spite of the fact that his guts were churning and his heart rate rising.

'Sir, they have named Barzakh.' The words came in a rush.

'Get out! Get out you miserable worm!' Khan thundered.

The General drained his glass, his good mood a thing of the past. He threw the glass against the wall where it shattered into a thousand pieces. With that, he calmed down and picked up his mobile phone. He unlocked it using a four digit code, and started making phone calls to the men who had visited him at Tilbury. In all six cases the phone went to answer machine. By the time he had reached the final call he was again in a towering rage and came close to smashing the phone on the desk. He curbed his anger. He told himself to think. How bad was it?

First things first. He leant forward and pressed a switch on the intercom on his desk.

'Come in here.'

The door opened almost immediately and the same aide who had told him about the raids appeared. 'Yes, my General. Sir.'

'How many cells do we have in Britain who can attack the soft underbelly of the non-believers?'

'Em,' the aide licked his lips, thought for a moment and then replied. 'We have seven cells left who are equipped and ready to attack. We were planning to use them over a number of weeks, to keep the British occupied with their own problems. At the same time we will recruit...,'

'Yes, imbecile! I know all that. My plans have changed. I want them to attack immediately!'

'What? All of them?'

'Yes, all of them. Send the orders.'

'Yes, sir. Yes.' The man bobbed his head, turned and practically bolted from the room.

The General nodded. The British would be too busy to take much interest in him. It looked very much as if the men he had met in Tilbury had been arrested. No matter. He would send men to Europe to make contact with the right people and re-establish the network. In fact, he began to think positively, it might be for the best. He would keep a bigger cut of the profits. The people in the network would be chosen by him. It delayed things by a few months but that was nothing in the over all scheme of things.

He had reported to the President that Rabbani had died from a heart attack. However, not before he had given the details of the combined Taliban and Barzakh attack in four months time. The date and location were untrue.

One thought had made him pause. Did the British know of his involvement? The more he thought about it, the more he was convinced they couldn't possibly know. What was there to know? Rabbani was a crook, he controlled Barzakh and now he was dead. While he on the other hand was the Chief of the Army and trusted by the President. A man with many friends and even more contacts in high places around the world. A man trusted by the West. No, he told himself. He was safe.

His family had just arrived. He had forgotten they were coming for one of his son's birthdays. Too bad. He was scheduled to depart for Islamabad by helo at 05.00.

TIFAT was locked in to all transmissions from the General's house. When the orders went out, Isobel and her geniuses tracked the messages to their destinations. Decrypting the messages was simplicity itself.

Malcolm Macnair picked up the receiver and speed dialled the personal mobile of the Commissioner of Police of the Metropolis. Although the position restricted the officer's authority to Greater London he also had certain national responsibilities such as leading the nation's anti-terrorism policing as well as protecting the Royal Family and senior members of the government.

'Hello, Malcolm, I take it this isn't a social call?'

'Hello, Phillip. I'm afraid not. We have intercepted seven attack orders to UK locations.'

'Christ! Where?'

'We don't know where the attacks are going to take place but we have identified the addresses of those who have been given the orders.'

'Who gave the orders?'

'Someone who will not be in a position to do so again.'

'Okay. I won't ask. Care to tell me where the orders came from?'

'You tell me.'

'Pakistan. Or possibly Saudi.'

'Good guess. Not Saudi.'

'No surprise there then.'

'We've e-mailed you the addresses. They've gone direct to your personal account.'

'Do you have a time scale?'

'There I have bad news. The attacks have been ordered to be carried out immediately. So I am afraid you'll have to move fast.'

'Don't worry. By the way, I haven't had time to thank you for what you did at Heathrow and please thank Commander Hunter for me. How are things going on the political front?'

'Let's just say I have matters contained. For now,' he added. 'Right. I'd better go and let you get on with it.'

Macnair broke the connection and turned his attention back to the operation. He looked at his watch. The team would be feet wet in six hours.

If they felt any tension none of them showed it. They looked as though they were about to embark on a relaxing holiday.

The gear was checked one last time. Wetsuits were donned and Hunter was given the thumbs-up. Scott Llewelyn appeared.

'Ready, Nick?'

'Whenever you are.'

'Five minutes. We're a mile out. The seabed is shelving quite quickly so I can't get you any closer. Just like we discussed, I'll surface, give you the green light, Petty Officer Charles here will open the hatches and away you go.'

'Thanks, Scott. We won't hang around. Thanks for the ride and the hospitality.'

Llewelyn nodded and smiled. 'Anytime. See you back here in four hours.'

'Any longer,' said Hunter, 'and we won't be coming back.'

The two men shook hands, the CO nodded to the others and then returned aft to the control room.

As was often the case the next two or three minutes dragged by. Then over the tannoy came, 'It's a go.'

The PO opened the first hatch, scrambled up the ladder, opened the second and climbed out. Don Masters followed. A buoyant canister was handed up followed by David Hughes. Another canister was followed by Jan Badonovitch, a third canister was followed by Peter Weir, a fourth by Matt Dunston, a fifth by Hunter and a last canister was handed up to him.

The night was pitch dark, the air was still and warm and the water flat calm. A perfect night, thought Hunter, for a clandestine swim.

The PO was already climbing back down the hatch. The team had their fins on and were clutching their canisters tightly to their chests. The sub began to sink slowly underneath the water and was gone within 90 seconds.

No words were necessary. The canisters were connected by 3m of thin, nylon rope. The team lined up in the order Hunter, Badonovitch, Dunston, Hughes, Weir and Masters, snorkels were adjusted and the swim started.

Hunter took a bearing on the lighthouse known as Ras Muari Light, also known as Cape Monze Light. Hunter knew that the tower had been a beacon to sailors for over 100 years. He aimed the compass 10 degrees right and they started.

They took long sweeps with their straight legs, a technique that achieved a deceptive speed, distance and endurance. Hunter had his canister attached to a rope which was in turn attached to a harness that fitted over his shoulders and around his waist. This left his hands free. He held the compass on a board in front of him using both hands. Alongside it was his Rolex Oyster Perpetual diver's watch. After 10 minutes he looked up to check the light. It was where he expected it to be, now 30 degrees to their left. The white cliffs of the shoreline were still a distant blur but much closer.

He put his head down, adjusted the course by a further 5 degrees to the right and they continued powering forward. Another 5 minutes and the check showed the lighthouse 60 degrees to the left and the cliffs less than half a mile away.

The next five minutes took them to within audible distance of the surf lapping the shore. The team unclipped their canisters and let the short lengths of nylon rope sink under the weight of the brass clips at either end. They spread out in a horizontal line. The beach was about 100m away. They each pulled their hoods off their heads to listen. All they could hear was the water hitting the shore.

Hunter and the others gripped the canisters by the loop of

webbing in the nose, extracted their silenced Glocks from their webbing on the left side and swam towards the shore. The Guns were 17s, with magazines holding 19 rounds of 9mm.

They continually stopped to look and listen. The sea was all they could hear.

Hunter arrived in the shallows. Ahead he could see the towering white cliffs. Every 10 seconds, the loom of the light from the lighthouse illuminated briefly the crags of the cliff. There was about 10m of small rock and a few boulders. The waterline was a metre up the gently sloping land. As they had expected, the area was free of sentries. With their feet on the seabed, the men removed their fins.

It was 03.24.

The team left the water and, bent double, headed for the cliff. From straight on, the cliff looked like a vertical climb. However, they knew from the sat photos they'd seen that it wasn't the case. The cliffs had been eroded over time and now sloped back at a steep angle but easy enough to climb.

At the base of the cliff, they stopped and opened their canisters. They each removed a collapsed rucksack and placed it to one side. They had debated whether or not to change out of their wetsuits into BDUs - Battle Dress Uniform. The weather had decided it for them. The wetsuit was designed to keep you warm and comfortable when in the water. As the temperature, even at that time of the night, was 30C or 86F keeping warm was the least of their problems. They had decided that comfort was more important. The BDUs were the usual mottled green and browns but these were lightweight and made for wearing in hot climes. They stripped off their wetsuits and pulled on underpants and t-shirt. Next, they strapped on Kevlar vests followed by the BDUs and then desert boots. They put the webbing back on and placed their silenced automatics under their left side, butts forward. Next, they smeared camouflage cream on their faces and hands, turning themselves into something that looked like beasts from the underworld. Into the specially designed leather holder in the right thighs of their trousers they placed a Ka-Bar. Access was quick and easy. They took out a personal radio, flicked the switch on and secured it in their left breast pocket. They put an earplug into their left ear and a throat mike around their necks. There were no wire connections.

'Okay?' Hunter whispered.

The others answered. The radios worked loud and clear. They emptied the canisters of the remainder of the gear into the rucksacks. Hunter put the compass into his pocket and strapped his watch on his right wrist. They were good to go.

They ascended the cliff two at a time. Hunter went up on the right side, Badonovich on the left. They went slow and easy. Silence was the order of the day. They had plenty of time; daylight was still an hour and a half away. There had been no change in the information from TIFAT. This meant there were 30 guards, 4 wives, 11 children, 11 servants and the General.

It was an easy climb until the last couple of metres. The slope went vertical and it took a few minutes for each of them to identify hand and footholds and make the climb. Hunter put his right forearm onto the ground at the top of the cliff and began levering himself over.

As he did so he caught sight of a pair of boots. If he stretched out his hand he could touch them.

57

Luckily for Hunter, the guard was standing with his back to the sea. The wall of the compound was about 10m away. The man was looking down at his feet. Hunter heard the splash of urine on rock. He didn't hesitate for a moment. He slid out his Ka-Bar, stepped up behind the occupied sentry, clamped his left hand over the man's mouth as tightly as he could, jerked the man's head back and sliced his throat open. He pushed him forward, holding onto his head so that the body hit the ground quietly. Badonovitch was standing to one side, his Glock in his fist, his eyes moving back and forth. The night was silent. Blood spurted onto the ground, creating a widening pool around the corpse's head.

Hunter whispered, 'One terr down. Let's go.'

Less than a minute later the other four joined them.

They were between the two towers situated in each corner of the wall, 250m in either direction, give or take a few metres.

Now they were away from the cliff edge the loom of the light didn't reach them, the shade cutting off the illumination at an angle that ran parallel to the shore. They put on their NVGs.

The razor wire was 4m above their heads. According to the security company documents, the wall also had infra-red beams going from one end to the other. However, as expected, the system around the perimeter had a flaw. The towers in each corner were manned and therefore could not be protected by any type of electronic device. It would be too easy for one of the guards to trip the alarm and for all hell to break loose. So the transmit and receive boxes for the infra-red beams ended next to the wall of the towers.

Peter Weir stepped back a couple of metres from the wall. He aimed his weapon at each tower.

'I can see both men,' he whispered. Cradled in his arms was an L129A1 Sharpshooter sniper's rifle. It used the 7.62mm NATO bullets and held 20 rounds in a detachable box. It was only 990mm long and weighed 4.5kgs and so was easy to lug around. This particular rifle had been equipped with the Trijicon ACOG 6X48 telescope sight. It was designed to be accurate out to 800m. In the hands of an expert like Weir it was deadly accurate out to at least 1200m. A fact that Weir had proven on numerous occasions.

Hunter and Badonovitch walked close to the wall. General Khan kept the approaches to the walls clear of any debris, rocks or plants. This was to prevent anyone approaching without being seen. It worked in the team's favour. The ground was flat and even. Not a stone turned, not a twig snapped.

Hunter would be making the first noise. At the tower, he stepped out about 3m and went, 'Psst! Psst!' He was looking up. He saw a man's head appear and look down. The man leant forward to look more closely and at that moment his head exploded in bone, blood and brains. Hunter had the presence of mind to leap backwards so that the blood and gore missed him by a few inches.

He took a mountain climber's rope from his rucksack. It was of kernmantle construction, a core of long twisted fibres known as kern and an outer sheath, the mantle, made of coloured fibres. It was a light grey, helping the rope to blend in with the colour of the cliffs and had a breaking strength of over two thousand pounds. He placed it at the foot of the tower.

Badonovitch stood next to the wall. Tied to his rucksack was a nylon bag. He quickly opened it. Inside were 6 by 1m double rods made from aluminium. The rods were 10cms apart and had two steps to each section. He slotted them together, placed it against the wall and Hunter went up like a cat. He was quickly followed by the Spetsnaz.

Hunter checked the body of the dead man. There was virtually nothing left of his head. The body had collapsed in one corner and so he left it there. The gun at his side was the ubiquitous AK74M with the GP-30 40mm grenade launcher attached. Grenades were in a box in a corner of the tower. There were 6 of them. There were also three more magazines. Each one held 30 rounds. They were well armed, of that there was little doubt.

'In the tower,' came softly through his earpiece.

'Roger that.' So that was three guards down. That left twenty-seven and counting. There was a scraping on the outside of the wall and Peter Weir stuck his head over the side.

Hunter didn't congratulate him on his shooting. He wouldn't expect it. He had just been doing his job.

They surveyed the grounds. The gazebos were surrounded by well-tended lawns. There were flower beds in strategic places. The beds, they knew, were a mass of colour. Under the influence of the NVGs the colours faded, blended and looked insipid.

The team stayed where they were, surveying the grounds. As expected, Hunter saw a man appear from the north-east and walk towards them. He had a rifle slung over his left shoulder, his hands were in his pockets and he was smoking. He was taking no interest in his surroundings, but why should he? The biggest danger to the attention of guards was the monotony. Nothing happened, nothing had ever happened, nothing was expected to happen. Result? You died.

This was proven to be the case when the sentry reached the bottom of the tower and looked up. Hunter was standing in full view. The sentry would be seeing what he expected. Before the man could say anything, Hunter pointed his Glock, pulled the trigger, there was a faint cough, twice, and the man died when two bullets smashed through the top of his skull.

Hunter and Badonovitch walked down the stone steps and into the grounds. The Russian grabbed the guard by his feet and dragged him into the bushes. That was 4 down and left 6 on duty. In the meantime, Hunter took out one of the plastic explosive devices he was carrying and placed it against the wall.

Hunter heard Matt Dunston's voice in his left ear. 'There are two at the gatehouse. They are sitting with their feet up, watching TV. No guns in sight.'

With two in the gatehouse and one in each tower, that left another two on patrol. According to the surveillance carried out by the satellites the patrol had a pattern. They walked around the house, along a footpath that circumnavigated the structure. It usually took them 10 minutes. Occasionally they took as long as 12 minutes but never less than 10. Now that they were on site it was obvious that the guards on patrol were unable to see each other. Hence contact would be by radio.

'Okay, Peter?'

'Ready, Nick.'

The sharpshooter had been scanning the other two towers. The one in the north-east corner was a simple shot of 500m. The one to the north-west was 800m and was visible over the roof of the central part of the house.

They had debated whether or not for one of them to walk up to the tower and distract the guard. There was a slight flaw in that plan. The guards walking around the house, if they arrived on site at the wrong time, could see whoever approached the tower.

Hunter checked the time. 03.46.

'Moving now,' said Hunter, quietly.

The guards had just gone out of sight around the western corner of the house. It meant they were walking towards the next corner with the gatehouse about 200m on the left. Hunter and Badonovitch headed for the south-east corner, out of sight from any of the guards.

They arrived at the corner and waited patiently. The first they knew of the approach of the guards was the waft of cigarette smoke. Hunter whispered, 'Standby.'

The guards could be heard shuffling on the concrete. They had about two seconds left to live.

Hunter stepped to one side, Badonovitch at his left shoulder. The guards were shoulder to shoulder as they walked around the corner. The TIFAT warriors were less than two feet away. They had debated whether or not to use Ka-Bars or guns. They chose the latter. 'Now,' said Hunter into his microphone.

The two guards stopped in shocked surprise. They were the last emotions they would ever experience. Simultaneously, Badonovitch and Hunter fired two rounds into their heads.

Peter Weir fired his first shot and killed the guard in the north-east tower before swinging the rifle to the left and taking aim on the other guard. There was no target.

He waited patiently. A second later, in the still night, he thought he heard the tinkle of breaking glass. The torso of the guard suddenly appeared looking over the side of the tower. Weir's breathing was shallow, his aim was steady and he pulled the trigger. The bullet entered the top of the guard's head and exited at his neck, taking with it the back of his skull.

'Both guards dead,' announced Hughes.

'We've taken the gatehouse,' said Dunston.

'We got our two,' said Hunter. 'That's all ten.'

The team congregated at the gatehouse. The first thing Hunter noticed as he approached the gates was the broken glass in the top half of the door.

'It was locked,' said Masters. 'We could see it wasn't bullet-proof so Matt broke the glass and Dave and I shot the guards.'

'Leave the TV going, sit the two guards at the table and switch off the lights,' Hunter ordered. With luck, anybody looking towards the gatehouse from across the compound would see what they expected to see.

Masters and Hughes did as ordered.

'Right, we need to immobilise the family and servants.' He took the rucksack off his back, opened it, took out a gas canister and rolled up plastic tubing.

David Hughes did the same only he removed two canisters and two lengths of tube. In all three cases the tubes were 8m long.

Peter Weir climbed the steps to the tower. From there, he had the best view of the compound. He could see the main front door, the one used by the family and two further doors, one each side, near the corners of the walls. The one to the left was the entrance to the General's quarters and the door on the right was for the guards. There were three other doors, in the rear, one for each part of the house. Although the doors were solid, there were windows of all sizes. The team knew they were made from double thickness, bullet-proof glass. That made them tougher than the walls.

It was 03.59.

'Don, you, Matt and Dave take the gas. Fill the family quarters.'

'What about the guards?' asked Masters.

'We don't have enough gas. They knew the risks when they signed up. There's twenty left plus Khan. I'll take care of the generator. Then I'll see about a visit to Khan. Jan, you deal with the armoury and Calor gas.' Hunter looked at his watch. 'Set timers for four fifty. No. Better make that zero five hundred.'

The team moved out. There was a major flaw in Khan's security system. Once the electricity was cut off there was no fail/safe. The system ceased to function. There would be no alarms, no awakenings and thus no protection.

The shed containing the diesel generator was halfway between the house and the gates. The gas shed was next to it. Both were made of stone, had wooden doors and were unlocked.

Hunter went into the shed. The generator was a large beast. According to the stainless steel plate on its side, it generated 2,500 kVA - kilovolt-amperes. A second generator stood alongside. Hunter turned off the tap to the diesel tank, placed an explosive charge on the side of tank and set the digital clock to 05.00. The generator spluttered and stopped.

It was 04.06.

He met Badonovitch outside. The Spetsnaz nodded and headed for the long, low building while Hunter headed for the door to the General's quarters.

'Boss,' said Badonovitch in his left year, 'it's an armoury. The place is packed with weapons, ammo and explosives.'

'Roger that.'

'Boss,' said Masters, 'the canisters are empty. We've checked the rooms. The family and the servants are out like lights.'

'Good. Cover the doors front and back. Just in case. I'm...' he got no further. The clacking of a helicopter descending out of the sky caused him to look up. He could clearly see its red port and green starboard navigation lights; the loom of the red strobe tail light was evident as were the white strobe on the top of the cabin and the white strobe beneath it. Even as he looked, the landing light came on. Hunter pulled off his goggles, blinking hard as the lights affected his vision for a few seconds.

'Problems,' was the only word he uttered.

58

THE SOUND OF the helicopter arriving awoke General Khan.. He looked at his electric radio clock and saw that the display was dark. He threw back the bedclothes and swung his feet onto the floor. He reached for his watch next to the clock and squinted at the luminous dial.

It showed 04.12.

His servant should have been in with a cup of tea at 04.10, to coincide with his alarm clock going off. No electricity! The incompetent fools! Someone would be made to pay. At least the hot water feeding the shower and the kitchen range were run on gas. There was also a cupboard full of Calor gas lamps. It wasn't the first time they had run out of oil for the generator. After the last time he thought the lesson had been learnt. It looked like it would have to be given again. Only more painfully this time.

He looked out of the window in time to see the helo land on the concrete pad behind the house. He reached for the bell pull to summon a servant. He had the rope in his hand when he heard gunfire. He stopped what he was doing and went rigid with shock. His brain wasn't computing what it was hearing. It was in denial for about a second. Then it started up again.

He grabbed his trousers and pulled them on over his pyjamas. He put on his shoes without socks and was struggling into his uniform jacket even as he rushed out of the door. His revolver was in its holster lying on his desk. What in hell was happening? Were they under attack? Or did some buffoon let loose with his rifle by accident? He dismissed the ideas as soon as it occurred. There were more shots. He recognised the sound of an AK74 on full automatic fire.

The helicopter had been a distraction.

'Peter?'

'Yes, Boss.'

'Take out the pilot and anybody else who appears.'

'Roger that.'

Men were piling out from the access door to the guards' quarters. The helicopter landed, its nose pointing at the main gate. The engine was already winding down, the navigation lights and the landing light went off as did the white strobe on the top of the cabin.

Hunter was caught in the light. One of the guards, seeing this apparition, stopped in utter astonishment. His AK74 was dangling down by his side, held in his left hand. Hunter reacted without thought. Instinct had been earned and honed over the years. He fired first. The bullet hit the man in the chest and sent him flying backwards. The silent cough of the automatic couldn't be heard above the fading racket made by the chopper.

Out of the periphery of his vision, Hunter saw the head of the pilot explode as he stepped around the nose of the helicopter. Hunter changed aim and fired at a second guard to the right of the man he had just killed. He fired twice and the guard collapsed.

Badonovitch came out of the armoury, took up a firing stance, and leant forward with the butt of the Glock gripped in his right hand and his left hand cradling his right fist. He fired two rounds into a man who was bringing his gun up to bear on Hunter. Suddenly there was silence. The helos lights were out and the compound was dark. Hunter moved fast. He threw himself to the right and landed in a bed of flowers, about 20cm lower than the lawn. It was just as well. Khan's bodyguards were well trained. Two of them opened fire at the spot Hunter had been standing only a second earlier. For Hunter, with his NVGs, the compound was lit like a stage. He could see one of the guards who was firing his weapon on fully-automatic kneeling outside the door to the house. He was either brave or stupid, Hunter decided, when he put two bullets into the man.

Dunston, Masters and Hughes were nowhere in sight.

Then, neither were any of the guards. There were 17 left plus the General.

General Khan had the presence of mind to pick up the phone and telephone the local police commander.

The phone rang and then a sleepy voice answered. 'This had

better be good or I will cut off your extremities.

'It is General Khan.'

'Sir,' the voice was wide awake. 'Sir, I beg your pardon. I didn't...I didn't know.'

'Shut up, you fool. I am at my house. I am under attack. Get as many men here as you possibly can. And I mean now or it will be your extremities that will be cut off and you will be eating them.'

The General slammed the phone down. The nearest station was 15 minutes away. Add 5 minutes to get the orders sent and obeyed and he would have to survive 20 minutes. Less, with a bit of luck. More, if the incompetents proved as useless as he believed them to be.

It was 04.17.

He had a bolt hole in the walls between the bedroom and the lounge. It was 6ft square and undetectable if you didn't know it was there. Should he get inside and wait for the attack to end? If he did, he wouldn't know what was happening. No, he needed to direct the battle.

What battle? It was deathly silent. The thoughts of his family intruded. What had happened to them? Were they safe? The thought formed and was dismissed. It didn't matter either way. If they lived or died was a matter for Allah. His task was to survive. That was what Allah wanted. If he didn't survive who would take the fight against the infidels to the level that was needed to achieve an Islamic world? There was nobody. Only him. No, Allah would see that he lived.

The door to the house was about 30m away. Hunter called in to the rest of the team.

'Matt, where are you?'

'I'm in the main doorway with Dave. Don is round the back. We found one door between the guards' quarters and the family's, as well as one door to the General's part of the house. The door to the guards' side is locked, with the key on the family side. The door to the General's side is unlocked. That other building next to the armoury is a garage. There are eight vehicles inside, all military, including a staff car.'

'Boss?' Masters' voice came over the ether. 'I'm opposite the backdoor to the guards' part of the house. I just saw the door open though I can't see anyone. Hang on, somebody is crawling out.'

Hunter didn't bother asking whether or not the REME was able to take the shot. He would have said if he couldn't.

'Got him,' said Masters. 'That'll help keep their heads down.'

'Right, listen up. I'm going in through the General's door.' Even as he spoke, Hunter was on the move. He crawled behind a bed of flowers.

Suddenly, glass was smashed in the windows of the house. There were eight windows downstairs and eight upstairs. All sixteen were broken. A hail of gunfire was let loose. None of it was directed at targets. The bullets sprayed the compound, some of it coming perilously close to where Hunter was lying.

It wasn't a bad tactic. There was no real hard cover to hide behind, whoever was shooting was invisible. If they had plenty of ammo then they had a good chance of hitting one of the team. One thing he was grateful for. They weren't firing their grenades.

'Peter? Can you see anyone?'

The words were hardly out of his mouth when Hunter realised the muzzle flashes from the fifth and sixth windows had ceased.

'Two down,' said Peter Weir.

That left 14.

The fusillade stopped for about 5 seconds and then a command was yelled and they started up again. During that brief lull, Hunter had crabbed away about a further 5m. He found himself behind a decorative plinth with a statue of a horse rearing up on it. The base was about a metre high, the horse about the same. Hunter paused and took stock.

He tried to look around the corner of the plinth but the bullets were flying like angry wasps. At the next lull in the shooting, Hunter decided it was time to risk it.

'Lay down covering fire,' he broadcast and then took off like an Olympic sprinter. He had taken only half-a-dozen paces when the bullets started up again.

He was running at an angle of about forty-five degrees to the house, heading for the door to the General's quarters when the bullet hit him.

He went head first onto the grass and rolled right. The bullet had hit him in the top of his left thigh. It stung like hell. He felt for the wound - couldn't feel a thing. He moved his hand up a bit and felt the sticky dampness and the tear in the top of his trousers. The bullet had missed his thigh and scraped along the edge of his buttock. The wound was a hindrance and not life threatening.

The bullets had stopped again and Hunter ran as fast as he could for the doorway. He knew the disadvantage of firing silenced weapons was that there was no gut-wrenching, fear inducing noise that helped to ensure people kept their heads down. On the other hand, it also meant the targets foolishly put their heads above the parapets.

'I hit one,' said Peter Weir.

'Got one,' said Don Masters.

That left 12.

Hunter hit the doorway and came to a halt next to Matt Dunston.

'You okay?' asked his friend.

'Hit in the top of the thigh,' said Hunter.

'Let me see.'

'It's okay.'

'Come on, Nick.' Even as he spoke, Dunston was reaching into his rucksack for the field dressing kit.

Hunter turned around and showed him his wound.

Dunston chuckled. 'Is that what's it's called nowadays? Top of the thigh? I'd say it was well north of your thigh.'

'Okay, Matt. I'll get enough from the others once we get out of here. In the meantime, slap a Band-Aid on it and let's get going.'

Dunston said, 'Drop your trousers.'

Hunter did so, Dunston taped the wound over with a plaster, and Hunter pulled his trousers back up and had the good grace to say, 'Thanks.'

'What's going on, Boss?' Badonovitch asked. 'You hit?'

The team had heard what he'd been saying and Hunter replied. 'It's nothing. Just a flesh wound. Matt and I are going into the house.'

He tried the door. It was locked. He aimed the Glock at the lock and pulled the trigger. He emptied the magazine and before he tried the door he changed the mag.

'Okay, Matt?'

'Whenever you are, Nick.'

Hunter hit the door with his shoulder and slammed it open. He threw himself to the right and went down onto the floor, breaking his fall with his left shoulder.

Nothing happened.

It was 04.31.

'Boss,' said Peter Weir, 'we've problems.'

'What sort of problems?'

'There are three vehicles coming this way and coming fast.'

59

GENERAL MACNAIR LOOKED at his watch for the umpteenth time. Even after all these years in command, sending men into dangerous situations didn't rest easily with him. It was a trait shared by senior officers the world over. He was in his office, his feet on his desk, a mug of coffee going cold at his elbow.

He knew the timetable along with the plan. But plans and timetables were all well and good but didn't take into account the "what ifs". These were the unknowns that could so easily go wrong. In theory the objective was simple; in reality it was highly complex and required a great deal of planning and even more luck.

He was in the operations room and, with the others, had been watching events unfold on the huge screen on the wall in front of them. The satellite picture had been clear enough for them to follow what was happening though they couldn't make out individuals. They had seen the team arrive at the wall and then the screen had turned to fuzz. Gareth was working flat out to get the picture back but so far without success. It wasn't uncommon to lose it like that. It was part of the luck. For now, it had gone bad. He looked at the clock on the wall opposite his desk.

It was now 00.33 British Summer Time. Four hours behind PKT or Pakistan Standard Time.

What was happening?

'Cars or lorries?'

'Can't tell. Cars. They just switched on their police warning lights.'

At that second the police sirens started.

'Do what you can,' Hunter ordered.

Peter Weir aimed at the lead car. For a nano-second he debated whether to shoot the driver or the car and decided on the driver.

A disabled car merely meant an attack on foot. He relaxed, aimed and fired. The target was 500m away. The second he pulled the trigger the car swerved to Weir's right. He fired twice more in swift succession.

The car behind was slowing. He fired twice and the car slammed to a halt. On one level, the occupants of the third car were lucky, on another they weren't. Their car rammed into the middle car and came to a halt with air bags erupting. It left them hidden by the car in front.

The rear doors of the second car opened and two men climbed slowly out. Weir lined up on the man to the left, fired and saw the man die. The second man stood looking in surprise across the top of the car and before he could move the marksman put a bullet through the top of his head.

Next, Weir fired a dozen rounds into the roof of the third car. One bullet struck the fuel tank and it exploded into flames. At that second, he saw more headlights in the distance.

'Nick, I've stopped three cars. Some uglies are down. But there's another five, maybe six cars coming fast.'

'How far away?'

'Maybe a klick.'

'Do what you can. I'll be as quick as possible and we'll get the hell out. Don? Anything happening?'

The firing had stopped.

'Nothing.' The words were barely out of his mouth when he said. 'Wrong. Have to go.'

There was a loud bang. Hunter knew the sound of a grenade exploding. He hoped one of the team had fired it. Then there were another two explosions in quick succession. He knew he was wrong.

Having studied the architect's drawings, Hunter knew the door opened straight into the huge living room. It would have been pitch dark if he hadn't been wearing his NVGs. He darted across to the stairs on the other side of the room and started slowly up them. Matt Dunston was five paces behind.

'Two men tried to come out the back after they fired grenades,' said Masters. 'Both are dead. According to my calculation that leaves ten.'

'Make that nine,' said Hughes.

'Eight,' said Badonovitch.

There were another half a dozen grenades exploding and then silence.

'Report,' said Hunter.

The three operatives responded that they were unhurt.

'Boss,' said Weir, 'the cars have stopped. It looks like there are at least twenty men. They aren't moving. I don't have a clear shot.'

'Roger that.'

Hunter was halfway up the stairs when an AK74 opened up on fully automatic. The bullets struck the wall behind him as Hunter flung himself flat onto the stairs. The magazine of an AK74 holds 30 rounds. Its firing rate is 650 rounds per minute. The mag was empty in under 3 seconds. The shooting stopped. Hunter looked over his shoulder to see Dunston collapsed on the stairs, blood seeping down the side of his face.

Hunter's dilemma lasted less than a second. He ran up the stairs, saw the door to the bedroom closing and ran full tilt at it. It took 12 strides to reach the door. Mustering all the kinetic energy and strength that he could, Hunter smashed into the door using his right shoulder. The door smashed open and Hunter threw himself into the room and onto the floor. The General was in the middle of the room. His rifle was in his hands and he dropped it to the floor.

'Don't shoot!' he yelled in Urdu.

'Where's Rabbani?' Hunter responded.

'What?' The General had his hands in the air and began to lower them.

'Keep your hands up, General. I asked you where Rabbani was.'

'What...What is this? What are you talking about?'

'Rabbani. Where is he?'

'Who are you?'

'Never mind who I am, just answer the question. We know about your plans to take over Rabbani's criminal empire. We know about you funding the terrorists and we know that you are responsible for the bombs going off in London. Now tell me where Rabbani is.'

'I don't know...'

He didn't get any further. The General was 10 paces away from Hunter and facing him. Hunter fired the Glock and blew the General's right knee apart.

The General screamed and collapsed onto the floor. He was moaning loudly, his hands clasped around the bleeding wound. His face was distorted with pain.

Hunter approached the man as he rocked from side to side.

'I asked you a question. If you do not answer me I will put a bullet through your other knee.'

'I don't know what you are talking about,' gasped Khan. 'Who are you talking about?'

'I delivered him to you. Now answer me.'

The General went rigid with shock.

'We know about Barzakh. We know about your plans to use Rabbani's criminal organisation to fund the fundamentalists. Now tell me where Rabbani is!'

'He's dead. Help me. Please. I beg you. Help me. The pain.'

'Boss, I don't know where they are coming from,' said Weir, 'but another three cars have just arrived. I've shot two of the men but I can't see any more targets. Dawn isn't far away.'

It was 04.39.

Hunter didn't need reminding. He weighed his options. His best friend was lying on the stairs, either dead or dying. The decision to continue the attack had been a hard one to take. But the risk of stopping to tend to Matt was far greater than taking Khan out and then looking after his friend. If Matt was still alive and two minutes meant that Matt died then he would have died anyway and there was nothing Hunter or anyone else could do to help.

Hunter had no choice but to believe Khan. However, there was one piece of information he needed. 'When and where is the attack by Barzakh taking place?'

'I know nothing about this Barzakh you mention.' He moaned. 'Please, the pain.'

Hunter thought of the deaths and injuries caused by the man writhing on the floor in front of him and asked, 'Is that you're last word on the subject?'

'Yes. I...'

The next shot went clean through Khan's left wrist, practically severing his hand from his arm.

The General screamed at the top of his lungs.

'Tell me where and when they are attacking. Or the next bullet will be into your right wrist, then your ankles and knees and I shall leave you here to die in agony. Which is it to be?'

With tears streaming down his face the General gasped, 'It is Peshawar. It is to take place commencing,' he moaned, 'commencing on the 23rd of July. Now, please, I have told you everything. Please help me.'

He pointed the Glock at the General's head. It was too dark for the man to see what was happening.

'Here's all the help you're going to get. Have a good time in Hell, General.' Hunter pulled the trigger and blew Khan's brains all over the floor.

He darted to the desk, grabbed the laptop, shoved it into his rucksack, ran back across the room and took the stairs two at a time. Blood was still pouring down the left side of Matt's face. His friend groaned. The sound galvanised Hunter. He slipped the rucksack off his back and took out his triage kit.

'Listen up,' he announced. 'Matt is down. Head wound. Still alive. I'll be out in two.' Even as he was speaking, Hunter ripped open the antiseptic wipes and as gently as he could wiped the blood off Dunston's face. The blood was seeping from a gash down the left side of his scalp. Like many head wounds it looked worse than it was. He hoped. Hunter wrapped a bandage around the wound and tied it off. Next, he took a ready to use hypodermic needle from the pack and injected its contents into Dunston's upper arm.

Hunter pulled Dunston into a sitting position, bent down, lifted him up onto his shoulders, jiggled him into a more comfortable position and headed down the stairs. He limped slightly. His own wound was bleeding. He could feel the blood trickling down his leg. It was irritating, though hardly painful.

'Coming out.'

He reached the front door. 'I've got Matt. He's still breathing. Sitrep.'

'Nothing out the back,' said Masters.

'Quiet out the front,' said Hughes.

There was nothing from Badonovitch.

'Jan?' Hunter said.

Still nothing for a few seconds and Hunter was growing concerned.

'Sorry, Boss. Two of the guards were trying to sneak out of a window. I hit one as he got to the ground and the other as he stood in the window. That leaves six.'

'Peter?'

'Real trouble, Nick. I figure there must be thirty or forty of them. They're grouping. I can see somebody pointing. I'd say he's the man in charge.'

'Can you take him?'

'I was about to do so. Hang on.'

A few seconds passed. 'Got him. The rest have scattered and gone to ground.'

'Jan, I'll cover from here. Go into the armoury and grab an AK and some grenades.' Tempted though he was to say hurry up, he resisted. The team knew precisely what they were doing. 'Dave, grab an AK if you can find one and spray the windows. Make them keep their heads down. 'Don, how much plastic do you have?'

'Three units.'

'Okay. Come round the back of Khan's quarters and meet me in the doorway. I'll give you two. Then booby trap the gate.'

'Roger that.'

The next few minutes crawled by. Masters appeared next to Hunter who handed over the plastic explosives.

'How's Matt?' Masters asked.

'Still breathing. I can't tell. We need to get him to the sub asap. Here, take these.'

Masters took the items and ran for the gates.

'Right, Nick. I'm ready,' said Badonovitch.

'So am I,' said Hughes.

'Put a grenade through each window. Dave, start firing and keep going. Peter, shoot at any and everything and see if you can disable more of their cars.'

'Will do. I'm down to the last fifteen rounds.'

David Hughes emptied a magazine in the official time of 2.7 seconds, replaced it in 3 seconds and emptied it again. Badonovitch had fired a second time before the first grenade exploded. He worked fast. The explosions then followed in three second intervals.

When the eighth grenade exploded, Hunter announced, 'Time to go.' He had Dunston on his shoulders and he began to run across the compound towards the south-eastern tower.

He reached the tower a few seconds behind Badonovitch. 'Jan, blow it,' he ordered.

The Spetsnaz stepped over to the explosive device Hunter had placed against the wall when they had arrived, switched it on, put the timer to 10 seconds and pressed the activate button. He and Hunter walked away; Hughes joined them and a few seconds later Peter Weir arrived. He hadn't bothered bringing his sniper rifle. Without bullets it was only so much dead weight. Instead, he had placed an IED under the stock. Anyone lifting the rifle was in for a final shock. What he did have was an AK74 and 4 grenades.

Masters arrived just as the explosives erupted. The shaped charge spent its force and blew a section of the wall away.

The team walked through.

'Dave, any more PE?'

'Two, Boss.'

'Don, booby trap the hole.'

Hughes handed over his two devices and Masters set about laying a trap.

The time was 04.51.

'Nick, let me take Matt,' said Badonovitch.

'I'm okay. Get the rope.'

The order was superfluous. David Hughes was already uncoiling the rope and securing one end around the base of a large boulder. He chucked the other end over the cliff. Hunter turned to the rope and staggered slightly. Dunston was a big man and the weight was taking its toll. Badonovitch, recognised as the strongest man in the party, said nothing, merely lifted Dunston off Hunter's shoulders. Hunter turned to protest and realised he was being ludicrous.

'Thanks, Jan.'

'Its okay, Nick. Now it's my turn.'

'You go first. Dave, then you, Don and Peter. I'll cover you. Peter, give me the AK.'

Hughes handed it over and Hunter hefted it in his hand. He fitted a grenade and went back to the hole in the wall.

Just then there was an explosion at the far end of the compound. The enemy had just encountered the booby trapped gates.

As the boom echoed across the compound, Hunter heard the yells of *Allahu Akbar*, there was indeterminate shooting and then wild yells.

Hunter found his vision getting hazy and realised that the pre-dawn had arrived and the darkness was fading. He ripped off the goggles and tossed them to one side. Next, kneeling beside the hole, he watched as dozens of men ran into the compound and stopped, looking around, obviously puzzled as to what was happening.

Hunter looked over his shoulder in time to see Peter Weir grab the rope and start down. Hunter turned back in time to see a man pointing in his direction. He didn't wait any longer. He fired the first grenade, loaded the AK and fired a second one. The first two landed amongst the men who were milling around as though directionless. The two grenades exploded sweeping shrapnel and blast across a wide area. Men went down screaming and cursing. Some never made a sound. They didn't have the time before they started their journey into the hereafter.

Hunter shifted his aim and fired 20 degrees left and then 20 degrees right. The blasts brought more screams then a commanding voice yelled and somebody opened fire in Hunter's direction. Bullets hit the wall to the right of him and sprayed concrete in all directions. The bullets missed but as other guns opened up the bullets inched closer.

Time to go.

It was 04.56.

60

HUNTER WALKED BACKWARDS down the cliff, going hand over hand down the rope. In seconds he was at the bottom. They had already taken Dunston's clothes off him and managed to get his wetsuit on.

The others were just finishing the transformation from soldiers to frogmen. With their blackened faces they looked like creatures from a horror story.

'Get going,' said Hunter, 'I'll be right with you.'

Masters had Dunston over his shoulders and he quickly walked down to the sea. Hughes was next to him. Once in the water they pulled on their fins and started out to sea, on their backs, on the surface.

Badonovitch went out far enough so that the water was up to his chest. He stopped and turned around and stood with his Glock held two fisted, aimed at the top of the cliff.

Hunter quickly tore off his clothes and dumped them to one side. He climbed into the wetsuit, grabbed a beacon from one of the canisters, put his Glock in its holster under his arm and ran for the water. He didn't reach it when the booby traps at the wall exploded. Rocks and debris flew everywhere. Some sailed into the air and landed at the foot of the cliff. If Hunter hadn't moved when he did he would have been bombarded by rocks as big as fists.

He waded into the water, turned to face the cliffs and pulled on his fins. He took out his Glock and did the same as Badonovitch. They swam backwards, rapidly, their guns pointing at the cliffs.

One thing the men at TIFAT acknowledged - Islamic fundamentalists might not have been over intelligent, but they were certainly brave. The dust had barely settled when men appeared at the top of the cliff. The angle and distance wasn't conducive to accurate shooting so both men pulled back on their triggers and kept them compressed for a couple of seconds. The

Glocks erupted and fired 4 rounds each. One of the men on the cliff was hit and, clutching his stomach, rolled over the edge. Another man half spun around before vanishing backwards. The dozen men who had been lining the cliff suddenly vanished.

The swimmers had gained a few seconds and they began to stroke the water as hard and fast as possible. A length of the rope they had used to drop down the cliff had been cut and tied around Dunston's chest and under his arms. Hughes and Masters had a firm hold and were dragging their friend through the water. The wetsuits gave sufficient buoyancy so that the body was floating but it was still hard going.

Hunter felt a twinge in his left buttock but ignored it. It was nothing to write home about.

The light was coming on fast but the distance was growing. The heads of their attackers appeared, guns were pointed and bullets flew through the air in a never ending stream. They all fell short of the team.

Then they saw some of their attackers grabbing the rope and starting down the cliff. Hunter wondered what they were going to do. If shooting from the cliff couldn't reach them, being at sea level was even worse. It was a complete waste of time. He watched four men run to the water's edge and begin to tear off their clothes.

The fanatics were coming after them.

A glance at his watch showed the time was 04.58.

The men waded into the water and began to swim after the team, carrying their AK74s above their heads. They were making little progress and there was little chance of them getting anywhere near.

The Pakistanis in the water were now out of sight. A gentle swell lifted Hunter and he craned his neck to look back. He saw one of the men, his hands held vertically above his head sink out of sight. He came up spluttering. Hunter dipped down and lost sight of them. A minute later a swell lifted him up and he craned his neck. He counted only three heads and they were getting further away. The only threat they posed was to themselves. If they didn't head back to shore they would drown and pretty soon at that.

The explosions were so close together they sounded

simultaneous. However, Hunter could just discern the three blasts individually. Some of the men on the cliff face were flung over the side, their bodies shattered on the rocks below. Others were killed where they stood. The sky rained masonry for the best part of 30 seconds and then the air over the compound was filled with a cloud of dust. The explosives set in the gas and diesel sheds had gone off.

Hunter hoped the General's family hadn't been injured. The house, in theory, was far enough from the blasts to withstand them. But the difference between fact and theory often meant the difference between life and death.

Hunter pressed the button for the beacon to start operating.

They all heard the bleep. It was loud and clear. At the same time the fuzz on the screen vanished and a picture of the compound reappeared.

'Where's the beacon?' Macnair asked.

'Just a sec, sir,' said Leo. 'Got it. I estimate it's about half-a-mile off shore.' His fingers flew across the keyboard and the picture on the wall changed. There was nothing but grey showing. 'That's the sea. There, got it!' A bright red spot showed on the screen. It was the beacon and it was inching its way across the screen and out to sea. Then the picture changed again and faint spots appeared. 'Six heat signatures as well. That must be their heads.'

The faint spots were intermittent. 'They come and go,' said Leo, 'because of the sea washing over them.'

'Excellent,' said Macnair. 'Send the Astute a flash signal. Give the exact location of the team. Leo, scan twenty miles in all directions and check for other surface vessels.'

'Yes, sir.'

Macnair sat at one of the consoles but was looking at the screen on the wall. Outwardly, he was ice calm, inwardly, his guts were churning. It was almost over. He hoped.

'Here's a reply, sir,' said Gareth, approaching the General. 'WILCO. ETA 1 hour.' Will comply. Estimated time of arrival, one hour.

Now all they had to do was wait. It was the hardest part. It always was. Macnair gratefully took a mug of coffee offered by one of the staff and nodded. 'Thanks.' He stared at the display.

How were they getting on?'

'It's in the laps of the gods, now,' said Isobel. 'We have more satellite pictures from the compound.'

'Put them up, will you?'

A picture of the compound filled the wall. The staff at their stations stopped what they were doing and stared at it.

'My God,' said Isobel, 'they did a good job.'

'As long as the primary objective was achieved,' said the General. 'This is just a bonus. So what have we got? Gareth?'

'Sir,' Gareth aimed his laser pointer at the screen. 'Let's start down in the south-east corner. You can see the hole in the wall. These red spots are mainly bodies. According to the sensors they are slowly cooling. Here and here are people walking around.' He moved the pointer. 'The sheds containing the gas, diesel and the building we thought was an armoury have all vanished. All that is left are the craters and rubble. You can see the house is damaged but mainly down this side where the guards were quartered. The main part of the house appears untouched but you can see holes in the roof. The heat signatures from the family quarters show all of them and the servants are accounted for. According to the sensors there is no reduction in body heat of any of the targets.' He moved the pointer again. 'This thing here was a helicopter. It wasn't there when we started so it must have arrived during the night. The gatehouse has been blown to smithereens. If we move up the picture to the north, along the main road to the compound you can see destroyed vehicles and a lot of dead bodies. There are some people walking around,' he pointed. 'There are two cars approaching.' They watched the screen as four men climbed out of each car.

Macnair would have given his eye-teeth to know who they were. 'Can we get a closer look?'

'Sorry, sir. That's as good as it gets.'

'Can you match the uniforms of the men outside the compound?' Macnair enquired. He took a sip of coffee.

'Yes, sir,' replied Gareth. 'Just a second.' He ran the image of one of the dead bodies lying on its back through some specialised recognition software. 'Got it. Local police.'

'That's not surprising,' said Macnair. 'Khan would want the locals on his side, be that civilian population or paramilitary and police. It makes sense. Hearts, minds, bribery and coercion, the mainstays of all dictators.'

Gareth said, 'This building is definitely a garage. You can see some vehicles now the walls have been caved in.'

'Has there been an increase in radio traffic? Anything at all?' Macnair asked.

'Yes, sir,' said one of the operatives at another console. 'Coming from the naval base at Karachi.'

'I don't like the sound of that.'

'We've intercepted orders telling the local admiral to get ships to sea and to search the area. The signals don't say any more than that. The ships have been sending their ETDs and apart from one vessel we are looking at four or more hours before anything can get underway.'

'What ships are we talking about?'

'Three Zulfiquar class frigates, one Alamgir class frigate and a Larkana class fast attack craft. The ship is named the PNS Larkana and will be underway in about an hour.'

'Armament?' enquired Macnair.

'The ship carries depth charges as well as two Type 76A 377mm/63 twin cannons and four 25mm 60s. It sounds pretty nasty.'

It wasn't only nasty but it could snatch defeat from the jaws of victory. The problem of how to deal with General Khan had been agreed between the Prime Minister and President Zardarim. They were supposed to be the only two people outside of TIFAT who knew what was going on. The attack was to be put down to militant fundamentalists who feared and loathed General Khan because of his successes against them. The idea was that once the operation was over, his memory would be honoured and quickly forgotten, as was the nature of such things.

However, that would all fall apart if the team were captured by the Pakistani navy. The political repercussions would be huge both for the British and the Pakistani governments. The least of it would be accusations of UK involvement in Pakistan's affairs. It was easy to imagine the manufactured offence felt by Muslims the world over. No matter how much proof was shown about Khan's intentions, far too many people would believe it was all a Western plot. That Khan was innocent of all charges and that the

President wanted rid of Khan because he feared for his position. It was easy to imagine what could happen.

Getting the team away safely therefore had greater implications than just saving their lives.

Don Masters said, 'There is nothing like a morning dip. Helps clear the cobwebs, it get the old endorphins circulating and, all in all, it's good for you.'

There was no response from the others. They were too busy saving their breath as they ploughed their way through the water. It had been a long night. These were amongst the toughest, fittest men that walked the planet but even their incredible stamina had a limit. Hunter, like the rest of them, was now working on energy fumes.

They were keeping a relatively straight line thanks to Hunter pointing his compass at the house and heading on a reciprocal course. He was glad to see the roof of the house still appeared intact.

They had finished the job an hour sooner than they had planned. The Astute was probably an hour away. She had to come in from outside Pakistan's territorial limit.

They had been in the water for 45 minutes. Hunter had kept an eye on the swimming Pakistanis who had disappeared one by one and were no longer a threat. Not that they'd been much of one from the start.

'Right, hold up,' announced Hunter. 'We're over a mile off-shore so the Astute should be able to come in. Any further won't make a jot of difference to us being picked up.' They stopped swimming and lowered their feet, lazily working their fins back and forth for additional buoyancy.

'How's he doing?' Hunter asked, swimming across to check on Dunston.

'Still breathing,' said Hughes, 'that's all I can say.'

It was about all they could hope for.

They fell silent. The adrenaline that had helped to sustain them was trickling away fast, taking their energy with it. Hunter could feel his eyes closing as the warmth of the sun heralded another hot day.

His head jerked up as he felt water lapping his chin and nose.

He spluttered, shook his head and finned harder, raising his body a few inches out of the water. At that moment he found himself on the top of a gentle swell. The team had drifted apart about 10m. He called out to them and as he did so he glanced towards the east.

A gunboat was bearing down on them, was less than a mile away and closing fast.

'Trouble.' Hunter called.

The others looked in the same direction as Hunter. Already the boat was only a few hundred metres away. The sound of her diesels was now loud and clear. Its smoke stack was belching fumes but that wasn't what was drawing their attention. It was the line of sailors along the deck, all of whom were carrying rifles. Hunter could see that the ship's guns were manned and pointing directly at them. The boat came to a halt about 100m away.

A loudhailer burst into life.

'A boat is being launched. If you try and resist arrest you will be shot. Do you understand? If you do, wave an arm in the air.'

Hunter had no choice. He waved.

61

SCOTT LLEWELYN HAD been told of the situation by Macnair. He had been patrolling just outside the 20 mile territorial limit ready to head towards the shore at the appropriate time. Macnair's message had him turning the sub and ringing on full speed before he read the part warning him PNS Larkana would be in the area soon.

He watched as their speed wound up to 30kts.

'Listen up,' he announced over the tannoy. 'We're in a hurry. The team we put ashore could be in trouble. They are at the r/v point or close to it already. However, we have been told that a Pakistani patrol craft could be heading their way at any time now. We need to get there first. Be ready to open the forward hatch, the aft hatch and the conning tower door. Guns,' he was talking to the Astute's Gunnery Officer, 'I want an M60 on the tower and I want a man at each hatch, armed with the Brens to make an appearance. They are not to climb out on to the hull but to show themselves and their weapons.'

The Astute was impenetrable to bullets whereas the gunboat was highly vulnerable. Especially to machine gun bullets of the calibre and rate of fire of the M60. Llewelyn tapped into his computer the name of the ship and read the details. Formidable against small craft. A nuisance rather than a danger to a submarine of the Astute class.

Llewelyn grinned. It wasn't quite what he'd signed up for but it was better than the boring patrols they spent most of their time completing.

'Vasco,' he said, using the nickname of all RN navigating officers, 'we'll get updates as to the team's position from Rosyth. According to the last signal we are,' he looked at the screen, 'forty-three minutes away.' He glanced at the speed indicator. Published design speed was 29kts. He was pleased to see the digital readout creep above that.

He was handed a signal. He tapped it into the plot and said, 'Come right four degrees.'

'Right four degrees, aye, aye, sir,' said the rating sitting in front of the control panel. 'Steady on course 353 degrees.'

The Astute might have been built for the 21st century, with its electronic gadgets and wizardry but some things never changed. Not in the Royal Navy.

Llewelyn knew he was about to put his head on the block and he felt strangely good about it. Posturing around the world in a nuclear powered submarine was one thing, taking action was another. Even if it was only in a small skirmish that didn't require a fraction of the potential the sub had to offer.

His instinct was to blast the patrol boat out of the water, his humanity and political savvy stopped him from doing any such thing. That, coupled with the likelihood of his court martial and long term imprisonment.

His gut reaction was due to the fact that General Macnair's last signal had informed him that the Admiral of the Port was a supporter of the terrorist group Barzakh, and that the captains of the ships under his command were probably in the same camp. Thanks to Macnair, he also knew that Barzakh were responsible for the bombings in the UK.

He looked at the screen displayed in front of him courtesy of the periscope. The screens gave him a 360 degree view. Distance to go, 7 nautical miles. Time to the r/v was 6m 38secs.

'When I give the word I want full astern.' He magnified the picture. He could make out the bobbing black heads of the team and the approaching gunboat. He waited patiently. There was nothing else he could do. 'Come right two degrees.'

'Right two degrees. Aye, aye, sir. Steady on course 355 degrees.'

Now came the tricky bit. He made it look easy but he was, in fact, a superb ship handler. He had an instinct that few people ever achieved. Scott Llewelyn had it in spades.

'Come right one degree.'

The order was repeated.

'Standby. Listen up,' he made the broadcast. 'We're surfacing in one minute. Standby hatches.' He paused. 'Standby. Full astern both.' He spoke with deadly calmness with no hint of his true feelings showing.

They could all feel the speed of the boat draining fast. He wanted to cut off the team from the gunboat. He actually smiled. He would love to see the faces of the officers and men on the patrol craft when the Astute popped up.

'Okay, lads. The upside is, we'll get medical help for Matt all the quicker.'

'Nick,' said Badonovitch, 'if there's an upside it means there is a downside.'

'The downside is we're in for an unpleasant time. However, *nil desperandum*. The General will have thought of something.'

'Your faith in the General,' said Masters, 'is touching.'

'Don't you have faith?'

'Definitely,' Masters managed a grin. 'The old coot will kick the doors in if he has to.'

'Amen to that,' said Matt Dunston. 'Where in hell am I?'

'Matt! Your conscious!' said Hunter, stating the obvious.

'My head hurts.' Dunston lifted his hand to his head to feel the bandage. 'What happened?'

'A bullet creased you,' replied Hunter. 'Luckily, your skull is so thick it didn't kill you. We got out of there and now we're waiting for the Astute.'

'I thought I heard a tannoy,' said Dunston.

'We've hit a setback,' said Weir. 'Look over there. We have company.'

Dunston turned his head. 'I see what you mean.'

They watched as an inflatable boat was launched. It carried a person at the controls and three armed men cradling rifles.

Hunter was about to say something when he grinned. The others looked around and also broke into smiles. The sea was churning, the water moving, a slight throb could be felt. It was a feeling they had encountered on more than one occasion.

'Blow tanks,' ordered the Captain. She went up like a whale hitting the surface. 'Open hatches,' he ordered as soon as the top of the hull was clear of the water.

He was already heading up the conning tower. Above him, he heard the hatch open and two of his men clamber out. They had the M60 between them. They slotted it into the bracket on the starboard side.

Llewelyn appeared next to the two ratings who already had the gun in position and pointed at the patrol craft. There was a moment of silence before the tannoy system from the boat erupted into life, starting with what he guessed was invective being thrown at them in a language he guessed was Urdu. Tempted though he was to reply, he said nothing. Llewelyn knew it would be unnerving.

Then came the threat in English that the gunboat would open fire immediately if the submarine did not move away and let the terrorists in the water be taken prisoner. The boat was 80m away.

'Petty Officer Potter.'

'Yes, sir,' said the PO holding the gun, looking along its sights.

'See the aerial on top of the bridge?'

'Yes, sir.'

He looked over the side. Four of the TIFAT team were already on the deck. One of them had to be helped. There were two still in the water.

'Rake it.'

The machine gun opened fire. The bullets swept in a short arc and the aerial disintegrated.

Llewelyn glanced at the deck to see the last of the men vanish down the hatch.

'Let's go. Leave the gun.'

The submariners vanished below. Even as the conning tower hatches were closing Llewelyn was ordering the blowing of the tanks. He heard the faint pinging of bullets striking the conning tower. It was like mosquitoes hitting the skin of a rhinoceros.

'Number One,' he said to the First Lieutenant, who was also the Officer of the Watch, 'you have the ship.'

'Aye, aye, sir. I have the ship.'

'Take us south and out of territorial water. Ring on 25kts.'

The OOW repeated the orders.

'I'm going forward,' said Llewelyn.

Hunter had already taken Matt Dunston to the Sick Bay. The rank and qualification of the senior person there was POMA(SM) - Petty Officer Medical Assistant, Submarines. His priority was radiation protection, his range of skills was impressive and included emergency medical care.

He welcomed Dunston with the words, 'Sit there, please, and I'll take a look.'

'Matt, I'll be getting changed. PO let me know how you get on.'

'Will do, sir.'

'Thanks, Nick,' said Dunston. 'And thank the others for me.'

'No need. You know that.'

Hunter went aft. The others had taken off their wetsuits, showered and changed. Drying off and having their feet planted on terra firma, even if in this case it meant the deck of a submarine, had given them renewed energy.

'What did the Doc say about Matt?' Masters asked.

'He didn't say. He's taking a look.'

'What about your wound, Boss?' Badonovitch smiled. 'Sitting might be a bit painful.'

The team exchanged grins and nods.

'Don't worry about me. I'll get it looked at later. Breakfast is ready. Have something to eat and get some sleep. I'll find out what's to happen to us.'

'Nick, welcome back,' said Scott Llewelyn.

'Scott,' Hunter smiled warmly, 'thanks very much.' They shook hands. 'You have no idea how glad we were to see you. You must have frightened the life out of the crew on the patrol boat.'

'We'll see later. We have film of the whole event. It's SOPs so that we can analyse what's gone right and what's gone wrong.' There was no mistaking the tone Llewelyn used. The unspoken words were "When presented at the court martial of the CO for some error or other."

'Why the firing?'

'I checked the Larkana's spec. They can only transmit ship to shore via the aerial on top of the bridge. We should have done sufficient damage to stop them yelling for reinforcements and telling them where we are or even what we are. Hence we're now legging it. We're not at max speed so we have a few more knots if we need them. I've told TIFAT you're all onboard. I gather one of your men was hurt.'

'Matt Dunston. It's a head wound. The bullet grazed his scalp. It looked worse than it is but he was out for the count for quite a while. I just hope he's going to be okay.'

'He's in good hands. The medic knows his stuff. Meet me in the wardroom and we can have breakfast and you can bring me up to speed.'

'Okay. Give me ten minutes.'

Hunter stripped off in the shower and took a closer look at the wound along his butt. It was deeper than he'd first thought. A small chunk of flesh had been lopped off about 3 inches above his thigh. It was seeping blood. He showered and dressed and made his way back to the sick bay.

'Sir?'

'Em, PO, where's Mr. Dunston?'

'Behind the curtains, sir. He's asleep.' The PO nodded at a lower bunk bed with curtains drawn across.

'How is he?'

'He should be as right as rain in a few days. The scalp wound is superficial but he also suffered a blow to the other side of his head. I assume it must have happened when the bullet knocked him sideways.'

Hunter nodded. 'He was right up close to a wall.'

'Then that explains it, sir. That was the cause of his being unconscious. I've checked his vision, his balance, his co-ordination and they are all okay. I finally gave him some pain killers. The scalp wound needed a couple of stitches and the bandage will have to be changed each day for a few days. But he'll be up and about tomorrow and none the worse for wear.'

'Good.'

'Anything I can do for you, sir?'

'Er, yes, PO. I was shot.'

'Pardon, sir?' The Petty Officer's surprise was evident.

'Just here.' Hunter half turned and drew a line across his left buttock.

'Not life threatening then, sir,' announced the PO.

'No. Except it's bleeding.'

'I'd better take a look.' He grinned. 'Better drop 'em, sir, and bend over. You know, sir, I never thought I would live to use those words, not to an officer, at any rate.'

'I'd appreciate it if you kept it to yourself,' Hunter replied, undoing his belt.

'Have no fear, sir. Here, we keep secrets just like in a confessional. Hmm. It looks like a couple of stitches are needed. I'll use two. They're dissolvable.'

'What does that mean?' Hunter held still as the PO cleaned the wound and deftly sewed it together.

'Precisely that. They'll dissolve in about a week. Saves having to have them removed.'

He finished his ministrations with a clean, padded plaster. 'I'll change it each day while you're onboard, sir. One thing, it'll leave a scar. There's nothing I can do about that.'

Hunter pulled up his trousers. 'Few people get to see it. Thanks PO. It's much appreciated.'

He headed to the wardroom. There, he made a beeline for the orange juice and drank a full glass in one long swallow. He filled a mug with coffee added milk and took an appreciative sip. Filling a plate with sausage, bacon, egg, fried tomatoes and baked beans, he then sat down opposite Llewelyn.

'Care to tell me what went down?'

Hunter began filling Llewelyn in on events.

He was halfway through his story when a rating knocked on the door and put his head in. 'Sir, signal, for you, copied Commander Hunter.' The man held out a clipboard.

Llewelyn perused his orders and then handed it over to Hunter.

'Thanks. Showing the flag in Simonstown?'

'Not usual, but we do get ashore occasionally. I suppose Simonstown is the closest friendly place. It's also far enough away so that we can deny all knowledge of what happened at Karachi. Not that anybody will be asking.'

'How far and how long to get there? Any idea?'

'I'd say a bit more than five thousand miles. Finish the story and then I'll go and sort out the navigation details.'

Hunter gave Llewelyn an account of the operation. It took less than 10 minutes. When he had finished, Hunter headed for his bunk where he immediately fell into a deep sleep.

62

SIMONSTOWN WAS 5,396 miles away. They would be transiting the ocean at 29kts. The Royal Navy's ETA was 08.00 in 8 days. The RN prided itself on making its promulgated time of arrival - the Astute would be there as announced. They would be welcomed by a band of the South African Royal Marines. Salutes would be exchanged, the South African Port Admiral would greet them, the British Consul from Cape Town would also be there accompanied, no doubt, by the Royal Naval liaison officer.

The news of the visit was greeted with cheers by the crew. The hospitality shown to visiting British sailors by the South Africans was the stuff of legend. Hunter knew it all too well, as did Scott Llewelyn. However, that's all it was - legend. Even so, a good time would be had by the majority of the crew.

Signals were already flying thick and fast as the Consulate in Cape Town went into overdrive to make it a memorable visit. A reception was arranged for the wardroom at the naval base. A list of names was transmitted to the sub and eagerly read by the officers. The seventy or so dignitaries and senior military officers' names were ignored. It was the names at the end of the signal they wanted - there were at least a dozen unattached nurses from the local hospital.

Invitations were arriving for sight-seeing tours, visits to tourist attractions, private parties and public junkets.

There was a strong bond between the South African Navy and the Royal Navy. A lot of goodwill would also be generated.

The only mention of the operation was a Bravo Zulu from the First Sea Lord. Bravo Zulu was shorthand for Well Done.

There was a lot on the news about what had happened. As planned, General Khan was being posthumously lionised by the Pakistani government. His death was being laid firmly at the door of the Taliban and Barzakh. They were presented with a problem.

The attack was being analysed to death. Every armchair tactician agreed it had been textbook stuff. Experts were questioned and made pronouncements that the attackers must have ranged from an elite half-a-dozen men to at least fifty.

The Islamists had a choice. Bask in the glory of such a successful attack or deny they'd had anything to do with it. Pragmatism won out. Denying it wouldn't change a thing. The General was dead. Hyping up their involvement made them sound like brave warriors who were able to plan complex and demanding operations and, most significantly, carry them out successfully.

The Taliban and Barzakh opted for the adoration and accolades of their followers.

There was only one problem with that which they ignored. They both claimed victory which merely added to more confusion as to what had really happened.

All of it suited the Pakistanis and the West. Macnair was delighted.

Hunter had handed over the saturated computer to the experts on the sub. They had extracted the disk and were able to transfer the contents to TIFAT for decryption and analysis. The information was damning in the extreme. Names coupled to past, present and future operations planned by Barzakh were going to prove invaluable when it came time for President Zardarim to face the Pakistani people. There was also the question of arrests, trials, convictions and punishment. Pakistan's courts would be tied up for months even years. Once the news got out, many of those named would act like lemmings, running to God alone knew where.

They were four days from Simonstown and Llewelyn was having breakfast when he was handed the signal board. 'Damn,' he said.

'What's up? asked Hunter, entering the room just then.

'The Defence Secretary is flying out to meet us as well.'

'Anything wrong with that?'

'Nick, have you ever been briefed on what your duties are in the event of the Def Sec descending on you?'

'I can't say I have.'

'I've met him. He's a real dick. Well, he'll get no fawning from me. The title sir is for senior officers only. Not jumped up politicians who are here today and gone tomorrow.'

'Especially one who has systematically done more damage to the navy than the French ever did?' Hunter queried.

'You got it.'

At precisely 08.00 HMS Astute's bows passed the breakwater into Simonstown Harbour. Hunter had been invited up to the conning tower to enjoy the pageantry. He had accepted with alacrity. He needed to feel the sun on his face.

Once they were secured alongside, Llewelyn made his way to the gangway with the gangway welcoming party. Bosun's pipes were blown, salutes made and received, handshakes exchanged and the party went in through the main doorway in the conning tower.

Hunter stayed out of the way. The RN liaison officer was a lieutenant commander and he arrived with a briefcase containing airline tickets and passports.

The team were due on the BA flight departing Cape Town at 19.45. It was non-stop to London arriving at 06.30.

Hunter had been looking forward to a day or two of R and R but it wasn't to be. Then he thought, sod it.

He phoned Macnair. 'Sir? With all due respect, I'd like us to have a few days here before we come home.'

'Nick, of course. Feel free. They're open tickets.'

The comment had taken the wind out of Hunter's sails.

'That's okay?'

'Of course. I was giving you the option. Cancel the reservations and come back sometime in the next, shall we say, five days?'

'Right. Thanks, sir.'

'How's Matt?'

'He's fine. Headache's gone and the scab is healing nicely.'

'Good. Give the lads my best and enjoy your stay.'

The connection was broken. Hunter grinned. Trust the old man. He phoned the BA desk at the airport and explained the change. Next, he found the team and imparted the good news to wide grins and nods.

'What are you suggesting we do, Nick?' Don Masters enquired.

'I don't want to stay onboard.'

'How about getting a hotel in Cape Town?' said Hunter.

'Sounds like a plan,' said Badonovitch, 'but we need to go shopping first.'

Hunter met Scott Llewelyn an hour later for a coffee in the wardroom.

'I just wanted to say thanks, Scott, for all that you and your crew have done. It's very much appreciated.'

'Think nothing of it Nick.'

'Any flak?'

'No. I don't think there will be. I've had a word with the senior rates to tell the lads to keep quiet about where we've been and what we've been up to.'

'It's bound to come out at some point,' said Hunter.

'Thanks to the Taliban and Barzakh it doesn't matter. The peasants won't believe it because they don't want to. They want to believe the propaganda put out by the Islamists. And the vast majority of the world's leaders won't care. Khan is history. It's time to move on to the next problem. Besides which, if there is any fallout, it'll be the responsibility of people way above my pay grade.'

'I spoke to General Macnair. A file on General Khan's activities is being put together and will be forwarded to a raft of the good and the great.'

Llewelyn snorted. 'Not so good and only in their imaginations are they great.'

'Amen to that. But think on this, Scott. What if Khan had succeeded and he had made President? Imagine a President of Pakistan, Islamic fundamentalism to rival the Wahhabis in Saudi Arabia and Sharia law. Where would it go from there?'

'That's the really scary thing,' said Llewelyn. 'These people think in terms of hundreds of years. If it takes a thousand years for Islam to be the world religion then so be it. It means a never ending war.'

'It's compounded when you think what could happen if they got their hands on nuclear weapons.'

'Which is what would have happened. Pakistan has nuclear missiles.'

'Precisely. Anyway, enough of the philosophical debate. That's for after dinner drinks. Speaking of which, how about giving me a call when you get back to Faslane? We can go out for a beer or two.'

'Better still, we'll have you over for a barbeque.'

'Deal. Right. I'd better be going. The taxis are waiting and the lads will be getting impatient.'

The two officers made their way to the gangway and shook hands. Hunter saluted as he walked over the brow.

He climbed into the front taxi. 'Cape Royale Hotel, please,' he ordered.

The team were going to be treated to large doses of luxury, courtesy of TIFAT.

The flight home was four days later. They hadn't done much apart from exercising using the gymnasium and spa, swimming in the sea, lolling on the beach and drinking too much in the evening. Badonovitch and Masters on the second night pulled a couple of air stewardesses working for Virgin Atlantic. They had a three day stop-over and the two TIFAT warriors were hardly seen again by the other four.

When they departed, they flew business class. The plane was only half full, the service good, the food okay, and the free drinks refused.

The flight was on time, they sailed through immigration and customs and caught the next available flight to Edinburgh.

They were back at Rosyth in time for lunch.

63

'WELCOME HOME, NICK,' the General greeted him when Hunter walked into his boss's office.

'Thanks, sir. It's good to be back. I picked up the newspapers in London. I was amused to find that Khan has been placed on a pedestal.'

'POTUS and the PM have both made statements that his assassination was proof what a brilliant job the good General was making in the fight against fundamentalism.' Macnair was referring to the President of the United States. 'President Zardarim had been happy to go along with the fiction. As you'd expect, the truth is seeping out all over the place which is inevitable but it doesn't matter. We've pledged support for the Pakistanis, along with the Americans, in the fight against Islamic terrorism. Though that support is short of actual troops.'

'So what sort of support is it?'

'Verbal.'

'Not a lot of use, sir, with all due respect.'

'True. That's for the public. Covertly, we're up to our necks.

'SAS, SEALS et al?'

'Precisely.'

'Where's the EU in all this?'

Macnair leant back in his seat and put his interlocked hands behind his head. 'Where do you think?'

'Running for the hills.'

'I couldn't put it better myself. That stupid cow, Baroness what's her name, the High Representative of the Union for Foreign Affairs and Security Policy and Vice-President of the European Commission, has been going on about the need for tolerance and understanding and the rest of the claptrap. When will these morons learn? We are dealing with people who cannot be reasoned with. Who have no conscience when it comes to murder, torture and carrying out some of the vilest acts ever committed in the history of mankind.'

Hunter merely nodded. 'Sir, how long will they be able to keep up this fiction about Khan? Surely something is bound to slip out.'

'Good question. If there is enough obfuscation coupled with continuous lies about the man then it's possible the Pakistani government will be able to keep a lid on it. Thanks to the fundamentalists claiming responsibility it's possible it will all go according to plan. If arrests are made, which presumably is what is happening even as we speak, then the truth about Khan will be bound to come out. Probably. But as long as they keep on about what a great man he was it should all swept under the carpet. Now that they've gone down that route let's hope so anyway. Anyway, our name is out of it.'

'For now. Too many people know about our involvement. Like the crew of HMS Astute,' said Hunter.

'There's nothing we can do about that. There's no point in worrying about something that hasn't happened. I'll deal with it if I have to. I'm off home. I'm taking what you navy types call a make and mend,' said the General.

Hunter smiled. 'I'll go through my paperwork before I do the same. Not that there's much.'

Later that day Hunter phoned his parents in Balfron. He was pleasantly surprised when his sister answered.

'Hi, Nick.'

'Lems! What are you doing home?'

Lems was the name he had given his sister, Louise, when they had been growing up. Where the name had come from nobody remembered, but it had stuck with Hunter who was the only person to still use it.

'I flew in last night. I've a five day stop-over so came home.'

His sister was a pilot at Griffiths Airlines. The company had started trading back in the fifties and had evolved from the luxury end of world travel to the budget airline sector.

Hunter knew his sister had recently been promoted to Captain. He also knew that few, if any, people working at the airline knew of her family connection with the business. Although the holding company was listed on the stock market and was one of the footsie 100, a large number of the shares were still held by the family. Individual holdings were inexorably being diluted as the shares passed through the generations, but Louise and Hunter still held enough of them to be described as wealthy.

Hunter packed a few things in his grip and headed out. He had changed his car for what he intended to be the last time for at least 5 years. He now had a Range Rover Sport. The SUV was large, roomy and comfortable. Its maximum speed ensured he could break the speed limit by a significant number of mph and its fuel consumption was reasonable though it would never be voted "best car" by the UK's Green Party.

He drove through the gates, turned left and headed towards Kincardine Bridge. An anti-cyclone, forecast to last for the next few weeks, had settled over the south of England. With it had come sunshine and virtually no wind. Not a day to be at sea, sailing, thought Hunter.

Once over the Bridge he hit the M9 and put his foot down. He wound the Rover up to 80mph for a few minutes and then eased back to 75. It was a comfortable speed to cruise at. He turned off the motorway at junction 10, circumnavigated the two roundabouts and reached the A84.

Seconds later he was forced to drop his speed to around the 40mph mark. That irritated him. If there was a tractor or other farm vehicle on the road, that was one thing. As it was, he could see it was a car, a dozen vehicles in front, meandering along. There was little chance of overtaking a string of cars so he kept his impatience underwraps, switched on the radio and listened to the news on radio 4. The pm programme had just started. He passed the Safari Park and turned left on to the long straight B8075 before turning on to the A811.

It was as he drove through Arnprior that news about events in Pakistan came on the radio.

'Thanks to the work carried out by General Pervez Khan, the murdered Head of the Pakistani Army, many arrests are taking place across the country. Some of those arrested are senior officers in branches of the military some even close to the General. Although in the normal course of events that would be sufficient to raise questions as to General Khan's actual involvement, President Zardarim has made it clear that the General was killed due to his success in the war on Islamic fundamentalism that his country is engaged in. Many eulogies to the General have been posted on Twitter, Facebook and other media and social media outlets. There is no doubt the General was held in high regard. Some of the attempted arrests have resulted in gun battles between the terrorists and the Pakistani military forces.'

Hunter tuned out and left the announcer droning in the background.

Once he reached Balfron, he wound his way into the village and down the hill that was Buchanan St. Just before Shearer's garage he turned right into the driveway of the white house and pulled up behind it.

Climbing out of the car, the first of the welcoming party was waiting for him.

'Winston,' exclaimed Hunter as their golden Labrador sprang up and placed his forepaws on Hunter's chest and tried to lick his face. The dog's tail was going nineteen to the dozen and it was obvious he was excited to see him. Hunter ruffled the dog's neck and stroked his head, equally pleased to see Winston.

The back of the house had been extended some years earlier and now had an extra en-suite bedroom. It was the room he usually occupied when he was at home. Only this time, he was about to learn, he wouldn't be getting it.

'Nick!' His sister rushed out of the house, hugged him and planted a kiss on both his cheeks.

Louise was 2 years younger and a couple of inches shorter than Hunter with a slim, well proportioned figure. Her hair was black, straight and cut short to just below her ears. She had deep blue eyes, a wide mouth with a ready smile, a straight nose and a determined chin. Hunter was fully aware men found her highly attractive. She was wearing hip hugging black trousers and a white, sleeveless blouse.

'Hi Lems, it's great to see you.' He glanced over her shoulder as a man appeared.

Louise turned her head and said, 'Nick, this is Christopher Bletchley. Chris, my brother Nick.'

The two men shook hands.

'I've heard a lot about you, Nick,' said Bletchley. He was the same height as Hunter, with fair, wavy and unruly hair that reached over his ears. He had brown eyes, an aquiline nose, a square, dimpled chin that gave him film star good looks. He looked fit and tough. Hunter instantly wondered about him. It wasn't for long.

'Chris is a Captain in the SBS,' said Louise.

Hunter grinned. 'It's a real pleasure to meet you, Chris.'

Bletchley returned the grin. 'Me too. At last I meet the living legend.' It was said without a hint of malice but with a tinge of mockery. He had a faint, Welsh accent.

'Don't believe everything my sister has told you. She makes it up.'

The Special Boats Service Captain shook his head. 'Nick, Louise has told me virtually nothing about you.'

Hunter frowned. 'Then where do you get this legend rubbish from?'

Bletchley cocked his head to one side as he looked piercingly at Hunter. 'Nick, what TIFAT does is the stuff of legend. Ninety-nine percent of the UK's special services, hell, the rest of the free world's special services, would give their souls to be a part of you lot. I know I would.' He cast a glance at Louise, shrugged and added, 'That's about as much sycophantism as I can stomach.'

Hunter nodded. 'That's more than I can. But it's very nice to meet you. I take it you're dating?'

'Dating? Nick,' said Louise, 'you are so funny. Did we time warp back to the fifties? We've been going out for nearly three months.'

'Oh? How come I haven't heard about it?'

'Nick, do you think I tell you everything that I'm up to?'

'No, I guess not. Which is probably just as well.'

'By the way, you're in your old room. Chris and I have the extension.'

'Fair enough. Mam, Dad! Hi!'

His mother came into the garden and gave him a hug and a kiss while his father shook his hand behind his mother's back.

His mother, Sian, was still a striking woman, also with short black hair but, at 61 years of age, with a few streaks of grey. She was dressed in a knee length, short-sleeved, flowery dress and was looking radiant.

His father was a couple of inches shorter than his son, brown haired and brown eyed. He often joked that his genes had never stood a chance against those of the Griffiths family, hence his kids were blue-eyed and black haired.

'Welcome home, son,' said his father in his soft, Newfoundland accent, still noticeable even after all the years he had been away.

'Great to be home, Dad.'

'Drink?' asked his mother.

'Beer will be ideal.'

'I'll get it,' said Bletchley and stepped back into the kitchen.

'Isn't he adorable?' Louise whispered to her brother, ignoring the looks her parents swapped.

'I'll reserve my judgement,' Hunter whispered back. 'Thanks, Chris,' he broke off as he was handed a bottle of Coors. 'Just what I needed.'

'The barbie is lit,' said his father. 'The salad is made, the table is laid, the white wine is in the fridge for those who want it, the red wine is on the table, the coals are hot and the steak marinated. It's time to cook.'

They ate in the garden. The food was simple, the steak tender and succulent and the conversation kept flowing. The undercurrent, the events in Pakistan, wasn't mentioned until the meal was finished, the table cleared and their wine glasses had been replenished.

'Okay, son, let's hear all about it,' said his father sipping at his wine.

Hunter shrugged. 'There's not a lot to tell.'

'Were you in Pakistan?' Bletchley asked.

Hunter nodded. 'Yes. It was my team that did the work.' He knew he could be open with what he had to say to his family as he had rarely kept anything from them. At least, his mother and sister tended to get the highlights, his father got the details.

He wasn't sure what he could or couldn't say in front of Bletchley. Then he rationalised, the man had signed the Official Secrets Act. Also, he would know to keep his mouth shut. So he told them what had happened. Not in detail, but enough to keep the conversation going until well after dark.

Finally, it was time to hit the sack. Before they did, Hunter and his father called Winston and they set off in the direction of the River Endrick. Their walk was a ritual they had fallen into years ago. They strolled in companionable silence until they crossed the bridge and turned right onto the pathway beside the river. Winston was in his element, running, sniffing and coming back for a neck rub.

'What do you think of Chris?' his father asked him.

'Seems a pretty good bloke. An SBS Captain is a respectable achievement and probably means he has a future ahead of him. What about you?'

'We've only just met him. I'm undecided but your mother has taken a shine to him. She says he's just what Louise needs to keep her in line.'

'She's hardly a wild thing now she's an airline pilot and a Captain to boot.'

'True. I guess I like what I've seen of him.'

'Me too.' Silence reigned for a few seconds then Hunter chuckled. 'Oh, I get it. You want me to check him out, is that it?'

'Do you mind?'

'Of course not. I would have done it anyway. I'll let you know what I trawl up.'

'Actually, don't. I'm going to go with my instinct. He has an MC plus a mention so he must be pretty special.' A Military Cross plus a Mention in Despatches said a lot about a man. 'Also, Louise seems to think highly of him, so just leave it.'

'Okay, Dad, whatever you say.'

'Care to share any more details about the op?'

'In all sincerity, there's nothing more to tell.' He hadn't mentioned blowing off the kneecap and wrist of General Khan. That was one detail too many.

'Why are you scratching your butt from time to time?'

Trust the old man, thought Hunter. He rarely missed a thing.

Playing for time, Hunter replied, 'Scratching my butt? I hadn't realised. Maybe because it's itching?'

'Yeah, sure son. Don't worry, I won' tell your mother. She worries enough about you as it is, though she's good at hiding it.'

'Okay. It's a flesh wound. Nicked me, that's all. It's just about healed but it itches from time to time.'

'Stitches?'

'A couple. They dissolve and are practically gone already. It's no big deal.' He didn't mention the bullet in the chest.

They finished their walk and made their way back to the house. There, his father said goodnight while Hunter made himself comfortable at the garden table and poured himself a whisky and soda with ice.

Winston sat at his feet, his tongue hanging out, his eyes closed, his nose and head twitching as he dreamt his canine dreams.

Hunter watched as his sister came out of the house and sat opposite him. She poured herself a soda water.

'Well?' she asked.

'Yes, thanks,' said Hunter, grinning, knowing what she really wanted to know.

'Very funny, Nicholas Hunter. What do you think of Chris?'

'Seems alright. I suppose. For a marine, that is. You have seen a marine doing up his shoelaces, haven't you?'

'What on earth are you talking about?'

Hunter stood up, placed his left foot on the chair and bent down to tie his right shoelace. 'See? That sums up a Royal marine.'

'Ha, ha, very funny. Seriously, Nick.'

'Seriously? I like what I've seen of him. Dad told me about the medal and mention but Chris didn't say anything about them.'

'He never even told me. One of his friends did.'

'I think that says a lot.'

'Good. I'm glad. Especially as I am going to marry him.'

'You're what?'

'Quiet! Not so loud. I'm going to marry him.'

'Do Mam and Dad know?'

'Of course not silly. But then Chris doesn't know either. Not yet, anyway.'

Hunter laughed.

'Quiet! Nobody's to know. But I am going to tell you what I want for a pre-wedding present.'

'What may that be?'

'I want you to get Chris into TIFAT.'

64

WHILE HE SIPPED his drink, Hunter thought about it. After a few seconds, he asked, 'Why do you want Chris in TIFAT?'

'Because he wants it.'

'Have you thought that maybe he's going out with you as a means of getting to me?'

'I did wonder, but only for a second. I'm sure it's not the case. He's only mentioned it once and that was pretty much in passing. I happened to mention where you worked and he said it was his career objective to go there. You know, pillow talk.'

'Please, Lems, I don't want any details.' Hunter held his hands up in mock horror.

'Idiot,' she replied with a smile. 'Please, Nick. Will you do it?'

'I'm not sure I can.'

'Why ever not?'

'It's not my shout.'

'But Nick...'

'But me no buts. I'll tell you what I will do. I'll have a word with the General and see if he'll go for it. We have need of an officer of Chris' calibre so it may be okay. I'll see what I can do.'

'Oh, Nick! Thanks very much. I'm sure he'll be a great asset at TIFAT.'

'We'll see. I'm not promising anything, but I'll ask. What about you?'

'What about me?'

'Is it what you want?'

Louise shrugged. 'I'm not sure. I told you, I love him. The idea of him putting his life on the line doesn't appeal to me in the slightest, but I know it's what he wants. So I'll support him.'

'Fair enough. Listen, Lems, don't say anything to Chris. Just in case.'

'I won't. Thanks, big brother. I really appreciate it.' Louise left the table and went back indoors.

Hunter stayed where he was for a while before he too went upstairs to bed. He was in the large back room where the boiler was stored. The bed was large and comfortable. He went out like a light.

Hunter was up at a few minutes past 06.00. He dressed in his running gear and hit the road with Winston excitedly running just ahead of him. They went up the hill, along Dunmore Street, at the end they cut right, continued down the hill, right again, up to the T junction and continued towards Boquhan. Once there, he turned right and headed back into Balfron from the other side of the village. He never had worked out the distance but as he had done the run in 14 minutes he decided to go round again.

Winston, on the other hand, decided he'd had enough. The dog gave him a look as though to say, 'Are you kidding?' and went back behind the house for a well earned drink of water and a doze.

Before he could get going he was joined by Chris Bletchley. They matched stride for stride. Hunter increased his pace. So did Bletchley. Hunter did it again. So did the other man. Bletchley opened up and Hunter had to put his foot down. They practically sprinted the last few hundred yards from the Endrick to the house. Bletchley won.

Both of them stood bent over, hands on their knees, gasping for breath. After a couple of minutes the Royal Marine said, 'Louise said you were a pretty good runner.'

'Swimming is more my thing,' Hunter managed to gasp out.

'I guess it's mine as well. Care for a workout?'

Hunter knew what he meant and nodded. 'Let's use the garden.'

They walked up behind the house and into the top garden. It was pretty much shielded by a hawthorn hedge his mother had planted years earlier.

'Any style?' asked Bletchley, smiling.

'What do you think?'

'I guess not.'

They went hand-to-hand, toe-to-toe, move-to-move for a fast and intense 10 minutes. Both men were panting, bruised and tested to their limits.

'Draw?' Hunter asked.

Bletchley stood up straight and said, 'Draw. Thank God.'

'Thank him for me too. To be honest, I don't think I could have managed another minute.'

'Me neither. I was fighting on empty.'

Hunter narrowed his eyes and burst out laughing. 'The pair of us are lying through our teeth.'

Bletchley laughed as well. 'I guess we are. But it's always good to keep something in reserve. That can often mean the difference between living and dying.'

'I have the same philosophy.' Hunter made up his mind there and then. If Bletchley wanted it, a job at Rosyth was his for the taking.

After shaving, showering and changing into lightweight trousers, white short-sleeved shirt and loafers, Hunter joined the rest of the family in the garden. It was already warm and promised to be another beautiful day. The workout had given him an appetite but a glass of orange juice, a bowl of Corn Flakes and a slice of toast was all he wanted.

Never one to let the grass grow under his feet, after breakfast, Hunter took Winston for a walk and, using his mobile, phoned General Macnair at home.

'Sir? Sorry to trouble you. I have a favour to ask.' He told him about Chris Bletchley. 'I think he'll be a great asset, sir.'

Macnair was made from the same mould as Hunter. 'Leave it with me. I'll get his records pulled. Does he want the job?'

'I think so. He hasn't asked me, but from the way he was talking I would say yes, he would.'

'I'll call you tomorrow.'

'Thanks, Sir.'

Hunter returned to the house. They had a lazy day. His father and mother left them at 17.00 to go across the road and down to the bowling club. They had become members the year before and both confessed to liking the game.

The following morning, Bletchley and Hunter did a workout similar to the previous day. This time, running two circuits, Hunter beat the Royal Marine by a dozen strides. At the unarmed combat they called it a day after nearly 20 minutes and agreed to a draw.

Hunter took a call around noon.

'Sir?'

'I've spoken to Captain Bletchley's Commanding Officer. He said a lot of highly complimentary things about him.'

'What about a transfer to us?'

'He was very unhappy about that. However, Sergeant Smithers and Corporal Thatcher have both requested a transfer back to their old unit at Poole. The CO knows them, of course, and rates them both. So he's agreed, two for one, as it were. If Bletchley wants in, he can come.'

'When?'

'Next Monday.'

Hunter chuckled. 'Who'll tell him?'

'It had better be his CO. He can give him the option.'

'Ask the CO if he'll phone at thirteen hundred, will you, please? Tell him that's the only time Chris will be available.'

'Any reason?'

'I want to see his face.'

Lunch was a light affair of egg and tuna salad.

'Why do you keep looking at your watch?' asked Louise, 'Planning on going somewhere?'

Her brother grinned. 'No. Just waiting for a phone call.'

Bletchley's mobile rang at 13.04. He looked at the screen. 'It's the old man.' He pressed the receive button. 'Sir?'

As he listened his eyes turned to Hunter. They narrowed. He said, 'Yes, sir. When? I have one hour? Who asked for me?' He listened to the answer. 'I see. Thank you, sir. I'll get back to you as soon as I can.'

He broke the connection and sat in silence for a few moments staring at Hunter. The rest of the family were watching him. Their puzzlement was obvious.

'Who was it, Chris?' Louise asked.

'Like I said, my boss.'

'Your boss? You mean your CO?' she queried.

'Correct.'

'What did he want? Are you being recalled?'

'No. I've been offered a posting.' He swapped his gaze to her. She looked stricken. 'Where to? Not Afghanistan or somewhere?'

'No. Quite close to here, actually.'

'To...' she looked at her brother who was watching the other man with a deadpan look. 'You mean TIFAT?'

Bletchley nodded. 'The very same. Is this your doing, Nick?'

Hunter thought about his reply before nodding. 'Guilty as charged.'

'I can't accept it.'

Curiously enough, it was what Hunter had expected. He also figured he knew why.

'You think I did you a favour? Because of Louise?'

'Why else?'

'Then you're a fool and that isn't something I took you for.'

'What do you mean, I'm a fool?'

'If you think for one second I'll risk the lives of my men by having somebody join us who I don't have complete faith in then you're off your cotton picking head. I'm the senior ops officer. I pick the men for the teams. We run four teams at Rosyth. Each team works together so that in a short period of time they know they can count on the others and know their abilities. I ensure they complement each other. The job is yours if you want it. There's no obligation to take it. One thing to be aware of. We're pretty informal but at the end of the day I'll be your boss.'

Bletchley looked at Hunter for a second before he nodded. He turned his gaze to Louise.

She looked uncomfortable for a moment, and then sat up straight, looked Bletchley in the eyes. 'You said you wanted it. I knew Nick wouldn't do it because I asked. I wouldn't want him to.' She paused and then added, 'And neither would you. But we look out for each other in this family.'

'Do you want the job?' Hunter enquired.

By way of response, Bletchley lifted his phone and speed-dialled. 'Sir? I'll take the job.' He broke the connection and grinned. 'Thanks, Nick. Thanks very much.'

Hunter grinned back. 'Don't thank me yet. You've just joined the toughest and busiest fighting force in the world.'

'Thanks, dear brother.' Louise leant over and kissed Hunter on the cheek.

An hour later Hunter took a stroll through the village up to the post office. It was 14.01 and it had reopened after closing for lunch.

There was nobody else there apart from the man behind the

glass at the counter.

'Hi, Arif. How're you doing?'

'Nick! It's a pleasure to see you. What can I get you?'

'A book of stamps, please. My mother has birthday cards to send.'

'Here you go.' Arif handed over the stamps.

He was from Pakistan and, Hunter knew, worked hard and was an asset to the village.

'Nick, tell me, were you in Pakistan?'

Hunter was suddenly wary, though he was sure he knew where Arif's sympathies lay.

'No. Why do you ask?'

'Nick, I've known you, what? Three years? I know you work for TIFAT in Rosyth. Half the village knows.'

'Arif, I've told you before. I'm just a desk jockey. You know, ordering supplies, counting paperclips.'

'Yeah, and I'm Santa Claus.'

'You have the right build for it,' Hunter grinned.

Arif grinned back. 'I'm dieting. The wife insists.'

'Then stop eating the Mars bars,' quipped Hunter.

'Seriously, Nick, were you there?'

Hunter shook his head. His phone blipped. 'Excuse me a second, Arif.' He took out his mobile and read the screen. He frowned. 'I've got to go. See you next time.'

'Okay, Nick. Take care. Desk job counting paperclips. Huh, that'll be the day!'

Hunter hurried down the hill and into the house.

'Chris!' he called out.

'Nick?' Bletchley came through from the kitchen, a dishtowel in his hands. He raised it up and said, 'Your sister is training me.'

'Training over. Your transfer has just been pulled forward by a week.'

'Huh? What are you talking about?'

'They've just sent a Bikini Amber alert. As far as we're concerned it means a general recall.'

'But I haven't been transferred, yet.'

Hunter asked, 'Do you want the job?'

'Of course I do.'

'Then get yourself into gear and let's go. The General can

sort out the paperwork later.' Hunter grinned. 'For Queen and Country, Chris.' He knew he wouldn't have it any other way. At times like that, one phrase often came to mind. It was from Shakespeare's play, Julius Caesar.

Cry havoc and let slip the dogs of war.

It was appropriate. He was glad to be one of the dogs.

Bletchley quickly packed a bag and joined him in the car.

Once out of the village, Hunter turned on the blue lights hidden under the grill of the Land Rover and hit 100mph along the A811. It was a modification for all TIFAT vehicles agreed after the last operation. This was the first time Hunter had used them.

He couldn't help wondering what lay ahead.

The End

The Seventh Circle

by Paul Henke

JUSTICE! When Richard Griffiths' world is turned upside down he expects the justice system to take action. But the powers that be have another agenda and Richard finds himself embroiled in the sinister world of terrorists and international politics. Justice is denied him. He has no choice but to take matters into his own hands. His thoughts and actions consume him as his quest for justice turns to a deep rooted desire for revenge.

But soon the hunter becomes the hunted. The consequences quickly spiral out of control. As action leaps from Europe to the Middle East and then the USA, the pace never slackens. Breaking free of the circle of hatred and retribution will take all Richard's courage and determination. Will it be enough?

This is Henke at his page-turning best – thought provoking and action packed.

ISBN: 978-1-902483-12-2

Corruption

By Paul Henke

A Nick Hunter Adventure

Paul Henke's new TIFAT thriller has Nick Hunter and his cousin, Richard Griffiths, trying to fight corruption in the European Union, orchestrated by members of the EU Parliament. From the UK to Switzerland the pace is non-stop as they fight organised gangs hired by the EU bureaucrats to protect their corrupt regime.
Corruption is an action-packed, edge-of-the-seat, thriller laced which begs the question - how much is fact, how much is fiction?

When Richard Griffiths meets attractive Andrea Nelson he is expecting nothing more than a holiday romance. But soon he is embroiled in a sinister web of deceit and corruption which reaches into the highest levels of the European Parliament. As atrocity follows atrocity,Richard's cousin, Commander Nick Hunter RN, of The International Force Against Terrorism is called in to chase down the villians before more innocent lives are lost.

In a fight against time this is Henke at his page turning best.

ISBN: 978-0-9558966-9-9

A Million Tears

By Paul Henke

The first book in the Tears Saga

A Million Tears is a mighty epic, the first of five books chronicling the life of the Griffiths family.

This is a tale of love and hate, murder and suicide, poverty and wealth – the story of a family whose devotion for each other helps them to succeed where others fail.

Dai's world was confined to the close-knit South Wales mining community where the most exciting event in his 10 years of life was a trip to the market town of Pontypridd. But he has his atlas and he has his dreams . . .

'A Million Tears' is the realisation of those dreams. From the hardship and poverty of Wales in 1890 to the optimism and wealth of America, the Griffiths family strive for success. Follow Evan, the head of the family, as he fights his way from coal-miner to businessman to politician. Dai, whose search for adventure takes him to the exotic corruption of the West Indies and Sion, who has to grow up fast to survive the brutality of the west. There's Uncle James who will stop at nothing to save the family and finally Meg, the rock of the family, the constant in all their lives.

This is a compelling story of adventure and love, tragedy and survival. A wonderful story by a master story teller.

ISBN: 978-1-902483-08-5

Mayhem

By Paul Henke

A Nick Hunter Adventure

The Nick Hunter adventures continue faster and greater than ever. TIFAT is now an established organisation in the old Royal Naval base at *HMS Cochrane*, Rosyth in Scotland. When Israel is threatened by an overwhelming force from the countries that surround it Macnair has to take action. As terrorist incident follows terrorist incident a pattern emerges. The usual suspects when it comes to sponsoring terrorist activities are closely examined but the evidence makes no sense.

Only when David Golightly, Deputy Prime Minister of Israel, contacts Macnair does the jigsaw begin to take shape. The perpetrator is a powerful and rich Israeli whose ambition it is to create a Greater Israel at any cost. Millions will die unless he is stopped; innocent men, women and children who are pawns in the hands of their Middle Eastern leaders.

From the Highlands of Scotland, across the Alps, into Italy and south to Israel the action is a non-stop rollercoaster. Fact and fiction mingle to make a breathtaking story you won't want to end. The twists and turns are as ingenious as ever as Hunter races across the bleak landscape of Northern Israel pursued by enemies who will stop at nothing to kill him. If he doesn't succeed, mayhem will engulf the whole of the region.

ISBN: 978-1-902483-02-3

Acclaim for Paul Henke

A Million Tears
'The summer's best holiday read ...' Scottish and Universal Newspapers
'An unquenchable thirst for daring and creativity ...' The Sunday Times

The Tears of War and Peace
'Henke isn't just talented, but versatile too. His books are very convincing. As good as Stephen King, Wilbur Smith, Tom Clancy and Bernard Cornwell.' Burton Mail

Debacle
'A gritty political thriller . . .' The Times
'A political thriller that combines international terrorism, the military and high finance. A roller-coaster of a thrilling ride.' The Sunday Post
'Has that absolute tang of authenticity – a rattling good yarn.' Chris Serle, BBC Radio
'Move over Tom Clancy. Henke has turned his own amazing real-life experiences into blockbuster novels.' The Sun

Mayhem
'A non-stop action adventure set in Scotland and the Middle East.' The Edinburgh Evening News
'A cracking good yarn. Non-stop action from beginning to end.' Central FM radio
'Fiction becomes fact in Paul Henke's action thrillers. A superb read.' The Northern Echo

Visit Paul's website: **www.henke.co.uk** for up to the minute news and special offers.